## RED-HOT STEEL

One by one the crews of Green Section followed into the hell of bursting shells and trident thrusts of tracer. Harvey's rocket struck a davit and a lifeboat swung crazily down to dangle by its bows. Matthews' cannon fire smashed into the wraparound armour of a pom-pom and killed two gunners. Paget's rocket hit a capstan on the stern and hurled murderous chunks of metal in all directions. Fragments of wood and metal flew from the Mosquito and a long tongue of flame leapt out from its starboard engine. Skimming over the black water like a fiery meteor it suddenly broke up and plunged down like a stone. The horrified Adams heard a voice call out "Oh, my God" and took a few seconds to realize it was his own . . .

*633 SQUADRON*
*OPERATION VALKYRIE*

# 633
## SQUADRON

## OPERATION
## VALKYRIE

### BY
### FREDERICK E. SMITH

✠

633 SQUADRON
OPERATION VALKYRIE
*A Bantam Book / published by arrangement with the author.*

*PRINTING HISTORY*
*First published in Great Britain by Cassell and Company, Ltd.
in 1978*
*Bantam edition / June 1979*

Bantam Books are published by Bantam Books, Inc. Its trademark, consisting of the words "Bantam Books" and the por-
trayal of a bantam, is Registered in U.S. Patent and Trademark
Office and in other countries. Marca Registrada. Bantam
Books, Inc., 666 Fifth Avenue, New York, New York 10019.

PRINTED IN THE UNITED STATES OF AMERICA

*to*
*my old friends*
*Betty and Arthur*

# ACKNOWLEDGMENTS

The author wishes to acknowledge his debt to the following works of reference:

Richards and Saunders, *Royal Air Force 1939-45* (H.M.S.O.); Bekker, *The Luftwaffe War Diaries* (Macdonald); Sir Charles Webster and N. Frankland, *The Strategic Air Offensive against Germany 1939-45* (H.M.S.O.); Captain Haukelid, *Skis Against the Atom* (Kimber).

And, last but not least, to acknowledge the personal help given him by Fredrik Kayser, valiant member of 'Gunnerside,' the Norwegian team that so effectively destroyed the first deuterium oxide stocks at Rjukan.

F.E.S.

The six Norwegians in workmen's clothes were clustered round the unshuttered window. The seventh, a massive bearded man with a thatch of fair hair, had his hand on the catch of the stout wooden door. As the door swung open a flurry of snow swept in and hissed against the wood stove.

A young man, wearing a white snow smock, stumbled into the doorway. The giant's deep voice rumbled over the howl of the wind. "What's the panic, Elsenstein? Germans?"

The frightened youngster nodded. "A patrol. They're chasing Arne."

The occupants of the hut reacted immediately, throwing on camouflaged smocks and grabbing up Sten guns. The giant pulled the youngster inside and helped him off with his skis. "How many?"

"I can't be sure, Jensen. But I saw four."

Skis in their hands, men were already crowding into the doorway. Jensen caught one man by the arm and pulled him back. "Not you, Paul. We'll take care of it."

The Norwegian he was addressing was a man in his early thirties whose high forehead, thin cheeks and flat, black hair suggested an academician rather than a man of action. Yet although he was no more than five feet eight inches tall and thinly built, his intense eyes and quick movements hinted at great reserves of nervous energy; a man whose will power alone would drive him further than most. His cultured voice reinforced his academic appearance. "Why not? I've been trained for the work."

The giant shook his head grimly. "You know what our orders are—you don't take any risks. You stay here with the kid. It shouldn't take us long."

Paul Lindstrom opened his mouth to argue, then turned away. Climbing into his ski smock, Jensen grabbed up a Sten gun and a pair of skis and yanked the door open.

As the door slammed behind him, Lindstrom walked to the open window. The hut was perched on a mountainside, on the fringe of a large conifer forest that covered its upper slopes. The main party of Norwegians had already disappeared into the forest. Jensen, covering the snow in giant strides, was in hot pursuit.

The youngster, who had now regained his breath, moved

up to Lindstrom's elbow. "Which way was Arne coming?" Lindstrom asked.

Elsenstein pointed at a ridge that ran down the mountainside. "He was making for that higher ground. But he might have taken cover in the woods by this time."

Jensen had already disappeared among the trees. Gazing at the snow-covered mountains and the steel-grey sky, Lindstrom had the sensation he was stranded at the farthermost reaches of a world where the sun was dying and all life was doomed. A gasp alongside him destroyed the fantasy.

"Arne hasn't taken cover! He's trying to draw them away from us."

A tiny figure on skis had just cleared the ridge and was frantically contouring the mountainside two hundred metres below the hut. As the pursued man drew nearer he waved a frantic arm to alert his compatriots. Five seconds later four more skiers cleared the ridge. Clad in German ski-troops' uniform, they were spread out in a fifty metre arc. As Arne passed the hut and headed towards the cover of another snow ridge, the leading German stopped, dropped on one knee and fired. The shot, a flat sound at first, came reverberating back as the German commenced his pursuit again.

Nudging Elsenstein, Lindstrom spun round and grabbed up a rifle. "Get ready in case Jensen isn't able to stop them."

By this time the German patrol was no more than four hundred metres away, skimming along the fringe of the woods like as many birds. As another man paused to take a shot at Arne, a fusillade of automatic fire rang out from the trees. The kneeling man collapsed immediately. With hoarse shouts the remaining three Germans turned down the mountain in an attempt to escape.

It was the signal for Jensen's entire party to emerge from the wood. As automatic guns fired again, two more Germans pitched into the snow and lay motionless. The last man stumbled, dropped his Mauser, but managed to keep going. Shouting something to his party, the giant Jensen went after him like a bloodthirsty Norse god. A burst of fire at close range flung the German over, his body riddled with bullets.

Arne had paused on the opposite ridge on hearing the firing. Seeing the ambush had been successful, he turned and made for the hut. With exhaustion taking its toll, he

2

was the last man to arrive and almost collapsed into the arms of Jensen. Fighting for breath, he was carried inside. Almost thirty seconds passed before he was able to speak.

"Helga sent me. . . . She says the Germans have decided to move all their stocks."

There was a gasp of dismay from the circle of men. Showing more concern than anyone, Lindstrom dropped on his knees beside the exhausted man. "Does she know when?"

Propped against Jensen's arm, Arne's sweat-streaked face stared up at him. "She says they're making elaborate arrangements. So it might take a couple of weeks. But no longer."

Jensen gave a Nordic oath. "Two weeks! Christ, we're going to have to move. Shall we radio London?"

Lindstrom was already on his feet. "No, it's too important for that. I'll take the Shetland Bus. But it'll have to be tonight."

Jensen turned to one of his partisans, a wiry young man with the face of a pugilist, who showed doubt. "Not tonight, Steen. There's less than four hours of daylight left."

Jensen's growl was like overhead thunder. "I want a boat tonight! Or there'll be hell to pay. You tell Anderson that."

Clearly intimidated by the giant's anger, the partisan turned to Lindstrom. "It's quite a long way to the coast, sir. Can you ski that far?"

"Just guide me there," Lindstrom said curtly. He turned back to Jensen. "You do realize that when that patrol doesn't return to base the Germans are going to comb these mountains?"

The bearded Jensen grinned, showing strong, white teeth. "Don't worry about us, lad. You get over to London and tell 'em what the bastards are doing. In the meantime we'll see what else we can find out." He swung round to his tense party. "All right, lads. Get your equipment together and let's move out."

In less than ten minutes the party was ready to leave. Outside the hut Jensen drew Lindstrom aside and gripped his arm affectionately. "Take care of yourself, lad, and watch out for patrols when you get near the coast. When you reach London, tell them they can rely on us whatever they decide to do."

Shaking his hand, Lindstrom followed his guide down the mountainside. Led by the giant, the rest of the partisans began skiing southwards. In a few minutes the only evidence that human life had violated the virgin slopes was the four bodies lying in the snow.

Davies glanced with surprise at the two M.P.s guarding both ends of the corridor. Security was always tight at High Elms but today it bordered on the claustrophobic. The Air Commodore's car had been stopped three times since entering the estate and a Provost Lieutenant had demanded the password from him before he had been allowed to step out into the courtyard. That same Lieutenant was now opening the door of the library that Davies knew so well. "Air Commodore Davies is here, sir."

The library, a long rectangular room with panelled oak walls, ran to French windows opening out on to a terrace. Two men were standing beside a long conference table that stood in the centre of the room. One was the Brigadier, Davies' contact with the Special Operations Executive, an elderly man of distinguished and soldierly appearance. General Staines of the American 8th Air Force stood alongside him, a massive figure of a man with short, spiky hair. Davies, who had worked with Staines on both Operation Rhine Maiden and Operation Crucible, knew the Texan well.

A man of great composure, the Brigadier was hiding his anxiety admirably as he shook hands with Davies and then turned with a smile to the American. "You two have met before, I believe."

Staines had a voice that sounded like ball bearings rolling about inside a tin can. "You can say that again. And it's always meant trouble." His powerful handshake made Davies stiffen. "It's good to see you again, Davies. How're you keeping?"

"I'm fine, sir." Davies ran his eyes over the Texan's massive frame. "I don't need to ask how you are."

Staines grinned. "I keep in shape. You know why, Davies? It's those cigars I smoke."

Davies, who had sampled one of the Texan's cigars and felt queasy for days, winced at the reminder. "I wouldn't recommend them as a general pick-me-up, sir."

The Texan's huge laugh rolled round the library. "You know something, Davies? You'll never be constipated if you smoke 'em. They work better than Number Nines."

The Brigadier moved forward. "May I offer you a drink, Davies?"

4

Although it was not his habit to drink before dinner and the dusk had not yet closed in on the February afternoon, Davies could adapt when the occasion demanded it, and the huge whisky that sat on the table in front of Staines suggested this was such an occasion. "Thank you, sir. A very small whisky."

Handing him a glass, the Brigadier motioned him into a chair. "I'm grateful you got over so quickly, Davies. This is something of an urgent conference."

From the presence of Staines, Davies had already made that deduction. "What's the problem, sir?"

The elderly soldier sank somewhat heavily into a chair. "A rather serious one, I'm afraid. Do you remember the Swartfjord affair last year?"

Davies could not hide a start. "I could hardly forget it, could I? Not after the losses we sustained."

"Quite. It was a terribly costly affair. A tragedy, in fact."

The soldier's expression made Davies glance at Staines. Seeing the American's genial face was now equally grave, Davies felt a sudden chill.

"You're not telling me that business has flared up again?"

The Brigadier nodded. "I'm afraid it has, Davies."

"But how could it? We destroyed the processing plant. Buried it beneath a mountain."

The Brigadier sighed. "I'm afraid there is more to it than that. The processing plant was obliterated and remains obliterated. But the element it was processing there still remains a problem. As you know, it is a product of hydroelectric power and the power station in the Swartfjord wasn't the only one in Norway that could produce it."

Staines, whose eyes had been darting from one man to the other, broke in with some urgency at this point. "Hold your fire a minute. You're talking as if Davies knew all about this stuff."

"He does, General," the Brigadier told him.

The Texan's frown deepened. "But I thought this was supposed to be one of the best-kept secrets of the war. I only got the lowdown myself a few days ago."

"I am sure it is, sir. But from the way things went last April we had no choice but to take Davies into our confidence. Naturally, we received full security clearance."

Staines sank back into his chair with a grunt. "All right, then you know what'll happen if Jerry gets the stuff processed and in use before we do. But from now on, Davies, even between ourselves, the only name for it is the IMI element. Understood?"

"I understand, sir." Davies turned back to the Brigadier. "Am I to take it, then, that another hydro-electric power station is now producing it?"

The elderly soldier rose to his feet. "I have a guest who will put the entire picture to you. He arrived an hour ago but after his tiring journey I insisted he had lunch before he met you. I'm sure he'll be ready to see you now."

Leaving the library, the Brigadier returned a couple of minutes later with a serious-faced young man wearing the uniform of an American major and carrying a briefcase. He led the newcomer over to Davies. "Lindstrom, this is Air Commodore Davies. Davies—meet Major Lindstrom of the American SAS. He has just got back from Norway."

The correctness of Lindstrom's English was tempered by his slight American accent. "I'm very pleased to meet you, Air Commodore. The Brigadier has told me it was your Mosquito squadron that carried out the raid last year on the Swartfjord plant. Please accept my congratulations. People all over Norway still talk about it."

Although not averse to receiving compliments about his much-beloved squadron, Davies was too much of a professional soldier not to frown at praise. "I'm glad to hear it. Because it cost a lot of good boys." Then, feeling he hadn't reacted with sufficient grace, Davies tried to make amends. "The Brigadier says you've just come out of Norway. How? By ship?"

"Yes. The Norwegian Linge—that's their Resistance Movement—run a daily boat service to the U.K. They call it the Shetland Bus. They got me across to Scotland and the RAF flew me down here."

Davies had personal knowledge of the fishing smacks and the like that made the perilous journey. Time and again the Germans caught the small boats outside the restricted area and blew them up but the tough Norwegians kept on coming. The younger man's accent was reminding him of Finn Bergman. "You wouldn't be a Norwegian yourself, would you?"

Seeing Lindstrom's hesitation, the Brigadier answered the question for him. "Major Lindstrom took up residence in America three years before the war when a large chemical corporation over there offered him a post as a physicist. When the Americans heard that the Germans were building up large stocks of IMI, he was asked if he would return to Norway to investigate. He volunteered, received specialist training, and began working with the Norwegian Linge in 1942. He helped Bergman with information about the Swartfjord plant last year."

Davies' respect for the academic-looking young Norwegian was growing by the minute. "You seem to have found yourself a dangerous job, Major."

Lindstrom's shrug had an element of contempt. "The people who live over there take far greater risks. People like my sister for example."

"Your sister?"

"Yes. She is acting as an agent in Rjukan. By mixing socially with the staff of the power station there she picks up a great deal of information. She is the reason I'm over here now."

Staines decided it was time to get proceedings moving again. "Until today the Air Commodore hadn't known there was a similar threat from another hydro-electric power station. Fill him in with the details, will you?"

Nodding, Lindstrom drew a map of Norway from his briefcase and opened it out on the desk in front of Davies. He laid a finger on a point on the province of Telemark. "The power station, the Norsk Hydro, is here, near the town of Rjukan. We've known it was producing IMI for a long time and until the Swartfjord processing plant began operations we saw it as our main threat. Late in 1942 a force of B.17s were sent out but they did no real damage. The British tried next, sending out gliders and airborne troops whose job was to land forty miles away and carry out a Bruneval-type operation on the station. It was a complete disaster with many of the gliders crashing into the mountains. The troops that survived were captured and later shot as spies.

"A Norwegian called Ronnerberg next offered to try. He gathered a party of Norwegian volunteers in Britain, gave them hurried training, then landed them in Norway by fishing boat. From there they made their way to the valley on foot. All carried suicide pills in case of capture. They managed to reach the valley undetected but then had to climb down an almost precipitous cliff face. While the main party kept guard, Ronnerberg and three others entered the basement where the IMI tanks were stored, overcame the guards, and attached limpet mines to the IMI tanks. Then they withdrew and managed to escape from the valley before the mines exploded. Knowing there would be a massive manhunt, they dispersed. A few reached Sweden and eventually made their way back to the U.K. The rest, led by two men called Skinnarland and Haukelid, stayed behind to keep watch on the IMI situation at the Norsk Hydro. Among other things my group has been busy collating and assessing the information Skinnarland sends to London."

Davies had been listening in fascination. "Ronnerberg wasn't able to sabotage the power station itself?"

"No. There was a limit to the weight of explosives his men could carry but in any case the exiled Norwegian Government weren't able at that time to sanction the destruction of another power station. The one your men destroyed in the Swartfjord caused great hardship in the province."

"So stocks of IMI have been building up again?" Davies said.

"Yes. Today we believe they are as large as when your squadron and Ronnerberg carried out your respective raids."

"But why hasn't something been done about them?"

"For a combination of reasons. As you can imagine, after Ronnerberg's raid the Germans made the valley virtually impregnable against ground attack. They also took warning from your Swartfjord raid and filled the valley with flak defences. It is true that had an IMI processing plant existed in the valley, as it had in the Swartfjord, we would have taken any risks but without such a plant the stocks themselves represented no immediate threat. But the news I've just had from my sister changes everything."

There were lines around Davies' eyes and mouth that had not been there earlier. A unit commander who normally had no difficulty in rationalizing losses against rewards, the Swartfjord tragedy was one operation he had never been able to forget. His voice sounded hoarse as he glanced up at the Norwegian. "You're not telling me they've built a processing plant there?"

"No. Not there."

Davies felt his muscles slacken a degree or two. "Where then?"

"In Bavaria. No doubt they feel now it is safer in the heartland of Germany. Allied agents have been keeping an eye on it and report it is almost completed. My sister's news confirms it. She says the IMI stocks are to be shipped out of Rjukan in two weeks' time. Perhaps less."

Staines leaned his massive bulk over the table. "Davies, those stocks mustn't reach Bavaria or the Heinies could beat us to the finishing post, and then it's Goodbye Mr. Chips. Somehow we have to destroy 'em either before they're shipped out or when they're in transit."

The Brigadier's quiet, very English voice added its own brand of gravity. "You'll gather the importance of this, Davies, when I tell you the C.-in-C. received a message this morning with one of Winston's red tags attached to it. That's why I immediately called this conference."

The red tags referred to had the words ACTION THIS

9

DAY emblazoned on them and represented Churchill's most feared directives. Shaking his head, Davies turned back to Lindstrom. "We couldn't destroy the processing plant in Bavaria?"

"No. Naturally we've considered it but our agents say it has been constructed in an almost impregnable position. Moreover we have to consider the possibility it is an elaborate hoax and the real plant is somewhere else. Or they could even be duplicated. The only way we can be certain the threat is eliminated is to destroy the stocks themselves."

Staines nodded at the briefcase on the desk. "Let's look at the photographs you've brought."

The men crowded round a large photograph of the valley that Lindstrom laid on the desk. Staines gave a whistle. "Jeez! It looks more like a job for a submarine. Where are the IMI stocks supposed to be?"

"Until now we've believed they were still in the power station's basement. But my sister's heard a rumour they might have been moved into concrete bunkers some distance away. The only way we can find out the truth is to take new photographs and compare them with the old."

Davies beat Staines to the question by a whisker. "But if the power station is too difficult a target and in any case the Norwegian Government won't sanction another raid against it, why would Jerry do that? The basement's the safest place they could be in."

The young Norwegian nodded. "That was the position until we learned about the Bavarian processing plant. Now it has been decided that no matter what hardship is caused, the stocks must be destroyed."

Staines was frowning down at the photograph. "Maybe so but if we couldn't clobber it a year ago, how can we clobber it now? It looks as big as a fortress."

Lindstrom's academic tone suddenly changed as his eyes lifted to Staines. "It is well over a year since it was bombed. Haven't we developed better bombsites and bigger bombs in that time?"

The strong hint of criticism made Staines frown. "You think the Heinies don't know that?"

The Brigadier, more aware than anyone how emotionally involved the young Norwegian was with the destruction of the stocks, intervened tactfully. "It is just feasible the stocks have been moved into bunkers, gentlemen. The Germans need that power station as much as the Norwegians and so while the stocks remain inside it, it has always been a target for attack."

Never one to beat about the bush. Staines came straight to the point. "We're waffling around this, aren't we? What do you want us to do? Try to find out where the stocks are and then have a crack at them? You do realize we'd have to bomb at high level? There isn't a hope of getting the penetration otherwise."

With the Swartfjord raid in mind, Davies was thanking God this was true. Studying the photograph again, he turned to the Texan. "We could try 2000 lb. armour piercing bombs, sir. With the right terminal velocity they'll penetrate nine inches of armour or sixteen feet of reinforced concrete."

The big Texan shrugged. "Great. Only how do we drop 'em? They're too long to go into our B.17s' bomb bays and your Lancs couldn't go because it would mean a daylight raid and they'd be shot to hell."

"Can you adapt your B.17s? Carry them outside the bomb bays perhaps?"

"No. We tried that once when we were thinking of attacking the Heinie submarine pens but the boffins couldn't find a way. We could ask them to try again but I wouldn't put any money on it."

"Then what about 500 lb. semi-armour piercing? If they were dropped from 30,000—as they'd have to be to get their full terminal velocity—we'd be above most of the flak defences."

Staines gave a lop-sided grin. "Who is 'we'? You or us?"

"We could give it a try, sir, if you like."

Staines shrugged his massive shoulders. "If it comes to a high-level daylight raid using A.P.s, it's obviously our job. Only how can I expect my boys to land bombs on a target so well hidden? Don't forget it's February—the bottom of that valley is probably in shadow twenty-four hours a day." His eyes moved to Lindstrom. "Am I right?"

The Norwegian nodded reluctantly. "A side valley does admit some sunlight but only for ninety minutes. Of course, this only applies if the stocks are in bunkers at the foot of the valley. The power station, being higher up the mountain, gets more daylight."

"Ninety minutes," Staines grunted. "Well, I suppose it's a possibility even if it's a goddam slim one. But all this is a bit academic until we know where the stocks are kept. So

11

let's look at the other possibility—of hitting them when they're in transit. Has your sister any idea what the Heinies have in mind?"

Lindstrom shook his head. "That's something she'll be trying to find out at this moment."

"So there's no way we can be making plans in that area," Staines muttered. "The snag there, if we leave it too late and they work out some special method of transportation, we could be caught with our trousers down."

"On the other hand, if we attack the stocks in the valley and mess it up, they'll be alerted we know they're moving the stocks and they'll take those special precautions," Davies pointed out.

"That's right. Heads we lose and tails they win." Staines turned to Lindstrom. "You tell us what you'd like us to do."

The young Norwegian hesitated. "I wouldn't like the valley to be raided unsuccessfully because then I'm certain the Air Commodore is right and greater precautions would be taken when the stocks are moved. After all, there hasn't been an attack for a long time and so security must have relaxed a little. At the same time it is true that the longer we wait the greater risks we take. While we're waiting for news of their transport plans, I'd like a specialist pilot to fly over the valley. He could take photographs which we can compare with the ones taken a year ago and at the same time he can assess the chances of a direct attack. That way we'll be keeping all our options open."

"I'll go with that," Staines said immediately.

Davies had been working on similar lines. "If you like I'll send one of my Mosquitoes over with a F53 camera. We'll also brief the pilot and navigator to keep their eyes open for any new-looking buildings. If we're crafty we can make it look as if they're taking photographs of Rjukan or some other nearby town. Then, when we've heard the crews' assessment and studied the photographs, we can all meet again."

Staines glanced at the Brigadier, then nodded. "That's fine with me, Davies. Only make it snappy because the whole business is a nightmare to London and Washington and they're breathing down our throats."

"I'll lay it on for tomorrow, sir," Davies said. "Weather permitting, of course."

12

## 3

"It's a man's life we're talking about, sir." Henderson, the Station C.O., was a big Highlander who invariably said what he thought. "I'm dead against it."

Davies, with two red spots high on his cheekbones, was showing resentment as well as anger. "Do you think I like it? Moore's the best squadron commander I have. But you tell me what choice I've got."

"I have told you, sir. Get Benson to send one of their high-level Spitfires over. That's their job."

"Jock, for Christ's sake. . . . To begin with I need a man with Moore's experience to make some assessments for me. Apart from that, it's so hush-hush I can't even tell you everything that's behind it. So how can I brief some run-of-the-mill pilot at Benson?"

"They're not run-of-the-mill pilots, sir. They're all very experienced men."

"All right, maybe they are. But they haven't the kind of experience I need."

"I've an entire squadron of experienced men here, sir. Why can't we use one of them?"

"I've just explained. To do the job properly Moore needs to be told as much as I've told you. Security won't allow less senior officers to have that kind of information. I can't be blamed for that, can I?"

Henderson walked to his office window and stared out. In general his relationship with Davies was good. A professional airman himself, Henderson knew a hard-driving, tenacious commander when he saw one, and Davies was all those things and more. At the same time experience had taught the Scot that Davies, who had personally created 633 Squadron, would sometimes commit his men to dangers beyond the normal call of duty. How much of this was due to Davies' confidence in his beloved unit and how much personal ambition. Henderson had never been able to decide but at moments like this he trod very warily. Taking a deep breath, he turned.

"If the job's as important as you say, sir, I suppose Moore will have to go. But I do feel someone ought to go with him. He doesn't need to know what Moore is looking for but he can act as wing man in case Moore runs into trouble."

Davies half-opened his mouth, then gave a reluctant grunt. "Who had you in mind?"

"Harvey. He's one of the few men here who has experience of Norwegian conditions. And he's the last man to chatter about the job."

There was a time when the very mention of Harvey, A Flight Commander, would have been enough to make Davies' hackles rise but since the Yorkshireman's heroic attack on the Rhine Maiden installation that had almost cost him his life, Davies' opinion of him had been considerably upgraded. The small Air Commodore scowled, then gave a reluctant nod. "All right, I'll agree to that. But you know how he likes to know the ins and outs of everything, so if he starts asking questions, tell him to belt up."

"I'll take care of that, sir. But what about Adams? We'll have to bring him in too, won't we?"

Adams was the Station Intelligence Officer and one of his tasks was to provide the latest intelligence about enemy radar detectors and flak positions. Hesitating for a few seconds Davies nodded. "It'll be a help and Adams is a trustworthy old bugger. All right, alert him and Moore and I'll tell 'em all I can. We'll bring Harvey in later. In the meantime you can tell your boys to stand down. I want them in good shape in case an urgent job comes out of all this."

Adams, his greatcoat collar up round his ears, pushed open the ante-room door. "Hello, Tess. Is the Squadron Commander in?"

The pretty, curly-haired Waaf sergeant sitting behind her typewriter gave him a smile. "Yes, sir. Do you want to see him?"

"I got a message he wants to see me. Will you check?"

The girl disappeared into the adjacent office, to emerge a few seconds later. "Please come in, sir."

A young Wing Commander was sitting behind a desk full of papers as Adams entered but rose immediately on seeing him. Although 633 Squadron was as informal as most RAF active-services stations, its informality never affected Ian Moore's natural courtesy. Immaculately dressed, of medium height and build, he was a good-looking man with fair hair and a small scar on his right cheek. Only a close observer would have noticed his slight wince as he straightened. Moore had been wounded and shot down during Operation Crucible the previous autumn and the femur of his right thigh, knitted around a steel pin, still gave him severe twinges when the weather was cold. His quiet cultured voice gave no sign of it as he greeted Adams and motioned him into a chair.

"Sorry to disturb you, Frank, but I've had a call from Pop Henderson. Did you know Davies is here?"

"Yes. I noticed his car as I came over. Is something special on?"

"It looks like it. He wants to see us both in the C.O.'s office. They're going to give me a ring when they're ready."

Adams, a pipe smoker, shook his head as Moore held out a cigarette case. "You don't know what it's about?"

"I've no idea at all. Except that Townsend has been told to D.I. the reconnaissance aircraft in double quick time."

Adams' curiosity was growing. "The recce kite? What can he want that for?"

"Townsend's also been told to get Harvey's aircraft ready. So your guess is as good as mine."

"Has Harvey been told anything yet?"

"Only that he has to stand by and join us in the C.O.'s office later. It all sounds very hush-hush."

As always when Davies was loose on the station, Adams had a feeling of unease. Not a professional airman like Henderson, he had always found it more difficult to forgive the small Air Commodore for the risks he took with his élite squadron. At the same time Adams was intelligent enough to know that it was men like Davies who won wars.

In many ways Adams was an enigmatical man. Hating war passionately, he should not have minded that his middle age and spectacles kept him from combat duty and yet Adams minded very much. To have to advise young men how to risk their lives as profitably as possible seemed indecent to Adams who felt his greatest daily risk was stepping out of his bath, and there were times when he would have given ten years of his life to wear wings and fly with them. With this desire in no way matching his anti-war sentiments, Adams had long given up trying to understand himself. Perhaps he would have had more success if he had realized he was an incurable romantic.

"I heard cheers coming from A Flight offices as I walked over," he said. "And Monahan and Evans came running past me as if their trousers were on fire. Davies hasn't brought Myrna Loy with him, has he?"

15

Moore smiled. "No, but he's done the next best thing: he's stood the squadron down. I phoned the good news to Harvey and Young five minutes ago."

Adams showed none of the relief such news would normally bring. "That doesn't sound too good either, does it?"

"You try telling that to the boys. I'll bet they're already queueing up to phone their girl friends."

The ringing of the telephone silenced Adams. Moore took the call, then nodded. "Yes, sir. Adams is with me now. We'll be over right away."

Adams met his eye as he replaced the receiver. "Are they ready?"

"Ready and waiting," Moore told him. Limping across the room, the young squadron commander took his cap from a wall peg, then turned and smiled at the uneasy Adams. "Let's go and find out what Davies has cooked up for us this time."

The tall, good-looking American with the shock of black hair was busy adjusting his tie before a cracked mirror propped up on a window ledge. The furniture in the small billet was sparse: two beds with their respective cabinets, a couple of wooden chairs, and a large cupboard that doubled as a wardrobe. Photographs of half-naked girls smiled from its unpainted doors. A piece of threadbare carpet lay between the beds: a couple of uniforms hung from hangers above them. A flying suit lay crumpled in a far corner where it had been flung.

With the short February afternoon drawing to a close, a naked fly-speckled bulb dangling from the ceiling was providing the American with light. He was humming as he twice knotted his tie and twice pulled it apart. Tommy Millburn, one of the squadron's ace pilots, was making the most of the stand-down and was preparing for a foray into Scarborough.

The sound of the door opening made him glance around. A diminutive Welsh navigator with a young-old face was coming in from the dusk outside. His sharp features looked pinched with cold as he jerked a thumb over his shoulder.

"What's going on? We're stood down and yet there's a hell of a panic in No. 1 hangar. Chiefy's got a whole bloody team working on Harvey's aircraft and the recce kite."

Millburn paused, tie in hand. "Did you ask Chiefy what for?"

"All he's been told is that they have to be ready by to-

16

night. I suppose it's one of Davies' stunts. Whenever he comes here there's trouble." Pulling off his scarf, the Welshman flung himself on his bed. Johnnie Gabriel, known to all and sundry as Gabby or The Gremlin, was clearly in one of his darker Celtic moods. Noticing Millburn's well-groomed appearance he gave a disparaging grunt.

"You're putting on the shine tonight, aren't you?"

Millburn knotted his tie for the third time. "This is it, boyo. The big pay-off. Susie nearly jumped out of her knickers when I got through on the phone and told her the news. Her folks are going out this evening, so we'll have the place to ourselves."

"And they won't have got past the front gate before you've got her upstairs in bed. Right?"

Millburn grinned. "What's your guess?"

"That's all you ever think of. Sometimes I think you ought to see the M.O."

Millburn began sniffing. "You catch that smell?"

Gabby looked around. "What smell?"

"Sour grapes, boyo. What's the matter? Does she still prefer young Matthews?"

Millburn's reference was to a particularly comely young Waaf who had recently been posted to the squadron. A tall girl, she also had Junoesque proportions, and Gabby, who liked his women tall and well-fleshed, had been glassy-eyed ever since. At the Welshman's scowl, Millburn grinned again. "She probably hasn't seen you yet. Try standing on a chair the next time."

"You think that's funny, Millburn?"

"Not as funny as your face, kiddo, when a dame turns you down. You look so goddammed surprised. Any other guy in your shoes would be used to it by this time."

As the conversation suggested, the two men, who flew together, were inseparable friends. Gabby's reaction confirmed the relationship. "You think you're something, don't you, Millburn? God's gift to women. One of these days you're going to take a hell of a tumble."

Millburn rubbed his newly shaved cheeks with lotion. "I'm having a tumble tonight, boyo. Right in that big double bed of Susie's."

"I hope her folks come back early and catch you at it," Gabby said vindictively. "That's what you need. Exposure."

"That sounds like me talking to Susie. I'm always telling her that."

17

"Funny, funny," Gabby grunted. "Why the hell don't you remuster? The Yanks are always saying they'd like to have you. So why don't you give them a break?"

Millburn ran a comb carefully through his dark hair. "Maybe I will when they run short of dames up here. But so far the supply seems O.K."

Muttering his disgust, Gabby threw himself back on his bed. "I don't know what she sees in Matthews. All he talks about is Harry Roy and dance bands."

"Maybe she likes dance bands."

Gabby's thoughts had already moved elsewhere. "In any case he's not that tall."

"Who? Harry Roy?"

"No. Matthews. Come to think of it, I don't give him more than a couple of inches."

Millburn grinned. "Maybe he stands tall in other ways."

"There's that mind of yours again," Gabby accused. "You can't keep off it, can you?"

The American made a gesture of apology. "Sorry, sahib. I hadn't realized you were chasing Liz Barnes for an intellectual conversation."

"I'm not chasing her," Gabby snarled. "She's already said she'll go out with me."

"When?" Millburn challenged.

Gabby hesitated. "Tonight. Or Wednesday."

Millburn grinned. "I get it. Matthews is Duty Officer tonight and on Wednesday he's agreed to play the drums at Machin's party. She's playing you for a sucker, boyo. You won't get as much as a nibble of her ear after you've paid for her dinner." Seeing Gabby's glare, Millburn turned. "All right, if you're so keen and confident, why the hell aren't you taking her out tonight?"

The reason for the Welshman's frustration came out in a rush. "Because that old cow in charge of her section has confined her to camp for a week. That's why."

The American gave a roar of amusement. "So that's it. When did she promise to go out with you? After she was grounded?"

"No, last week. What's so funny, Millburn? If it was you, you'd be biting broken glass."

"No, I wouldn't. I'd be thinking of ways of getting round it."

A hopeful gleam entered Gabby's eyes. "You wouldn't like to help out, would you?"

One look at the Welshman, who had swung his legs

eagerly to the floor, was all Millburn needed. ."Oh, no. I'm not risking a courtmartial so you can get your horrible little red hands on Liz Barnes. That's right out."

"But nobody would know," Gabby argued. "I wouldn't bring her here until all the boys were out or in the Mess. And I'd keep the door locked."

"I said no! You try it and I'll break you all over the airfield. I mean it, boyo."

The scowling Gabby threw himself back on his bed. "So I'm supposed to stay here all night listening to Much-Binding-in-the-Marsh while you're in bed with Susie."

Millburn walked between the beds and took his tunic off the hanger. "That's about the size of it. Unless you want to bed her down on the airfield perimeter. Frozen grass down her knickers ought to work wonders for you."

Gabby gazed up in dislike. "That after-shave of yours smells like a gorilla's armpit."

"What's that mean? You want to use it?"

"Me? I don't want everyone thinking I'm a Nancy Boy."

Climbing into his tunic and greatcoat, Millburn set his cap at a jaunty angle and made towards the mirror again. Halfway there he suddenly paused and grinned. Straightening his face, he turned back to the disconsolate Gabby. "You thought of the dispersal huts? They've all got beds in them, haven't they?"

"Of course I've thought of them. But there's always some sod on duty."

"We're on stand-down, remember?"

"So what? That Corporal of ours keeps the key. And he'll never hand it over so I can take a girl in there. He's a bloody Biblepuncher."

"I wasn't thinking of him. Monahan's Corporal isn't above having a Waaf in his hut. I know he's done it himself. And his hut's at the far side of the airfield."

Gabby was now listening hard. "Why should he let me use it?"

"Because I pay him to service my car, that's why. You like me to have a word with him?"

Hope was suddenly radiating from Gabby's face. "When?"

"Tomorrow. I'll arrange it for Wednesday. Matthews will be busy at the party and everyone else will be too drunk to miss you. That's it, boyo. You're in."

Gabby stirred, then rose on one grudging elbow. "I suppose that's decent of you, Millburn."

19

Millburn waved an indulgent hand. "Don't mention it, kid. Just think about Wednesday and leave it all to me."

The restored Gabby sank back on his bed. Dreaming of the bliss to come, he failed to notice Millburn's expression as the American turned and made for the door. Pausing there to glance back, Millburn took the precaution of removing the key before making his exit. Outside a loud chortle broke from him as he made his way towards the transport pool.

# 4

Davies peered out of the window. "We could be in luck. The Met. boys say this anti-cyclone stretches right across the Atlantic."

"They don't know if it's reached Norway yet, sir," Adams reminded him.

Davies let the curtain fall and turned back. "No. But it's drifting that way. So if for any reason we have to go there again we should have a few days of decent weather."

The hint of further Norwegian operations made Adams wince. Of all the squadron personnel with experience of the Swartfjord tragedy, no one had been more affected than Adams, paradoxically because his role had been the passive one of waiting in the Operations Room and listening to the slaughter of his friends. When he and Moore had entered the C.O.'s office fifteen minutes ago and Davies had broken the news that the IMI threat was alive again, Adams had felt almost physically sick.

Davies' eyes were on Moore and Harvey who were standing at the far side of Henderson's big desk. "I'm fully aware that this is a dangerous sortie. In fact if it wasn't so damned important I wouldn't dream of sending only two of you. But we can try to eliminate as many risks as possible. So I want you to go out at ultra high-level."

Harvey, a man with few affectations and a face like one of his moorland fells, gave a grunt of protest. "We'll be a lot safer at low level, sir."

"Why?" Davies demanded. "Who's going to catch you at 35,000 feet plus? Even Junkers 88s and 190s with nitrous oxide can't get up that quickly."

With an accent that was almost truculently Yorkshire, Harvey tended to sound more aggressive than he was. "They won't need to be that quick if their detectors pick us up halfway across the North Sea."

"There's no evidence Jerry's got detectors that efficient in Norway."

"There's no evidence he hasn't either. If this target's as important as you say, he must have it well protected."

Scowling at this sample of northern logic, Davies turned to Moore. "What do you think, Moore?"

Debonair and easy-going as he was, Moore could be as outspoken as any man when the situation called for it.

21

"Harvey's had more experience over Norway than any of us, sir. I have to take notice of what he says."

As Davies did a turn round the office Adams was reminded of the time before the Rhine Maiden affair when the Yorkshireman and Moore, respective products of poverty and privilege, had found little in common but dissent. Since the operation, however, in which Moore had shepherded the critically wounded Harvey home, their relationship had totally changed. Now, although Harvey would probably have died rather than admit it, the two men were the closest of friends.

Adams' eyes were drawn down to the black mongrel at Harvey's heels. Giving a restless whine, it was nuzzling its head against the Yorkshireman's leg. During Harvey's long confinement in hospital, Adams had taken care of Sam and it would have been interesting to know who had gained more from the arrangement, the bereft Sam or the lonely Adams. But, as Adams had always known, Sam was a one-man dog and since Harvey's return to active service the dog had been paying the Intelligence Officer less and less attention.

Pushing the animal impatiently away, Harvey pursued his case. "If this anti-cyclone hasn't reached Norway yet, it's a million to one there'll be cloud below 35,000 feet. So if you want photographs we'll have to go down in any case once we've crossed the coast."

Davies scowled at the two pilots. "You're both dead set at running into Jerry's defences, aren't you? Leave it for the moment and let's look at your flight plan." He pulled a notebook out of his pocket and handed it to Moore. "As this is a hush-hush job we're not using your specialist officers. I had this plan drawn up before I came and you can show it to your navigators later. You'll find it contains all you need."

Moore was scanning through the pages. "ETA—1305? Isn't that rather late in the day, sir?"

"That's one of our problems. Apparently it's not daylight in Norway until around nine-thirty at this time of the year and the light doesn't reach the bottom of the valley until after noon. The shadows are back by 1415 so it's vital you keep to those times."

Moore nodded and turned a page over. "I see Rjukan is about 200 kilometres from the coast." As Harvey gave a grunt, Moore glanced up wryly at Davies. "That's a fair way inland, sir."

22

"Maybe you see now why I want you up at high level. If you stay up there all the way, you can get your photographs and be out again before Jerry can reach you."

"But I thought you wanted an assessment of the valley as well as photographs."

"So I do," Davies grunted. "But an assessment's no good to me if neither of you are alive to bring it back. As I've explained, Moore, this can't be a hit-or-miss operation. It's so important Bomber Command have been ordered to lay on mine-laying operations in the Skagerrak and the Baltic to draw Jerry's fighters south and eastwards. The Banff Wing are also co-operating by flying sorties against targets in the north. On top of that you're getting an escort on your way back. So if we do a rough costing, a million pounds or more and a fair number of lives are going to be spent making sure you come out unscathed with the information we need. Does that explain why I can't let you take a single unnecessary risk?"

Even the phlegmatic Harvey looked impressed by Davies' statistics. "If it's that important, sir, our best chance is to go in low and come out low. No question about it."

At times like this Davies wondered what perversity of creation had attached the north of England to the south. "Not being a complete idiot I've another reason for preferring you to keep up aloft. Apart from the valley's flak defences which might be as heavy as the Swartfjord's, we mustn't let Jerry guess we're interested in it. If you two come screaming through it at zero height, he'll have to be blind and stupid not to guess, won't he?"

Motioning Harvey to keep quiet, Moore took a glance at the map of Norway that was spread over Henderson's desk. "You said earlier Rjuken had a number of important industries. Supposing we circle it a couple of times as if taking photographs, then dive into the valley and fly westwards. With any luck they'll think we're only doing it for cover."

Davies was remembering he had suggested a similar stratagem to Staines although at that time he had thought only in terms of high level. Now temptation in the guise of the two pilots was reminding him how much more information a low-level reconnaissance would provide. Testily Davies compromised.

"You two are hell bent on suicide, aren't you? All right; this is the way you'll play it. If the weather's clear right across to the target, you'll stay up high and do the best you can. That's an order. If there are clouds, you'll use your own initiative. If that means a low-level run down the valley, you'll make it as innocuous as possible." The small Air Commodore turned from Moore to Harvey with some sarcasm. "Happy now?"

Harvey's shrug said it all. The entire argument had been academic because once over Norway the weather would make high-level flying a farce. Trying to hide his irritation and failing abysmally, Davies snatched the notebook from Moore. "Now we've got that nonsense settled, let's get down to specifics."

## 5

The two Mosquitoes were flying in echelon with Harvey little more than fifty yards behind Moore's starboard wing. As he felt his aircraft yaw unsteadily in the rarified air, the Yorkshireman dropped back after fifty yards. Since leaving Lossiemouth, where they had topped up their tanks, the two Mosquitoes had been climbing steadily towards their maximum ceiling. From the turbulent layers of air near the sea they had passed into the troposphere where all the variations of weather take place. Here their contrails had streamed out and shredded away in a 50 m.p.h. wind that was swirling around the edge of the high pressure area. Now, nearly halfway across the North Sea, they were almost in the stratosphere and the high winds that had been causing problems to their navigators were beginning to slacken. Far below, the sea looked like a vast frozen plain in the winter sun. Above the sky was a deep blue with the sun a molten ball.

To the uninitiated the appearance of the Mosquitoes would have been puzzling. Their upper surface had been painted in crazy streaks of black and white and below they were a uniform cerulean blue. With a yellow halo around their spinning propellers, they yawed more and more unsteadily as they climbed into the icy stratosphere.

Inside the two aircraft the crews were suffering all the discomforts of high-level flight. Without pressurized cabins, they were wearing air-tight masks and pressure waistcoats beneath their bulky flying suits to assist the passage of oxygen to their lungs. Although the Mosquito was normally a warm aircraft, the subzero temperature outside was affecting their nervous systems. Instruments kept blurring before their eyes and as the aircraft climbed even higher their sense of remoteness grew. The normal roar of the Merlins was reduced to a distant ticking as if the Mosquitoes were toys and they were children playing inside them.

As well as studying the instruments and searching the immense sky for enemy aircraft, the crews were assessing the weather conditions. Apart from a few cirrus clouds that had drifted below, the visibility was almost unnaturally clear for a North European winter day. Ahead, however, the look of the horizon made Hopkinson, Moore's navigator, glance down at his padded flying suit and oxygen equipment. "It doesn't look as if we are going to need these much longer, skipper."

Hopkinson, a Cockney who had been shot down with Moore the previous year during Operation Crucible, had been more severely wounded than his pilot and had returned to the squadron only a month ago. It was a return Moore had never been more thankful for than today. A peerless navigator, with eyes like a sparrow-hawk, Hopkinson was the ideal man to find a valley in the labyrinth of fjords and mountains that was Norway.

Behind J-Jimmy, the squadron's photographic Mosquito that Moore was flying, Harvey was eyeing the long banks of cloud ahead with satisfaction. Everything Harvey had seen of Norway convinced him their chances of success were doubled if they crossed the coast at low level. The fact that the clouds had appeared before enemy radar detectors could have picked up their approach enhanced his satisfaction.

"I think you're right, Hoppy," Moore said. "But we'll hang on a few minutes to make sure."

Levelling out from their climb, the two Mosquitoes droned on. The first of the clouds that swept below looked like islands against the lighter hue of the sea but the dense mass ahead suggested the aircraft had reached the eastern fringe of the huge anti-cyclone. After a couple of minutes Hoppy glanced back at Moore. "We'd better not leave it any longer, skipper, or their detectors will pick us up."

Nodding, Moore waggled his wings twice. With the Mosquitoes bound by radio silence on the outer leg of the mission, it was a prearranged signal to descend. As their noses dropped and the altimeter needles began to swing back, Lacy, Harvey's navigator, gave a sigh of relief. For the last ten minutes he had been experiencing sharp pains in his left shoulder and elbow and wondered if it could be the dreaded bends. With Harvey playing the role of wing man, Lacy had flinched at the possibility he might force the formidable Yorkshireman to abandon his friend and return to base. At a lower altitude the danger of bends would vanish.

With the decision made, Moore took the Mosquitoes down rapidly and all four men began swallowing to ease the increased pressure on their eardrums. At seven thousand feet Moore loosened his face mask. Hoppy followed his example a few seconds later, taking deep breaths of fresh air. With the clouds shadowing it, the sea had now

26

changed colour and texture. An icy grey-green patchwork, its wavetops snapped at the Mosquitoes as they sank down to an altitude of only three hundred feet. As they crossed one of the diminishing sunlit patches, their shadows appeared, chasing them like sharks.

Moore pointed at the cloud banks ahead. "How high are they, Hoppy?"

Hopkinson squinted through the wet windshield. "I'd say around 4,000 feet. Maybe a thousand more."

"Then we should be O.K."

Hopkinson had the Cockney's mordant sense of humour. "With mountain peaks everywhere? It's going to be a doddle, skipper."

Moore smiled at him. "I've every confidence in you, Hoppy."

"You have? Then what am I worried about?"

Back in D-Danny Harvey glanced at his navigator. "How long to ETA, Jack?"

Lacy consulted his log. "Thirty-four minutes."

A sudden whiplash of hail reminded both crews they were flying into a Norwegian winter. With his wipers barely able to clear the windshield and the danger of icing present, Moore took the Mosquitoes up to 1,500 feet. Wise to the conditions, Harvey fell back to the limit of his visibility. A couple of minutes later when the squall passed the two aircraft sank down to the sea again.

Land was sighted three minutes later. At first the crews thought it was a low-lying cloud but as they raced towards it they saw it was a rocky, uninhabited island. Hoppy answered Moore's enquiry with a nod. "Enemy coast ahead, skipper."

More skerries flashed past. Disturbed by the thunder of engines, seagulls rose in clouds from them. As a fishing boat appeared, rolling in the heavy swell, a man leaned out of the wheelhouse and waved. Hoppy grinned at Moore. "At least the natives are still friendly."

The mainland appeared a minute later, a study of virgin snow and brutal soaring mountains. Leaning forward, Hoppy pointed at a wide gap at eleven o'clock. "Try that fjord, skipper."

Moore banked and made for it. A grey-painted ship making for the same fjord appeared, her bow wave white against the grey sea. As J-Jimmy rocketed past Moore noticed a couple of multiple pom-poms either side of her bows but before the startled German crew could react the

27

Mosquitoes' speed carried them past. At the same time all four men knew a radio warning would already be tapping out.

Land rose on either side of them, belts of dark pines and slopes of scree. A small hamlet, linked to civilization only by the sea, was perched at the foot of a mountain slope. Moore caught a glimpse of a wooden jetty, Falumred houses, half-a-dozen anchored fishing boats and a cluster of oil tanks. Five seconds later there was a triumphant shout from Hoppy, "We're all right, skipper. There's the cement factory."

Glancing starboard again, Moore saw a large dust-covered building with an overhead chain of cable cars running down from the mountainside. His comment was heartfelt. "Hoppy, you're a wonder!"

A hundred yards behind in D-Danny Lacy was pointing at the same factory. "He's found our entry point, skipper. Bang on the button."

Harvey's gruff comment held a fellow professional's respect. "That's bloody marvellous navigating."

Bellies lowering to a few feet above the water, the Mosquitoes raced up the fjord. Mountains rose dizzily on either side, patchworked in icy scree, dark pines, and snow drifts. Isolated farm houses standing at the water's edge flashed past, wooden-framed with high sloping roofs. A girl in a red coat was standing alongside a half-dozen goats. She waved excitedly but before the grinning Hoppy could reply J-Jimmy banked steeply round a mountain spur.

Six miles inland from the sea the water of the fjord was like glass, reflecting the stark colours of the enclosing mountains. With the two Mosquitoes flying line astern, the air-blast of their propellers shivered a wake along it. As they penetrated deeper into the fjord steep gorges and waterfalls appeared on either side. Ahead the mountains closed in around another hamlet and Hoppy glanced at Moore. "I think that's the end of the fjord, skipper. We go over the top."

Moore nodded and drew back on the control column. The Mosquito soared upwards and levelled out over a wilderness of mountain peaks, woods and lakes. Glancing at his altimeter, Moore saw with surprise that it registered 2,000 feet: the terrain had been climbing steadily since they crossed the coast. "Is this our plateau?" he asked Hopkinson.

The Cockney was frowning over the Norwegian name.

"It's the fringe of it, I think, skipper. The Hardanger something or other."

Moore was recalling his flight plan notes. The Hardangervidda, the largest and highest plateau in Europe. Four thousand square miles of desolation with only its perimeter served by roads and even those needing constant attention by snow ploughs in the winter. An icy, windswept wilderness that ironically was easier to cross on foot in the winter because the low temperatures hardened the bogs and the deep snow levelled off the rocky terrain. Except on its fringes, a place inhabited only by reindeer and equally hardy animals.

In D-Danny Harvey was showing his experience by keeping a full half-mile behind his leader, so allowing himself time to follow J-Jimmy's manoeuvres. Trying to keep as low a profile as possible, Moore was making for a second valley that ran diagonally across his flight path. Already the altitude had taken its effect on the plateau. Dwarf birch and shrubs were mantled with snow, and where the bitter wind blew, patches of black rock alternated with snow drifts. Lakes were frozen over and waterfalls columns of ice.

Almost without warning, the ground plunged dizzily into the steep valley. Grateful for its cover, the two Mosquitoes flung themselves into it like meteors. Towering, moss-covered walls of rocks flashed past. Swinging round mountain spurs bearded with shrub, the aircraft penetrated deeper into the plateau. Alternating his eyes between the map strapped on his knee and the valley ahead, Hoppy pointed a finger. "Take the starboard fork, Skipper."

Moore saw the valley was bifurcating. To the left a hamlet squatted on a flat apron of terrain. The road that ran from it wound alongside a frozen river. The second leg of the fork appeared little more than a cleft in the mountain wall. Moore's voice was dry as he swung J-Jimmy towards it. "I hope you're right, Hoppy."

The mountains closed in like the walls of a prison: the trapped aircraft engines reverberating across them. Long minutes passed, then the walls gave way to a large, frozen lake. Before the four men could relax Hoppy was leading J-Jimmy into another equally steep valley. Harvey grunted an oath as he swung D-Danny in pursuit. "Let's hope the little bugger knows what he's doing!"

A small town signalled the end of the second valley. Showing relief his map reading had not failed him, Hoppy

29

jerked a thumb upwards. "That's the last of our cover, skipper. The rest of the valleys until we get near Rjukan run north and south."

Leaping out on to the plateau, the Mosquitoes flew as low as their pilots dared. Their altimeters were now showing 3,500 feet. Here, near the centre of the Hardangervidda, the landscape had changed. Low, treeless hills interspaced by bogs and lakes ran as far as the eye could see. With the altitude giving full scope to the iron Norwegian winter, every stretch of water was frozen solid.

After the relative security of the valleys, all four men felt as exposed as flies crawling over a white tablecloth, and the two navigators increased their surveillance of the sky above. At this altitude the cloud ceiling was less than two thousand feet. Although it gave welcome cover to the low-flying aircraft, the men were aware a hundred 190s could be hiding inside it. Moreover, slanting streaks of sunlight, dramatically illuminating hill tops and patches of snow ahead, gave warning the clouds were breaking to the east.

A brilliant rainbow appeared, arcing spectacularly against a bank of clouds. Thirty seconds later hail rattled furiously against the Mosquitoes' windshields. When the fierce squall passed, Moore turned to Hoppy. "Any sign of Rjukan yet?"

The Cockney shook his head. The scabrous hills on either side held snow only in drifts or ravines: the rest had been denuded by the high winds of the Hardangervidda. As the two Mosquitoes leapt over a hill and along a drift, plumes of snow appeared behind their propellers. Wild grouse rose from a clump of bushes and scattered in all directions. Hoppy tapped Moore's shoulder. At two o'clock a deep gorge split the plateau. "I think it's the River Mane. If it is, it goes stright to Rjukan."

A few summer houses appeared, snow-covered and empty. A man was dragging a toboggan loaded with firewood along an icy strip of road. Then a drifting patch of sunlight ahead lit up the town, an untidy spread of houses and factories in the wilderness. As the Mosquitoes swept over the suburbs Norwegians ran from their houses and waved in excitement.

Guided by Hoppy, Moore made for the factory area. As he began circling it at less than a thousand feet, the first of the town's defences began to react and three black puffs of smoke burst aft of Harvey. They were followed by winking flashes as other guns began opening fire.

With the alarm well and truly given, Moore broke radio silence for the first time. "Frank, can you see the generator factory?"

Harvey waited a few seconds before answering. "Sorry, Ian, I didn't catch that."

"I asked if you could identify the generator factory."

"Aye, I think so. Isn't it that dirty big building at eleven o'clock?"

"According to my map that's the steel wire plant. I want the generator factory."

"Then it must be the one with those three sheds alongside it."

"Get me photographs, will you?"

"O.K., skipper. Lacy's taking them now."

It was a conversation meant solely to mislead. It was well known that German monitoring stations were using English-speaking operators to pick up R/T talk between hostile aircraft, and it was hoped such an operator would be in attendance around Rjukan. If one was not, no harm would be done.

Moore circled the factory area a last time. Radar sets were now warmed up and 37 mm shells bursting uncomfortably close to the Mosquitoes. "How are you doing, Frank? Have you finished photographing that factory yet?"

"Yes, skipper. We're finished."

"O.K. Then let's go home."

The two aircraft banked away, followed by tracer and a line of bursting shells. Tense in his seat, Hoppy was giving bearings to Moore. Below the last of the suburbs fell away. At ten o'clock a huge lake high up on a mountain shone in a patch of sunlight. "That's the reservoir," Hoppy said. "The power station's lower down."

Fifteen seconds later Moore could see it, a massive seven-storied building standing on a plateau halfway down the mountainside. Penstock lines, pipes that conducted water at enormous pressure into the power station's turbines, could be seen linking the building to the reservoir above. A road cleared of snow ran in a loop from the station to a bridge that spanned an awesomely steep gorge. A local railway track ran westward along the mountainside. Gausta, the highest mountain in southern Norway, could be seen past J-Jimmy's wingtip.

In the few seconds left before the Mosquitoes reached the valley, Hopkinson was examining the power station

31

through high-powered binoculars. "See any concrete bunkers nearby or below?" Moore asked.

"No, just outhouses," the Cockney told him. "And none of 'em look recently built."

"Then get down to your camera. The photographic experts will have to sort it out." Moore switched on his R/T again, hoping his words sounded sufficiently innocuous. "We'll take it in turns to give cover on the way back, Frank. Your turn first."

With Moore carrying the wide-angle, high-speed camera, it had been decided beforehand that if reconnaissance were carried out at low level, Harvey would stay above and give protection. Accordingly, as the enormous valley loomed beneath the Mosquitoes, Harvey swept straight on. Moore, giving Hopkinson a look of reassurance he did not feel, took a deep breath and pushed the control column forward. Bringing snow avalanching down the cliff from the thunder of its engines, J-Jimmy dived over the rim and went plunging down.

## 6

In the few seconds left to him before all his concentration was needed, Moore found himself recording impressions as if his own mind had become a camera. The black birch woods that clothed the higher reaches of the opposite mountain like the pelt of some enormous animal. The long, multi-storied building that looked more like a fortress than a power station. The outbuildings, large by normal standards but dwarfed by their massive parent structure, that clustered round its base. The narrow bridge that spanned the precipitous ravine. . . . The enormous desolation of it all. Staring down into the ravine, Moore decided that the Norwegians who had climbed down its sheer, ice-bound cliffs to sabotage the station must have been giants of men.

Until now, to avoid drawing attention to itself, the station had remained quiet but when it became apparent J-Jimmy's curving flight would take it almost overhead, its defences leapt into action. The command to open fire seemed to come from the station roof itself where a chain of glowing shells soared upwards. A few seconds later every gun within range began firing. Tracer squirted up from rocky aeries; shells came pumping up from clumps of trees. Bracketed by bursting steel, J-Jimmy rocked like a cockleshell in a storm. Hopkinson, busy with the camera, gave a startled gasp. "Christ, skipper, what is this place? Hitler's secret hideout?"

While one half of his mind was frantically trying to stay alive, Moore was making an assessment of the valley's defences with the other. Everything appeared to be there: batteries of 20mm in both double and quadruple mountings; predictor-guided 37mms and 88mms. To avoid the net of steel the LMGs were throwing up, he swung over to the opposite side of the valley but there was no escape from the chains of shells that were bracketing him.

From above it looked as if the entire valley was spewing up shells and that no aircraft could possibly survive. Harvey's alarmed voice crackled in Moore's earphones. "Ian, for Christ's sake get out of there. It's suicide."

Inside his padded high-level flying suit, Moore was drenched in sweat as he fought to control the bucking Mosquito. Across the valley the power station was almost abreast of him and he was trying to make out its details through the curtain of red-cored explosions and smoke. A blinding flash and crack sent a piece of steel slicing through a wing root. Another explosion beneath his starboard engine smashed away a metal fairing. Harvey's voice came again. "Get out of there, Ian! For God's sake, get out."

Hopkinson added his own plea. Although a veteran of nearly seventy operations, the Cockney's face was bloodless. "Haven't you seen enough, skipper?"

Moore's reply was sharp with tension. "Get those photographs taken. I want the valley floor as well."

"I've taken 'em, skipper. What I can get, that is."

A rounded mountain peak was sweeping up ahead. As another explosion made J-Jimmie falter, Moore made his decision and banked towards it. As its scree-covered slopes and scrub swept below, the hell of shells began to ease. Hopkinson was just expressing his relief when Harvey's shout checked him. "Bandits, Ian! Four o'clock."

Moore swung immediately to starboard. He was not a second too soon: a long burst of cannon fire ripped past his port tailplane. Hopkinson, who had left his camera, was staring back. "190s, skipper. Two of 'em."

The German pilots were experienced men who had fought in North Africa and Italy. Instead of attacking in line astern, they swept down in line abreast, so driving the pursued aircraft on to one another's guns. Realizing the danger, Moore dived immediately and the second Focke Wulf's cannon fire lanced above his cupola. Yet air space was limited: the mountain slopes were less than five hundred feet below.

Up aloft, Harvey was not without his troubles. At least twenty-five per cent of the flak had been directed at him and now a further two 190s were giving him their attention. One was already swinging on to his tail; a second was making up ground avidly. Yet with his friend and squadron commander in danger, none of this entered the Yorkshireman's calculations. He put D-Danny's nose down and went hell-for-leather after the Focke Wulfs who had Moore caught in a steel trap.

In fact the move proved to be the right one. The valley's defences opened up again as D-Danny dived across it and the two 190s, with no desire to be shot down by their own guns, swung away. Bracketed by black and white explosions, Harvey flashed across the valley and at a range of less than a hundred yards fired both his cannon at the nearest enemy fighter. Its unsuspecting pilot never knew what hit him. With its engine still giving full revs, the 190 went straight into the mountainside. Petrol, bursting from its tanks, made torches of half-a-dozen birch trees.

Putting his weight on the control column and rudder, Harvey swung aggressively towards the second 190. Bewildered by the recklessness of the attack its pilot broke off the action and vanished behind a mountain shoulder. Harvey tucked himself in behind J-Jimmie. "You two all right?"

Moore exchanged glances with the thankful Hopkinson. "We are now. Thanks, Frank."

Keeping as low as they dared, the Mosquitoes flew back across the Hardangervidda. Both navigators were gazing back at the black shapes darting about beneath the clouds like wolves casting for scent. The black and white camouflage on the upper surfaces of the Mosquitoes made them difficult to pick up against the snow-covered plateau.

The specks disappeared behind a mountain top but as the terrain flattened all four men wondered if their Mosquitoes were visible on the German monitors. If they were, it could not be long before the 190s were given their vectors. Survival might well depend on them finding the fjords that led to the sea before this happened. With Hopkinson guiding their withdrawal, the strain was heavy on the little Cockney.

Ten long but uneventful minutes passed. Then, as they flew through a patch of sunlight, Lacy caught sight of half-a-dozen blurred specks dropping down like gannets. "Bandits, skipper! Six o'clock high."

Harvey gave a muted curse but, along with Moore, his reaction was immediate. Both Mosquitoes sank down until their bellies were only feet above the frozen rocks.

The Focke Wulfs were type A-4s armed with Mauser 151s, cannon with a very high muzzle velocity. The leading aircraft opened fire at six hundred yards. Its hose of 20mm cannon shells exploded in a birch wood a quarter of a mile ahead of Moore, tearing off branches and cutting a swath of boiling snow. The shells ceased abruptly as the German pilot, seeing the frozen ground rushing up at him, hauled back frantically on his stick. As he went rocketing upwards, his ears were assailed by curses from his flight commander for his neglect of elementary combat principles.

While the shaken pilot regained his nerve, the rest of the Focke Wulfs spread out into a wide line. The principle

35

was that of a party of horsemen chasing a fox. The outer riders would prevent escape, the inner ones would effect the kill.

Equipped with the BMW 801 engine, the Focke Wulfs had slightly the edge in speed on the Mosquitoes at ground level. Even so that edge was only marginal and both navigators had time to watch the 190s as they crept within range. In the sunlight that was still illuminating them they looked like evil but beautiful insects with their outstretched cowlings, long transparent cupolas, and short wings. Harvey at the controls of D-Danny was cursing his helplessness. While the odds against the Mosquitoes made it imperative they seal as many avenues of attack as possible, the zero height they were flying made any retaliatory action impossible. "Where the hell is that bloody fjord?" Harvey demanded of his white-faced navigator.

The dark shadow that split the terrain appeared just as the foremost 190 tried its first burst of fire. With the range still too long, it swung away like a badly-aimed whip but served notice that time was fast running out for the Mosquitoes. Hoppy's yell came like a stay of execution. "There it is, skipper! At two o'clock."

Moore was already banking towards the gorge. With a growl of relief Harvey followed, his wingtip only feet above the snow. As the ground fell away beneath them and they dived into thick shadow, Harvey grinned at his relieved navigator. "Now let's see what the bastards can do to us."

The relief for the two navigators, helpless to do anything but grip their seats, was short-lived. The bottom of the narrow fjord with its semi-darkness was a frightening place for fast-moving aircraft. Nor did it deter the German pilots. Unable now to attack in line abreast, they plunged down after the Mosquitoes one by one. The tremendous din of the engines brought minor avalanches of snow and scree down the steep cliffs.

Two hundred yards behind Moore, Harvey felt D-Danny shudder under the impact of shells. Gritting his teeth, the Yorkshireman settled the Mosquito down even lower. Hardly daring to look out of his cupola, Lacy caught a glimpse of black rocks, ice floes, and foaming water. A second burst of cannon fire, glowing vividly in the shadows but this time well above D-Danny brought a grunt of satisfaction from Harvey. To force their fighters to attack bombers from below, the Germans set their fighters' guns up two degrees. A typical piece of Jerry thoroughness that could sometimes be used against him.

Ahead Moore banked steeply as he followed the fjord southwards. At the far side Harvey saw the ghostly column of a waterfall that reached down from the heights above. At its base was a massive ice stalagmite. Making straight towards it, Harvey held his course until the last moment, then rolled the Mosquito on its side and hauled back on the column with all his strength. Wings groaning with the strain, D-Danny changed course and swept after Moore.

The German pilot flying even lower than Harvey and with his eyes intent on his prey, saw his danger too late. The red flash as he crashed into the stalagmite lit up the gorge like a bomb. The Focke Wulfs' deputy commander, a brave man but not a foolhardy one, took the message. The *Tommi* fliers were fighting for their lives, a circumstance that did not apply to his men. Regretfully he gave orders to abandon the action.

Harvey's exultant voice gave the news over the R/T. "They've chucked it up, Ian."

Moore met Hopkinson's relieved eyes. "Thank God for that. Then let's keep our heads down and get back home."

Davies, Henderson, and Adams were waiting beside a jeep when the two Mosquitoes appeared. Motioning the two men to join him, Davies leapt into the driver's seat. The first Mosquito circled the field once and then came in over the southern perimeter. Spray rose like smoke as its tires touched the runway. As it turned off to its dispersal point, Davies revved the engine and drove at speed towards it.

Moore and Hopkinson were being divested of their parachute harnesses when the jeep arrived. For a moment Davies' eyes followed Harvey's Mosquito as it taxied past them on the runway. Black scars ran along its fuselage and there was a large hole in its tail fin. Grunting to himself, Davies jumped down and crossed over to Moore.

"How did it go?"

Moore was suffering the hearing affliction that all crews suffered on landing. Shaking his head at Davies, he took a deep breath and swallowed to clear his sinuses. Realizing that in his anxiety he might be taking security risks, Davies drew him away from the mechanics who were now clustering around J-Jimmy. "Did you get there all right?"

Moore was unzipping his bulky flying suit. "Yes, sir. We got there."

"Thank Christ for that. Did you get a good look around?"

"I think so."

"And photographs?"

"Hoppy took them. Although I was only able to make one run past the power station."

"Why? Was the flak bad?"

Understatement was Moore's way. "Pretty bad, sir."

With his vital questions asked, Davies found time to show concern. He motioned at J-Jimmy's missing fairing and the sharpnel-damaged wings. "Pretty bad? You look like a dog's dinner. Did you get all that in the valley?"

"Most of it. We also had a spot of bother with a flight of 190s."

"High level or low?"

"Low. We ran into clouds halfway across. So we had to go low both ways."

A second jeep drew alongside the Mosquito. The station's photographic section were arriving to collect J-Jimmy's pack of film. Seeing the distinguished company that surrounded the aircraft, the corporal driver and his Waaf passenger leapt out in great haste. Davies swung round on them testily.

"What do you two think this is? Sunday afternoon in Cheltenham? I said I wanted those photographs in a hurry."

In his haste to obey the young corporal caught his foot on one of the mooring hooks and went down boots over breeches. Redfaced, he scrabbled in the wet grass for his tools. "Yes, sir. Sorry, sir."

Turning back to the smiling Moore, Davies lowered his voice. "If you went in at low level, does that mean you weren't able to do that spoof bit over Rjukan?"

"No; we did it as planned. Although whether it fooled Jerry is another matter."

"Could that be why the 190s latched on to you?"

"I don't think so. I think their detectors or Observer Corps picked us up on the way out." Moore glanced across the airfield where the tall figure of Harvey could now be seen talking to his mechanics. "It's a good thing I'd Harvey with me. I wouldn't have got back otherwise."

"You mean because of the 190s?"

"Yes. They had me boxed in until he shot one down. Another flight made contact with us as we neared the coast but we lost them in a fjord."

"How many were there?"

"I counted six. There might have been eight."

"Christ, you've been lucky," Davies muttered, taking a fresh look at the battered J-Jimmy. "I'm sorry I had to send you, Ian, but this was one time I had no choice."

Standing alongside J-Jimmy with Adams, Henderson was clearly growing impatient at the length of Davies' private conversation with his squadron commander. Moore took a step towards him. "Let's hope the photographs make it worthwhile, sir."

Davies checked him. "The Brigadier and I will be debriefing you, not Adams. How soon can you be ready?"

"I'd like a drink and something to eat, sir. I'd also like a bath."

For the first time Davies noticed the pilot's fatigue. "Fair enough. By that time the photographs should be ready. You'll be coming with me to see the Brigadier and General Staines, so it could be a late night."

"Do you want Harvey and the two navigators to come as well?"

"No. It'll be a top security conference. But check with them first there's nothing you missed. All right?"

"Yes, sir."

"Good man. Now go and have a stiff brandy. No, wait." Proving he was not as insensitive as he sometimes appeared, Davies grinned in the direction of the frowning Henderson. "Better have a quick word with Jock first. He's dying to know what happened."

The atmosphere in the library at High Elms was tense as Lindstrom slipped yet another photograph into the magnification unit on the table and bent over it. Standing at his elbow Staines met the Brigadier's eyes and gave an impatient shrug. A full ten seconds passed before the Norwegian sat back. "Well," Staines barked. "What's the verdict?"

Lindstrom looked up. His thin, intellectual face showed bitter disappointment. "As far as I can see there are no new buildings. We'll have them checked by experts, of course, but I don't think there is any doubt. Do you want to take a look?"

Slipping into his seat, Staines peered into the eyepiece. As he fed in one of the latest photographs, he gave a start. A combat airman from his spiky hair to his polished boots, Staines was a man who noticed first things first. "Just look at that flak! Jesus!" He glanced up at Moore who, along with Davies, was standing at the other side of the table. "How the hell did you get out of that valley, Moore?"

An immaculate figure again after a bath and a change of clothes, the young squadron commander smiled. "I think they blew us out, sir."

"You're not kidding! What do you reckon they've got in there?"

"Just about everything. Double and quadruple 20mms. 37mms and 88mms with predictors. Dozens of LMGs. They start at the entrance and run along both sides of the valley. There's a particularly high concentration on and around the power station itself."

Full of respect, Staines' eyes were moving over Moore's double DSOs and his DFC. "I hope they gave you turkey and cranberry sauce when you got back."

"Hardly, sir. But the Spam was tender."

"Spam!" the Texan grunted. "You serve with a tight-fisted outfit, Moore. I think you ought to move over into my bunkhouse. We'd feed you better than that."

With Davies unsure whether to smile or frown and in the end doing neither, Staines turned back to Lindstrom. "So from these photographs you believe the rumours are wrong and the stocks are still in the basement?"

"It looks that way, sir."

"So once again we can't destroy them at source?"

"Not unless you feel you've now got enough strength to blow up the power station from the air."

"We didn't exactly cover ourselves with glory the last time, did we?" Staines grunted. "And I don't see what's changed since except their defences have gotten stronger." He glanced back at Moore. "What's your assessment of a large scale B.17 attack?"

Moore's verdict made both the Brigadier and Lindstrom wince. "I believe it would be a disaster, sir. Firstly the power station is too massively built to be completely destroyed and that would mean no one could be certain whether the stocks were destroyed or not. Secondly, you'd need a perfect day for a high-level attack and as we're dealing with Norway that's most unlikely. Thirdly, it's very awkwardly sited and the valley is in shadow most of the day. Fourthly, you'd be under attack all the way there and back. I believe their monitors or Observer Corps picked us up flying across the Hardangervidda. At high level you'd be picked up much earlier."

"And you say they've got A-4 Focke Wulf units there?"

"That was the type that attacked us. They're armed with high-velocity cannon and I'm pretty sure they're using nitrous oxide boost."

"So the sons of bitches would be waiting for us as soon as we crossed the coast." Staines paused thoughtfully. "Unless we jammed their scanners."

"That might work if the station was nearer the coast. But it's a long way inland."

Staines nodded. "That's almost word for word what they said after the last mission. Except someone used the word impossible." His gaze shifted to Davies. "In my book that rules out my B.17s. And your outfit too, unless you've any bright ideas."

Davies, whose zeal and ambition were at war with his memories of the Swartfjord massacre, could only glance at Moore, who shook his head.

41

"If you're thinking of our going in at medium or low level, we'd stand even less chance. We wouldn't be able to achieve any penetration and we'd run into every gun in the valley. I can't see any way we could be successful."

Saying something in Norwegian that sounded like a protest, Lindstrom turned and walked a few paces from the table. In the silence that followed the screech of a bird in the elms outside could be heard. The Brigadier, whose expression had been growing more strained by the moment, stood like a graven statue. Staines, looking uncharacteristically anxious, pulled himself together and tried to lift the conference from its depression.

"O.K., we can't hit those stocks in the valley. Then let's consider the chances of hitting 'em in transit. Lindstrom, how long is it going to take your sister to find out the shipment details?"

Regaining his self-possession, Lindstrom turned. "I can't say, sir. It might be that Skinnarland finds something out first."

"O.K. Can't London or your sister ask him what progress he's making?"

Lindstrom's reply surprised everyone but the Brigadier. "Neither Skinnarland nor Haukelid knows my sister exists. They know nothing about my group either."

"You mean you don't work together? For Christ's sake, why? Don't you trust them?"

There was an undertone of impatience in the young Norwegian's voice. "Trust doesn't enter into it. Skinnarland and Haukelid are two of our best agents."

Tactful as always, the Brigadier took over the explanation. "As Skinnarland and Haukelid were the ones taking the greater risks and because this IMI project is so important, SOE decided a second group should be built up in case Skinnarland's group was infiltrated or destroyed. That is how Major Lindstrom and his sister became involved."

All this was clearly news to Staines. "You're saying the two groups have no contact at all?"

"No direct contact. This way, if anyone is captured and interrogated by the Gestapo, he cannot give away information about Major Lindstrom's group."

"But Lindstrom's party know about Skinnarland."

"Not all. Only Lindstrom, his sister, and two other men."

Intrigued by this subtle example of intelligence work, Staines could not hold back his blunt question as he

42

stared at Lindstrom. "O.K., four of you. What happens if you are captured?"

The slimly-built Norwegian's reply was almost matter-of-fact. "We carry our precautions with us."

No one felt a need to ask what those precautions were. Davies cleared his throat. "Your sister must be a very brave girl, Major."

"What does she do in Rjukan?" Moore asked. "Or would you rather I didn't know?"

Lindstrom turned to the pilot. Although he had clearly been disappointed at Moore's assessment, with both men young and both taking extreme risks with their lives, it was apparent since their introduction that evening they had found a mutual respect.

"She's also a scientist, Wing Commander, but unlike Skinnarland she's not connected in any way with the power station. But in her work and social life she often meets technicians and scientists from the Norsk Hydro and that's where she gets her information."

Staines was fascinated by the presence of two autonomous groups of partisans. "O.K., she passes her information on to London. But surely with two groups working on the same project they must know something of what the other is doing or they could waste time overlapping."

"One group has to know," Lindstrom conceded. "As we knew about Skinnarland and Haukelid before we took on the work, we were the obvious choice."

"But, goddam it, knowledge means contact. And you said you hadn't any."

"No. The Brigadier said we had no *direct* contact. It works this way. Helga's right hand man, one of the two who know about the other group, keeps a radio watch on Skinnarland's transmissions to London. As he is tuned into the same wavelength and knows Skinnarland's code, Helga knows at any time what the other group is doing. If she misses anything, of course, London informs her but this seldom happens."

Staines grinned at Davies. "Got the picture?"

The small Air Commodore, who had been listening in fascination, gave a grimace. "Thank God I'm a simple airman."

"Amen to that." Staines turned back to Lindstrom. "All right, let's get back to business. Now we know we can't hit the stocks before they're moved, are you still hoping we

43

can help or are you resigning yourself to another sabotage job like Ronnerberg's?"

The answer was much as the Texan expected. "How can I say that before I know what method the Germans will use to transport them?"

Muttering under his breath Staines heaved his bulk from his chair and did a full turn of the library before halting in front of the Brigadier. "My orders are to stay here until I know for certain whether I can help or not. But I've got a goddam Air Force to run. Can't you give me any idea how long it's going to be?"

The elderly soldier sighed. "I wish I could, sir. I know both Skinnarland and Lindstrom's sister will be doing everything in their power to find out. We've reason to hope one of them might come through with news tonight but on the other hand it might take them another day or two. It's impossible to be precise."

Staines lifted his big hands. "A day or two." Then he gave a grunt of resignation. "All right. I'll let Spaatz know. I take it you can fix me up with a bed here?"

"Of course, sir. That's already taken care of." The Brigadier turned to Davies. "Will you be able to stay too, Davies?"

With Davies in receipt of orders that tied him to the Brigadier until the problem of the IMI stocks were resolved, the request was a mere formality. "Yes, I'll be staying. But you can get along, Moore. You must feel like a good rest after that operation. Take my car. You can get someone to drive it back tomorrow."

Realizing he had been dismissed Moore was reaching for his cap when Staines' gravelly voice checked him. "Don't forget that offer of mine, Moore. Turkey and cranberry sauce instead of Spam. How can you lose?"

Moore smiled back. "I'll bear it in mind, General." His eyes moved to the Brigadier. "I wonder if I might have a quick word with you before I go, sir."

With the philosophy that officers of lower rank, however high in his esteem, should have no secrets from their seniors, Davies seemed about to ask a reason for the request. Instead he frowned and stood aside for the Brigadier to take Moore's arm and lead him towards the door. "Of course, my boy. Would you like to use my office?"

"No, sir, there's no need for that. I was just wondering if you'd had any news of Anna Reinhardt recently. Harvey is certain to ask me."

44

to squadron losses, and the Intelligence Officer had clearly been shocked to learn the ghosts of the Swartfjord were at large again. Harvey too had his compelling reasons and one at least concerned the Rjukan valley. A Flight Commander with an almost parental attitude to his crews, the Yorkshireman would be wondering if he was to lead them on another suicidal Norwegian mission. Adams' question confirmed Moore's belief.

"We've been wondering all night what decision Davies has reached about Rjukan. Can you tell us?"

Remembering Harvey had not been told as much as Adams, Moore chose his words carefully as he handed glasses to both men. "Yes, I think I can do that. We shan't be raiding the valley."

Adams' reaction was heartfelt. "Thank God for that. Frank says the flak was murder."

Harvey grinned cynically. "All the same, I'll lay odds it's not the flak that's put Davies off."

Aware that the Yorkshireman's comment was also a question, Moore searched for a way of changing the subject. "That reminds me—I haven't thanked you yet for knocking that 190 off my tail. Have you put in your claim yet?"

Harvey took the hint without resentment. "There's plenty of time for that. Those 190s weren't bad, were they? They've never got that experience up there. I'll bet they've been drafted in from France or Germany."

Moore nodded. "I think you're right. Why don't you two take the weight off your feet?"

Adams had already noticed there was only one spare chair. Sensitive as always to his non-combatant role and guessing how tired both pilots must be, he chose the bed. Dropping into the chair, Harvey downed half his whisky in one swallow. "They were closing on us all the time. It was a bloody good job Hoppy didn't miss that second fjord. Those are nice jobs, those A-4s, Ian." The Yorkshireman's feelings towards his enemy were straightforward and uncomplicated. "Too good for those bastards."

"They were all 151 cannon jobs, weren't they?"

"My tail unit says so. It's a miracle it didn't drop off."

Adams was sitting very still. The RAF's way was either understatement or self-deprecation and normally the two men were classic examples of both. That they should be discussing the mission in this way told Adams it had been

47

one of outstanding danger and both of them still had tension to work out.

Harvey's rugged face cracked into a grin. "I thought you were going to dive right into that river. Did you realize how narrow that gorge was?"

"Not until we reached the bottom."

"You know something? It scared me more than the 190s."

"It didn't scare you more than it scared me. What did their leader crash into? When we saw the flash we thought at first it was you."

"You'll never guess. He pranged into a frozen waterfall."

I will never understand myself, Adams was thinking. I loathe war as an abomination and yet I sit listening to these two men like a fascinated child and long to emulate them.

Harvey finished off his whisky. As Moore reached for his glass to fill it, the Yorkshireman grinned again. "I'll bet Davies is cheesed off he can't use us."

Moore shook his head. "I don't think so. Not this time."

"Don't give me that. He's never been put off by high casualties. Not that glory-hunting bastard."

Moore caught Adams' eye. The small Air Commodore had been a part of the SOE project that had involved Anna in the Rhine Maiden affair, and Harvey had never forgiven him for it.

"No, that's not fair, Frank. There's always been a good reason when he's thrown us in at the deep end. And in the long run it's always paid off."

"Has it? What about that train operation you carried out when I was in dock? The one that forced you into the Crucible affair with the Yanks?"

"That wasn't Davies' fault. The C.-in-C. himself insisted something had to be done to improve U.K.-U.S.A. relations. And it did pay off in the long run, didn't it?"

"What about the cost?" Harvey demanded. "I lost half my flight and you didn't come out of it exactly fit for the Olympics, did you?"

"I agree. Davies plays for high stakes and that can be costly. But no one can deny he gets results out of all proportion to that cost."

"You're saying he sees war as bloody mathematics."

"Yes, and surely that's what it is. I don't like it any

48

more than you do, but if the loss of eight or ten men can save the lives of thousands, you can't say it isn't a good exchange."

Harvey's scowl deepened. "I still say he's a ruthless little bastard who uses men for his own ambitions."

"Isn't all ambition ruthless? War only makes it seem worse because it's dealing with life and death."

With the conversation having turned philosophical, Adams felt more qualified to join in. "I'm not that keen on Davies myself but here I have to agree with Ian. If man wants to live competitively, he has to choose ambitious men to lead him. We can only have different leaders if we choose a different lifestyle."

Harvey's memories of his under-privileged family and their suffering were never far below the surface. Deep-set and bitter, his eyes turned towards the bed. "You think that's ever likely to happen?"

Adams sighed. "It might, one day. But I agree it's never seemed so far away."

"It's a million years away, Frank. Put Davies in civvies and the only difference is he'd be starving his workers to death instead of killing 'em with flak."

With the conversation unexpectedly probing old scars, Moore turned it against himself by winking at Adams. "You know what he's hinting at, don't you? That I'm going to behave the same way when the war's over."

For a moment there were centuries of class hostility in the look Harvey gave him. "That wouldn't surprise me, Moore, not with that chain of shops you have. You'll join the local Rotary and they'll have you as one of the boys in no time at all."

Moore's attractive smile spread. "I'm already working on it. DROs to the managers every morning and glass-house for the workers. I'm surprised no one's thought of it before."

"They have. Where've you been all these years? Dining at the Savoy?"

Moore's eyes twinkled at the tense Adams. "Didn't you know he's the original Luddite? Boots, braces, spanner in the works, the lot."

Unexpectedly the Yorkshireman's scowl turned into a broad grin. "I never realized those 190s might be doing the workers a favour. Why did I put my big foot in it?"

Realizing Harvey's aggression had been only another

symptom of battle reaction, Adams relaxed. "You two had me worried for a moment. I thought you were wearing different uniforms."

"We've never worn anything else," Harvey grunted. "His pin stripes and my dungarees."

Adams tried to match the big Yorkshireman's repartee. "They both look pretty much alike to me."

"That's your eyes, mate. You need another pair of specs." As Adams laughed ruefully, Harvey drained his glass. "So Davies spent a million quid this morning for nothing. You know something, Ian—it doesn't sound like him. Anyway, thanks for the whisky."

Nodding at Adams he moved towards the door. There, as if having an afterthought, he turned back. "I don't suppose the Brigadier said anything about Anna, did he?"

Ready for the question, Moore nodded. "Yes. They heard from her quite recently."

"How recently?"

"Four or five weeks ago." To soften the blow, Moore went on quickly: "It seems all SOE agents are under orders not to communicate too often for safety reasons."

"Do you believe that?"

"It seems to make good sense."

In Harvey's world a man did not show his wounds in case the predators moved in. "And that was all?"

"Yes. I'm sure she's all right, Frank."

The Yorkshireman nodded and turned. "Thanks, anyway. I'm turning in now. Good night."

"Good night, Frank."

Adams waited until the door closed and the pilot's footsteps died away. "He's worried sick about her, isn't he?"

Moore sat motionless for a moment, then rose and limped towards the whisky bottle. "Yes, he is. Let's have another drink."

The tap on the kitchen door of The Black Swan came just as its innkeeper, Joe Kearns, was putting the fire screen in front of the hearth. Guessing who his visitor was, he crossed the stone floor and drew back the latch. Standing on the step, Adams had a slightly owlish appearance as his eyes adjusted to the light. Seeing the Intelligence Officer was half-drunk, Kearns opened the door wider. "Hello, Frank. Come on in."

Adams supported himself against the door jamb. "Hello, Joe. I'm very late."

Kearns, a widower, was a Northcountryman in his middle fifties with ruddy cheeks and thinning, white hair. A man with a slow, contemplative voice, he drew a second chair in front of the fire. "You've been later than this, lad. Sit yourself down."

Muttering something indistinguishable, Adams climbed out of his greatcoat and dropped with some relief into the chair. Eyeing his flushed face, Kearns came to a decision. "Let me give you a coffee, lad. The kettle's boiling."

Adams stared at him with some dignity. "You don't think I'm drunk, do you?"

"No, lad. Not drunk. But you have had a few tonight. And that's not like you."

"I'd like a few more," Adams muttered. "You haven't got any Scotch under the counter, have you?"

Kearns hesitated. Then, deciding a normally temperate drinker like Adams must have his reasons, he left the kitchen and returned with a half-bottle of Scotch. Pouring out two generous glasses, he set the bottle alongside Adams. "Just one thing, lad. Promise you go straight to bed after this."

Nodding, Adams fished in his tunic pocket and held out his hand to Kearns. "Our Messing Officer had a delivery today. It was only a small one so I couldn't scrounge any more."

The innkeeper saw he was being given four ounces of Three Nuns tobacco. "That's nice of you, lad. I was getting short. You have a pipeful?"

Shaking his head, Adams took another sip of whisky. "I suppose you know our boys have been stood down for a couple of days."

"Aye, we could tell that from the way they've been comin' in here. That's why you found me up tonight— Maisie an' me only finished washin' the glasses fifteen minutes ago." Never one to embarrass Adams by asking about squadron affairs no matter how curious he was, Kearns went on: "What are you going to do, Frank? Take the chance to nip home and see the wife?"

Adams looked almost surprised. "Me? No, I've still got work to do." Then, with alcohol lowering the level of his restraint, his voice turned bitter. "There's no need, is there? She knows I'm safe."

51

Kearns needed to hear no more to know what was wrong with Adams. Bending forward, he refilled his glass. The Intelligence Officer's voice was thick as Kearns sat back. "My assistant got back yesterday. You know—Sue Spencer."

Kearns eyed his suffused face through a cloud of tobacco smoke. Sue Spencer was Joe Kearns' kind of woman, a tall, willowy girl with a sensitive face and a gentle voice. A very feminine woman and yet, according to Adams, very efficient at her work. "Aye, I know Miss Spencer. Didn't you say her fiancé has got back at last from France?"

"That's right. Just over a week ago. He's staying with his parents and I managed to get her a long weekend."

"It must have been a great day for her when she heard he was safe," Kearns reflected.

"Cloud Nine," Adams declared. "Never seen anyone so overjoyed. But something must have happened over the weekend. She goes quiet on me whenever I ask how Tony is."

"Maybe she's worried about his health."

"No, it can't be that. The Medical Board have passed him and he's returning to the squadron as soon as his leave's over." For a moment the frowning Adams sounded sober as he pondered on the girl's change of mood. "It has to be something else. Something she won't talk about."

Kearns was recalling what Adams had told him about Tony St. Claire. Sent off with the squadron to attack a German train in the hope of releasing the American prisoners it carried, St. Claire's Mosquito had been struck by a flak shell at the moment the pilot was releasing a rocket. Thrown off course by the explosion, the rocket had struck a wagon load of Americans and killed a number of them. A few seconds later St. Claire had crashed and been spirited away by partisans who were working with the squadron in the rescue attempt.

"A thing like that was bound to prey on his mind, Frank. Particularly as he's been hiding with the Resistance all these months. But now he's home he'll soon get over it."

"No, it's not that either. Or why wouldn't she tell me?"

"Because he's her fiancé and she's loyal to him. She's probably afraid that if it got out they wouldn't let him fly again."

Adams displayed the triumph of the inebriated as he shook his head. "Wrong again. There's nothing Sue would like better: she suffers hell every time he flies. You know what she said to me yesterday?" When Kearns shook his head, Adams leaned towards him. "She said it was monstrously unfair that men like Tony, who've suffered so much, should have to go back into combat when there are thousands of men wearing the same uniform who've never heard a shot fired in anger."

It was all very clear to Kearns now but before he could speak Adams raised an admonishing finger. "No, she wasn't having a go at me. She wasn't even thinking about me or she'd never have said it. She was just crying out at the unfairness of it all. And she was right. It is unfair."

Kearns sighed. "Frank, we've gone over all this before. And the answer's always the same. You're not to blame because you're too old to fly, any more than I'm to blame for being too old to fight alongside my son in the Army. It's a fact of life and we have to live with it."

Adams' aggrieved eyes stared at him. "But I don't seem able to live with it. I have for years but now it seems to be getting worse. Tonight when I was talking to Moore and Harvey I felt. . . ." Unable to continue Adams was reaching down for the bottle when shame checked him. "I'm sorry, Joe. I should never have come over in this state. I'm going back now to get my head down."

Kearns jumped up. "Don't be silly, lad. What are friends for? Sit down and get it out of your system."

Ignoring his protests, Adams climbed back into his overcoat and made for the door. "Thanks for the drink, Joe. I'll pop in and see you tomorrow."

Outside the slate roof and white-washed walls of the old inn were silvered by the moonlight. Crunching down the frozen gravel path, Adams paused at the gate beneath the leafless branches of the crab-apple. Across the road that ran to Highgate, a wooden fence denoted the northern boundary of the airfield. Standing there with his emotions intensified by alcohol, Adams was struck by the paradox. On this side of the fence life was supposed to be a thing above price. On the other side it was probably the cheapest commodity that existed and was spent accordingly. Two worlds, apparently a million miles away in concepts and values. Which, Adams wondered, was the true one? In the animal world it was all kill and be killed. Perhaps the world beyond the fence was reality and all the rest the stuff of dreams. If so, Adams thought, he was an even greater misfit than he imagined.

Deciding whisky and frost were bad companions he made for the camp entrance. As the sentry smartly presented arms, Adams' mood changed and he glanced round to see if anyone were looking. Seeing no one he patted the startled airman on the shoulder. "Very smart, young Hilton! Very smart indeed!" Beaming, hiccuping gently, Adams passed by and weaved down the perimeter road to his billet.

## 9

The Brigadier was an austere man and his bedroom in High Elms reflected that austerity. Except for a locker at his bedside, his only furniture was a bed, a bookcase, a tall-boy, a desk, and a single high-backed chair. The walls were empty of pictures except for two framed photographs, one of an Army major in his thirties and the other of a pretty young woman with a child on her lap.

A telephone linking the bedroom to the Communications Room stood on the locker. A small pocket alarm clock rested beside it. Its hands had just reached 3:10 A.M. when a high-pitched squeal sounded. By nature a light sleeper, the Brigadier was awake immediately.

"Yes. What is it?"

"It's London, sir. The call you're expecting. Shall I put them through?"

"Yes. At once."

The receiver clicked as the special line was fed into the circuit. The conversation that followed lasted nearly ten minutes before the Brigadier recalled the operator. "I want to see Major Lindstrom in my office immediately. Ask General Staines and Air Commodore Davies if they will kindly wait for me in the library. I want coffee served as soon as we are all present."

The arrival of the four men in the library reflected their different personalities. The borrowed pyjamas and dressing gown that Staines was wearing barely covered his massive frame but the man's personality more than made up the deficiency. Second into the room after Davies, his jowls already shadowed by the night's growth, he grinned at the Air Commodore. "You ever see Oliver Hardy wearing Stan Laurel's gear? Here he is."

Like Lindstrom and the Brigadier who hurried in a couple of minutes later, Davies was fully dressed. All received Staines' broad grin. "The privileges of rank, gentlemen. To be scruffy at 3 o'clock in the morning."

An orderly brought in a tray of coffee. Staines waited until he withdrew before turning to the Brigadier. "I take it you've got the news we've been waiting for?"

A precise man, the Brigadier had somehow found the time to shave. "Yes, sir. It was London. Forgive my disturbing you all but the importance of the news made it imperative."

Chest hair sprouting through his open dressing gown, Staines waved an impatient hand. "Forget the apologies. What does London say?"

Never one to neglect his guests even in moments of high importance, the Brigadier began pouring out cups of coffee. "It seems they had news from Skinnarland just after midnight. He says he has discovered the route and method of transport the Germans are using for the IMI stocks although as yet he doesn't know the date. However, he seems confident he will find that out soon. When he does, he believes his party will be able to sabotage this consignment themselves."

"How?" Staines asked.

"Skinnarland's information is that the consignment consists of seventy-odd containers which will travel by armoured train to Mael, a landing stage for the ferryboat service along Lake Tinnsjo. Here the tanks will be loaded on a ferry and taken to Heroya on the south coast where they will be shipped to Germany. Skinnarland and Haukelid believe the lake is the weak link in the chain and their plan is to blow up the ferry when it reaches the deepest part of the lake, which is around 1,300 feet. It will mean killing Norwegian passengers but in view of the imperative need to destroy these stocks the Norwegian Government has already given its permission. If the plan is successful, the containers will sink too deep for salvage."

Staines rubbed his bristly chin. "How are they going to blow the ferry up? Mine it?"

"Yes, Haukelid has volunteered and is taking a small party with him. We must hope he is successful because there is nothing we can do to help him."

"That's for sure," Staines reflected. "That far away there's no chance of us laying on a raid that could get there at the right time. But aren't they leaving their attack late? If it fails, the stuff goes straight on board a ship and off to Germany. Isn't there any way of sabotaging the train?"

The Brigadier handed coffee to Davies and Lindstrom. "Skinnarland has considered the possibility but it seems the problems are insurmountable. Two companies of special SS troops have been brought in as guards and two spotter aircraft are going to give constant aerial surveillance. Mining the track has been considered but the Germans might send a wagon ahead of the train that would detonate the mines prematurely. Also there is no certainty an explosion would demolish all the containers which are sure to be strongly built. Lastly, there is a danger to the local population. It seems the only feasible place where mines could be laid is between two towns, Tinnoset and Notodden, and as the train will also be carrying ammonia, the spillage and fumes could cause injury and death. Another fear is that the Germans would take reprisals against the towns if the train is sabotaged near them."

Staines shrugged. "So it's back to the ferry. O.K., that lets Davies and me out, doesn't it? All we can do is wait and hope."

The Brigadier's quiet voice checked him. "I'm afraid that's not all, sir." He glanced at Lindstrom. "Perhaps you'll take over, Major, and explain what else we've heard."

The academic young Norwegian moved forward. His accent seemed to bring his audience closer to the dramatic events in far-off Norway. "It appears my sister has also been in touch with London tonight, gentlemen. In addition to what Skinnarland has heard, she has been given some vital information by a scientist friend working at the power station. The stocks of IMI are not all going via the ferry to Heroya. Only half will go this way: the rest will be shipped shortly afterwards by an entirely different route. This is why London has been so long in contacting us. They have been seeking advice from Norwegian geologists taking refuge over here."

There was a murmur of alarm from his audience. "You're saying the Heinies are hedging their bets but Skinnarland doesn't know?" Staines asked.

"That's correct, General. As they're aware the Allies intend making an all-out effort to destroy the stocks before they reach Germany, they've decided to spread out the risks."

"Has Skinnarland been told this?"

The Brigadier answered for Lindstrom. "We've decided not to tell him. He has quite enough to worry about in dealing with the first consignment. In any case he hasn't enough men to split his forces."

"So who's going to take care of this second shipment?" Staines demanded. "Lindstrom's group? Or are we able to help this time?"

The young Norwegian hesitated before answering. "We shall do our best, General, but we are hoping you can help

57

because our problem is different to Skinnarland's. My sister's informant says the second consignment is sailing from the west coast instead of the south. And the stocks will go all the way by rail."

Staines' ears had pricked. "West coast? What port are they using?"

Before Lindstrom could answer, the Brigadier intervened again. "There's one thing you must know, General. We do not want the ship sinking at berth. That way we could never be certain the stocks could not be salvaged. Ideally we want to sink her within sixty minutes of her departure."

Staines gave a grunt of disbelief. "You're really making it easy for us, aren't you? Why sixty minutes?"

The Brigadier led the Texan and Davies to the map of Norway and pointed at one of the many tributary fjords that made up the head of the Hardanger fjord. "The port they are using is Kranvin, here. As you will see it is linked to the rail system so the Germans will be able to transfer the stocks straight on to the ship. Once loaded she will then sail down this tributary out into the main fjord and then to the sea. Our problem is this. Because of their glacial origin, Norwegian fjords are comparatively shallow at their coastal end but extremely deep inland. London has confirmed from geologists this is true of the Hardanger fjord."

Staines' face was a study as he glanced at Davies. "So you want us to clobber this ship after she sails and before she reaches the shallower end of the fjord. Is that it?"

The Brigadier nodded. "Well before she reaches the seaward end, I'm afraid, because the configuration also affects the banks of the fjord. For the first thirty miles they are sheer but afterwards they begin to shelve and islands appear. So here she might be able to beach herself even if she were heavily damaged. Or, if she sank, divers might be able to reach her."

Seeing Staines' expression, Davies took over. "Did your sister find out what ship they're using, Major?"

Lindstrom nodded. "It's a light cruiser that has been undergoing repairs further down the Hardanger fjord. She is serviceable again and will move up to Kranvin to take on the shipment."

Staines' interjection summed up his frustration. "A cruiser—a fast ship. Christ, then it's impossible. Goddam ridiculous, in fact."

58

There was a sharp edge to Lindstrom's protest. "We shall have an agent at Rjukan watching for the departure of the train. And another keeping surveillance on the landing stage at Kranvin. The first man can let you know when to start getting ready; the second will tell you the moment the cruiser sails. Surely this must help you."

"How?" the Texan demanded. "It's the last message that counts. Even if we could stand by with our engines running, which we can't, we'd still only have sixty minutes to get there. It's mathematically impossible."

Davies shook his head regretfully as the wrought-up Norwegian turned to him. "We might gain a half-hour or so on the B.17s but basically we have the same problem."

"Supposing my agent told you the moment the train arrived in Kranvin. Couldn't you take off then? The loading is bound to take some time."

Staines took the onus of answering from the rueful Davies. "Loading could take half an hour; it could take a full day. And then there's no guarantee the cruiser will sail straight away. How can his boys stooge about over Norway waiting for the pieces to fall into place? The Heinies have got monitors and air defences and they're bloody good. Anyway the cruiser would never sail until she got the all-clear."

Aware of the futility of his suggestions even before he made them, the Norwegian turned away. Watching him, Davies gave a start. "Wait a minute. What about tides? If they held her up for a few hours we might have a chance."

Lindstrom sounded as if he hated himself for the admission. "There are no tides in the fjords. At least none worth speaking of."

"Then there's no way we can do it," Davies confessed.

Seeing the young Norwegian's distress, Staines recovered his patience. Glancing down at the map, he traced his tobacco-stained forefinger round mountain ranges and lakes back to Rjukan. "The Heinies are going to have to do a hell of a lot of re-routing to keep on track all the way to Kranvin, aren't they? I suppose your sister couldn't be wrong about them using a train all the way."

It was clearly an effort for Lindstrom to shake off his disappointment. "If they're using a west coast port they must use the railway system. Many of the central roads are blocked by snow at this time of the year. But you are right about the time it will take. London has worked out that even if the second shipment follows on the heels of the first—which isn't likely—it will still take over fifty hours to reach Kranvin. So at least we have this extra time to prepare an attack."

"Two days en route," Staines muttered. "Maybe more." His shrewd eyes lifted to the Norwegian's face. "Isn't there any chance of your group laying on an ambush somewhere along the line?"

"I wish we could think of one." Lindstrom said bitterly. "My sister says the Germans are taking even greater precautions than with the Tinnsjo shipment, probably because the stocks will be in transit longer. They are using an armoured train and packing it with troops. As my group are only lightly armed, they'd be slaughtered if they tried to attack it, and anything less, like mining the track, wouldn't ensure the stocks were destroyed."

"What about mining a bridge or tunnel?" the Texan asked.

"They'd all be under heavy guard so any move we made would be radioed straight back to Rjukan and the train simply wouldn't leave. If neither of your Air Forces can help us, we shall have to try something but I've little hope of success."

Staines was frowning heavily. "If you can't hit the consignment on its way to Kranvin and we can't hit it in the fjord, what the hell are we going to do? All I can suggest is that we clobber the cruiser while she's waiting for the stocks in Kranvin. At least that'll hold up transportation for a while."

The Brigadier stirred. "Can you do that?"

"Yes. We'd have heavy losses on the way but my B.17s could reach Kranvin. Only I thought you weren't keen on any move that would scare Jerry off mass transportation. If we sink the cruiser, he'll probably send that consignment over to the Fatherland at a pint a time."

The Brigadier sighed and nodded. "This is our fear. So I don't think we can consider it until we've exhausted all other possibilities."

Davies thought it was worth a try. "I take it you've thought of an aircraft carrier? If one lay off the Norwegian coast, her aircraft could reach the cruiser before she left the thirty mile zone."

He felt no surprise when the elderly soldier shook his head. "The Navy would never risk a carrier within range of land-based bombers. In any case the cruiser would never take on the shipment if she knew a carrier was waiting for her."

"Then what about submarines?"

"Yes, our back-up plan calls for submarines to be stationed outside Heroya and we shall now do the same for the Hardanger. But unfortunately, as you will see from the map, this fjord has so many islands at its mouth that there are at least half a dozen ways the cruiser can escape to the sea. Add to that the German offshore minefields and our submarines' chances are not very high. Our only real guarantee the stocks don't reach Germany is to do what Skinnarland is hoping to do and destroy them before they reach the open sea."

The sound of Staines dropping heavily into his chair seemed to sum up the insolubility of the problem. Lindstrom broke the silence by turning to the Brigadier. "Will you arrange for me to be dropped back tonight, sir? I must find a way of breaking this deadlock."

The worried soldier stirred. "I doubt if they'll allow it, Major. The winds are very high at the moment and the moon isn't full until next week."

The sharpness of his protest betrayed the young Norwegian's frustration. "I must get back tonight, sir. You can see there isn't a minute to lose."

## 10

The gust of wind made the security S.P. at the door of the Nissen hut shiver and turn up his greatcoat collar. Inside the hut that served as Adams' "Confessional," the February sunshine that the anticyclone had brought was casting parallelograms of light on the linoleum floor. As the gale tore at the metal roof, Davies glanced upwards and grimaced. "Let's hope the weather's better over Norway or Lindstrom's never going to get his drop in tonight."

Three men, Henderson, Adams and Moore were sharing the Station Intelligence Office with Davies. He had arrived fifteen minutes earlier and immediately convened the conference. A map of Norway covered the large desk that Adams used when de-briefing the crews. The second desk, belonging to the absent Sue Spencer, Adams' Waaf assistant, was covered in photographs that Adams had managed to produce from his comprehensive files.

"Who's taking him over, sir?" Adams asked.

"The Brigadier got him a Stirling from one of SOE's special squadrons. He had to push them a bit—they wanted to wait until next week when the moon's full."

As a window rattled in the wind, Davies turned back to the map. "All right, you've all had time to think about it, so what about some suggestions? You can forget the Fleet Air Arm. The Navy says they haven't a carrier within two thousand miles and in any case they're all stretched to the limit. What they didn't say but we took as real was that even if they had one, they'd never risk it so close to the enemy coast."

Henderson's forefinger was moving along the deep inlet that ran to Kranvin. "I suppose there's no chance of a submarine getting into the fjord and torpedoing the cruiser when she's reached deep water?"

"No, we asked that. The Navy says Jerry's got the entrance of those fjords sewn up tighter than a bull's arse in fly time."

"Midget submarines?" Henderson ventured.

"They were also considered but there aren't any serviceable at the moment. In any case the crews would need special suits for the cold and there isn't time to develop them."

Moore, who had been examining the photographs on the other table, now moved towards Davies. "There seem a fair number of hamlets on either side of the Hardanger fjord, sir."

The Air Commodore nodded. "I suppose that's because it's an important inland waterway. Why?"

"I was wondering if we couldn't mine the channel across its deepest sector. The only snag there is that Jerry might hear us and guess what we're doing."

Davies started. "Mines! That's an idea."

Henderson showed markedly less enthusiasm. "We couldn't do it in daylight. And with all those mountains around, it would be suicidal at night."

Reluctant to throw out the only idea that seemed to have a remote chance of success, Davies became irritable. "We have to destroy those stocks, Jock. No matter what. I want everyone to understand that."

"Perhaps Lindstrom's group will see them off before they reach the ship," the Scot said hopefully.

"From what he told us, he hasn't a hope in hell. He'll have a go if necessary—he's that kind of man—but how do partisans with Sten guns and grenades stop and capture an armoured train? They'd be massacred."

Adams, who after Moore's suggestion had hurried over to a cabinet to consult his files, had now found what he wanted. "I'm afraid Jerry has quite a number of small bases along the Hardanger fjord, sir. Because of its length and the surrounding mountains, he finds it a safe place to maintain his minesweeper and patrol boats. So he'd be sure to pick up our aircraft flying back and forth across the fjord. And once he's guessed we're mining it, wouldn't he then decide to ship the stocks out from somewhere else?"

All the unfortunate Adams received for his pains was a scowl from Davies. "If he didn't scoop up the mines as fast as we dropped 'em, yes, he would. And then we could be worse off than ever. All right, if we can't mine the cruiser, what else can we do? We can't circle around the bloody country until it sails."

Adams' inspiration came as inspirations so often do, from nowhere. "But we could wait on the ground, sir, couldn't we?"

Davies stared at him. "Say that again."

"We could wait on the ground. About fifty miles away, so that the moment we're told the cruiser has sailed we could take off and attack it."

Davies' expression was almost comical as he turned to Henderson. "What's the matter with him? Is he drunk?"

It was all becoming as clear and bright as a bursting nova to the excited Adams. "It would work, sir. As long as we got there undetected."

"You're saying we should go over there, capture an airfield, and then squat on it undetected until the ship sails? You feeling all right, Adams?"

In his excitement Adams realized he had forgotten to mention the critical element of his plan. "No, sir. Not an airfield. We could use a frozen lake."

Davies looked as if he had been struck by a rubber truncheon. "A what?"

"A lake on one of the high plateaux. Unlike the fjords they're fresh water and they freeze hard because of the altitude. And there must be hundreds of them." Pushing forward, Adams pointed at the Hardangervidda and the country immediately north of it. "In this area. It's one of the most desolate parts of Norway. And we know it's not well-patrolled because that's where many of the Linge Movement operate. Lindstrom could find the right lake for us and we could go out a day or two before the stocks are due to arrive."

Davies turned and gaped at Henderson. "My God. He could be right."

The Scot looked too stunned to speak as Adams rushed on excitedly. "Wherever we went in this area we wouldn't be more than fifty miles from Kranvin. So we could afford to wait until Lindstrom's agent told us the cruiser had sailed and still arrive well before she was out of the thirty mile zone."

Henderson found his voice at last. "What are you trying to do, Adams? Kill off my entire squadron? How the hell can our aircraft land on ice? Are you suggesting we put skis on 'em?"

The mildest of men and one who hated risks being taken with his aircrew friends, Adams was bewildering himself with his enthusiasm. "No, that's not necessary. It's been done before without skis."

"Bullshit!"

"No, it has. 263 Squadron did it in 1940 when the Germans captured their Norwegian airstrip. And Gladiators are quite a heavy aircraft."

Henderson stared at Moore. "Did they?"

The immaculate young Wing Commander nodded. "Yes. Quite successfully, I believe."

Davies sounded hoarse. "Adams, that's bloody brilliant.

You might have found the answer." He swung back to Moore. "What do you think, Ian?"

Moore was smiling at the excited Adams. "I think it's worth consideration, sir."

"Too true it is. In one stroke it solves our problem of getting there in time." Davies' enthusiasm reached a new peak as he fairly beamed at the pink-cheeked Adams. "What are you taking these days, Adams? Monkey glands?"

Henderson clearly felt all this euphoria had to be punctured. "You're not really serious about this, are you, sir? That we go out like a flock of migrant birds and land on the first frozen lake we find?"

Davies was too excited to take offence. "Don't knock it, Jock. If we can pull this off, it'll be the greatest thing since the Wooden Horse captured Troy."

The phlegmatic Henderson was not easily won over by dreams of glory. "But what about all the problems? How would we get there undetected? How do we know if the ice would hold us? And what would we do about maintenance and supplies?"

"Those are secondary problems, Jock. The great thing is to find a way of bombing those stocks when they're vulnerable. It looks as if Adams has done just that."

In his alarm Henderson forgot whom he was addressing. "You want us to take the entire squadron behind the enemy lines, land, and then sit on our arses? If a single soldier spotted us, they could wipe us out. It's the craziest thing I've ever heard."

Davies' sharpening features gave notice the moment of *bonhomie* was coming to an end. "You got any better ideas?"

"No. But that doesn't mean . . ."

"Never mind the buts, Jock. It's the only idea that might work and so we're going to consider it in every detail. That means all of us. All right?"

For a long moment the Scot's resentful face stared at him. Then years of discipline turned the tide. "All right, sir, if that's what you want."

"It is what I want. Those stocks have to be destroyed. So let's get on with it."

With Henderson silenced, albeit unwillingly, Davies turned to Moore. "I can find out about the ice conditions—there are plenty of Norwegian scientists working with the SOE. And there's still time to get Lindstrom on the blower before they fly him out. If he feels it would work, he can

65

start his men looking for a suitable lake as soon as he gets over there. But what about you, Ian? You realize it would have to be a night landing?"

"I suppose Lindstrom's men would be able to put out storm lanterns for us?"

"If we supplied 'em, I don't see why not. If Lindstrom doesn't come up with any way of sabotaging the stocks himself, he'd probably move his entire group there. In any case, we'd need scouts and outposts round the lake to watch out for Jerry patrols."

"Then, as it's full moon next week, I think we'd have a reasonable chance of making a landing."

Henderson's grunt dampened the Air Commodore's euphoria. "Reasonable if you forget those Norwegian mountains and the chance the ice might give way."

Wishing to keep the Scot from further friction with Davies, Moore took his comment on face value. "As far as the ice goes I suppose we'd have to take the opinion of the geologists. Unless I went out first and tried it myself."

Before Henderson could protest, Moore went on quickly: "Detection and supplies could turn out to be our biggest problems. As Harvey and I found out yesterday, Jerry appears to have both short- and long-range monitors over there and they seem very efficient."

By this time Davies had the bit firmly in his teeth. "We could jam your approach. Jerry would guess something was up, of course, but he wouldn't know what or where. And he'd hardly guess you'd landed."

"We'd be in a mess if he sent out spotter aircraft," Henderson said. "Sixteen Mosquitoes on a frozen lake would stand out like sore thumbs."

"Obviously we'd have to camouflage 'em," Davies grunted. "The partisans could help there."

Realizing he had lost the fight, the big Scot, who had not an ounce of malice in him, prepared to do his best to make the operation a success. "I suppose we could use paint and camouflage nets. What about the other supplies? Would you air-drop them?"

"I think we'd have to. We wouldn't want too many aircraft landing there beforehand. We could either handle that ourselves or Staines would do it for us. He'd want to help anyway."

"We'd have to borrow two or three transports ourselves," Henderson pointed out. "We'd need some technicians with us. And someone would have to go out beforehand to sort out the supply drop and organize the landing. We couldn't expect the partisans to know our needs."

Davies nodded thoughtfully. "That's right. We'd need a man who knows the squadron's requirements inside out." He grinned at the Scot. "Feel like volunteering, Jock?"

Henderson did not hesitate for a second. "Of course, sir. Let's settle for that."

"Don't be a clot," Davies grunted. "We can't take chances with you. But think about it, because if we have to do this job time's at a premium and the chap will need some basic parachute training."

Adams, who had been listening in growing excitement, cleared his dry throat. "Will this man be a volunteer, sir?"

Davies glanced at Henderson and then nodded. "I suppose he'll have to be. It won't be the safest of jobs. Why?"

"Then I'd like to go, sir."

All three men started. Davies' first reaction was amused disbelief. "You! This some kind of a joke?"

"No, sir. I'd like to take it on. After all, I know the squadron's requirements as well or better than anyone."

Catching Henderson's glance, Davies moderated his tone. "That's true enough. But parachuting down into enemy territory is a young man's game. You and I are past it, Adams."

Adams had the feeling his complex personality had at last split into two. "The only other men on the squadron who know all its requirements are the senior aircrews and the C.O., sir. You can't risk any of them, whereas I'm expendable. If you will think about it, I'm sure you'll see I'm right."

In spite of what his critics said about him, there was a sympathetic side to Davies and Adams' plea had touched that side. At the same time, when his sympathy clashed with his duty as it so often did in wartime, he tended to over-compensate and so justify his critics' opinion of him. "How the hell can anyone like you parachute into Norway, Adams? I know you thought of this idea but that doesn't mean I have to let you spearhead it."

With his one chance of finding self-respect slipping away, Adams forgot where he was. "I can handle it, sir. Give me the chance, please. It's important to me."

Resenting this intrusion of emotion, Davies was frowning heavily. "What do you mean—important?"

Ashamed of his outburst, Adams was suffering an agony

of embarrassment. "I just mean I want to go, sir. That's all."

"So do I. So does Henderson. But we accept the facts of life and know we can't."

A complex man himself, Moore had watched the scene in silence. Having had many a philosophical conversation with the sensitive Adams, he knew his man well. As the Intelligence Officer turned miserably away, Moore glanced at Davies. "If I might express an opinion, sir, I think Frank is fully qualified to go."

Adams halted, hardly able to believe his ears. Davies looked equally amazed. "You can't mean that."

"I do, sir. No one knows our requirements better."

"I'm not disputing that. It's his age and physical condition that's the issue."

"But the rest of our ground officers are all specialists and they aren't that young themselves. We're going to need someone who knows all our requirements and has everything prepared. Also someone who can use on Aldis lamp."

"I know all that. But he's still too old for the job."

"Why? He's only going to organize things. The partisans will do all the hard work."

The frowning Davies glanced again at the motionless Adams. "If I didn't know you better, Moore, I'd think you were allowing friendship to come into this." He addressed his second sentence to Adams. "You do realize this job could be dangerous?"

"Yes, sir, of course I do."

"And you still believe you can handle it?"

"I don't see why not, sir."

"I can see a dozen reasons why not. Only I have to admit you've got all the qualifications." Hesitating a last time, Davies gave a growl of disgust. "All right, you can go. But for Christ's sake don't botch it up."

The look Adams gave Moore was pure gratitude. "Thank you, sir. I'll do my best."

"You'd better," Davies grunted. Looking as if he feared he was turning senile, he turned irritably towards Henderson. "I want a few minutes privacy while I try to get through to Lindstrom."

The three officers retired to the far end of the hut. There was admiration in the grin Henderson gave the still dazed Adams. "I thought you'd more sense than to want to be a hero."

Adams nodded jerkily. "So did I."

"It could be damned dangerous, you know. And it'll be bitterly cold over there." Henderson's eyes ran dubiously over the Intelligence Officer's stout figure. "You think you're going to be able to cope with those kinds of conditions?"

Adams tried to make a joke of it. "They say a bit of fat helps to keep you warm. So maybe for once it'll come in useful."

At the far end of the hut Davies, after a couple of sharp exchanges with telephone operators, was now in deep conversation. He joined the others five minutes later. "I got through to Lindstrom. He thinks it's a sensational idea and if his sister can't find out anything that'll make sabotage possible, he's prepared to co-operate with his entire group. In the meantime, so that all contingencies are covered, he'll send off half a dozen men to scout for a suitable lake. That means we have to be ready too." Davies turned his attention to Moore. "I want your boys to begin training immediately. The job is landing at night with the minimum of lights and assistance. Even with a full moon on its way, we can't guarantee there'll be no cloud. You got any ideas?"

Moore nodded. "As we can't be certain how ice will show up in different weather conditions, I'm wondering if we can do a 617 Squadron and focus spotlights down from both nose and tail."

Davies grasped the idea immediately. "You lot are in good form this morning, aren't you? You mean adjust the lights so when their reflections merge you know you're a pre-fixed distance above the ice?"

"That's right. Each navigator could be watching the lights and give his pilot soundings. If he can get the kite down to twelve or even eighteen feet, there shouldn't be any problem in making a reasonable landing."

Davies looked dubious. "Will it work that low?"

"I don't see why not, although we'll have to experiment. I'll get the electricians working on the kites right away and take the boys out tonight."

"Where to? Scotland?"

"No. Let's try it first where there aren't any mountains as distractions. I was thinking of somewhere like Southport if the tide's right. Wet sand should reflect the light much like ice will."

Davies blinked. "You're not thinking of trying to land there?"

Moore laughed. "No, sir. Just circuits and bumps to practise the drill."

"Sounds like a great idea. Adams can alert the Observer Corps." As Davies turned to the Intelligence Officer, his face reflected the unease a few minutes reflection had brought him. "I'm going to ask STS to give you a couple of days parachute training. It won't exactly make you a paratrooper but it might save you breaking a leg over there. So be ready to leave first thing in the morning."

Adams tried to hide his nervous swallow. "I'll be ready, sir."

Davies' gaze moved down to Adams' waistline. "You'd better try to get rid of some of that flab too. You might have some running to do among those mountains."

## 11

A gust of wind lifted the four-engined bomber bodily and threw her fifteen degrees off course. The pilot of the Stirling cursed as he heaved her back. He had been fighting strong winds for the last two hundred miles and his shoulders and arms were aching with the strain.

Far behind the Stirling the last of the coastal searchlights were playing uneasily on the underside of the clouds. As was the practice when conveying agents to Norway, the bomber had crossed the coast at high level and was now descending rapidly. Four thousand feet below, the Hardangervidda was sweeping into view. With the moonlight barely penetrating the clouds, its snow-covered wastes looked both desolate and forbidding.

As the Stirling reeled again, the pilot raised his face mask. "We can't drop him in this, Len. Tell him I'm turning back."

Halfway down the fuselage two men were huddled on leather cushions. One was Lindstrom, looking a bulky figure with his equipment, weapons, parachute, and white camouflaged suit. The second man was wearing a standard RAF flying suit. Both looked half-frozen from the cold of the long journey. Two supply-dropping containers rested on the metal floor behind them. A faint blue light made the men's faces look even more pinched and chilled.

Lindstrom, whose earphones picked up the pilot's message, answered himself. "I have to jump tonight, Flight Lieutenant. It's very important."

The pilot, an Australian, was not one to mince his words. "I'm the gaffer up here, Major, and I say we're turning back. I'm not carrying the can if you kill yourself."

"But surely you were told I had the right to make the decision myself?"

"I wasn't told that. Were you, Len?"

To Lindstrom's relief, the young man alongside him nodded. "Yes. Old Wilkie told me. Didn't you hear?"

The pilot released a fruity Australian oath. "Of course I didn't hear. I'm only the skipper of this bloody kite. You sure of this?"

"That's what Wilkie said. The Major was free to make his own decision."

"It's vitally important I land tonight," Lindstrom broke

in. "You've my word that whatever happens you won't take the blame."

"Your word's no flaming use to me if you're dead, Major."

"But the people I work for gave me permission. So how can you get into any trouble?"

The frowning pilot hesitated, then addressed his entire crew. "You guys are witness to this. The Major takes full responsibility. O.K.?"

Lindstrom relaxed as he heard a chorus of assent. The Australian's only reply was a grunt but the Stirling droned on deeper into the Hardangervidda. Five minutes later Lindstrom heard him speaking to his navigator. "You see any lights yet, Johnnie?"

"Nothing yet, skipper. But we could be a bit off course in this wind. Head five degrees south for a couple of minutes."

The Stirling yawed, then steadied. All the crew were now peering down at the wind-swept plateau. Four minutes later the Australian addressed Lindstrom again. "I reckon your contact's had more sense and gone home, Major."

"Keep searching, please." Lindstrom begged. "It's very important."

Changing course again, the black-painted Stirling droned on. Far over to the right a few flickering lights and a faint glow betrayed the presence of Rjukan. With the town's defences alerted, searchlights began playing on the underside of the clouds. The pilot's twangy voice sounded again. "I'm giving it ten more minutes, Major. Then I'm starting for home."

Although aware of the danger of losing himself in the wilderness, Lindstrom was contemplating making a blind jump when a call came from the front gunner. "There's a light at ten o'clock, skipper."

The Stirling swung to port. Dead ahead now, the tiny light flashed three times, went out, then flashed a short coded message. "We've made contact, Major. You still want to jump?"

Lindstrom was already removing his helmet. "Yes, I'm ready."

"O.K., it's your neck. I'm circling back. Get the hatch open, Len."

The Stirling banked steeply. An icy blast entered the fuselage as Lindstrom's assistant removed a floor hatch.

Through it the snowy wastes could be seen swimming dizzily past. Supporting himself on a metal strut, Lindstrom rose to his feet and began flexing his half-frozen legs. His assistant knelt beside one of the supply-dropping containers and waited.

The Stirling levelled out, dropped in a gust of wind, then steadied again. Waiting for his signal Lindstrom could feel his heart thudding. Apart from the physical risks of the drop, no agent could be certain his contact had not been captured and substituted by an enemy decoy. As the circulation began to return to his legs, a green light appeared above the hatch.

The assistant pushed out the two containers in rapid succession. Falling to the limit of their drag lines, their parachutes blossomed out and they swept downwards. Waiting his turn to leap through the gaping hole, Lindstrom could feel his cheeks freezing in the icy gale. Checking his static line was securely anchored, his assistant put a mouth to his ear. "Good luck, sir."

Lindstrom nodded and sat on the edge of the hatch. Taking a deep breath, he dropped forward. The icy wind that had been tearing at him became a hurricane as his body experienced the full velocity of the aircraft. Mountains, lakes and sky revolved dizzily as he turned a full somersault. The static line that was still attached to the Stirling ripped open his pack. A couple of seconds later his parachute opened and a violent jerk checked his headlong descent.

His first feeling as he hung in space was relief. In the dim moonlight he could see the containers sweeping southwards in the wind. Above, the black shape of the Stirling was banking as it turned towards England and safety. For a moment he felt envious of its crew. Then he pushed the emotion away and concentrated on the ground rising towards him.

The same wind that was sweeping the containers south was buffeting his own parachute. Twice in less than a minute it dropped sickeningly as air was driven from it. If a similar spillage occurred near the ground he knew he would be lucky to escape without broken legs or pelvis.

Unable to see the flickering torchlight, he could not tell whether he was drifting towards or away from it. As the drone of the Stirling died away he heard the bellowing of the wind and the whipping of the shroud lines above him.

With the ground no more than five hundred feet below, he estimated he was travelling as fast horizontally as he was vertically. Catching hold of his harness straps, he tried to turn himself in the direction of his horizontal drift.

He landed with a great snapping of branches in a patch of scrub. Snow filled his mouth and eyes as he pitched forward and a splintered branch scored his cheek painfully. With the wind already filling the parachute he would have suffered worse injury had not the silk canopy wrapped itself round a dwarf birch. Held there by the wind, it gave him time to press his harness release lock and squirm out of the straps.

Winded by his heavy fall, he took nearly a minute to recover and make for the parachute. He was only just in time: the wind had edged beneath it and already half of it was flapping clear of the tree. Conscious its discovery would bring an immediate manhunt to the plateau, he struggled to fold it but time and again it tore away like a living thing. When he finally succeeded in burying it among the bushes he was breathing heavily again.

The sound of a high-pitched whistle as the wind momentarily dropped made him grab for his Sten gun. As he peered over the scrub he saw a white-clad figure on skis advancing towards him and heard a shout. "Paul! Where the hell are you?"

Lindstrom pushed into the open. "Over here. By the trees."

The newcomer was Jensen, his beard rimed with frost. Grabbing Lindstrom's hand, he gripped it hard. "It's good to see you, lad. But you took a hell of a chance. I didn't think they'd let you jump in this wind."

The giant's massive presence seemed to push back the cold and the desolation. "I had to do a bit of arguing." Lindstrom motioned at the spare pair of skis Jensen was carrying. "Are those from the containers?"

"Ja. Your pilot knew his stuff. The wind brought them close to me."

"Where are they now?"

"In a clump of bushes and covered with snow. They'll be safe for a day of two." The giant noticed the contusion on the younger man's cheek. "That's a nasty scratch. Let me have a look at it."

Pushing him impatiently away, Lindstrom knelt down and began strapping on the skis. "Was Helga able to get away for the night?"

"Ja. She's waiting for you at the Poulsson's place. Only she has to be back in Rjukan by daylight. So we can't hang around."

"What's her latest news?"

Jensen grimaced. "Not good. As we expected they're going to send the Tinnsjo train out first. If the stocks get past Haukelid, I suppose there's the chance they'll send the second consignment the same way. Otherwise it's on an armoured train all the way to Kranvin. Helga says there's also talk of a hundred troops on board."

Lindstrom lifted his startled face. "A hundred?"

"Aye. And enough fire power in those flak wagons to blow a hole through a mountain. There's no way we can engage a force of that size, lad."

"Hasn't Helga found any loopholes?"

"She never gives up, that sister of yours, but this time the bastards seem to have got their security watertight. I'm worried at the risks she's been taking, lad. Arne says they're having a purge of all likely suspects as part of their security operation and I can't believe she's not on their list."

Lindstrom hid his concern by lowering his face and fitting on his second ski. "I'll talk to her about it. You don't think we can get the train by mining a bridge or a tunnel?"

"What's the point? They've already got every weak link under heavy guard, so even if we managed to plant mines they'd be alerted and come and defuse them. And mines along the track won't destroy the stocks. They're in specially built containers." The giant Norwegian was showing disappointment. "Can't London help us? I thought that was the idea of going over there."

"They had an idea just before I left," Lindstrom told him. "It sounds far-fetched but there's nothing else." As he quickly described Adams' plan Jensen showed renewed hope, then gave an excited laugh.

"That's the craziest thing I've ever heard. But it might work. Christ, yes, it might."

"Do you think so?"

"If they can get in undetected, why not? Anyway, it gives us a second chance if Helga can't find out anything new for us."

"Always assuming Haukelid sinks that Tinnsjo ferry," Lindstrom reminded him. "If he fails and the Germans use the same route for the second consignment, we could be back to square one again."

75

Jensen's face dropped. "Christ, yes, I'd forgotten that. But Skinnarland sounded reasonably optimistic the last time we heard him transmitting. So we'll just have to hope for the best there."

Nodding, Lindstrom heaved on his pack and slung his Sten gun over his shoulder. "As far as this lake idea goes, I'd like half a dozen men sent up to Hallingskarve immediately to look for something suitable. Then, if Helga can't find a weak link in Jerry's transit arrangements, we won't have wasted any time. Shall we get moving?"

"What about grub?" Jensen asked. "It's a long trip to Poulsson's place on an empty belly."

"I'm all right. I had a bar of chocolate on the plane."

Never subdued for long, Jensen gave his huge, fierce grin. "Some people do all right, don't they, lad? What's chocolate?"

As the two men turned eastward, a gale of wind hurled flakes of frozen snow and grit at them. Needles could not have been more painful to Lindstrom as they dug into his lacerated cheek. Half-blinded, leaning forward on his skis as he led the way, Jensen vented his feelings in rich Nordic oaths. "I hope the bloody Jerries are out in this tonight. Up to their sodding eyeballs looking for us."

## 12

Davies glanced down at his watch. "They're late, aren't they?"

Henderson checked the time. "Only a couple of minutes, sir."

Giving a non-committal grunt, Davies motioned at the wet beach that surrounded them. "At least we're lucky with the tide tonight. Moore didn't make a bad choice. I hadn't realized there was a beach this big in the country."

Adams, the third man in the group, had not realized it either. The wet sand, glistening in the moonlight, seemed to stretch for miles in all directions. A few blinkered lights, moving among the dark mass that was Southport and along the far side of the Ribble estuary, accentuated the men's isolation. The only sounds Adams could hear were the far-off murmur of the sea and an occasional rumble of machinery carried from the industrial heartland of Lancashire by the wind.

Given the responsibility of organizing the night landing experiment the same day it was devised, Adams had been compelled to move fast. His first task, after checking the tides were right, had been to alert the Observer Corps and obtain a safe cross-country route for the Mosquitoes. His next move had been to commandeer all the storm lanterns he could find and have them loaded on a large transport. Six unwilling men from the Signals Section had then been chosen to accompany the lanterns. Finally, leading the way in a staff car with Davies and Henderson as passengers, Adams had led his small convoy to Southport beach where the six airmen had laid out the storm lanterns in two rows a hundred yards apart. As the key man in the experiment, Adams had then positioned himself at the far end of the artificial runway and was now waiting, not without considerable apprehension, for the squadron to appear.

During the time the convoy had taken to assemble and make its slow way across the Pennines, the squadron's electricians had been working like proverbial beavers to fit and focus spotlights on each Mosquito's nose and tail. In turn Moore had briefed his crews on what was expected of them that evening. Not to his surprise he had been forced to parry question after question as the puzzled men tried to find a reason for the exercise.

As Adams had expected, his part in the proceedings had been complicated by gratuitous advice from Davies, some of which had made the usually mild-tempered Intelligence Officer bite his tongue. But at last it seemed the Air Commodore was satisfied with the dispositions of the men and all that was needed was the arrival of the squadron.

As Adams moved from one leg to the other, he felt water squelch in his left shoe and made a mental note to visit the cobbler on his return to Sutton Craddock. The wind, keening along the beach, made him huddle deeper into his greatcoat. Davies, similarly clad, gave a grunt and swung his arms. "Chilly, isn't it?"

Feeling he ought to say something, Henderson concurred. "Yes, sir. It is."

Davies turned to Adams. "Be colder in Norway, mind you."

Unsure how to reply, Adams took his cue from Henderson. "Yes, sir. I expect it will."

"It will. They say it can get so cold your breath freezes."

Conscious for some time that Davies was regretting his choice, Adams dragged his ears up from his coat collar. "It's lucky for me I don't feel the cold very much."

The cold and his inability to find a reason for changing his mind made Davies malicious. "It's probably that flab you carry."

If you've got a disadvantage, use it to advantage, Adams told himself. "It probably is, sir. It does have its uses sometimes."

. Davies gave him a stare. Adams was just congratulating himself when he heard a far-off drone. Davies' expression changed. "Here they are. Get your men alerted."

Lifting his Aldis lamp, Adams flickered it down the beach. A few seconds later his men began lighting the storm lanterns. The drone of engines, rising and falling in the keening wind, could be heard clearly now. Over in Southport and the adjacent towns, although wardens had been alerted that the aircraft were friendly, civilians began hurrying for shelters, expecting the sirens to sound at any moment.

Since leaving Sutton Craddock Moore had led the squadron out in line astern. He had crossed the Pennines at six thousand feet and had now dropped down to three. He led the squadron in an orbit at that height while Hopkinson read the message from Adams' flickering Aldis lamp.

"The wind's straight up the beach towards the river, skipper. He says we can start whenever we like."

Moore switched on his R/T. "Nightjay leader to squadron. Follow me at forty second intervals. Keep your kites steady and your eyes down. This could be tricky."

Breaking away he dived towards the Ribble. In the three-quarter moonlight its estuary was clearly visible. Banking over it Moore headed southward towards the beach where the improvised flare path was now fully lighted. "You watch the spotlights when I turn them on," he told Hoppy. "I'll keep my eye on Adams."

Adams' Aldis lamp had two functions, to pass on messages to the aircraft and to monitor their descent. Slow pulses meant a correct angle of descent. Fast pulses meant the angle was too steep. As the light winked at him, Moore brought A-Apple down to seven hundred feet and lowered her undercarriage and flaps. Below, the beach had a silvery sheen in the moonlight, causing Hoppy to glance at Moore as the pilot aimed A-Apple's nose between the parallel lines of lanterns. "What do we want spotlights for, skipper? This is a doddle."

Three quarters of a mile ahead, Adams had an excellent silhouette of A-Apple against the moonlight sky and saw she was making a nigh perfect approach. His relief was doused by Davies' sharp question. "You see Moore all right, Adams?"

"Of course, sir."

"You're quite sure?"

Adams understood. "My eyes are all right when I'm wearing the right glasses, sir."

"Just the same, they're something I'd forgotten. You'd better take a spare pair along with you if you go. Make a note of that. It could be important."

Adams' finger squeezed hard on the Aldis' trigger. "Yes, sir. I will."

Holding A-Apple steady, Moore was letting her sink as if to make a landing. When the beach was no more than two hundred feet below, Hoppy glanced at him. "You want to try the spotlights, skipper? We don't need 'em."

"Try them," Moore told him.

The two spotlights flashed on. One shone forward from beneath the Mosquito's tail, the other forward from her nose. Angled to meet on the runway ahead, their bright circles were lost in the coruscating sand. Seeing Hoppy shake his head, Moore let A-Apple sink until she was no more than fifty feet above the beach. Then, with a roar of engines, her nose lifted and she thundered over the three officers. As she banked away, an Aldis flickered from her cupola. Adams read the message aloud. "They couldn't pick up the spotlights. The beach is too bright."

Davies' face was a study as he turned to Henderson. "Isn't that typical? If we wanted a clear night the clouds would be round our backsides."

Henderson was studying the sky. Although it was clear near the moon, dark clouds were backing up over the sea. "With luck it won't last much longer, sir."

Moore decided to send down Teddy Young next. Young, now B Flight Commander, was a veteran of 633 Squadron: indeed he was the only pilot to have flown back from the Swartfjord. Gingerheaded and powerfully built, he was Australian from his love of horse racing to his sense of humour. As he peeled out of orbit, he grinned at his English navigator, Woodfall. "You know why we're doing this, don't you, Woody?"

"No, skipper. I've no idea."

"It's practice for landing on flat-tops. Davies is transferring us to the Fleet Air Arm."

With no more difficulty than Moore in skimming the moonlit beach, Young decided to introduce a touch of comedy. Holding his Mosquito down until the last moment, he leapt over the three ducking officers with less than twenty feet to spare. As the men wiped their faces of sand and spray, Davies glared after the climbing aircraft. "Who was that?"

Henderson, who had spotted the Mosquito's identification number, showed innocence. "I don't know, sir."

"Isn't Harvey number two?"

"That wasn't Harvey, sir. His kite's still wearing that camouflage from the Norwegian sortie."

Realizing he was right, Davies gave a grunt and dug wet sand out of his shirt collar. "You've too many comedians around these days. It's time you cooled their heels a bit."

The Scot grinned at Adams. "He probably didn't see us. There must be quite a few shadows on the beach."

"Didn't see us?" Davies growled. "With Adams flashing an Aldis lamp right in his face? Stop making excuses for the sod."

One by one the experienced pilots came down and completed the exercise with ease. When Millburn's turn came his voice summed up everyone's feeling. "What's the idea of circuits and bumps, skipper? Have we all gone back to OTU?"

As usual Moore was equal to the occasion. "Some need it more than others, Millburn. Down you go."

The American glanced at Gabby as he peeled away. "You any idea what it's for?"

"How should I know? Maybe we're rehearsing to fly into submarine pens."

Millburn grinned. "What—at night?"

Banking steeply over the estuary, he lowered his flaps and undercarriage and swept in low towards the lights. As he sank to within thirty feet of the beach, Moore broke in sharply. "Get your spotlights on, Millburn!"

"I don't need spotlights, skipper. I can see the crabs waving their pincers at me."

"Get them on, Millburn. At the double!"

The order came not a moment too soon. As Gabby turned the spotlights on, the moonlight disappeared as if governed by the same switch. As the bright beach suddenly went dark, Millburn lost all spacial awareness. Grunting with alarm, he shoved both throttles forward and T-Tommy shot upwards like a startled wild fowl. With the American's R/T still switched on, all the orbiting crews heard his curse. "Jesus; who put the light out?"

Checking the reprimand he was about to give, Moore dived down instead. "Stay in orbit, Number 11. I want to try this again myself."

The entire landscape had changed in colour and texture as he crossed the estuary for a second time. The beach was only a shade lighter than the land mass and its distance below the Mosquito difficult to judge. With the thinly spaced lanterns the only fixed reference points, Moore aimed A-Apple's nose between them and gently throttled back.

Adams, for whom the task had been ridiculously easy so far, now discovered A-Apple's silhouette was almost hidden in the bank of cloud and made a mental note to warn all crews to use their navigation lights when the moon was obscured. As he began transmitting a series of dots, Hopkinson tapped Moore's arm. "We're dropping too smartly, skipper. Hold her up a bit."

Without the moonlight Moore was finding it difficult to pick up the beach between the two rows of lanterns, but as he eased the control column gently back Adams' distant flashes lost their urgency. Unable to judge his height accurately, he told Hoppy to switch on the spotlights.

81

This time their reflections on the sand were clearly visible but with the rear light well ahead of the nose light it was apparent A-Apple was well above landing height.

Needing to keep his eyes fixed well ahead to hold the Mosquito steady, Moore had to rely on Hoppy to monitor the spotlights. "They're about fifteen feet apart now and closing . . . . Twelve feet . . . ten. . . . Keep her going, skipper. Nice and steady. . . ."

Ahead, the three officers were half-blinded by the oncoming spotlights. In his excitement Davies had a tight grip on Adams' arm. "He's getting bloody low, isn't he?"

Although Moore could see the converging splashes of light on the periphery of his vision, he knew that to turn his eye downwards, even for a second, could be fatal. Alongside him Hoppy, equally conscious that if the aircraft's wheels sank into the soft sand it would mean disaster, dared not blink as he watched the reflections converge. "About seven feet apart now, skipper. . . . Six feet . . . four. . . ."

With startling abruptness sand and spray splattered against the windshield. Hoppy's yell of alarm could be heard by every airman circling above. "Up, skipper! Get her up!"

Without time for thought, it was Moore's reflexes that saved both men's lives. Pushing both throttles forward before Hopkinson's yell had died away, he turned both airscrews to fine pitch and eased back on the wheel. With her flaps and landing wheels down it appeared to the breathless onlookers as if the Mosquito's wheels must drop into the sand. Instead she picked up and began to climb away with a startled scream of engines.

Down on the beach it was difficult to tell which of the three officers was the paler. "What happened?" Henderson muttered.

An Aldis lamp flickering from A-Apple thirty seconds later gave the explanation. "Moore says the bracket of a spotlight must have worked loose and given a false reading." Adams said. "As the same thing might have happened to another aircraft, he's taking them back to base."

With the responsibility of the Norwegian operation heavy on him Davies shifted restlessly. "Doesn't he realize what little time we might have left?"

Henderson stared at him. "He nearly killed himself, sir. You can't expect him to take the same risks with his men. Not when this is only a training exercise."

Davies grunted something, then pulled himself together. "No, I suppose not. Those spotlights have to be made safe. All right, Adams. Round up the men and let's start back."

Above, the drone of the Mosquitoes' engines was beginning to fade into the night sky. Aiming his Aldis down the beach, Adams ordered his men to take the lanterns back to the transport. As the lights went out one by one, the wind came sobbing out of the darkness and sent a shudder of foreboding through him. Hunching up his greatcoat collar and slinging the strap of the Aldis over his shoulder, he turned to follow Davies and Henderson. As he trudged across the wet sand he became conscious again of the water squelching in his shoe.

## 13

It was bitterly cold in Adams' Confessional the following morning. Although on his return he had awoken his indignant G.D., one Percy Jones, and told him to light the stove, so far its only contribution was an acrid smell of coke fumes. The naked electric lights also added in some indefinable way to the bleakness of the large Nissen hut.

All the three officers who had controlled the ground side of the previous night's exercise were present. They had barely had time to climb out of their car after their long journey and stretch their legs before the Duty Officer had run up and told Davies the Brigadier wanted an urgent word with him. After being closeted privately with Henderson's scrambler telephone, Davies had dismayed everyone by announcing they had fifteen minutes to grab a cup of coffee before reconvening in Adams' office. Moore was also ordered to attend.

Only Henderson had elected to have a bite of breakfast. Adams had rushed off to ensure his office was reasonably presentable, found it was not, and had been shoving files into drawers ever since. Moore, who had been working with the fitters on the spotlight brackets since his return, had gone off for a shave. Assembled now with the others he was the only man who did not look tired and dishevelled from his sleepless night.

Checking two security S.P.s were on station outside, Davies walked back to Adams' large desk. Two small red spots were burning high up on his cheekbones.

"As you've probably guessed, there's news from Lindstrom. He saw his sister during the night and made immediate contact with the Brigadier. From what she told him it seems unlikely she'll gain any more information about the shipments and as the Germans are making arrests all over Rjukan, Lindstrom wouldn't allow her to go back. As her absence means she'll become a suspect in any case, she's going with him and the rest of his group to find us a suitable lake. In other words, the operation is on."

Adams' heart seemed to leap and burn in his chest. To hide his own dismay, Henderson was frowning. "Isn't there a chance Skinnarland might still find something out?"

"You're forgetting—Skinnarland doesn't know about the second consignment. Anyway, with the first consignment due out shortly, he and Haukelid have already left to organize their own attack." Davies' excited eyes moved to each man in turn. "It's our baby now—bibs, nappies, and all."

In the brief silence that followed the cartilaginous sound of Adams swallowing could be clearly heard. Giving him a glance, Davies turned to Moore. "What's the verdict on those spotlight brackets?"

"It was vibration working them loose, sir. I've put fitters on strengthening them."

"Those spotlights are worrying me," Davies muttered. "Even if they're only switched on for a few seconds, they can be seen miles away."

"Perhaps we won't need to use them. We certainly won't have to if conditions are as good as they were last night. The problem comes when there's no moonlight—then it's difficult to pick up the ground between the lanterns. But if there's snow around, particularly on mountains, there could be more reflected light than we get here."

Davies jumped at the possibility. "That's a good point, Moore. Then are you satisfied this is the landing procedure to use?"

"It's not ideal, sir. But considering the short time we have and the circumstances, I don't see what choice we've got. However, I would like to see the lake first."

Davies chose to misunderstand. "With luck you'll get photographs once Lindstrom has made his choice."

"Lindstrom's not a pilot, sir, and he could make a bad choice. I need to assess the lake from the air and to make a trial landing."

Davies' flat refusal beat Henderson's protest by a good neck and shoulders. "That's out! I'm not risking you again."

"But we must establish the ice will hold us. Otherwise we might fly out, find we can't land, and lose our last chance of destroying the shipment."

"I know we have to find out more about the ice. But that's a job any competent pilot can do."

Moore's insistence made Davies lift his eyebrows. "With respect, sir, you're forgetting one thing. As Squadron Commander I have the right to know if an operation is feasible or downright suicidal. As in this case you don't know, I surely have the right to find out for myself."

Davies was beginning to breathe hard. "I grant you someone has to do a trial run for us. But it's not going to be you. I'm going to need you too much later on."

"I don't think you're being fair to me, sir."

"Well, that's too bloody bad, isn't it?" Davies snapped. "Because you're still not going. Got it?"

Pale-faced and very erect, Moore gazed at him a full five seconds before nodding coldly. "Very well, sir."

"Very well it is," Davis grunted. Irritated by the clash he turned to Henderson. "I'd like to use Millburn and Gabriel. They've got the flair for this kind of sortie. Any objections?"

Henderson prevaricated. "Are you going to give them an escort?"

"How can I? Jerry will be certain to pick up a gaggle of kites and then the exercise will be pointless. No, my idea is they fly out at night and stay at low level. As this anticyclone is still drifting eastward and the moon's nearly full, they ought to have decent weather most or all of the way."

"Does that mean you want to try a night landing?"

"Not on a test run," Davies grunted. "We'll time the operation so they reach the lake just after sunrise. Then they can do a survey before they land. Don't look so worried, Jock. I intend laying on plenty of spoofs for them."

As Henderson's face cleared, Davies turned to Adams. "How would you like to go with them? It'll save you parachute training."

Adams gave a start. "I, sir? In a Mosquito?"

"Why not? You won't have a drop to do and you'll be safer than in a Stirling. I'll borrow one of those VIP passenger jobs for you." Davies' grin had a touch of malice. "I believe one or two of 'em have even got perspex windows in the bomb doors so you can enjoy the scenery."

Thrown by the suggestion, the imaginative Adams was wondering which was the more fearful prospect, dropping earthwards with a faulty parachute or plunging headlong through broken ice. Deciding that at the worst he would die in cheerful company, he took a deep breath. "I'll go with Millburn, sir."

"Good man. That saves me getting in touch with the STS."

Leaving Adams certain he was going to regret his decision the moment the conference was over, the indefatigable Davies began issuing his orders right and left.

"If we're going to be ready for this job, we'll have to

work like beavers from now on. Moore, I want your boys to get in all the night-landing practice they can. Once you've got that spotlight problem licked, you can use this airfield. It'll save a lot of coming and going and also mean you'll have plenty of bods handy to do the chores."

"This airfield, sir?" Henderson asked, startled.

"Why not? You can use the east-west runway so everyone will be well clear of the Control Tower. Your job, Jock, is to get your specialist officers together and find out what stores we're going to need over there. I know this will be tricky because on no account must they know what our target is. You just tell them we're going to use a Norwegian lake for a couple of days and leave it there."

The big Scot grinned wryly. "It's hardly the kind of thing they get told every day. To put it mildly they're going to be curious."

"Let 'em be curious. If Jerry finds out about this, not only are we going to be dead ducks but worse the shipment's going to get through. So you tell 'em if they breathe the word Norway outside your office they're for the big drop."

Henderson nodded. "How do you intend getting the stores over there? Will you use the Americans?"

"I think so. Staines has put in a lot of time and I know he'd like his boys involved. But that's something we can talk about when Lindstrom's found a lake. In the meantime get your lists ready but tell your specialist officers I only want the barest essentials—we don't know yet what stores the partisans will need. So no barrels of beer or camp beds at this stage of the game."

"What about armament?" Henderson asked. "As it's a light cruiser we're attacking I suppose Lindsay will advise rockets."

Davies shrugged. "We'll have to bomb up here and carry them with us. What else can we do?"

Although the Scot had known it all along, it was a shock to hear it said aloud. "Land in the dark with a full complement of stores? Isn't there any way round it?"

When worried himself, Davies tended to use sarcasm as a disguise. "Yes, there's a way. We can take out three or four Bombays loaded with stores, bomb trolleys, hoists, armourers, the lot. Only I've a nasty feeling something might go wrong, haven't you?"

Henderson's cheeks turned pink with resentment. "This

is possibly the most dangerous operation we've ever tackled, sir. Don't blame me for trying to eliminate a few of the risks."

A small figure in his greatcoat, Davies walked over to the window. Although the sun was shining through it by this time, rime could still be seen clinging to the glass. It was a full fifteen seconds before Davies turned.

"You know, Jock, I sometimes think you all forget what this squadron means to me. When I first put forward the idea of a Special Service Unit, I was attacked all the way down the line. The bastards didn't fight clean either, not with Bomber Command, Fighter Command and Coastal Command all screaming for more aircraft. It was a miracle I made it, so do you think I'm going to risk its existence now without a good reason? For Christ's sake, Jock, a man gets a liking for the thing he fights for."

Totally unused to emotion from Davies, the three officers watched in silence as he walked back to the desk and picked up his briefcase. "I'm very much aware what I'm asking of you all but if Churchill says those stocks must be destroyed, that's good enough for me. I'd be quite prepared to send my son along if he'd finished his training."

Henderson cleared his throat. "I'm sorry, sir. I wasn't suggesting you were being callous."

Davies shrugged as he drew on his gloves. "I'm not blaming you, Jock. It's your job to fight for your boys. And in one way I suppose I am being callous. But I wish someone would give me an alternative."

When no one spoke he walked down the hut to the door. "Moore, I want you to start your boys practising as soon as it's dusk because the Brigadier wants all three of us at High Elms by 2130 hours. By that time he's hoping to have more news. Now I'm going for a couple of hours' kip and I suggest you do the same."

Lifting his greatcoat collar he opened the door and walked out. The S.P. outside presented arms with a thud of gloved hand on rifle stock. Inside the hut there was silence as the three officers were left gazing at one another.

Catching sight of Moore coming out of A Flight offices, Millburn ran after him. "You got a moment, skipper?"

Moore turned. "Hello, Tommy. What can I do for you?"

88

The tousle-headed American nodded at Gabby who had now caught up with him. "Our gremlin friend wants to ask you a favour."

The Welshman scowled. "I thought you were doing the asking."

Millburn grinned at the amused Moore. "I think he's shy. He's wondering how long you're keeping us on circuits and bumps tonight?"

"I hadn't thought about it. Why?"

"There's a rumour you've got a conference around 2100 hours. Will we be finished by then?"

Moore shook his head in wonder. "I don't know why we try to break Jerry's codes. All we need do is drop our grapevine into Berlin. Why do you want to finish at 2100 hours?"

"It's Machin's birthday and we'd planned a bit of a party for him," Gabby explained.

To his chagrin, Millburn let out a loud guffaw. "Don't let him fool you that's his reason. He wants Matthews busy on the drums so he can steal his dame away. I don't think he has a hope in hell but give the guy credit—he's a tryer."

Moore fought back a smile. "You've picked a bad time. Supposing you postponed the party for a week or two. Won't the scheme work just as well?"

"Not really, skipper. You see his problem is he can only make love around full moon. It has something to do with his being a gremlin. So he's tight on time."

Believing he should refuse, Moore was having second thoughts. With the entire squadron guessing something special was afoot, a party would help to stave off tension. On a grimmer note it might also be the last party some of the crews would ever attend. "If we start practising at dusk I suppose you will be getting a bit dizzy by nine o'clock. All right. You can make your arrangements for nine-thirty."

Gabby was looking delighted. His question was innocence itself. "Is your conference here on the station, skipper?"

"No, it isn't. But that doesn't mean you go wild and wreck the place. Is that understood?"

The Welshman looked hurt at the suggestion. "It's not that. It's just the boys can't relax if they think Davies might be dropping in."

Moore nodded. "Fair enough. He'll be miles away. Tell Machin I'm sorry I can't come." Famous for his generosity at Mess parties, Moore pulled out a notebook, scribbled on a page and tore it out. "Give this to the Messing Officer. It should help to keep things moving."

Glancing over Gabby's shoulder, Millburn gave a whistle, then a broad grin. "Half a dozen bottles of Scotch? He'll have to raid Pop Henderson's private store for that. Don't ever get yourself posted, will you, skipper, or we'll all have to resign."

The soaring decibel count in the Mess that night made Young shout as he pushed a glass of whisky at Harvey. "Ian's contributed six bottles. Get stuck into it before these young bastards drink the lot."

The evening's night-landing exercise had ended but with its results needing assessing, the two flight commanders had been closeted with Moore for the last fifteen minutes. In that time the younger members had well and truly launched Machin's birthday party. One group, singing their heads off, surrounded the piano where Lindsay, the Armament Officer, was demonstrating his virtuosity by playing every request thrown at him. A second, more active group, were playing a favourite RAF game. At one end of two parallel lines of men, an apple was floating in a bucket of water. At the other end two blindfolded men were being whirled round before attempting to walk the gauntlet and pick the apple up in their mouths. Prevented from wandering off course by the flanking men they reeled along to cat-calls and cheers. Halfway towards the bucket they collided with a sickening clash of heads. As they fell, men dragged them aside and prepared the next pair of victims.

Young was grinning at the horse play. Harvey, a man made older than his years by his harsh childhood, was showing forebearance rather than amusement. As he raised his glass, Young turned to him.

"You got any ideas about this blind-landing bullshit?"

The Yorkshireman shook his head. "None that make any sense."

"You don't think we're being trained to pick up agents?"

"In Mosquitoes? Not unless Davies is going daft."

"Then what else could it be?"

Never one to waste words, Harvey only shrugged.

"It's bloody dangerous," Young went on. "If Prentice hadn't got that R/T warning he'd have gone straight in. You know he burst a tire?"

"So Moore said. You think his night vision's O.K.?"

"It's more likely those flaming spotlights," Young grunted. "They've only got to shift a degree or two and you've got a bum reading."

Across the room a blindfolded navigator had been twirled round so fast he lost his balance and staggered into the arms of an attractive Waaf. As a chorus of cheers sounded, Young grinned. "I might join that game in a minute."

Further down the bar was a small group of hardened drinkers, with Millburn, Hopkinson, and Gabby conspicuous among them. Usually talkative when in liquor, Gabby was preoccupied tonight. Alongside Lindsay, a burly young man with a mop of fair hair was seated behind a drum kit and enthusiastically beating out rhythm to the piano. Matthews, whose ambition to be a dance band drummer was almost an obsession, had been given permission by the Adjutant to bring his kit into the Mess and was making the best of the occasion. Standing as close to him as twirling drum sticks would allow was a sultry brunette of Junoesque proportions. Since her posting to the Parachute Packing Section, Gwen Thomas was the undisputed belle of the station. Exuding sex like a strong perfume, she drew disbelieving stares from senior officers down to the lowest erk. For some reason better known to herself, she had so far given her attention to the vigorous and enthusiastic Matthews but her reaction to the many glances being thrown at her tonight suggested his tenure was precarious. Like many of the Waafs present she was not commissioned. In some ways 633 Squadron was a law unto itself and it was not uncommon for other ranks to be invited to non-military functions.

Seeing where Gabby's eyes were riveted Millburn nudged Hopkinson's arm. "Watch this," he whispered. "It's going to be something."

He approached the rapt Welshman. "You got the booze, boyo?"

Gabby tapped the side pocket of his tunic and nodded.

"Then why're you wasting flying time?"

Although he had four whiskies inside him, Gabby was looking uncharacteristically apprehensive. "I'm letting her get warmed up, that's all."

"Don't give me that. You're scared. And I don't wonder. Even a drummer boy's better than a Welsh gremlin."

The scowling Gabby turned. "Why don't you transfer, Millburn? Won't the Yanks have you?"

"They're in a tough spot, kid. They want my expertise but not my competition."

Gabby's caustic reply was forgotten as the sultry Gwen caught his eye again. Millburn grinned. "You don't need to worry. I've already put in a word for you."

The Welshman looked immediately suspicious. "What have you said?"

"I said back home they call you the Swansea Stallion. It worked like a charm. She nearly jumped out of her knickers."

Gabby glared. "I'll kill you if you've messed it up for me, Millburn."

"Messed it up? She can't wait for you to get your little red hands on her. Get over there and see if I'm not right."

Muttering under his breath Gabby drained his glass, braced himself, and started across the room. Millburn winked as Hopkinson moved closer. "It's working out nicely. Just watch."

Across the room the girl was swaying her hips to the rhythm of the drums as Gabby approached her. At first she shook her head at his request but as the Welshman persisted she allowed him to draw her away to a corner of the Mess where the crowd was less dense. In the conversation that followed, Gabby's gesticulations at his tunic pocket, at the unsuspecting Matthews, and at a door that led outside made it obvious what he was suggesting. At first the girl appeared to resist and when she swung her voluptuous way back to the piano, Hoppy gave a grunt of disappointment. "She's turned him down."

Millburn was watching Gabby. Looking furtive he was edging his way along the opposite wall. Reaching the door he glanced back to make certain Matthews was still preoccupied with his drumming and slipped out. Millburn winked at the Cockney navigator. "No; it's right on track. Keep your eyes on the girl."

Still swaying to the music, Gwen allowed a minute to pass before she began to edge unobtrusively away. Watching the engrossed Matthews she slipped through a second door that led outside through the kitchens. Slapping Hoppy gleefully on the back, Millburn turned to the bar. "That's it, kiddo. All we do now is wait for him to sling his hook and then we move in."

"Did you get the pistol from the armoury?" the grinning Cockney asked.

"No trouble at all. I said we needed it for the night-landing exercise."

Outside, the anticyclone that was drifting slowly across Northern Europe was displaying itself in a purple sky, a fattening moon, and frost on every blade of grass. Waiting behind the far corner of No. 1 hangar, Gabby, who in his

93

eagerness had neglected to collect his greatcoat, was finding his ardour at some risk in the freezing wind. As he took a quick swig from a half-bottle of whisky, the muffled-up figure of Gwen Thomas appeared in the moonlight. With a grunt of relief, Gabby let out a low whistle. Catching sight of him the girl crossed the empty tarmac apron and joined him in the shadow of the hangar. Her complaining voice made him lift a warning finger to his lips. "I must be out of my mind, Johnnie Gabriel, comin' out here with you. What are you up to anyway?"

It was a painful fact that Gwen Thomas' voice and intellect did not match her other vital statistics but with Gabby's plans not including any lengthy dialogues his ardour was in no way dampened. His main problem, with the girl's physical charms affecting his nerves and self-confidence, was living up to the exacting role Millburn had set for him, for Gwen's presence convinced him the American was right and she was as sexy as she looked. Taking a deep breath, Gabby decided it was the Swansea Stallion or bust.

"Up to? What do you think I'm up to?"

In the shadow of the hangar the girl's eyes were assessing him. "From what I hear a girl isn't safe with you. Maybe I ought to go back to the Mess."

Grinning, Gabby steered her towards the perimeter path. "Who wants to be safe, love? Isn't excitement more fun?"

For a moment she resisted him. "It all depends what you mean by excitement, Johnnie Gabriel."

"Why don't we go and find out?" he suggested.

She hesitated, then allowed him to push her forward. "I don't see why we can't go to your billet. At least we'd be warm in there."

Eyes glinting like a ferret, Gabby squeezed her hand. "You'll be warm where we're going, love. Wait and see."

The dispersal hut that was his objective stood six hundred yards round the western perimeter. Warm air met their cheeks as Gabby produced a key and threw the door open. Ahead of them a coke stove glowed redly in the darkness. As Gabby furtively locked the door on the inside and lit a paraffin lamp, two wooden-framed beds swam into view. Shelves ran round the walls, littered with tools, oil cans, tins of grease and miscellaneous equipment. A teapot, a packet of tea, a bottle of milk and two filthy tin mugs stood on a tea chest. Pin-ups of half-naked girls filled every spare inch of the walls. The war air was heavy with the odour of coke fumes, petrol, and anti-freeze oil.

Gwen was staring round the hut in disbelief. "You think I'm goin' to spend the evenin' in here? You must be out of your mind."

Terrified the fish was going to escape when so close to the hook, Gabby moved fast. "At least let's have a cigarette and a drink first."

She pointed at the two filthy mugs. "In those?"

Fumbling under one of the beds Gabby drew out a cardboard box containing a couple of cream cakes, two glasses, and a bottle of soda water. Muttering something and refusing to take off her greatcoat, Gwen dropped on the other bed. "One drink, that's all. Then I'm gettin' back."

Gabby handed her a cream cake first. She took a tentative bite, then glanced up in surprise. "It's real cream, isn't it?"

Remembering his role, Gabby laid a finger on one side of his nose. "That's right. Influence, love."

In spite of herself, Gwen looked impressed. "I haven't had real cream for years. Where did you get them?"

The drink Gabby handed her was three parts whisky and one part soda water. "Just stick with me, love, and you'll do all right."

She took a sip and grimaced. "Are you tryin' to get me drunk?"

Gabby grinned. "Now why would I want to do that?"

"Don't think I don't know all about you, Johnnie Gabriel, because I do. Even your friends talk about you."

"What do they say?"

"That you're worse than a randy tom-cat." The girl stared around the hut in distaste. "I don't know what I'm doin' in here. I'm used to men treating me right."

"I'll treat you right, love. The best way a man can treat a woman."

"You don't half think you're something, don't you?"

"If you know you're good at something, there's no sense in keeping quiet about it, is there?"

She wrinkled her nose. "Listen to him. The great lover. I'll bet you're like all the rest of 'em. Just talk."

Deciding things were going well, Gabby moved over and sat beside her. "You want to find out?"

"In here? That'll be the day."

"It's not my fault you're confined to camp, is it? Anyway this bed's clean."

As he pulled back the blanket she saw there were two clean sheets underneath. "My Gawd, you're sure of yourself, aren't you?"

"Nothing tried for, nothing won," Gabby suggested.

"Better men than you have tried, Johnnie Gabriel."

With his ardour demanding action or else, Gabby decided to call up an old and trusted ally. "I'll bet they have. You're the best looking girl I've seen in years."

As she turned and her black hair brushed her face, Gabby felt an electric shock go right down his spine. "You expect me to believe that?"

"It's true, love. I've never seen a figure like yours."

She stared down at herself. "What's so special about my figure?"

Deciding that if the Swansea Stallion missed a cue like this he would be discredited forever, the dry-mouthed Gabby leaned forward and began undoing her coat buttons. "If you keep still I'll show you."

She allowed him to remove her greatcoat and tunic. Swallowing hard, he had the first three buttons of her shirt undone when she suddenly slapped his hand. "That's enough, Johnnie Gabriel."

Even if her protest had been genuine it would have been too late. With the feel of her huge breasts beneath his hands, Gabby lost all restraint. Kissing her wildly on the neck and shoulders, he threw her back on the bed and rolled on top of her. For a moment he heaved like a ship in a storm as she struggled. "What do you think you're doin', Johnnie Gabriel? Let me go!"

With her weight matching his own, it is highly doubtful that Gabby could have held her had not passion brought an end to her resistance. As she sank back with a moan the trembling Gabby whose heart was hammering like a pneumatic drill, managed to pull off her blouse and slide up her bra. Goggle-eyed at the treasures that heaved out, the small Welshman buried his face in them while he struggled to remove her nether garments. The result was a tumultuous tangle of clothes and limbs, with the moaning Gwen trying to give advice while Gabby, refusing to release what was already in his grasp, struggled to attain more. When her last garment finally slid to the floor, her cry of relief turned into impatience as Gabby hurled himself back on her. "What are you doin'? You've still got your trousers on."

Realizing she was right, Gabby tried to unbuckle his

belt with one hand. Kicking frantically, he succeeded in getting his trousers and underpants down to his knees but no further. With his libido urging him on, he would have settled for that had not Gwen's legs been trapped beneath him, so making his goal unattainable. Cursing, he rolled sideways, dragged the guilty garments off, and hurled them to the far side of the hut. Clad only in his socks, he threw himself back on the pulsating Gwen. With an acreage of heaving flesh beneath him, there was the problem which part should claim his attention. It was settled by Gwen dragging his sweating face between her breasts and sliding her hands down to his buttocks. As Gabby prepared to enter Paradise, she suddenly stiffened. "Listen! What's that?"

Buried to the ears between her lush breasts, Gabby was incapable of breathing, much less hearing. Digging his toes against the frame of the wooden bed, he drove himself upwards. The girl let out a loud moan and her nails dug fiercely into his back. For a moment the only sound in the hut was heavy breathing. Then Gwen's eyes, black in the lamplight, opened and stared up in alarm. "There is something! I think it's on the roof."

Although the small Welshman could hear nothing but the pounding of his heart, one thing he knew for certain. Nothing, be it werewolf or Count Dracula outside, was going to rob him of his hard-won victory. "You're hearing things," he panted. "It's just the bed creaking. Try to relax." Before she could argue he put his mouth over her lips and tightened his grip of her.

On the roof outside, crouched precariously with his stocking feet in the gutter, Millburn signalled down to Hopkinson who had just helped him make the climb. A group of young officers, who had crept up on the dispersal hut with the two practical jokers, grinned expectantly as the Cockney reached up and handed Millburn a loaded Very pistol. Bracing himself, the American slid cautiously along the roof until he was within reach of the smoking chimney. As he signalled the onlookers to be ready and attempted to shift his grip on the pistol, it slipped from his hand and fell with a clatter on the tin roof. Snatching it up Millburn wasted no time. Pointing it down the chimney he pressed the trigger.

Gabby's refusal to take note of the girl's alarm was now paying handsome dividends. With her nubile body moving in unison with him, the creaking of the wooden

bed was keeping all outside sounds at bay. The Welshman's first intimation all was not well came when Millburn
dropped the Very pistol. As he paused to listen, there was
a sudden deafening explosion followed by a crash of metal
as the stove doors burst open.

The girl's scream and the convulsion of her body shot
Gabby out of Paradise like a cork from a bottle and
pitched him ignominiously on the floor. Gaping at the
stove he saw a huge green fireball fizzing among the em-
bers. A couple of seconds later a cloud of dense black
smoke came belching out. Coughing and choking, the startled Welshman dragged the girl from the bed. "It's a
bloody incendiary! It must be! Get out of here."

Pulling herself away, Gwen grabbed her greatcoat and
threw it on. Still dazed at his fall from bliss to catastrophe,
Gabby was fumbling in the dense smoke to find the lock.
Her eyes streaming, the girl yelled at him stridently. "Why
did you have to take the key out? Hurry up and get it
open!"

Finding the lock at last, Gabby tore the door open and
dragged the coughing Gwen after him. With the dense
smoke billowing out he failed to notice Millburn waiting
at the door with a blanket for the girl in case she needed
it. As the furious Gwen tore away from the naked Welshman, a great cheer rose as Gabby staggered out into the
moonlight. Knuckling his streaming eyes, he caught sight
of the arc of hysterical young officers. Aghast, he swung
round, saw Millburn comforting the girl, and the truth hit
him like a bludgeon. "Millburn! You!"

The American gave him a wink. "Hiya, kid."

Stunned by the wickedness of the deed, Gabby's voice
was hoarse. "That was a Very light you fired, wasn't it?"

As another hysterical yell broke out, Gabby went berserk, dancing up and down in his socks like a malevolent
leprechaun. "I'll kill you, Millburn. I mean it. I'll kill you."

Half-crippled by laughter, the American held up a hand
and backed away. "Steady, boyo. You'll give yourself ul-
cers."

Gabby had now found the weapon he wanted, a three-
foot length of angle iron lying in the frozen grass. As he
snatched it up, Millburn pushed Hopkinson in front of him
and ran hard for the distant hangars. Brandishing the angle
iron, white buttocks twinkling in the moonlight, Gabby tore
after him, leaving men falling over one another in their
hysteria.

## 15

The rising sun was an orange halo around the peak of a distant mountain. In the west the moon was a frail bubble floating in the lightening sky. Two men, armed with Sten guns and wearing camouflaged smocks and skis, were standing on the top of a hill. Two miles behind and below them an icy ribbon of road ran northward alongside a frozen river. The hillside that swept upwards from it had deep snow drifts in every hollow and against every pile of rocks, a legacy of the prevailing wind. The western slope of the range was covered in scrub and ran for a mile or more down to a large frozen lake.

The two skiers were Lindstrom and Jensen. There was an air of suppressed excitement about them that suggested they had received some momentous news. The giant Norwegian was nodding down at the lake. "That's the best we've been able to find, lad. And it looks as if we've found it just in time. Arne's already settled in and ready to receive messages from Kranvin and Rjukan."

The lake visible from the hill top was roughly pear-shaped and about one and a half kilometres long but at the far side a narrow neck led into a second lake. Jensen read Lindstrom's thoughts. "It's shaped like an hour-glass, with the two lakes about the same size. So whichever end they come in, they'll have a fair runway if they go through the neck."

"It should be long enough," Lindstrom agreed. "Where's this hiding place you mentioned?"

Jensen pointed along the southern shore of the lake. Two parallel hill ranges soared above it, the one bordering the lake covered in stunted trees. "You can't see it from here but at the other side of the neck a river cuts through those hills and flows into the second lake. As it's frozen now and sheltered by high ground and trees on either side, I reckon they can run their aircraft into it."

"Where's Arne got his radio?"

Jensen nodded at the neck that joined the two lakes. The southern side was a precipitous bluff that fell a sheer two hundred feet to the ice. "The woods on that side are full of summer cabins we can use as billets. There's one on top of that bluff and Arne grabbed it right away. He reckons he'll get good reception and transmission from there."

"Did you say you'd already been in touch with London?"

"Ja. I sent 'em full details of the lake." At the glance Lindstrom gave him, the giant shrugged. "You said I could make a decision myself. As things have turned out, it's a good thing I did."

Lindstrom nodded and switched his gaze to the hills flanking the northern boundary of the lake. Although stunted trees grew on the lower slopes they were more barren than their counterparts opposite. "How high do you estimate these hills are?"

The bearded Norwegian shrugged. "I'm guessing but I'd say those northern ones are around three hundred metres and the southern ones around two-fifty. That's measuring from the lake, of course. Why? Do you think they're too high?"

"Not if the wind stays easterly. They've got a good run in from the west. What about enemy outposts?"

"The nearest one's at Horge, thirty-odd kilometres away on the Laerdalsoyri-Fagerness road. That's the beauty of this place. There's nothing to guard."

"Is there any chance they could see the lights when the aircraft come in?"

Jensen nodded at the hills that marched away northward. "There's plenty of high ground in between."

"Where's the next outpost or depot?"

"They've got men guarding bridges and tunnels on the main northern and southern trunk roads, of course, but they're well clear of here. The place we have to worry about is Gol, fifty kilometres south. Jerry's got some medium tanks there and half a regiment of ski troops."

"How would they get to us if alerted?"

Jensen turned and pointed down at the distant ribbon of road. "Along there. They could either stay on it and climb this hill to reach the lake or they could turn up a secondary road that runs at the back of those southern hills. My guess is they'd take the secondary road. They'd have problems getting armour up through this snow and they'd be as exposed as hell on the lake. The secondary road runs through a narrow wooded valley and would take 'em straight to the river. So that would be their best bet."

Lindstrom's eyes were on the woods that clothed the southern shore of the lake. "Unless they came at us eastwards through those woods. That would also get them to the river, wouldn't it?"

The giant smiled grimly. "Trust you to be awkward, lad.

100

Yes, that would be their first move and we wouldn't have enough men to stop them. That's why you have to ask for mines when you call for the air-drop."

The younger man gave a slight start. "Mines?"

"Ja. Both anti-tank and anti-personnel. If London gives us the time we can sow 'em round that hillside. It wouldn't keep Jerry out for more than a day or two but that'd be long enough to get the aircraft away."

"Then you think you could hold them on the secondary road?"

"We could if we mined it and they didn't send an army in." The big Norwegian grinned. "We'd have to, wouldn't we, or they'd swarm up the river and catch our flying boys in bed."

Lindstrom was assessing the size of the woods. "How long will it take you to sow those mines?"

"It's a bloody big job, and now we know for certain the first shipment's moving out this afternoon we haven't a minute to waste: there's always the possibility the second one might be sent off at the same time. So I'd like the air-drop tonight. I know they'll have to move like hell but that's their problem. I'll filter my boys in this evening so we'll be ready to start work right away. Only will London sanction the drop before they get confirmation that the ferry's been sunk? If Haukelid botches it up, Jerry might decide there's no need to use the cruiser."

Lindstrom's academic face tightened. "It's a chance they have to take. If they wait it'll be too late."

"Don't forget the ice hasn't been tested yet," Jensen reminded him.

Lindstrom nodded. "I'll get Arne to send a message right away." Picking up his ski sticks, he turned again to Jensen. "Make sure you've got everything you want on the list we send them. I must keep our broadcasts down to the minimum."

Jensen knew why. Any increase in clandestine radio traffic at this time could hardly fail to warn the Germans it concerned the movement of the IMI stocks and so might lead to even greater security. In addition they would have mathematicians working day and night trying to break the code and every extra broadcast aided their work.

Jensen tapped his shock of hair. "I've had it up here for days, lad. Plenty of ammunition, both Sten and anti-tank. Mortars and shells. Yankee bazookas. Grenades. Mines. I

101

suppose they'd better throw in a few stretchers and medical supplies too. And what about a case of whisky? They owe us that, don't they?"

Lindstrom stared at him. "What are you thinking of doing? Attacking Oslo?"

Digging his ski sticks into the snow, the Norwegian sent himself catapulting towards the lake. His grim laugh floated back. "It's my one chance to get myself an arms cache, lad. Then I can really have fun with the bastards."

The S.P. presented arms with a snap as Henderson led his small party to the door of Adams' Confessional. Returning the salute, the Scot opened the door, only to see Davies in close conversation with Adams at the far end of the hut. "I'm sorry, sir. We'll hang on if you haven't finished."

Motioning him to wait, Davies turned back to Adams. "What do you think? Is everything clear?"

Adams hesitated. "I think so, sir."

"Thinking so isn't enough, man. You've got to be sure."

Adams made himself more positive. "It's all right, sir. I am sure."

Davies nodded. "Fair enough. I suppose you can always get through to me on the blower if you think of anything else before you leave." He turned to the newcomers. "All right, Jock. I'm ready now."

The three men accompanying Henderson were Moore, Millburn, and Gabby. They followed the Scot to the large desk where Davies handed him two large photographs. "We've been lucky. The Norwegians in London have been working like navvies since Lindstrom's message came through and these are what they've flown up to us. Apparently they were taken during a geological survey before the war."

Henderson took the photographs to the window. Staring down he frowned, then studied them again. The impatient Davies watched him. "Well. What do you think?"

As always the Scot gave his opinion bluntly. "I don't like the look of those hills."

"We're hardly likely to find a Norwegian lake without hills, are we?"

Henderson handed the photographs to Moore, "Maybe not, sir, but it doesn't make them any safer."

Moving to Moore's elbow, Davies pointed at the top

102

photograph. "That western end's pretty open. You could go in that way, couldn't you?"

"We could try, sir. Providing the wind was right, of course."

"They say it blows from the east two days out of three," Davies said hopefully.

"Then it doesn't look too bad. But we'll be in a better position to judge after Millburn and Gabby have filed their report."

His reminder made the small Air Commodore take the photographs away and turn to the curious Millburn and Gabby. Although he had already ear-marked the couple for the mission, its dangers had made him request the men's acceptance rather than demand it. With Davies knowing his men well there had been little risk in the gesture. At the same time he felt a spot of *bonhomie* was called for.

"Sorry for all this prelim stuff, chaps, but now we can get down to business. As you'll have gathered, this is the lake you're going to visit. I want plenty of photographs taken and I want to know all the snags, if any, of making a night landing. Then I want you to go down and land yourselves. As it'll be daylight you shouldn't have too much trouble."

The puzzled Millburn accepted the photographs Davies was holding out. Gabby, who had not yet forgiven the American for his knavery with the Very pistol, felt that as navigator he should have first look at them and scowled as Millburn's tall figure blocked his view.

"Do you know how long the lake is, sir?" Millburn asked.

Davies studied the intelligence that had been sent to him with the photographs. "The two lakes together are about two and a half kilometres long. So you should have a fair margin to play with."

Henderson's unease showed itself again. "Don't forget it's ice they're landing on, sir."

"I haven't forgotten, Jock. I've been in touch with Maintenance Command and they've come up with a pair of special low-pressure tires with a metallic tread. With their airfields often frozen hard, the Canadians called for the design when they began building the Mossie under patent. The tread bites into the ice and according to MC gives a reasonable grip. They've promised us the first pair this afternoon and are busy rounding up a batch for the rest of your kites." Realizing immediately he had made a security slip, Davies turned back with some haste to Millburn and Gabby.

"We've decided your ETA is to be just after sunrise. This means you'll have night cover most of the way, yet when you arrive there should be enough light for you to take your photographs—the hills at the eastern end are quite shallow. It also means that with the Jerries eating their frankfurters or whatever the buggers eat for breakfast, your chances of being seen are cut down. However, we're not relying on luck. A detailed flight plan is being worked out for you and you'll be briefed on it this evening. One thing I must stress, however. At all costs Jerry's attention must not be drawn to this lake. That's why you're going to fly all the way out under his radar detectors. And when you reach the lake you must keep low while you take your photographs. Is that absolutely clear?"

Millburn glanced at Moore before asking his question. "The skipper and Harvey think they were picked up when flying at low level. How can we be sure they don't pick us up too?"

Davies hid his fear well. "The Hardangervidda is a high flattish plateau and you're flying well north of it. This means you'll get cover from the long fjords and high mountains. On top of that there's nothing but a wilderness around this lake so Jerry's not going to expect an enemy kite to settle down there."

The shrewd Gabby was quick to grasp the inference. "Then this lake hasn't any importance to Jerry, sir?"

"No. And that's the way we must keep it."

Gabby's curiosity was too much for him. "Then what's our interest, sir?"

For a moment it seemed the testy Davies would give short shrift to the question. Then, remembering the men were volunteers about to undertake a perilous mission, his expression changed. "Yes, I can tell you that, Gabriel. You're going to land Mr. Adams on it."

The remark did not register immediately. Then Gabby gave a dubious grin. "Is that a joke, sir?"

Davies gave the discomfort Adams a malicious smile. "No, it's no joke. You're flying Mr. Adams in and leaving him with a group of partisans. And if you breathe a word of this to a living soul I'll have your guts for garters."

Henderson hid a smile. Had the two airmen been told

they were to take Alice into Wonderland they could not have looked more surprised. Wondering how he could dampen down the men's curiosity while gaining the information he wanted, Davies decided there was no way small risks could be avoided if bigger ones were to be avoided later.

"There's one more job I want you to do. A river splits the southern hill range and runs into the western lake. Naturally it's also frozen. I want you to take a look at it and see if aircraft can be hidden there."

"Do you mean more than one aircraft?" Millburn asked.

"Yes," Davies grunted. "I want you to estimate how many."

"An entire squadron, sir?" Millburn asked innocently.

Davies glared at him. "Stop fishing, Millburn. You'll be told the whys and wherefores later. I want you off the lake and on your way home thirty minutes from your ETA. That's because the Americans are providing a flight of long-range Mustangs to escort you home. You'll get rendezvous details later but you won't pick up the Americans until you cross the coast. So keep your heads down. I've told Chiefy to keep your VIP Mossie under guard at the far side of the field so no one will see its special tires. As it has a camera pack fitted, Moore's going to issue a cover story that you're doing a special recce for him. That's all for now. I'll see you again at the briefing this evening."

As the two men saluted and turned, Davies checked them. "This job couldn't be more important. So do all you can to get through but at the same time try to get back safely. We must have this information as quickly as possible."

The S.P. on the door, muffled up in his greatcoat, recognized the two men as the most informal officers on the station as they emerged and his salute was little more than a gesture. Reconciled by their curiosity, neither men noticed him as they turned towards the Mess. Gabby's gnome-like face was a mixture of cynicism and bewilderment.

"You can't help but like his style. Take any risk to get through but stay alive long enough to tell us what we want to know. Who does he think we are? Bulldog Drummond and Sexton Blake?"

Millburn grinned. "Speak for yourself, boyo."

"That's what I should have done in the first place, isn't it? Why the hell had you to volunteer, Millburn? Have you

105

got a paternity order hanging over you or something?"

"I thought you'd like a bit of excitement. I mean, things must be getting tough when a guy has to bed his dame in a dispersal hut.'"

Gabby scowled at the reminder. "I ought to navigate you right over a Jerry airfield, Millburn. Maybe I will." His expression altered. "What's going on, for Christ's sake? What's Adams going to do?"

"Maybe he's a secret service agent in sheep's clothing," Millburn suggested.

"Adams? That'll be the day. And why does Davies want a hiding place for the aircraft?"

"Nothing to it, kiddo. While Adams is capturing Quisling single-handed, you and me will be up the creek stewing reindeer steaks. Where's your imagination?"

While all this speculation was going on Davies was dropping another and bigger bombshell in the Intelligence Office. "You weren't here when I told Adams that Jerry's moving out the first consignment late this afternoon, were you, Jock?"

For a moment the air seemed to freeze. Henderson glanced at Moore, then shook his head. "No, sir. I wasn't."

"Sorry to drop it on you like this but obviously I couldn't mention it in front of Millburn and Gabriel. Skinnarland got word of it and Lindstrom picked it up. It means the air-drop is scheduled for tonight so the stuff will be there when Adams arrives. It also means we have a maximum of two days to get there ourselves. There's a fair chance we might have longer because Lindstrom feels pretty certain Jerry won't send out his second consignment until he knows the fate of the first but obviously that's something we can't rely on."

As the implications sank in, Henderson looked shocked. "That means we have to be ready by tomorrow night at the latest. I was banking on at least one more day."

Davies was showing considerable sympathy. "I know it means a hell of a lot of work, Jock, but it's not impossible. You should be getting all your extra equipment within the next twenty-four hours and if anything doesn't arrive, you've only to buzz me. Rolls-Royce has promised you a special coolant and a low viscosity oil. MC are sending you these special tires and heavy-duty accumulators. They've also promised us warm clothing. It'll all gel together if you impress on every officer and every NCO that 1800 hours tomorrow is the deadline. Naturally you'll have to go into full security right away and cut all outside contact. One job to do immediately is pick your maintenance crews—the very minimum you need. Don't go asking for volunteers. I want your best technicians, not pot hunters. They'll fly out in the three Mitchells I'm borrowing."

Henderson looked like a man having a bad dream. "I'm not only thinking about us. What about Staines? How can he get all our supplies ready for tonight?"

Davies grinned. "We haven't been sitting on our arses these last few days, Jock. As soon as we received your list, MC began sending stores down to his squadrons in East Anglia. Sorry I wasn't able to tell you but you know how tight these high-security jobs are."

"So Staines has got everything ready?"

"Not everything," Davies confessed. "Lindstrom has made a request for ammunition, guns and mines. At this late hour he's not likely to get all he wants but Staines is doing his best and the Yanks usually move fast when the pressure's on."

Henderson had heard only one word. "Mines?"

Davies' grin was slightly lop-sided. "What's wrong with mines? The more precautions they take over there the better."

"But isn't it a risk to drop all this stuff tonight before we're certain the operation is practical or that Jerry is going to use the cruiser? You said yourself he might change his mind if the ferry gets through to Heroya safely."

Davies' expression changed. "The C.-in-C. realized that as well as anyone but he's still authorized the drop. He knows Lindstrom's men must have at least twenty-four hours to sow the mines and prepare their defence positions. In any case I've the feeling we might be asked to attack the ferry if Jerry sends his second consignment that way. There's no reason why we shouldn't. They can always contact us over there."

With Henderson still boggling at the administration work involved it was left to Moore to read through Davies' last remark. "You're not thinking of coming with us, are you, sir?"

"Of course I'm coming," Davies snapped. "This is a once-or-nothing job. I only wish we were going tonight. I'm worried in case this weather breaks." Turning back to

Henderson, he gave a sympathetic grin, "There's just one more thing if you can stand it, Jock. A swaddie called Captain Jackson is paying you a visit this afternoon."

By this time Henderson was beyond surprise. "A swaddie? What does he want?"

"He doesn't want anything. He's coming to give your boys a spot of infantry training. We don't know what lies ahead over there, so it might be useful if they know one end of a Sten gun from the other."

Henderson cast a dismayed glance at the expressionless Moore. "How am I going to explain him away?"

Davies shrugged on his greatcoat. "Anyway you like, except with the truth. Say there's a new Ministry order that all aircrews have to undergo military training in case they're shot down." Picking up his briefcase Davies went to the door. "I have to get back to the Brigadier now. But I'll be back in time for Millburn's briefing."

# 16

The staccato rattle of automatic fire sounded clearly as the door opened and Adams entered the Nissen hut. Sue Spencer, standing at the window, turned towards him. "It's the crews on the small arms range, isn't it? What on earth's going on?"

Shutting out the icy breeze, Adams crossed over to the coke stove and extended his hands. "They're getting a bit of basic infantry training. It's Davies' idea."

The girl, who had been with the squadron long enough to know that Davies never acted without reason, showed her curiosity. "But why do aircrews suddenly need infantry training?"

Wishing his heart would not surge at every reminder of the mission ahead, Adams felt it confirmed what he had long believed: that he was totally unsuited for any enterprise that smacked of danger. A patriotic man, it made him wonder if he were not being selfish in accepting the mission and whether, regardless of the damage to his self-esteem, he should not relinquish it to a more suitable man.

Since lunch he had been in his billet writing a long letter to his wife. He had wanted it to contain some tenderness but being unable to mention the imminent operation he had found himself inhibited. For a long time now letters between Valerie and Adams had been of the My Dear Frank, My Dear Valerie variety and any sudden infusion of sentiment would be certain to make Valerie's pencilled eyebrows lift.

Adams' wife was fifteen years younger than himself, a slim waspish woman with a narrow, elegant face, an expensive taste in clothes, and a roving eye for younger, combatant officers. Long ago relegated to the role of a provider, Adams had no illusions about her feelings for him and in turn he always felt a sense of relief when separation put an end to her carping. At the same time he was the kind of man to whom a long relationship always creates affection and a sense of loyalty. Adams had never been able to decide whether these emotions constituted love or not but certainly in their manifestations, a compulsion to aid and protect whatever the cost, they seemed to bear a kinship. One of his worries at the moment was

109

whether he was being fair to Valerie in volunteering for a mission that might deny her his protection in the future. The inner voice that told him Valerie would always cope, and after a suitable show of grief make excellent use of her freedom, in no way expurgated his sense of guilt. Adams was a permanent victim of his loyalty: one reason why he was a lonely man.

He walked down the hut to his desk and sat down. He pulled out his pipe before answering her. "I've permission to tell you now, Sue. Come over here."

She moved to her desk and stood facing him. Watching her Adams thought yet again what a graceful, gentle girl she was. He opened his pouch and took out a pinch of tobacco before glancing back at her.

"We're going over to Norway, Sue."

At first she did not take his words literally. "You mean we're going to carry out a raid over there?"

"We are eventually but that's not what I mean. We're going to land our aircraft over there."

She gave a start, then a bewildered laugh. "This is a joke, isn't it?"

"No, it isn't a joke." Leaving out his part in the operation and all mention of the IMI stocks, Adams told the girl the rest. When he finished her face was pale.

"I've never heard of anything so crazy. It only requires one German soldier to see them and every man will be killed or captured. Whoever thought of it? Davies?"

Adams shook his head. "No. I did."

She gave a gasp. "You! I don't believe it."

"Sorry but I did. You see it's vitally important to sink this warship and there's no other way it can be done."

"But how can one cruiser be worth the loss of an entire squadron? What's it carrying to make it so important?"

Adams struck a match and put it to his pipe. "All I'm allowed to tell you at the moment is that this cruiser must be sunk. And this is the only way it can be done."

"By landing sixteen Mosquitoes behind the enemy lines? How can Davies agree to such a thing?"

Adams shrugged. "Desperate needs lead to desperate measures, Sue."

"Desperate measures are one thing. Suicide is something else. How are the aircraft going to land? If they go over in daylight they're sure to be seen."

"We've been practising night landings with spotlights

while you've been away. We're also hoping to help them down with an Aldis—something in the way naval aircraft are flagged down. It's rough and ready but as we're hoping for moonlight we think it'll work."

"But how can you know the ice will hold?"

"The boffins are confident it will but to be quite certain Millburn and Gabby have volunteered to fly out and try it."

The girl gave an angry shake of her head. "I think you've all gone out of your minds. Thank God Tony isn't back. He's only just escaped from the Germans. I don't want him a fugitive again."

Adams sighed. "I don't blame you. I don't like the risks the crews will be taking myself but Davies assures us they're necessary."

A professional herself, Sue was trying to understand how the scheme could possibly work. "What about petrol and oil? What about running up the engines and testing them? Surely you're not expecting the partisans to have aircraft fitters among them?"

"No, we'll be taking a few technicians with us. And there'll be an air-drop of supplies beforehand."

"Then who's going to organize everything over there? Someone will have to take overall charge. And who's going to signal the aircraft down?"

Adams had never expected to make the announcement in so small a voice. "Me."

She gave another gasp. "You?"

Adams glanced down at his pipe and discovered with no surprise that it had gone out. "Why not? After all, it was my idea. And I've as good a knowledge of the squadron's requirements as anyone."

She was looking horrified. "They can't let you, Frank. They just can't."

Adams' aggrieved eyes lifted to her. "Why not?"

Although a sensitive girl with knowledge of his personal problems, she was still too shocked to choose her words. "I've never heard of anything so stupid. How can they possibly let you go?"

"Why not? Because I'm too old? Or too fat?"

She saw now she was wounding him and her tone changed. "Of course not. But men who are dropped behind the enemy lines have to have special training. And learn how to go down by parachute. You've never had any of that, have you?" -

"I'm not going down by parachute. I'm flying out with Millburn and Gabby tonight."

She gave a violent start. "Tonight? But that's even worse. What if the ice breaks?"

He shrugged. "Then it's good riddance, I suppose."

"Don't talk like that. I won't let you."

He opened his mouth to answer, then changed his mind. Her voice was accusing. "I know why you volunteered. And it was stupid. A man like you doesn't need to prove himself."

Adams took off his spectacles and began cleaning them. "That's where you're wrong, Sue. So very wrong."

"But why?"

"God knows. But this is my one chance to do more than talk and fill in pieces of paper and I'm taking it." He managed a wry grin. "Even if it kills me."

Without spectacles his myopic eyes gave him a curiously vulnerable appearance. A knock on the far door brought them both relief. A young ACII, his face spotted with acne, came to attention and handed Sue a letter. "It came in the afternoon post, Miss."

The girl's expression was enough to tell Adams whom the letter was from. "Aren't you going to read it?" he asked when she laid it on her desk.

Seeing he was as relieved as she by the interruption, she tore open the envelope. Thirty seconds passed before Adams, fumbling with pipe and matches again, noticed the girl had finished reading but was still gazing down at the letter. "Is everything all right?"

It was a moment before she answered him. "Yes, of course it is." Turning towards her desk she half-stumbled as if unable to see clearly. He rose sharply and caught her arm. "What's wrong, Sue?"

She smiled brightly at him. "I slipped, that was all."

"I don't believe you. Tell me what it is."

She laughed. "With you flying out to Norway in a few hours? And the rest of the squadron following soon afterwards. At least give me the credit of being able to see things in perspective."

He was watching her closely. "Then there is something wrong?"

"A little thing, yes. But nothing I hadn't found out last weekend. And I'm sure it'll sort itself out in time."

"If it's such a little thing, why can't you tell me? It won't go any further."

112

That he could show concern for her at such a time made her eyes moist. "I think I've said it before, Frank. You're a wonderful person."

Adams did his best to keep the moment light. "Tell me! A last request before I go and capture Norway single-handed for the Allies."

She laughed again. "I'll tell you. But only when you come back." When he gave a wry grimace, her voice broke. "You will come back, won't you, Frank? Please come back."

## 17

The night air was icy as Knut Haukelid and Rolf Sorlie climbed out of the car. Both were carrying rucksacks and were heavily armed with Sten guns, pistols, and hand grenades. Haukelid, a tall and powerfully built man, went to the driver's window and spoke in a low voice. "Remember—if you hear shots, you drive off at once. Otherwise you wait two hours. If we're not back by then forget about us and get away." His eyes moved to the second man in the passenger seat. "If that happens, you get to Sweden and then to England as fast as you can, Larsen. Professor Tronstad needs you over there."

When both men nodded, Haukelid turned to Sorlie. "Come on then. Let's get it over."

The night was as silent as a held breath. Across the Tinnsjo fjord the snow-covered mountains were outlined luminously against the indigo sky. The high-pressure area on which Davies' hopes rested was holding but to the two saboteurs it was a deadly threat as they made their cautious way down the road. Ice, crunching under their feet, seemed as loud as rifle shots and both men flinched as a dog began barking on the far side of the fjord.

Dark and shuttered houses began to appear. Alert for the slightest sound they froze as a night bird rose from a hedge with a clatter of wings. The silver sheen of water was now visible below them. For a hundred yards the road dipped steeply, making walking difficult on its icy surface. As they whispered to one another, their breath floated away like smoke.

The wooden houses dropped back, isolating them on a moonlit patch of snow. Pausing to listen, they ran for a clump of trees on its fringe. As they reached them, a low whisper made both of them grab for their pistols. "It's all right. It's me, Syverstad. Watch out when we reach the railway station. The Jerries have posted a guard there."

The three of them could hear the murmur of voices in the booking hall of the small station as they crept past. Half a minute later they reached a bridge that led down to the quay. Berthed against it was the Hydro, the ferryboat that was their objective. The laughter and music that came from it made the silence of the town seem the more unreal.

Frozen snow lay thick on the bridge. Nodding at his companions to cover him, Haukelid crept across. All three men winced at the crunching of the ice. When they were safely across, Haukelid motioned at the booking hall. Taking advantage of every shadow, they slipped into the dark entrance and paused. Sorlie put his mouth to Haukelid's ear. "Where the hell are the sentries? They can't have left it unguarded."

Sorlie's bewilderment was shared by his two companions. Their contacts in Rjukan had confirmed that two special companies of SS troops would be travelling down with the consignment all the way to Mael and that the spotter aircraft would be keeping a constant surveillance on both the train and the track. Everything indicated the Germans were being typically and ruthlessly thorough in their protection of the precious stocks and yet the ferryboat, the vital link to the next staging post, appeared to have been overlooked. It was an oversight so much out of character that all three men felt it must be a trap.

When five minutes passed and nothing moved on the quayside, Haukelid turned to his men. "Cover me. I'm going on board. If I wave, come right over. If I start firing, run like hell away from here."

Their nerves raw with tension, Sorlie and Syverstad watched Haukelid start across the moonlit quay. Expecting a challenge or fusillade of bullets at any moment, Haukelid's heart was beating hard as he approached the ferryboat. The music and voices seemed to be coming from the crew's quarters forward and when no one challenged him he edged towards the bows and climbed on to the deck. Seeing an open companionway door, he stood alongside it and listened. The voices were loud now and he could see lights. Hearing a toilet flush he waited no longer and waved an arm. Thirty seconds later Sorlie and Syverstad were standing beside him. Sten gun held in one hand, Haukelid led them down a flight of steps. Peering round a corner in the dimly lit passage he saw a party of six or seven men playing cards in the crew's mess. Motioning to his two men, he led them in the opposite direction towards the third-class accommodation. Out of sight now, he halted the men alongside a hatch. Earlier that week, dressed as a workman, he had taken a trip on the ferryboat and had gained two vital pieces of information. One was that it took the ferry twenty minutes to reach the

115

deepest part of the fjord which was opposite Hasleviken. The second was that this hatch led down to the bilges in the ship's bows.

As the three men began to remove the hatch they heard footsteps on a companionway behind them. Before they could reach the doorway a middle-aged man of heavy build appeared. Seeing the three armed partisans facing him, he gave a violent start. "What are you doing here?"

His question, delivered in the local accent, reassured them he was a Norwegian. Haukelid motioned him to keep his voice down. "Who are you? The night watchman?"

The man nodded nervously. "What's going on?"

"We're in a bit of trouble and we need a place to hide. We can rely on you, can't we?"

With ferryboat crews' often having to close their eyes at illicit cargoes, the watchman's fears began to disappear. "Do the Jerries know you're in these parts?"

"No. We shook them off a couple of hours ago. You won't get involved if you help us now."

Reassured, the man pointed at the hatch. "You've picked one of the best places. It leads down to the bilges."

"Can we go and take a look?"

"Yes. Only don't be long if you're not staying down there."

Removing the hatch Haukelid motioned Sorlie to go ahead of him but caught Syverstad's arm as the second partisan was about to follow. "Stay with the old chap and keep him talking," he whispered. "We'll do the job as quickly as we can."

He followed Sorlie down the steps. As they crawled forward the air turned foul with the stench of diesel oil and bilge water. When the bows came within arms' length, Haukelid wriggled round and emptied out the contents of his rucksack. Pushing himself along with his elbows, Sorlie came alongside him and did likewise. In the light of the torch Haukelid was shining a nineteen pound charge of plastic explosive; lengths of wire, electronic detonators and two simple alarm clocks appeared.

With the ever-present danger that German guards might arrive, the two men worked as fast as they dared, although in the cramped conditions the work was difficult and dangerous. The wires were linked to the detonators, the detonators to the charge which was hidden in the bilge water, at this point over a foot deep. Haukelid, who had masterminded the plan, had chosen the bows for the

116

explosion so that as water rushed in, the propellers and rudder at the stern would rise and make it impossible for the ship to be beached before she sank. He was also hoping the railway wagons containing the IMI stocks would roll off the ferry if she tilted sufficiently.

The last act of the two partisans put them in their greatest danger of the night. Acutely conscious that any failure to detonate the charge could mean the stocks reaching Germany and the entire course of the war changed, they had decided to use two alarm clocks in case one failed. Pre-set to go off at 1045 that morning, the time Haukelid estimated the ferry would reach the deepest part of the Tinnsjo, both had been turned into electric devices that would trigger off the charge the moment either hammer struck its bell. However, the gap between hammer and bell of either clock was no more than a third of an inch and any slip that brought the two together would blow the men to fragments. They were drenched in sweat when the clocks were safely secured to one of the ribs that made up the bows of the ferry.

Cleaning up any tell-tale traces of wire and tools, they crawled back over the bilges and emerged from the hatch to find Syverstad still chatting to the night watchman. Expecting the man to ask why they had been so long, they were relieved to see him grin at them. "Well, did you find what you wanted?"

Seeing the warning glance Syverstad gave him, Haukelid smiled back. "Yes, we found it all right. There are some great hiding places down there."

Syverstad intervened quickly. "I've been telling him we have to fetch some things from Rjukan before we can go into hiding. But he says we must be aboard before eight as Jerry is loading on a special train around that time."

Haukelid held out a hand. "We're grateful for your help. You won't be forgotten, I promise you."

The man looked almost bashful. "We try to do our little bit, sir. Even if it's only turning a blind eye at the right moment."

Slapping his shoulder, Haukelid led his men off the ferry. None of them spoke until they crossed the bridge, then Haukelid turned to Syverstad. "Do you think he suspects anything?"

Syverstad shook his head. "He didn't seem to. I think the poor devil's a bit simple."

"He doesn't sail on the ferry, does he?"

117

"No. He lives in Mael. He goes off duty just before the train's due in."

"All the same, the Germans are sure to interrogate him after the ferry goes down," Sorlie muttered. "It seems a shame we couldn't warn him to do a bunk."

Haukelid's glance was wry. "What about the crew and the passengers who're taking the ferry? They're all just as innocent but what the hell can we do?"

It was a thought that kept the Norwegians silent until they reached the clump of trees. There Syverstad halted. "I'll have to get back now. Take care, you two."

Haukelid shook his hand. "Thanks for all you've done, Gunnar. Good luck."

Before he vanished among the trees Syverstad turned back. "You know something? I still don't understand why Jerry forgot to put a guard on that ferry."

Haukelid grinned at him. "Don't look a gift horse in the mouth. Get going while our luck holds."

The two remaining men sighted the car ten minutes later. Larsen showed his relief when they opened the rear door. "Where have you been? We were only giving you ten more minutes then driving off."

Both men were surprised to see they had been away two hours. Sorlie dumped his rucksack into the car, then shook hands all round. His task was to return and help Einar Skinnarland. "Watch yourselves on the roads," he said. "Jerry might be taking special precautions tonight."

Haukelid, whose orders were to make for Sweden and then England, gripped his hand tightly. "The same goes for you. He might have patrols out. Give Einar our regards and tell him to keep his eyes and ears open. If we're lucky, the Jerries are going to go berserk in a few hours."

The two friends' eyes held for a moment, then Sorlie slipped away. The car started up, throwing out clouds of condensation into the icy air. Tires crunching, it vanished round a hill shoulder. The hum of its engine could be heard for a long time. When it finally died away the only sound came from the restless dog on the far side of the fjord. It was howling now and the sound was eerie as it echoed among the hills.

## 18

That same night, while Haukelid was driving towards Sweden with his mind on the fateful deadline of 1045, further north a lone Mosquito was winging its way into the heartland of Norway. Entering the Sognafjord at a precisely calculated ETA, keeping less than three hundred feet above the moonlit water, it had swept up the spectacular fjord for nearly eighty miles while the sky began to lighten and the snow on the flanking mountains took on the pallor of dead skin. By the time the fjord began to narrow, a red pennant of cloud could be seen ahead. Following Gabby's glance, Millburn nodded. "It'll be sun-up in ten minutes. Where the hell's that terminal?"

The men's first objective was the hamlet of Revsnes, ferry terminal for the main trunk road that ran from far-off Oslo up to the north-west coast. Farmhouses and tiny hamlets had been seen at intervals along the fjord but Gabby, whose eyes were reddened from hours of concentration, was searching for a jetty and a road that ran for a few miles along the fjord before turning southeast. As another cluster of houses swept past and Gabby shook his head, Millburn turned irritable. "How long past our ETA now?"

"Only a couple of minutes."

"Only? You sure you haven't lost us?"

"You want to try navigating in this place, Millburn. Every bloody mountain looks like the last one."

"What have mountains to do with it? Davies said if we followed the fjord we were sure to hit that road. You sure you haven't missed it? Because if you have we're heading for Russia."

Gabby, who wasn't at all sure, decided attack the better form of defence. "Stop bellyaching and help me. I'm not a bloody St. Bernard."

Millburn gave the small Welshman a disparaging glance. "That's for sure. If you climbed into his pouch alongside the brandy, he wouldn't know the difference."

Almost to his surprise Adams found he was smiling, and not for the first time during the long flight felt grateful for the company he was keeping. Since being helped into the adapted bomb bay of the VIP Mosquito, emotion after emotion had been harassing the middle-aged Intelligence Officer. With this his first operational flight, his awareness that soon he would be entering enemy skies where hundreds of fighters and thousands of guns would be hungry to shoot him down had first taken priority over everything else. But as the long hours had passed and discomfort and cold had taken the raw edge off this fear, other fears had moved in. If the experts' calculations were wrong about the ice, the Mosquito would soon become a coffin plunging himself and its crew into an icy grave. And even if that obstacle were overcome, his somewhat ill-defined role in Norway had then to be faced. Here the conscientious Adams could not decide which fear was the greater: fear of the enemy or fear of failing in his duty to his friends.

If he was grateful for the intercom, Adams was less sure about the perspex windows that had been fitted into the curving bomb doors. Locked as he was in the aircraft's belly, the view downwards would have been vertiginous even at high level. At low level, with the Mosquito's speed starkly displayed, it was intimidating.

It was also hypnotic. Feeling it would be more comfortable to stretch out during the long North Sea crossing, Adams had brought four leather cushions with him and after take-off had abandoned the somewhat cramped seat and lain full length on them. Discovering he tended to roll over when the aircraft banked he found that if he lay on his stomach and put an arm through a door strut he could hold steady against all but the most violent manoeuvres. In this position, however, Adams' face was right over the perspex windows and once he had caught sight of the roller-coaster view below he was hooked.

Eyes wide, he had watched moonlit waves sweeping past so close that sometimes their spray had dimmed the perspex. He had seen the brutal rocks of skerries rear out of the sea as if trying to disembowel him. When the Mosquito had plunged into the fjord he had discovered that if he pressed right down and contorted his neck he could catch a glimpse of the mountains that rose on either side like the walls of a prison. It was true that occasionally, when Millburn had flung the Mosquito round a mountain spur and rocks had swum dizzily before him, Adams had closed his eyes but like a child fascinated by his fear he had opened them again almost immediately.

At the moment, alerted that Gabby was having difficulty in finding Revsnes, Adams was doing his best to help. To his right he caught sight of a fishing boat chugging stoically upstream. As it flashed past and Millburn banked five degrees starboard to follow the winding shore, there was a triumphant yell from Gabby. "That's it. There's the jetty. And the road."

Adams tried to press down even further but the Mosquito's angle of flight denied him a view of the hamlet. There was relief in Millburn's reply. "You'd better turn Catholic and light a candle to St. Christopher, boyo. You were lost and you know it."

Adams knew the fjord spread out into a labyrinth of tributaries at this point but feeling the Mosquito bank to starboard again he knew Millburn was correctly following the road along the southern fjord. Gabby was sounding aggrieved. "Anyone else would apologize."

"Stop telling everyone how wonderful you are and get your head down," Millburn told him. "When does that road turn inland?"

"At the end of the fjord," Gabby muttered.

"How far's that?"

"About ten miles."

"OK. Watch out. I don't want to go shooting past it."

Less than two minutes later the Mosquito went into a sixty degree turn, sending Adams rolling over in a heap as it levelled out. Grabbing the strut again, he drew himself back and saw they were now flying along the foot of a steep valley. A hundred feet below a road ran along a frozen stream, its surface discoloured a dirty brown. Millburn sounded critical. "You're sure this is the main road? It looks as if it's made of gravel to me."

Tired after his hours of concentration, Gabby was in no mood for criticism. "You saw where it came from. What else could it be?"

Adams could see a frozen bank of snow flanking one side of the road. A helpless passenger so far, he was glad he could offer some advice at last. "Most of the roads in this part of Norway are made of gravel, Tommy. I understand they haven't come up with a macadamized surface yet that doesn't split in the winter. As it's being kept open by snow ploughs, I'm pretty sure it's the right one."

With Millburn reassured, the Mosquito raced on. The views were breathtaking as the road led the aircraft into steep wooded valleys and over high mountain passes. The secondary road for which they were searching appeared less than two minutes later, snaking up through a series of hairpins on to a barren plateau. Aware this was the moment when German monitors might spot them, Millburn sank down to less than a hundred feet. At that height the Mosquito's speed became a true one with clumps of bushes, rocks and frozen lakes flashing beneath as if on some enormous conveyor belt. Although the half-buried telegraph poles indicated the narrow road had some importance, its icy surface suggested it did not receive the same attention from the snow ploughs as the trunk road to the north.

Ahead Gabby saw two shadows moving around a clump of rocks. Seconds later they became reindeer feeding on moss. Taking fright they turned tail and fled. Millburn nodded after them. "Did you know Father Christmas lives in these parts?"

"I suppose those were Dasher and Blitzen," Gabby said sarcastically.

"That's right. Maybe when we land we can leave a message. You know—what we want for Christmas."

"I should do that. Ask the Norwegians to deliver it. They'll like your sense of humour."

Millburn gave a wicked grin. "Why don't you ask for a kit of drums? It's worth a try, boyo."

Before the scowling Gabby could reply a number of mountain huts appeared alongside the road. A barn with overhanging eaves and an earthern roof drew Gabby's attention and he rummaged among a pile of sketches and photographs on his knee. Fifteen seconds later he turned to Millburn. "We're O.K. Follow the road for another three or four miles and the lake should be on our right."

A narrow frozen river had now joined the road and ran alongside it. On either side scabrous hills marched southwards. As the altitude dropped a few hundred feet, trees began appearing again, first singly, then in belts on the hillsides. Aware that in a few minutes he might be dead if the ice did not hold, Adams was trying to control his hammering heart by imagining what his wife's reaction would be if he were killed on active service. Valerie would go through the rituals—beneath her sophistication she was as conventional as the rest of her class. But would her underlying emotion be resentment that he had left her with only a squadron-leader's pension or would it be relief she was now free to pursue younger men without the gossip that had followed her previously?

Adams' thoughts were swept away as Gabby gave a

shout and the Mosquito banked steeply to starboard. As it skimmed a hill crest, Gabby turned to Millburn triumphantly. "That's it, Yank. Spot on."

In the few seconds before Millburn sank down into the protecting basin, the configuration of the lake could be seen clearly: its two pear-shaped segments joined by a narrow isthmus, the heavily wooded southern hills, the more barren hill range to the north. If further identification was needed, it was provided by the area of glazed ice that ran down its centre. To aid the squadron to land the partisans had cleared a narrow runway, mingling the displaced snow with the virgin surrounds to avoid a tell-tale outline. In addition they had done their best to follow the natural shoreline. The effect was to create a smaller version of the lake, camouflage that could not stand close scrutiny but might well deceive an enemy pilot unaware what he was seeking. While Millburn expressed his doubt that the runway was long enough, Adams was marvelling at the work it represented at such short notice.

The morning sun had now cleared the horizon and although the lake was still in shadow the slanting rays were emphasizing every shadow of the dark trees and every fold of the snowy hillsides. A faint mist swirling over the northern hills was tinted a delicate pink and here and there crystals of ice on the trees sparkled like jewels. Adams thought he had never seen a sight more beautiful or more dangerous.

In the cockpit both airmen were already at work. While Millburn began a wide, exploratory orbit, Gabby started taking low-angle photographs. As he flew through the narrow isthmus, the American examined the steep cliff on its southern flank before entering the second lake. Here the frozen river that cut through the southern hill range could be seen clearly. Millburn lowered a wingtip to give Adams a better view. "How many kites do you reckon could be stacked in there, sir?"

Adams nearly said the entire squadron, then remembered Davies had not committed himself. "The mouth looks pretty wide. And it goes right back into the hills. I'd say as many as Davies wants, wouldn't you?"

As Millburn levelled the Mosquito he caught sight of a yellow arrow of cloth lying on a clump of bushes near the river. "They're ready for us," he told Adams. "They've laid out a wind arrow." As he rolled the aircraft over again to give Adams a better view, there was a cry of indignation from Gabby. "What the hell are you doing, Millburn? How can I take photographs if you keep on playing silly buggers?"

"Stop bellyaching," Millburn told him. "You've got one more circuit and that's your lot. I don't intend missing those Mustangs on the way back."

The American kept his word, then turned and flew south along the river valley. "I suppose we'd better take a quick recco at that lane Davies mentioned."

The two-mile deep hill range they flew through had two folds, the heavily wooded one that swept down to the lake and a second one that plunged into a narrow valley running parallel to the lake. The lane that ran down this valley was the secondary road Jensen had pointed out to Lindstrom. Turning east over it Millburn followed it to its juncture with the north-south Gol road, then swung back to the lake. "O.K., that'll do. Let's go down and meet Father Christmas."

With danger the constant companion of aircrews, Adams had often wondered how they were able to carry out their multitudinous tasks with such sang-froid. Now, with the hills sliding beneath him and the life-or-death landing only seconds away, his respect was profound. For a moment the rising sun shone blindingly through the perspex windows as the Mosquito banked steeply to port. As Adams shielded his eyes, he heard Millburn's voice. "I'm going round to land now, sir. We'll be coming in towards the sun."

Prone sometimes to irrelevant thoughts, Adams reflected that it would have been pleasant if ingrained habit could have been forgotten at such a moment and Millburn had addressed him as Frank instead of sir. Although Millburn was his equal in rank, Adams' age and more sedate temperament always drew the courtesy title from the American and it had never made Adams feel older than today.

The thought flew from his mind like a scared cat at Millburn's next words. "Make sure you're in your seat and your belt's fastened, sir. This could be a bit dicey."

Adams glanced at his seat, then decided against it. If the ice gave way, neither seat nor belt would help him. There had been some advice given during briefing about opening the escape hatch before jettisoning the hood in the hope the invading water would aid rather than hinder their escape, but Adams like the other two had paid little attention to it. All three men knew that if the Mosquito broke through, the freezing water and the ice ceiling above would make a mockery of escape.

There was a heavy rumble of hydraulic jacks and the note of the engines changed. Even had he not known the undercarriage was being lowered Adams would have guessed Millburn was beginning his landing approach. Throughout the long and uncomfortable flight his stomach had determined the manoeuvres of the aircraft better than his senses and now its sudden buoyancy told all. Trying to steady his heart by holding his breath, Adams closed his eyes and waited.

The sunlight outside disappeared as the Mosquito entered the slanting shadow thrown by the eastern hills. Its engine note fell once more, this time sufficiently for Adams to hear the scream of the airfoils. When his stomach floated again he knew the flaps had come down and touchdown was near. For a moment the Mosquito surged forward as Millburn blipped his engines, then the scream of airfoils came back. Lying with eyes tightly closed Adams could feel air pressure thumping the fuselage beneath him. The hypersensitivity of his senses reminded him of something he had always believed but never experienced: that a man is never so alive as when in imminent danger of death.

It was Adams' last irrelevant thought before there was a heavy grunt beneath him followed by a jolt that seemed to shudder the Mosquito from nose to tail. To the imaginative Intelligence Officer it signalled the fracturing of the ice and a plunge to oblivion: in fact it was merely the flexing of the undercarriage in what was a near perfect landing. Expecting an onrush of black water at any moment Adams was amazed to hear the slithering and rumbling of wheels and the jubilant shout of Millburn.

"What do you know, boyo? It's holding!"

Although equally relieved, Gabby refused to indulge the American's euphoria. "Wait until we've stopped rolling before you count your chickens, Yank."

Millburn muttered something uncomplimentary. Unsure how the Mosquito would react on ice and conscious a skid at this speed could mean disaster, he was handling the controls like a tightrope walker handling a balancing pole. Adams, who by this time had found enough courage to open his eyes, saw nothing but ice flashing past the windows but by contorting his neck he managed to glimpse a rocky cliff and realized the Mosquito was racing through the isthmus. The speed of its passing and Gabby's voice warned him that all danger was not past.

"If you don't pull her up soon we're going to over-run the bloody runway."

Unable to take his eyes off his task, Millburn vented his tension in a growl of rage. "If you don't shut up, you little bastard, I'll skewer you on one of those pine trees."

Although the Mosquito's impulsion was beginning to slow down, she was no more than seventy yards from the eastern end of the swept area before Millburn dared touch his brakes. The effect was an immediate skid to port. Cursing, the American applied left rudder and when that had no effect he gently blipped his starboard engine. The Mosquito's prompt response was to skid in the opposite direction and she was still sliding when she ran off the runway. As snow cascaded over her tail and fuselage, she performed a gentle ground loop and came to a halt.

## 19

The sweating Millburn released his breath. "We should have had the brakes checked. Unequal drag shows up too much. And the runway could be longer. Otherwise it worked fine." Then he remembered Adams. "You all right, sir?"

Down below Adams had never felt more talkative. "Yes, I'm fine," he shouted. "That was a marvellous landing, Tommy."

Although sharing Adams' relief, Gabby had no intention of inflating Millburn's ego. "It was a lousy landing. He came in too fast. I think he was scared."

With tension removed, Gabby's accusation brought nothing more than a grin from the American. "Tell me something, boyo. When gremlins turn green, does it mean they've filled their trousers? Because if it does you'd better get out of here fast."

The falsetto note in Adams' laughter made him decide to eschew humour until his nerves settled down. "Can you see anything of our welcoming party?" he asked.

His reminder made Millburn open up one of the feathered engines. With snow pluming out behind it, the Mosquito swung round and began taxiing back down the lake. As it neared the steep cliff two men appeared on its far side and waved the aircraft towards them.

Seeing the partisans' urgency both airmen remembered where they were and felt a sudden nakedness on the broad expanse of ice. Blipping his engines, Millburn taxied the Mosquito past the cliff and swung her into the river mouth a hundred yards beyond it. As hills and trees closed in on either side, they relaxed again.

While Millburn manoeuvred the aircraft round for a quick take-off, the curious Gabby stared out at the two partisans. From the description Davies had given, he recognized the smaller man in American uniform as Lindstrom, although the young scientist's face was bruised from his parachute drop and shadowed by a growth of beard. The second man, massive and heavily bearded, was wearing the uniform of a Norwegian Army captain. As Millburn cut his engines the giant's bellow, delivered in atrociously pronounced English, reached up to them. "You were takin' your time out there, weren't you? Do you want the bloody Jerries to know you've arrived?"

Millburn grinned at Gabby. "There's nothing like a warm welcome, is there?" As he, Gabby, and Adams climbed down to the ice, the American turned to the giant Norwegian. "Don't panic, Olaf. If they come, we'll look after you."

Jensen's bearded face was a study. "What did you say?"

"I said don't worry about the Germans. We'll look after you."

As the giant gave a growl of disbelief, Lindstrom said something to him in Norwegian. When Jensen turned back he was wearing a fierce grin. "So you are a funny man, Englishman. Are your friends funny too?"

Gabby made a grimace. " 'Englishman!' You're promoted, boyo."

"That'll be the day," Millburn grunted. He turned to Adams. "You all right, sir?"

Adams, whose first impression of Norway had been the bite of the wind on his face, nodded. As he introduced himself and the two airmen to Lindstrom, he noticed three other partisans watching them from the river bank. One was wearing a thick anorak and hood that half covered his face. The other two, like Jensen, were wearing Norwegian Army uniforms and Adams knew they were members of the Linge Movement. When acting as agents or saboteurs they were forced to wear civilian clothes but when they engaged the enemy in the mountains or on the high viddas, they chose to wear their national uniform. Trimmed down to bone and gristle by the rigours of their existence, unshaven and unkempt after their recent trek to the lake, they looked archetypal freedom fighters and the sensitive Adams felt his non-military appearance must be amusing them.

His eyes moved down the frozen river where distant figures of more partisans could be seen. They had paused a moment to watch the Mosquito taxi in but were again busy carrying toboggans down from the river bank and unloading them. It was a sight that assured Adams the Americans had carried out the air-drop during the night as planned.

He turned back as Lindstrom introduced him to the huge Jensen. "Steen works closely with my sister. He's also in touch with many freedom fighters and for this job he's called in as many as he can get."

Jensen grinned at Adams. "You'll like my boys. They enjoy fighting Germans."

Adams wondered if the giant was gently ribbing him. From the tilt of his neck he felt he was talking to an oak tree. "Where did you learn to speak English, Captain?"

"Me? Before the war I landed my fish in England. In Hull and Grimsby. I did that for fifteen years until those bastards came." The Norwegian's jovial tone changed. "Now I keep myself busy doing other things."

As his hand entered a steel trap, Adams felt vaguely glad he was not a German. Alongside him Lindstrom was waving the partisan in the mud-stained anorak to join them. At first he thought he was being introduced to another section leader but as the partisan threw back the hood he noticed Millburn give Gabby a nudge. Glancing back, Adams saw the newcomer was a woman.

"This is my sister, Helga," Lindstrom told him. "Things were getting too hot in Rjukan, so we insisted she got out before it was too late. Helga, this is Squadron-Leader Adams who is going to remain here with us."

Although the woman's face was scuffed by the bitter wind and fatigued by the rigours of the journey, Adams thought her eyes were the bluest he had ever seen. "I'm very happy to meet you, Miss Lindstrom. Although I didn't expect to have the pleasure."

Her scientific background showed in the quality of her English. "I didn't expect to be up here either, Squadron-Leader. At least not a week ago. But that is war, isn't it? It's a great relief to us all that you made a safe landing. We believed the ice was strong enough but one can never be certain of such things."

Adams liked her direct and friendly approach. He motioned Millburn and Gabby towards them. "I had nothing to do with that part of it. These two did all the hard work."

She shook hands with both men. Millburn was clearly impressed. "How did you make the journey up here, Miss Lindstrom? On skis?"

She smiled at him. "Part of the way, yes."

"It's a tough country to ski in, isn't it? All we saw were hills and mountains."

"Not for us. Most of us can ski as soon as we can walk. But we didn't ski all of the way. We travelled some distance by train, although the Germans don't approve of resistance fighters using the railways."

Millburn liked her sense of humour. "They're a mean bunch, aren't they?"

She laughed. "We think so."

Lindstrom had been listening to Millburn's accent. "You're an American, aren't you?"

"That's right."

"In the RAF?"

Not even his intense curiosity could quell Millburn's sense of humour. "Yeah. I thought they needed stiffening up a bit. Now they won't let me go." His eyes moved to the smiling Helga, then back to Lindstrom. "How come you're wearing American uniform, Major? Or are you an American too?"

The questioning look he received from Lindstrom reminded Adams he had better put him in the picture. "I'm sorry, Tommy, but you're not supposed to ask any questions."

The American grinned. "It was worth a try. Wasn't it, Olaf?" he asked Jensen.

The giant Norwegian gave a growl. "Don't call me Olaf. My name is Steen Jensen."

Millburn ran his eyes up and down the man's huge frame. "Your Mommie and Pappy made a mistake. Olaf suits you better."

Adams turned hastily to Gabby before the frowning giant could reply. "Get my stuff out, will you? And the package."

Climbing back into the Mosquito, Gabby handed a rucksack, a sleeping bag and a Sten gun down to Millburn. He followed them with a small wooden crate. As Adams nodded, Millburn presented the crate to Lindstrom. "It's a gift from our C.O. He hopes it'll keep you warm at night."

Jensen pushed eagerly forward. "What is it? Scotch?"

Millburn winked at him. "You've got a good nose, Olaf. Six bottles."

Although the American was a powerful man himself, the playful slap Jensen gave him sent him stumbling across the ice. "Six bottles? Then you can call me Olaf, Yankee. As often as you like."

As the eager Jensen broke open the crate, Adams turned to Gabby. "You'd better get your photographs taken of this river. Time's running out." As Gabby nodded and pulled a hand camera from his flying suit, Adams drew Millburn aside.

"What's your verdict on this lake? Is it possible for aircraft to land on it at night?"

Millburn kept his face expressionless. "It depends what kind of aircraft you've got in mind. Lancs might have a bit of a problem."

Knowing that two men as intelligent as Millburn and Gabby could not fail to put two and two together, Adams was finding his security brief absurd. "I can't stop you guessing, but for God's sake don't make it so obvious. You know perfectly well I'm not talking about Lancasters."

Millburn grinned. "O.K. Yes, Mossies should make it. Providing the runway's extended, there's still some moonlight, and we get the kind of ground support we've been getting during practice."

Feeling relief, Adams threw away the last trappings of security. "What about this river mouth? Can we hide our aircraft inside it?"

"Yeah, I think so. It's about wide enough to get them in two abreast. But they're going to be sitting ducks if Jerry spots us."

"We'll have camouflage nets to hide them," Adams told him. "So tell Davies we can use the river as a hide-out, will you?"

The intrigued American could contain himself no longer. "What's going on, sir? You can tell me the rest, can't you?"

Adams backed away. "No, I can't. If Davies wants you to know more, he'll tell you all during your briefing." Before Millburn could ask any more questions, he turned to Gabby.

"Have you finished?"

Gabby nodded. "I've taken a full spool."

"Good. Then you'd both better get back. Tell Davies everyone here seems in good spirits and that I'll do my best to see the landing is a success."

"Don't forget to see the runway's extended." Millburn reminded him. "I'd say a couple of hundred yards to be on the safe side."

The two airmen said their farewells to the three Norwegians, then turned to Adams again. The respect they showed him made the apprehensive Intelligence Officer feel, for the moment at least, that his offer to spearhead the operation was worthwhile. For once Millburn sounded serious. "Take it easy, sir, and watch yourself."

Adams led them to the Mosquito. "We'll throw a party when this is over. Now off you go or you'll miss your rendezvous with the Mustangs."

131

The three partisans followed Adams out on the lake to watch the Mosquito's take-off. As it passed over them with a crackling roar and waggled its wings, Adams was reminded of an incident in his childhood when his parents had left him for a fortnight with strangers. They had driven off before dawn and the young Adams, lying in bed listening to their receding car, had felt the loneliest child on earth.

Lindstrom's voice made him start guiltily. "We'd better get back among the trees, Squadron-Leader. There's always the chance a German patrol might be about. And Helga has a meal ready for you before you take a look at the stores."

"Did you get everything you wanted?" Adams asked as he fell into step.

Lindstrom ignored Jensen's growl of denial. "We think so although men are still bringing in the containers. Fortunately the Americans made the drop right on the target area."

"What about the mines?"

"They were the first thing we looked for." The young scientist pointed at the steep, wooded hill they were approaching. "We've got men sowing them around the far side as fast as they get them. We're hoping to have the job finished by tomorrow at the latest."

Adams realized there were more partisans in the area than he had thought. He turned to Jensen. "You sound disappointed. Is there something they've forgotten?"

Jensen scowled fiercely. "Why couldn't they send more Sten and anti-tank ammunition? Don't the fools realize the more Germans we kill the easier the job's going to be for them later?"

Helga, who seemed totally unawed by the bearded giant, gave a cry of impatience. "Stop talking that way, Steen. The squadron-leader will think we're a crowd of blood-thirsty cut-throats."

Jensen looked almost sheepish as he stood aside to allow the girl to take a path that led up through the trees. "The squadron-leader can't think we're doing this for our health, kjaere."

"Call me Frank, please," Adams protested as he followed Jensen up the path. "It makes things easier somehow."

It was a remark that met with Jensen's approval. His teeth shone whitely through his beard as he glanced back. "No bullshit, eh, Frank? I like that." Winking at

132

Adams, he threw a sly glance at Lindstrom. "Maybe it calls for a little sip of Scotch, ya?"

The first Mitchell came in low over No. 1 hangar and touched the runway with a flurry of spray and a squeal of brakes. As it turned to taxi back, Davies threw in the gears of his jeep and accelerated across the grass. As he halted alongside the B.25 a ladder dropped to the ground, followed by a young air-gunner who held the foot of the ladder while Staines descended. His fur-collared flying jacket made the American look even broader than usual. Pausing to chat to the air-gunner, he caught sight of Davies and gave a shout of welcome. Jumping from the jeep, Davies met him halfway and shook hands.

"This is a pleasure, sir. I hadn't expected to see you today." Unable to contain himself a moment longer, Davies drew the American aside. "I take it you have heard the news?"

The slant of Staines' big jaw suggested immense satisfaction. "Why do you think I drove to your Mitchell base and bummed a lift up here? That Haukelid must be a hell of a man, Davies. He blew up the ferry right over the deepest part of the fjord." He grinned at the excited Air Commodore. "You know what this means, don't you? It's a million to one now that the Heinies will use that cruiser."

Davies nodded. "We'll be ready by tonight, sir. I was waiting for the Mitchells to arrive so I could brief all the crews together. With any luck we'll be airborne on schedule."

Staines' heavy eyebrows came together. "We? That doesn't mean you're going, does it?"

Davies was forced to pause as a second Mitchell, airfoils whining, swept in to land. "Yes, sir. I got permission two days ago."

Staines gave a growl of frustration. "And I argued with Spaatz for half an hour and got nowhere. I always thought you were the outfit with the red tape. You're lucky, Davies. It should be a hell of an adventure."

"There is a bit of difference between an Air Commodore taking a risk and a general," Davies pointed out.

The American's scowl showed he found the statement poor comfort. He was watching spray flying from the Mitchell's wheels as it touched down. "You've had rain here today."

133

Davies' expression betrayed his secret apprehension. "Only a shower. About an hour ago. Apparently there's a warm front moving in from the Atlantic. But it seems the weather's holding over there."

"My boys say the air-drop went well. Has Lindstrom confirmed it?"

"Yes, he has. His only bleat is they'd like more Sten and anti-tank ammunition, so we're taking a few boxes with us tonight."

Staines grinned. "Did you hear we dropped 'em a few bazookas?"

Davies gave a start. "Surely you're not expecting there'll be armour?"

"No, but there's no harm in playing safe, is there?" Staines gave his infectious laugh. "We've got an army unit playing soldiers only half a mile from my HQ and I've got a top sergeant who could steal the knickers off Helen of Troy. So I sent him out in a jeep yesterday morning and he came back with some bazookas and a few boxes of shells. They'll always come in handy later if Lindstrom doesn't need 'em now." The Texan paused while the last Mitchell swept in to land. "I notice you've had these B.25s stripped down to the buff. That doesn't mean the boffins are having second thoughts about the ice, does it?"

Davies stared at him. "Not unless you've heard anything." When the American shook his head, Davies went on: "We were told that the lake's altitude should ensure it's strong enough to take Mitchells but that we should also play safe and send them in as light as possible. So we've taken out all guns and non-essential equipment and are only carrying three crewmen. And we're limited to six technicians a plane."

"You think it's safe to go out unarmed like that?"

"We haven't much option, have we? Don't forget we'll have Mossies all around us. By the way, thanks for your offer to lend us aircraft. If we hadn't had our own Mitchell squadron prepared to help, we'd have been glad of it."

The Texan shrugged. "If that IMI consignment gets through, we'll both be facing the same problem, Davies."

The small Air Commodore was only too aware of his heavy responsibility. "I take it you'll be seeing the Brigadier while you're here?"

"Of course. I'm AWOL until tomorrow morning. I want to be with him when you land. What time's your ETA?"

"0300 hours."

"And your code word if all goes well?"

"Summertime. Wintertime if for some reason we can't get down. In that case we'll try again tomorrow night."

"What about when you clobber the cruiser?"

"Culloden if we sink her. Bannockburn if we botch it up."

Staines' grin proved he was no mean student of British military history. "Your Scots lads are going to be a bit schizophrenic, aren't they?" Then, as a sudden gust of wind sent a piece of paper flying past them, his eyes rose to the bleak afternoon sky. When he glanced back at Davies his mood had changed.

"There's one thing I'd like to emphasize, Davies. If it begins to look for some reason or other that you can't clobber that cruiser, don't hope for the best and leave it to the last minute to warn us. It's vital our backing-up forces know where they stand."

"I understand, sir."

There was another pause as Staines gazed down the airfield. Following his eyes Davies saw a faint mist was beginning to hide the distant poplars from sight. When Staines broke the silence he seemed to be musing rather than making a statement. "On the other hand the odds against our backing-up forces doing the job must be more than ten to one."

Fully aware what he was being told, the usually confident Davies frowned and shifted restlessly. "What can I do over there if the weather closes right down on us, sir? I can't order my boys out to certain death."

More perceptive than his rugged features hinted, the big Texan took Davies' arm and steered him towards the jeep. "Let's forget the goddam affair for half an hour and take a look at that Mess of yours. The heating in that B.25's on the blink and I'm half-frozen."

## 20

There were unfamiliar faces in the Operations Room at Sutton Craddock later that same day. Seated in a small but apprehensive phalanx behind the usual complement of aircrews was a motley selection of ground staff. At a quick glance about fifty per cent were senior NCOs. Davies had argued that with the Mosquitoes going out in first-class condition one or at the most two men of each trade ought to be able to cope with any minor breakdowns that might occur. The only exceptions were engine fitters and to a lesser degree armourers, and that explained the number of less exalted ranks sitting alongside the curious NCOs.

The lugubrious old sweat McTyre and the cherubic-faced Ellis were among these "erks." Like the rest of the ground staff they had been working at top pressure most of the previous night and throughout the day and the sudden order to report in the Operations Room with the aircrews had dropped among them like a cat among exhausted pigeons. It was true that very occasionally a senior NCO might be asked to attend an aircrew briefing on a point of technical advice, but there was no precedent for the attendance of humble airmen. With McTyre never one to see the sun when there was a wisp of cloud, his prognostications had spread alarm to the innocent Ellis.

"It's the bloody invasion, mate. Five bob to a penny. They want advance airfields over there, so we're bein' sent to grab 'em. Stands out a mile."

In the circumstances even the impressionable young Ellis could be forgiven his credulity. "But how can we get airfields for them? We're not paratroopers or infantry."

McTyre's glance had been half-pitying and half-triumphant. "You forgotten that infantry training we've been getting? That's your answer, mate."

"But I didn't fire off more than twenty rounds," the youngster wailed. "And I only hit the target twice."

"You think they care?" the old sweat asked darkly. "We're cannon fodder, mate, just like the last war. While the Jerries are knocking us off, the bloody officers will creep up behind and get away scot free."

"But why us, Mac?"

"Don't you know anything, mush? The last war was fought to thin out poor buggers like you and me so they

136

wouldn't have to fork out unemployment pay. So far this war's disappointed 'em so they're usin' the invasion to put things right."

Curiosity and varying degrees of unease were not confined to the ground staff. The last week with its night-landing exercises, its mysterious modifications to the Mosquitos, its infantry training, and the constant shuttling to and fro of Davies had already convinced the crews something big was afoot. This evening, as they filed into the Operations Room, their eyes had been drawn to a huge map of Norway that hung beside a blank cinematograph screen. The Swartfjord operation still cast long shadows over 633 Squadron and the uneasy buzz of conversation among the crews after they had greeted the entry of Davies and Henderson showed their tension was a full notch tighter than usual. Nearly every man was drawing on a cigarette and the smoke was forming an artificial ceiling above them. With scale models of German aircraft dangling amid the haze, an imaginative observer like Adams, had he been present, might have imagined the aircraft were about to pounce on the assembly.

The tension was not aided by the muttered conversation Davies was having with Moore. Seated at the large table alongside them were Henderson, Sue Spencer, and a number of specialist officers. Two large blackboards stood behind the table, both covered with sheeting.

Reaching a decision, Davies nodded at Moore and rose to his feet. The buzz of curious voices ceased immediately and the hush became palpable as the Air Commodore advanced to the front of the platform. An actor to his fingertips, he gazed at the assembly for a full five seconds before addressing it.

"Good evening, gentlemen. Sorry we've had to close the station down and made you miss your dates, but now and again we have to give the war our attention and this is one of those days."

The odd titter that broke out told Davies much about the mood of his audience. Had it been relaxed he might have played the briefing in a low key and let the operation build up its own nervous energy. But with the crews already on the edge of their seats, Davies wanted to avoid anything anti-climactical. He was not sorry for he had seldom experienced more personal excitement before an operation.

137

"All right, chaps, I can see you're anxious to know why we've been playing silly buggers all this week, so I won't keep you in suspense any longer. You're quite right—we have got something rather special for you. So special, in fact, that whether you pull it off or not they'll still write you into the history books. You'll find out why in a moment."

A loud murmur broke out as he moved back to the desk and took a pointer from Sue Spencer. It ceased abruptly as he reached the map of Norway, something that was not lost on Davies. In his own way a student of psychology, the Air Commodore was a great believer that the morale and performance of aircrews had much to do with their conditioning beforehand. Aware that the Swartfjord raid had been a disaster as well as a triumph for the squadron, he had been faced with the problem of whether he should link it with the present operation (as in fact it was linked) or leave out all mention of it in his briefing. Davies' own feelings were that men fought better when following in the footsteps of illustrious predecessors but he was intelligent enough to realize this might apply more to professional soldiers like himself than to wartime volunteers. In the end he had sought the advice of Moore, who, like so many other fliers in the squadron, was a volunteer reservist. To his gratification Moore had agreed the two operations should be linked and until this moment this had fitted nicely with Davies' need to emphasize the importance of the mission. Now, listening to the chilled hush, he was less sure of himself although he was never one to falter once a decision was made. Taking a deep breath, Davies crossed the Rubicon.

"Norway, chaps. Not a country we visit very often and yet the reason this élite squadron was formed. Here in the Swartfjord the Jerries were refining a product that might have won them the war. So we came up here to Yorkshire and we trained and we trained and finally flew into a black valley lined with guns and destroyed the factory, stocks and all. This is history now, I know, but history has a way of repeating itself and that's why you're all here today."

A feather could have been heard to fall as Davies faced his youthful audience. "It won't be news to you that Jerry is a determined and resourceful enemy. Although we buried the Swartfjord factory under a mountain, he was

138

already producing similar stocks in another part of Norway. For reasons that don't concern you, they didn't represent a threat to us while they stayed there but now our agents tell us they're to be shipped to Germany in a cruiser. This changes the entire situation and our boffins tell us that if these stocks reach Stettin or wherever the cruiser will make for, the situation will be as dangerous for us as it was in April last year."

With this vital point emphasized, Davies paused to allow it to sink in. "So you see we've got a mission every bit as important as the Swartfjord job. From our point of view it would have been simpler if we could have caught the cruiser out in the open sea and clobbered her there. But things aren't that simple. To begin with no one knows the exact time she will sail which means no one knows what time she'll come out into the open sea. On top of that I don't need to tell any of you that the sea's a hell of a big place and so even if we had intelligence of her movements we might still not find her. So to be certain of making contact we have to attack her in the fjord. Even that isn't as straightforward as it sounds because if we sink her at her anchorage we've no guarantee the stocks can't be salvaged. The same problem exists in the fjord except for one stretch about thirty miles long. Here the banks are too steep for beaching and the water too deep for salvage. So that's our contact point." Seeing men staring at one another, Davies decided a question might give him a lead-in for his next startling announcement. "Some of you look a bit lost. Is there anything you want to ask me?"

Half a dozen hands shot up immediately. Davies chose the nearest. "Go on, Heron."

"If we don't know what time the cruiser's going to sail, sir, how can we time our arrival to contact her in this stretch of fjord?"

Davies grinned his satisfaction. "Right on the button, Heron. We racked our brains for days to solve that one. It's the reason you flew to Southport and why you've been making yourself a general nuisance here. Tonight you're flying over to Norway and there you're going to land on a frozen lake and wait until you hear the cruiser has sailed. Then you'll take off, reach her in half an hour or maybe less, and give her the works. If all goes well she'll sink in the deep channel and take her damned stocks down with her."

There was an incredulous hush as he finished speaking. Then an outcry such as Henderson had never heard from his crews.

"What's he talking about? How can we land on a bloody lake?"

"In Norway? Doesn't he know Jerry's over there?"

Fully conscious of how outrageous the proposition seemed until examined in depth, Davies had come prepared to show forbearance and he allowed the crews a few seconds to vent their feelings before putting up a hand. "All right, chaps, you've said your piece. Now listen to me. It'll work. Milburn and Gabriel have proved it."

Necks craned as men tried to see the named airmen. Davies' voice pushed them back into their seats. "They've been excused the briefing to get some shut-eye but you'll get a chance to talk to them later. In the meantime keep quiet and let me get on." As the outcry subsided, Davies turned back to the map. "You'll be getting detailed instructions from Wing Commander Moore in a moment but here is the broad outline of the plan. The lake we're going to use is about here. It's been chosen because it lies in a particularly desolate stretch of country with a minimum of German outposts. The hills around it aren't very high and we know the ice will hold because Milburn and Gabriel have very courageously tested it for us. You'll follow exactly the same landing procedure that you've been practising here. A crowd of Norwegian partisans, who'll be our watchdogs while we're over there, will set out a runway of storm lanterns, although we've every hope of moonlit conditions. In addition Squadron-Leader Adams, who flew out with Milburn, will be there to give us the wind direction and guide us down."

There was another stir among his audience. A disbelieving voice let out a yelp. "Adams?"

Davies could not help a grin at the commotion he was causing. "Yes. He volunteered and was flown out by Milburn last night."

Another hand shot up. "Will we be using our spotlights, sir?"

"Yes. I've just told you—we're using exactly the same landing procedure."

"But isn't there a danger we'll be seen?"

"I told you earlier that there are no German outposts in this area. The partisans scouted it very carefully before choosing the lake."

From the corner of his eye the wary Davies saw Harvey lean sideways and mutter something to the officer beside him. As flight commanders, Harvey and Young were seated in two chairs at one side of the assembly. Aware of the Yorkshireman's almost parental attitude to his men, Davies had made certain both officers had been given a preliminary briefing that afternoon. As he had expected, both had expressed dismay at the high risks involved but whereas Davies felt Young had said all he had to say at the private briefing, he was by no means certain this applied to the blunt Yorkshireman and he welcomed the distraction a young navigator provided.

"Won't the Germans be able to pick us up on their monitors, sir? And if they do, won't they be able to trace us to the lake?"

"They could but for one thing," Davies told him. "I've arranged for three flights of Lancasters equipped with Mandrels to fly up and down the Norwegian coast until we land. In case some of you don't know, Mandrels are the latest radar jammers. So Jerry's monitor screens will go haywire while you're flying in and by the time they're clear again you'll have landed. He probably won't even guess you're there, but even if he does he'll assume you've gone back home with the Lancs."

"What about fuel, sir?"

"That's all taken care of. The Yanks did an air-drop last night and with any luck everything we need should now be in the hands of the partisans. That's another of Mr. Adams' jobs—to see everything is sorted out and ready for us in case we have to make a quick scramble." His eyes lifted to the phalanx of ground crew at the back of the room. "By this time you must have guessed why you're attending this briefing. Although our kites will be going out as shipshape as they've ever been, they're going to need light maintenance and refuelling while over there and that's why you're coming with us in those three Mitchells you saw arrive today. I hope you all feel as I do—that it's an honour to be taking part in such an important operation."

Watching Davies' performance from the large table on the platform, Henderson wondered how much of his last comment was tongue in cheek. Although a couple of senior NCOs, whom Davies had been forced to take into his confidence earlier, had expressionless faces, the majority of NCOs and erks looked horrified at the prospects

141

before them. Fighting back a grin at their glassy-eyed expressions, Henderson listened to Davies rounding off his briefing. "You'll all be getting detailed instructions from your senior NCOs later but if you have any general questions, let's have them now."

A horny hand rose. "Chiefy" Powell, the grizzled NCO who kept the squadron's engine fitters on their toes, had served in India and the Middle East before the war and was as unperturbable a technician as ever changed a spark plug. His unruffled voice, with its Lancashire accent, acted as a tranquilizer to the apprehensive youngsters around him.

"Just one little point, sir. Did you have a chance to talk to the Rolls-Royce people about the temperature problem?"

"Yes, Chiefy. The Engineering Officer has seen them and they acted smartly. They put a Merlin into a refrigerator and dropped the temperature down to what we expect in Norway. They've offered a few other suggestions which the Engineering Officer will explain to you later but in the main they think you should be all right using the oil they've suggested and the heavy-duty accumulators."

Powell lowered his hand. "Then we shouldn't have any problem, sir. Thanks."

Davies blessed the country for producing men like Powell. "Of course you won't, Chiefy. Any more questions?"

A tentative hand rose from behind Powell. "How are we going to defend ourselves, sir?"

"The band of partisans are looking after the defence side of things. But of course you'd be expected to help 'em if the need arose. The Armoury have orders to issue every man with a Sten and a hundred rounds of ammunition. And you'll get warm clothing from the stores. Anything else you want to ask me?"

If the ground crews had been shaken before, they were speechless now. McTyre, still wearing oil-stained overalls like many of his mates, leaned towards the round-eyed Ellis. "You hear that, mate? It's worse than I thought. The bastards can't wait to get us shot. They're dumping us in Jerryland."

Hearing his hoarse whisper, Davies dropped on him. "You got a question, McTyre?"

Although caught by surprise, McTyre was a natural

survivor. "Yes, sir. Just one. It's going to be chilly over there. Where are we supposed to nap?"

Hearing a laugh or two, Davies helped to ease the tension. "You like your sleep, do you, McTyre? The answer is you'll nap where you can. Some might have to sleep in the kites, others might be lucky and get a hut. But no doubt that's something else Mr. Adams will have sorted out for us before we arrive."

Glancing at his watch, Davies crossed over to the two blackboards and pulled away their covering. One contained an artist's sketch of the lake and the hills surrounding it. The other supported a blown-up photograph of the river mouth. Davies' pointer rested on the latter. "This is where we're going to park the kites until we need them. As you see, it's the mouth of a river that runs into the western lake. It has hills and trees on either side, and if we park near them and spread our camouflage nets sensibly we ought to be invisible from the air."

"Up the creek!" a wit muttered from one of the aircrew benches. Davies joined in the laughter, "Right up it, lad. *Tee Emm* will devote an entire edition to you, when you get back."

This time the laughter was more relaxed. Satisfied, Davies walked back to the table. "Later on you'll all come up here and study these pictures in detail. Take notes, sketches, anything you like. You'll also be getting separate photographs from Flight Officer Spencer and a cinematographic show in the bargain. But first Wing Commander Moore will have a word with you on flight procedure."

Nodding at Moore, Davies sat down. The young squadron commander moved to the front of the platform. Immaculately dressed as always, cultured of voice, he might have been a young managing director explaining new company policy to his staff rather than a combat pilot about to lead his crews on a desperate venture. His first words, Tess, described as whimsical.

"We've really been playing it tight to the chest this last week or two, haven't we, chaps? I'm sorry for all the mystery but as you'll have gathered from the Air Commodore, tight security is essential."

With his audience duly placated, Moore's tone changed. "I want you all to listen very carefully because we can't afford the slightest mistake. You'll be getting details of our

143

ETAs in your navigators' wallets but first I want to run over the mission in general terms in case you have any questions."

There was a subtle change in the mood of the aircrews as they listened to Moore. It was their battle leader talking and his exploits with them had earned their professional respect. Only a cough or two broke the silence as he glanced down at a piece of paper.

"Let's take our armament first. We'll make our first attack with rockets but the possibility exists the cruiser might need armour-piercing bombs or semi-APs to see her off. So some of us will be carrying a couple apiece. I don't need to stress this brings up the problem of the weight factor but after doing a bit of juggling our engineering wizards appear to have solved it very well."

The extraordinary versatility of the wooden Mosquito could hardly have been better illustrated than in Moore's first three sentences. Originally designed as an unarmed bomber, it had shown such potential in its trials that new marques had come in rapid succession off the drawing board. Among these was the fighter-bomber, a compromise version that carried four 20mm Hispano cannon as well as two 250 lb. bombs in the rear of the bomb bay and two 500 lb. bombs in place of wing tanks. With his élite squadron called up to perform a variety of tasks, Davies had approached the De Haviland company to see if they could give him an even more versatile marque.

Their answer had been ingenious. With the fighter-bomber's four cannon breeches extending too far back into the bomb bay to make the carrying of large stores possible, the designers had replaced them with two Brownings and two short-barrelled cannon. This had restored the bomb bay close to its original length and yet left the aircraft with enough fire power to hold its own against most enemy fighters. Facilities for wing rockets had also been provided. It is true that to cope with all these armament variations the cockpit layout was somewhat cramped but most pilots and navigators suffered the discomfort gladly for the flexibility the aircraft gave them. This special marque of Mosquito was not issued to any other squadron in spite of the many indignant appeals that were made—possibly, as Davies believed, because the cost of its modifications was too high. At the same time he had no problems getting replacements: the latest to be equipped with four cannon to increase fire power. Clearly the powers-that-be had decided the squadron's remarkable record justified the expenditure.

Anticipating anxious questions about the weight factors, Moore was explaining the problem in some detail. "It goes without saying we shall have to fly out with our stores on board, which means we have to land with them. Ideally, then, to compensate for the extra weight, we'd like to be landing with empty fuel tanks. But against this we need to conserve all the fuel we can because the Yanks have been limited in their air-drop by what the Norwegians can drag to the lake by toboggan. This is why we've had a few headaches before getting it all sorted out. As it's a little complicated I want you all to listen carefully.

"On the way out we're going to land at Sumburgh in the Shetlands to top up. But, all skippers note, this applies only to the kites carrying rockets. They're the ones responsible for fuel conservation: it has been estimated by the time they reach the lake they'll still have a reasonable reserve and yet their landing weight will be inside the safety margin. The kites carrying bombs are something else. To compensate for their extra load their tanks should be low on arrival. So they'll leave here with a carefully calculated fuel load and will be landing at Sumburgh only for coffee."

"What if we run into any trouble on the way across, skipper?" The question was delivered in a rich Australian twang.

"We're not cutting the margin that fine, Teddy. There'll be enough for headwinds and the odd spot of enemy trouble." Moore switched his gaze to the hushed ground crews. "Armourers note—the stores won't be armed. So if anyone makes a bad landing, they won't explode and blow him back to the U.K."

"Let's hope the rockets and bombs know that." It was Young again, quipping to the silent Harvey.

Moore smiled. "If I were you, I'd go round and tell them, Teddy."

"I might just do that, skipper."

As Davies coughed, Moore glanced at his notes again. "We shall be flying at economical cruising speed all the way to the lake. This would be necessary in any case because of the three Mitchells that are going out with us. We'll be using all sixteen Mosquitoes and we'll fly in battle formation with the Mitchells tucked in between A and B Flights." Moore slanted a humorous glance at the seated Davies. "The last thing we want to do is lose our Air Commodore."

Davies took in good part the boos and cat-calls that followed. "Naturally, we'll be keeping radio silence all the way." Moore continued. "If we have to communicate we'll do it either by Aldis lamp or Very pistol. You'll find the appropriate codes in your wallets. But even then communicate only in an emergency. There's always the chance Jerry's night fighters might spot us."

On the front bench, Larkin, a stringy New Zealander and one of the squadron's old hands, leaned towards his navigator and whispered something, only to pause as Moore went on: "After leaving Sumburgh we shall make straight for the lake. Weather permitting we shall cross the coast at 8,000 feet and drop down to 5,000 once we've cleared the flak defences. We shouldn't have any trouble from guided night fighters for the reason you've been given but if any of you are attacked, fire single red Very lights and we'll try to help."

Here Larkin lifted his hand. "What's the latest Met. report, skipper?"

"Pretty good considering. We might run into a few squalls on the way but over in Norway the anti-cyclone seems to be holding."

"If it's as bright as it's been here recently, isn't it possible Jerry might see us or pick us up on his short-range monitors?"

"We don't think so, Andy. They don't have the depth of night fighters or radio beacons they have on the Continent. And if they fly blind they're far more likely to head for the Lancasters who'll be attracting all the coastal searchlights. With luck they won't even know we're there."

Larkin subsided into his seat. "Fair enough, skipper."

Moore turned back to the intent crews. "Our ETA at the lake is 0300 hours. I know it's an ungodly time but it's been chosen because that's when the moon is at its zenith. If the sky's clear we shouldn't have any trouble getting down because there should be plenty of reflection from the ice. If it's cloudy, then we might need Squadron-Leader Adams and his storm lanterns. As you've heard he'll give us the wind direction. If it's blowing from the east or south we shouldn't have any problems because we'll be approaching over shallow hills. If it's veered to the north or west we'll have to be more careful, as you'll see from the photographs. If you have to make a cross-

146

wind landing, watch for drift on touchdown. We're being issued with special tires, but we can't expect too much from them."

Another hand rose. "Won't the lake be snowbound, skipper?"

"No, that's taken care of, Butterfield. The partisans have swept a runway for us that follows the contours of the lake so it looks as natural as possible. It seems they're old sweats at camouflage, so we're going into good hands."

When the questions ceased, Moore explained the landing procedure. "I shall land first and according to which way the wind is blowing taxi to the far end of the lake and then follow the shore line back until I reach the river mouth. There I shall park inside beneath the trees. The rest of you will land in numerical order and repeat the procedure. Make certain your landing lights are turned off when you reach the river but leave your navigation light on—we don't want any collisions. Our aim is to end up dispersed along both banks of the river but don't let that part worry you too much. By the time you land Squadron Leader Harvey and I will be out on the ice and we'll lead you to your place in the creek." Anticipating a reaction, Moore gave his attractive smile. "Some might say we've led you into it already but let's hope they're wrong."

When the nervous laughs died Moore moved on to the second part of the operation. "I can't tell you exactly how long we'll be over there before the scramble comes. It all depends how quickly Jerry gets his stocks to the cruiser. But agents will be monitoring their progress and as soon as the ship sails we'll be notified. It won't be the panic it sounds because we shall have had an earlier warning when the stocks reach her and it'll take some time to load them. We estimate that if we are ready for take-off by the time the cruiser sails, we ought to make contact with her when she's in the middle of the deep channel. So on the first alert we get our kites out on the lake and on the second we scramble. We clobber the cruiser and then fly straight home. Simple really."

As aircrews grinned wryly, an indignant hand rose from the back of the room. "What about us lot, sir? What're we supposed to do when you've all gone?"

Moore's eyes twinkled. "You won't be abandoned, Mc-Tyre. You'll take off in the Mitchells the same time we do but you'll head straight for home. All right?"

"If you bear up bravely they might even give you a DFC," a wit shouted.

Harvey did not join in the laughter that followed. As it subsided he caught Moore's attention. "I take it the Norwegians have warned you how quickly the weather can change over there. I've seen fog come down like pea soup and last for a week. Has that been taken into account?"

With Harvey one of the few men on the station who had experienced Norwegian conditions firsthand, it was not a comment to be taken lightly. Aware everyone knew this, Davies rose. "Have you anything more to say, Moore?"

"I don't think so, sir. Not at the moment anyway."

"Then I'd like to answer that question."

Moore nodded and the two men exchanged places on the platform. However much the Air Commodore's opinion of Harvey had modified since the Rhine Maiden affair, the glance he gave the Yorkshireman was still vintage Davies.

"The Met. people think there is a good chance this anti-cyclone or at the worst its aftereffects will last long enough for us to complete this job. At the same time only a liar would pretend the weather isn't a gamble. But if I haven't made myself clear, I'll spell it out again. These stocks have to be destroyed whatever the risks. And those risks include the weather. All right?"

About to reply, Harvey felt Young kick his ankle and he sank back. Aware how the short dialogue had dampened the atmosphere Davies changed his tone as he turned to the silent assembly. "Don't look so serious. This could be a damned good scrounge. After all, you could be over there for a couple of days with nothing to do but lie in your sleeping bags. So don't forget to take 'em. We might even manage a few home comforts too. Some of you will be going out with empty bomb bays so I've no objections if you winch in a barrel or two of beer. Don't overdo it, mind," he went on as a stir of interest ran round the room. "I'll expect your flight commanders to check on everything you carry."

With the mood of the assembly restored, Davies walked back to the table. "All right, you can start coming up here now. It's a pity we haven't had time to build a papier-mâché model of the lake but I think we've enough photographs to make up for it."

148

For a full hour crews clustered in groups round the table and on the floor of the room, receiving detailed instructions from their specialist officers and collecting their wallets and maps. When all counsel had been given and all questions answered, they trooped back to their seats to view the films Sue Spencer had ready for them.

By the time the film show was over the perilous aspects of the mission were so submerged under the weight of the briefing that even the ground crews appeared to have lost their nervousness. Sensing this, Henderson, whose traditional role as O.C. of the station was to give the final address, kept his tone lighthearted.

"That's the lot, gentlemen. With luck you all know what to do. As a matter of fact, you're on a good thing this time because I'm coming with you."

Waiting for the groans that did not fail him, the big Scot grinned. "You ought to be glad. With me there you've someone to carry the can. All aircrews can stand down now and go to bed—you've a long night ahead. Sorry I can't do the same for the ground crews but you'll be able to nap on the way out. Off you go, then, until I see you tonight."

As benches rumbled back and men began rising Henderson caught Moore's eye and remembered. "Oh, yes, there's one last thing. The code name for the operation is Valkyrie."

## 21

Unsteady with fatigue Adams stumbled on the frozen path and fell to his knees. Hesitating a moment, Lindstrom reached down and put a hand beneath his armpit. "Are you all right?"

Adams nodded shamefacedly. "Yes, I just slipped, that's all."

The path the two men were following wound upwards through the wooded hillside. Through the frozen trees Adams kept catching glimpses of the lake. Although it was only late-afternoon, the sun had already disappeared and dusk was greying the hills. As the path grew steeper Adams, whose chest felt sore from his exertions in the bitter cold, was forced to pause for breath. To his left a number of small huts had appeared among the trees and he motioned at them.

"What are these huts? Holiday cabins?"

"One or two of the larger ones probably were," Lindstrom told him. "But most were used before the war by fishermen or reindeer hunters to keep their tackle in. You find them scattered all over Norway. They're proving a godsend to our Resistance."

A hut with an earth-covered roof appeared in a small clearing ahead. On its north side wind had piled up snow into a four foot ridge. Frozen into the snow was a pair of antlers, remnants of a kill made by an earlier band of partisans. Kicking his boots against the wooden step, Lindstrom pushed the door open and motioned Adams inside.

Although the air was thick with the smell of wet clothes, smoke, fish-oil, and half a dozen less definable odours, its warmth was balm to the half-frozen Adams. With the hut lacking glass windows and with its wooden shutters closed, the only light came from a paraffin lamp standing on a rough table. A pallet bed, two crates that served as chairs, and a couple of wooden chests made up the furniture. A stove stood beneath the chimney with piles of birch stacked round it to dry. A large pot of simmering water was standing on its flat top. A few tools, a large axe among them, leaned against one wall. Moss and earth sealed the cracks between the split logs but here and there pinpoints of light could be seen.

Adams, who had been up to the hut earlier to have a meal, saw that Helga was sitting beside one of the packs the Mitchells had dropped. Her eyes took in his weary appearance as she smiled at him. "How has everything gone?"

Suppressing a groan Adams unslung his Sten gun and leaned it against a wall. Unused to carrying firearms, he had found it had impeded his movements all day. "We think we've collected all the supplies now. But there's still some sorting out to do before the boys fly in tonight."

Nodding, the girl began pouring boiling water into two tin mugs. Glancing at her brother, she motioned at the open pack alongside her. "Do you know what's in there? Dried fruit, tobacco and *chocolate*. Imagine it. Chocolate!"

Lindstrom turned to Adams who had flopped down on a crate. "Some of Jensen's men have been living on pemmican and fishmeal porridge for months. So this is quite a day for them."

Helga passed a steaming cup of coffee to Adams. "This is something none of us has tasted for months either. Real coffee. Not like him"—and she pointed accusingly at her brother—"he lives on the fat of the land when he's over in England."

Lindstrom smiled as he received his own cup of coffee. "Jealousy will get you nowhere, kjaere."

Tired though Adams was he could not fail to notice the change in the young Norwegian since he rejoined his sister. Until then Adams' impression had been of an austere man with an almost fanatical determination to emulate Haukelid and destroy the remaining IMI stocks. The energy he had shown throughout the day, at one moment supervising the sowing of the mines at the opposite side of the hill and in the next helping to drag toboggans from the dropping zone, had exhausted Adams just to witness it. Now, in the presence of his sister, a softer, more humourous side to his character was evident.

Adams' eyes moved back to the girl. With her anorak and hood discarded, it could now be seen that she was a few years older than her brother—Adam's guess was thirty-two or three. Her features were strong but intelligent with wide-set eyes and a firm chin. Her thick blonde hair, which appeared to have a natural wave, was cut short in pageboy style. Although practically dressed for the conditions in a thick fisherman's jersey and warm slacks, her figure retained a shapeliness that was neither bulky nor over-fragile.

Adams realized Lindstrom was addressing him. "What do you think of our HQ hut?"

The weary Adams managed a smile. "It's homely at least."

"We were lucky to find one with a table and a bed in it. The Germans went around Norway just before Christmas emptying the huts of anything our Resistance might find useful. As they missed this one we thought we'd double it up as Helga's hut and our HQ." Lindstrom smiled at his sister. "It has the advantage we can have coffee while we plan the Germans' downfall."

"Sometimes I think that's the only reason he brought me along," Helga told Adams. "So I can feed them and give them hot drinks."

The perceptive Adams could feel the strong bond between the Norwegian and his sister. "It certainly was a surprise for me to find you here. I don't know how a woman can stand up to these conditions."

Helga's eyebrows rose. "You don't think a woman's place is by the kitchen stove, do you, Mr. Adams?"

Adams hesitated. "I don't think so."

"Are you sure? I saw your expression when you noticed me this morning." Seeing Adams' discomfort, Helga laughed. "I wouldn't worry about it too much, Mr. Adams. You've plenty of support here. If my brother had his way I would spend my life in a nunnery. He still can't accept that a woman can do most things a man can do if she's given the chance."

Grimacing at Adams, Lindstrom finished his coffee and moved towards the door. "I've had this kind of talk ever since I was a boy. There's no wonder I've got an inferiority complex." As the weary Adams moved to follow him, the Norwegian waved him back. "No, you've done enough for the moment. Stay and get some rest."

"I'd better come," Adams muttered. "There's still a lot to do."

As Lindstrom caught Helga's eye, she intervened with exactly the right weight of persuasion. "It isn't wise to do too much on your first day over here, Mr. Adams. The climatic change and the altitude can cause sickness. Stay a while and tell me what things are like in Britain today."

Adams wanted to resist but the flesh was too weak. "Just a few minutes then. I must have everything ready when the boys fly in."

A draught of icy air struck Adams as Lindstrom opened

152

the door. "We'll be ready in time. Tell Helga what the women in England are wearing these days. She'll pretend not to care but in fact she'll lap it up."

Ducking as the girl pretended to throw a mug at him, he scuttled outside and closed the door. "You and he are very close, aren't you?" Adams said as Helga laughed and turned away.

She returned to the stove before answering. "Yes, I suppose we are. As children we used to play together like a couple of boys. Until he was twelve I could ski faster than him and that used to make him very cross." She paused. "Would you like another cup of coffee?"

"I'd love one," Adams told her.

She took the mug from him, then rose to take a tin off a shelf high on the wall. Watching her, Adams was thinking that her heavy masculine garb would have overpowered some women but as her full breasts pushed out the fisherman's jersey it seemed to emphasize rather than diminish her sex. Until that moment Adams had believed it was only the slender and fragile women who attracted him. Now he realized that his tastes were more catholic than he had realized.

The look he received as she reseated herself made him wonder if she had read his thoughts. Yet no evidence of it showed in her voice as she sweetened his coffee and handed it to him. "Was Steen down there when you left?"

"No. They found more mines in the dropping area and he took another party of men round the hill to plant them."

She gave a low laugh. "Poor Steen. He hates Germans so much I almost think he would be glad if they found us here and attacked us."

"Why is that?" Adams asked.

"It's a common enough story, Mr. Adams. His wife and only child were killed in a bombing raid at the beginning of the war. He never talks about it but it changed his life. He left the sea and went up into the mountains where he has hunted Germans ever since." Before Adams could ask more, she changed the conversation. "What will happen tonight? Will your squadron be able to land safely?"

Adams hoped he sounded more confident than he felt. "I hope so. The weather appears to be holding and they're first-class crews." Remembering the news he had heard that day he tried to make a joke of it. "We'll have to pull it off, won't we, after what Haukelid has done?"

The news of the other group's success had been picked up by the camp's radio operator just before noon. With Jensen and the two Lindstroms the only other partisans who knew about Skinnarland's venture, the man had been compelled to give them the news in private. Their excitement and relief showed again in the girl's expression.

"Isn't it marvellous news? I've never seen Paul so excited before. We've all been praying Haukelid could do it but at times it seemed too much to expect."

"I think we felt the same," Adams said. "You must be very proud of them."

"We are. Very proud." The girl paused, then said: "Paul says it was your squadron that did the raid in the Swartfjord last year."

"Yes, it was. Last spring."

"You can't imagine the effect it had on people over here. They say villagers put flowers on the men's graves right through the summer. You lost nearly the entire squadron, didn't you?"

"Just about. Only one aircraft returned." As a shudder ran through the girl, Adams changed the subject. "They told me in England about your work in Rjukan. Weren't you afraid of being caught?"

"I suppose that now I look back on it, I was. But things never seem so bad at the time, do they?"

Adams, to whom the prospects of torture were terrifying, shook his head. "To me it takes enormous courage. Paul says you used to question some of the high-ranking German officers at parties. Weren't you afraid they would suspect you?"

"Not really. To begin with, one seldom had to ask outright questions, only ones that guided the conversation in the right direction." As the girl opened the shutters of the stove to feed in logs, its glow betrayed her smile. "You see, Mr. Adams, men are very vain about their achievements and they love to tell women below a certain age how important they are. Moreover the Germans are invaders, and so, no matter how they strut about, they cannot help having a subconscious guilt at being here. This makes them even more inclined to brag and postulate. So I did not find it difficult to pump them until the SS were brought in. Then it did become dangerous."

"I'd have been terrified," Adams said. "I couldn't do it in a thousand years."

She made an impatient gesture. "Of course you could.

154

If invaders were on your soil you would do exactly the same."

Adams, who had expected to meet no one but armed and desperate men during his mission and instead found himself having a tête-à-tête with an attractive woman, made a suggestion wholly out of character. "Do you have any of that whisky here?"

"Yes. Steen brought a bottle up. Would you like some?"

"Let's both have some. In our coffee. To toast the success of our collaboration."

She gave a laugh of delight as she poured a generous tot into their mugs. "A charming suggestion, Mr. Adams, Skoll!"

Adams lifted his mug. "Skol."

A short silence followed in which Adams heard the logs crackling and hissing in the stove. Then Helga gave an amused grimace. "I think I have given myself too much, Mr. Adams. One is not used to drinking whisky in occupied Norway."

Although no drinker himself, Adams waved away the suggestion. "Drink it. It'll do you good."

He could feel the comfort of the liquor spreading through his limbs and dulling the edges of fatigue. Outside, a wind that had been keening all day, was rising as the night came and sliding razor-sharp draughts through the walls. The girl motioned him to draw his seat nearer the stove. "You're not seeing our country at its best, Mr. Adams. It is a pity."

Obeying her, Adams felt the warmth of the stove on his cheeks. Suddenly and inexplicably, he felt enormously at home in the desolate, ice-bound hut. "Tell me about it."

"You've never been here before?"

"No. The few times I went abroad before the war I went to France. My wife likes the sun, you see."

"Your wife? What is she like?"

"Valerie? She's tall and slim and likes clothes . . ." Loyal by nature, Adams found he did not know what else to say about Valerie. Instead he reached out for the bottle and poured another generous tot into both their mugs. Helga's blue eyes stared at him. "What are you doing?"

Adams could not have explained had he tried. "You were going to tell me about Norway."

"Oh, yes. I wish you could see it in the summer. The lakes are so blue and the meadows so green—it is very beautiful, Mr. Adams."

"I'm sure it is. Please go on."

The whisky was lowering the threshold of her restraint. In the lamplight her expression was soft and full of memory. "The skies are very lovely too, with the snow-capped mountains floating among them." With a laugh, she lowered her blonde head. "It sounds silly, I know, but sometimes I think of Norway as a great cathedral. It has that kind of silence and the same vaulted ceilings that seem to lift you up until you are no longer in contact with the world. When you go among our mountains, as I used to do, their size and their silence purify you." Then she laughed again. "Did you ever hear such dreadful chauvinism?"

Adams cleared his throat. "It's not chauvinism to me. I understand it very well."

Her eyes lifted to his face. "Of course you do. You are English and who loves their country more than the English? But isn't it sad that we both have to fight and kill for our love?"

Adams was beginning to feel he had known this girl all his life. "It's not just sad, it's criminal. I think that every time I watch our boys going out on a mission."

"Yes, I am sure you do. But you also envy them, don't you?"

He gave a start. "How do you know that?"

"I saw it on your face this morning when your crew took off. You envy your pilots just as sometimes I envy Paul and Steen. Yet I hope you never have to kill, Mr. Adams."

Every nerve in Adams was alert. "Why?"

"I'm not sure. It is just a feeling. Some men do not mind killing—it does not scar their minds. But I think it might scar yours."

"Could you kill?" Adams asked.

"To free my country, yes. I might have to. But I daren't think what it might do to me."

Adams would never have believed that in a few short minutes he could feel so close to another human being. "Your country might be occupied but to me you're the freest person I've ever met."

Her glance made his cheeks turn warm. "Thank you, Mr. Adams. That is one of the nicest things I've ever had said to me."

"Frank, please." Adams begged. "Mr. Adams makes me feel so old."

Her laugh warmed him. "Old? How silly. But of course I will call you Frank. And you will call me Helga."

A gust of wind buffeted the hut and rattled the metal pipe of the stove. The sound jolted Adams back to the present. "I must get back. I can't leave all the work to them."

He had barely reached his feet before fatigue compounded by alcohol sent him reeling towards the wall. As he leaned in dismay against it, Helga caught his arm. "This is stupid. I insist you lie down and rest. Let me help you."

Humiliated but helpless, Adams had no option but to obey. As he sank back on the bed, she reached out for a blanket. Her voice softened as she laid it over him. "Your friends in England would not know this but with your working so hard it was bound to happen. The change in climate is too severe, but if you sleep now you will feel better this evening."

Adams tried to speak but suddenly the effort was too much. As his heavy eyelids closed and he felt the soft pressure of her hand on his shoulder, his thoughts turned whimsical. In the space of less than half an hour he had spoken to a nostalgic girl, a woman freedom fighter, and a mother figure gentle in voice and deed. In a frozen hut deep behind enemy lines he was feeling more relaxed and contented than he could remember. Did it not all prove what he had always claimed—that it was a mad and irreconcilable world? Without being certain why, Adams found great comfort in that thought as the warm pressure remained on his shoulder and sleep drew him into its sepia embrace.

## 22

A-Apple yawed unsteadily and dropped a full twenty feet. Hopkinson gave Moore an anxious glance. "Ice again, skipper?"

Moore nodded. "Warn the boys to fan out, will you?"

The Cockney glanced out of the dark cupola. Three black shadows were rising and falling on either side of A-Apple. Lifting his Aldis lamp, Hoppy flashed his message to port and starboard. Yawing unsteadily, the three Mosquitoes banked away before resuming their flight path.

Rime ice had first been noticed on the initial leg of the mission to Sumburgh, a glazing on the upper wing surfaces that if allowed to grow would eventually destroy the shape and lift of the airfoils. On landing Moore had been characteristically decisive. Every available man, including his own aircrews, was mobilized to rub the leading edges with glycol.

Along with two mechanics, Moore and Hopkinson had been working on A-Apple when Davies had appeared on the tarmac below. Illuminated by storm lanterns, the Air Commodore's small frame seemed diminished by the bulky clothes he was wearing.

"What do you think, Moore? Is it going to get worse?"

A large rag in one hand and a tin of glycol on the wing alongside him, Moore glanced down. "It depends how lucky we are, sir. I think we got this flying through that cloud near Lossiemouth."

Davies' anxiety had shown in his terseness. "Hurry it up, won't you? We must get out there before the Lancs make tracks for home."

The task had wasted fifteen precious minutes but with the future weather unpredictable, Moore had felt it essential. When all the crews reported their aircraft clear of ice, he had taxied back over the fog-shrouded field and swung A-Apple on to the flarepath. With their navigation lights glowing like eyes, the rest of the squadron had drawn up in position behind him. When Control gave permission for take-off, Moore had given a last word to his crews. "Don't forget that hill ahead. And if you get any more icing, keep well apart."

Heavy with its load of stores and ammunition, A-Apple had clung to the runway longer than usual and sheets of icy water had hissed against her spinning propellers. Her undercarriage had grunted and grunted again before she had finally broken free and banked triumphantly eastwards.

One by one the other aircraft followed him. Smith, flying Zero 4, had received a fright when his starboard engine had let out a high-pitched scream on starting. Realizing his starter motor had jammed on engagement but hating the idea of being left behind, he had taxied round the airfield with the others in the hope the cogs would disengage before the engine seized up. Taking off on virtually one engine, he had climbed to 1,000 feet before the engine note had dropped back to normal. With the cogs chewed off his starter motor, his engine was free again. How he would be able to start the engine in Norway was a problem Smith pushed to the back of his mind.

In an attempt to avoid further icing Moore had led the squadron out at 3,000 feet and for twenty minutes the ploy had been successful. Then a squall of hailstones had struck from nowhere, smothering the windshields and rattling bulletlike against nose cones and engine nacelles. It had lasted no more than two minutes but aware all the crews would have visibility problems, Moore had given a lead by switching on his own navigation lights.

Short although the squall was, it had brought a chill of apprehension to Davies. Along with Henderson and six of the ground staff, he was a passenger in one of the B.25s that were flying line abreast between the second and third echelons of Mosquitoes. With accommodation at a premium due to the bomb bay being filled with light but bulky essentials such as sleeping bags, tents and heaters, the men were scattered all over the Mitchell. Two were lying in the bomb bay crawlway, three were squashed into the rear of the fuselage where the camera was normally housed, and a sixth unfortunate was lying beneath the pilot in the bombaimer's crawlway.

With the Mitchell carrying no mid-upper or ventral gunner, makeshift seats had been provided for Davies and Henderson just aft of the main spar. With their backs to the engines, they faced the three technicians wedged in the empty camera compartment. Bitterly cold in spite of their protective clothing, illuminated by the ghostly light of a faint blue bulb, the men were sprawled out in the resigned posture servicemen assume when there is nothing they can do to influence their fate. Every now and then

159

their aggrieved eyes would stray to the equally frozen officers, silently condemning them for this violation of the ground staff's union.

Excited beyond measure at being back in action again, Davies had been as restless as a terrier with fleas during the flight from Sutton Craddock to Sumburgh. After Sumburgh the cold and the background drone of the engines had seemed to subdue him and the relieved Henderson had been able to close his eyes. The respite, however, had been short lived. With his batteries recharged, Davies had found new grounds for nervousness in the hail that rattled against the B.25's metal skin. Complaining about the lack of intercom facilities, he had climbed into the mid-upper turret to take a look outside, then squeezed past the mechanics in the crawlway to talk to the pilot. On his return he looked anxious. "That damned hail's started to ice us up again, Jock. I hope to Christ we don't run into any more."

Not for the first time Henderson wondered how a man who could plan an operation as thoroughly as Davies could turn so fretful once that operation was under way. Practical as always, the Scot left his seat and had a word with Corporal Chapman, one of the squadron's radio mechanics. In turn Chapman prodded a marble-faced young ACI who unrolled a blanket and pulled out three large thermos flasks. Half a minute later Davies was being wooed by Henderson's reassurances and a steaming mug of coffee.

"It's probably coming from that front that's moving eastwards, sir. From all we've heard the high pressure's still holding over Norway."

Davies was not so easily comforted. "It's not just our landing tonight, Jock. We have to get off that lake and we don't know how long it's going to be before the green light comes. We'll need to be bloody lucky if this front holds off that long."

Henderson sighed. "On the other hand we could be on our way in twenty-four hours or so. Surely all we can do is hope for the best."

Conscious the Scot had effectively sabotaged the weather as a source of concern the resentful Davies turned his attention elsewhere. "I hope these B.25 pilots are up to the job. We'll be in a hell of a mess if we lose our ground crews."

Expecting to see three horrified faces staring at them,

160

Henderson made frantic signals for Davies to keep quiet, only to realize the sound of the engines deadened their voices. "What's the matter?" Davies grunted. "You think they'll all run away or something?"

Attempting to grin, Henderson wished to God he would settle down. "It's a pretty scary experience for them, sir. We don't want to alarm them any further."

Davies scowled down the dimly lit fuselage. "It's not every day ground crews get a chance to be in on the action. They ought to be damned grateful."

The Scot was trying to imagine the likes of McTyre feeling grateful for their present plight. "Let's hope they see it that way, sir."

The Mitchell pilots to whom Davies referred belonged to an RAF squadron used for mine-laying in the Baltic. As soon as the Air Commodore had realized he might need larger aircraft, he had requested that three of its crews received the same training as 633 Squadron. Given no hint of what lay behind the order, the crews had received their first intimation in a special interview with Davies soon after their landing at Sutton Craddock. Believing until then that their training could only have something to do with landing the agents in Occupied Europe, the crews' feelings can be imagined.

With the shadow of the past heavy over them, the crews of 633 Squadron could not be said to be relishing their mission either. Veterans like Harvey and Young, the only pilots to have returned from the Swartfjord, were showing unusual touchiness, and even Millburn and Gabby were not indulging in their customary banter. Having done one landing on the lake already, the weary couple were only too aware of the death trap it could become if their parked aircraft were sighted by the enemy.

The remainder of the squadron were suffering according to their experience and temperaments. Nearly all were apprehensive but experienced crews led by pilots such as Machin, Smith, Larkin, Monahan, Roberts, and Van Breedenkamp had all learned to harness their fear so that it sharpened their senses and quickened their reflexes. Even the frail Allison, Matthews' navigator, who never faced a raid without worrying what would happen to his invalid mother if he were killed, had learned not to let fear impair his efficiency.

Less fortunate men came in two types: the rare ones who never felt fear and the ones who had not yet

161

conquered it. Probably only the burly Matthews, the would-be danceband drummer, belonged to the first group. Matthews did not think himself immortal because that very thought entails some degree of death awareness. Matthews *felt* his immortality and so was in danger because fear is an essential element of survival.

The second type of man was represented by Hugh Prentice, a young pilot who had been posted to the squadron six weeks ago along with a second pilot, Collins, and two navigators. After giving the four men intensive training, Moore had put them into his operational reserve where crews were blooded on simple missions before facing the rigours of day to day combat. In the meantime, however, he had lost two aircraft in a raid on Rotterdam and when Davies had arrived and demanded full squadron strength for Norway he had been forced against his will to include both reserve crews in the operation.

His concern was less for Collins and his navigator than for Prentice. Prentice was a thin, intense man who appeared to live on his nerves. It was not a temperament that necessarily ruled him out as a successful combat pilot: with the right guidance Moore knew that such men could often drive themselves harder and longer than their more phlegmatic comrades. His concern was that neither he nor his flight commanders had had the time to give that kind of guidance.

Had Moore known it, his concern was well justified. Flying in S-Sammy in the last echelon, Prentice was drawing uneasy glances from his navigator, Lawry. A man with thin black hair plastered on top of a somewhat bony head, Prentice had twice been physically sick in the interval between briefing and take off. With crews intensely loyal to one another, Lawry had managed to help him through the last take-off rites without anyone noticing his state of nerves. When all had gone well as far as Sumburgh, Lawry had started to believe the worst was over and that the demands of the operation were destroying the tension they had created. Then had come the take-off in which Prentice had first almost run his heavily loaded Mosquito off the flarepath and then narrowly missed the hill ahead. From then on he had hardly replied to his navigator's instructions and in the subdued blue light of the instrument panel his bony face had an unhealthy sheen and pallor.

Ahead in A-Apple Hoppy was tapping Moore's shoulder

and pointing at 10 o'clock. Although the sky above was turning luminous as the clouds thinned Moore could see nothing ahead but a solid black horizon. Yet with Hoppy's keen eyesight a legend in the squadron, he knew something was there and moved his eyes a few degrees away, an old trick of night flyers to draw on the less blunted areas of the retina. Immediately he saw the faintest of luminous wands waving in the darkness. They vanished the instant he glanced back. Hoppy's voice held a note of relief.

"It looks as if the Lancs are still around, skipper."

Moore nodded. "They'd better be. How's our ETA now?"

"We're at least thirty minutes adrift. It's these bloody headwinds we're getting."

The headwinds to which the Cockney referred had proved stronger than the Met. report had suggested and had extended the delay experienced at Sumburgh. In normal circumstances Moore would have called for an increase in speed because although the conservation of fuel was an important factor, it was far more important that the squadron touched down before the patrolling Lancasters switched off their Mandrel jammers and went home.

Yet it was the one thing Moore could not do. Although an excellent medium bomber, the heavier Mitchell was unable to match the speed of the remarkable Mosquito. And with only one aircraft needing to be picked up by enemy detectors for suspicion to be aroused and investigating patrols sent out, there was no point in letting them find their own way to the lake. Nor, with radio silence strictly enforced, could Moore ask the Lancasters to give them extra time.

"We'll just have to hope we get there within the safety margin, Hoppy. Or that the Lancs play it safe and give us an extra fifteen minutes. They must have noticed the headwinds too."

The coastal searchlights could now be seen with direct vision. They had shifted and were almost directly ahead as the distant Lancasters patrolled the southern sector of the coast.

"What's your new ETA for the coast, Hoppy?"

"About nine minutes, skipper."

"Then we'd better start thinking about those mountains. Warn the boys, will you?"

As Hoppy's message flickered out, A-Apple went into a shallow climb. As Moore had hoped, the rime ice had

163

shredded from his wings at the lower altitude and by this time, if the Met. people were right, the squadron should be well past the moist front that was creeping eastwards. When A-Apple reached 8,000 feet without further problems and the moon broke out from the luminous sky, Moore decided the forecast was right. "We're high enough now to clear all the coastal mountains, aren't we, Hoppy?"

The high mountains that ran along Norway's western coast were often too steep to hold snow and so were invisible to aircraft at night. Hoppy, although in hospital during the Swartfjord raid, had flown in all the missions preceding it. Only too aware therefore of the murderous trap the mountains could be, he was squinting intently through the windshield. "We ought to be, skipper. Although you can't fly over 'em too high for me."

A cluster of searchlights had suddenly appeared at 2 o'clock as the patrolling Lancasters passed close to a naval base and tiny sparks began bursting in the sky. As both men's eyes moved to them there was a brighter flash, then a red fireball that sank down and vanished. Hoppy gave a curse.

"Why the hell are they flying so near the coast, skipper?"

Moore's voice had a flat sound. "I suppose they're trying to give us as deep a penetration with their jammers as possible. Keep us away from their searchlights. They must have a heavy flak concentration there."

A few seconds later the searchlights blinked out as the Lancasters droned out of range. Immediately the horizon seemed to rise in a solid black wall. "See anything?" Moore asked.

Conscious of how the headwind might have drifted him off track, the worried Hopkinson shook his head. "Try two degrees to port, skipper."

A-Apple yawed, then steadied again. Behind it, the lifting black shadows followed suit. The moonlight was bright now and frosting the sea. As the sky cleared from horizon to horizon, Hoppy voiced his satisfaction. "At least we shouldn't have any problems landing on the lake, skipper. Providing we find it," he added as Moore gave him a wry glance.

To both men's relief the fjord appeared at eleven o'clock half a minute later, a scimitar of moonlit water biting deeply into the black land mass. As Moore headed for it, a cluster of searchlights leapt into the sky again and be-

164

gan fanning out. Turning a couple of degrees to starboard, Moore headed for the long mountain range that ran along the fjord's southern flank. As its brutal peaks began sweeping past, Lacy, Harvey's navigator, turned to the Yorkshireman with a grimace. "It looks even colder than last year. So let's keep out of trouble this time."

Harvey gave his dour grin. "What's the matter? Don't you like winter holidays?"

The long mountain range was a monochrome of glaciers, black rocks, and drifts of snow. To port, frosted glimpses of the fjord could be seen. The Mosquitoes, rising and falling gently as if lighter than air, had their wings and propellers edged in silver. A complex man with an imagination on a par with Adams', Moore was thinking how at any other time the sight would have held the senses with its beauty.

Halfway along the fjord another battery of searchlights leapt up. Although the enemy's long-range detectors were jammed, the sound of the Mosquitoes' engines had alerted their crews. Hoppy nodded at the waving beams. "With their detectors on the blink, they'll all be as jumpy as hell tonight."

Moore knew that a red alert would have sounded throughout the entire German defence system but with the enormous area the enemy needed to explore, his efforts would almost certainly be concentrated around the industrial areas and military bases. The distant flicker of searchlights that kept springing up in all directions suggested this was already happening. "We should be all right inland, Hoppy. It's a desolate area and they won't expect anything as daft as a night landing on a lake."

With the coastal defence well behind, Moore brought the squadron down to 5,000 feet. Below, a tributary of the fjord could be seen running northwards. As Moore ignored it and followed the main fjord deeper inland, Hoppy leaned forward. "There's a light, skipper. Dead ahead."

Once again Moore had to gaze off centre before he picked up the pinpoint of light. It was high up on a mountainside beyond a southern tributary of the fjord. As Moore swept over the frosted water Hoppy triggered his Aldis lamp. When the light flickered back the code word the Cockney nodded his satisfaction. "That's it, skipper. Valkyrie."

Waiting until the light was beneath him, Moore turned five degrees to starboard. Four minutes later the mountains and steep valleys below began giving way to a plateau of hills and lakes. Sharing his attention between navigation instruments and the ground, Hoppy gave another grunt of satisfaction as he jabbed a finger forward. "There's our second marker, skipper."

The light ahead flickered back the code word to Hoppy's enquiring Aldis. "How long now?" Moore asked.

"Less than two minutes, skipper."

The coastal searchlights had long disappeared and apart from a few faint beams probing the sky to the north, the signalling light was the only sign of life below. At the same time all the crews were painfully aware of German thoroughness and Hoppy's comment was a fair reflection of their feelings. "Let's hope those Norwegians know what they're doing, skipper. Because if there's a Jerry outpost within fifteen miles of the lake they're going to hear our engines even if the hills hide our lights."

The lake was sighted a minute later, instantly recognizable because of its shape. On Millburn's advice the partisans had extended the runway another two hundred yards while keeping to their stratagem of following the contours of the shoreline. While a distinct aid to camouflage it had the less desirable effect of making the lake look smaller than it was. Although all the crews knew the ice did extend beyond the runway no one was certain how far or what effect deep snow would have on an overshooting aircraft. In D-Danny Lacy was expressing his disquiet.

"You think we're going to get into there, Frank? It looks a tight squeeze to me."

Although Harvey was always ready to express criticism before an operation if he felt it justified, he was the last man to spread alarm once that operation was under way. "The Yank did it yesterday, didn't he? And they're supposed to have lengthened it since."

"But that was in daylight."

Harvey cocked an eye to the northwest where a bank of cloud had appeared out of nowhere. "So what? If the moon stays out we should be O.K."

The twin lakes were now sliding beneath Moore's port engine. Waggling his wings, he put A-Apple's nose down. To ensure Adams did not betray himself to any patrolling night fighters, it had been decided he should give no signal until Moore identified the squadron. Levelling off a thousand feet above the snowy hilltops Moore swept down the lake while Hoppy signalled with his Aldis. As A-Apple banked southward a light began flickering from the eastern shoreline. Twisting his neck, Hoppy read the message. "It's Adams all right, skipper. He says the wind's almost due east."

Relieved his men would be spared the more dangerous approach over the eastern hills, Moore led the squadron in a low orbit while the storm lanterns were lit. From the speed of the operation it was obvious Adams had a number of partisans working for him. Unnoticed before, a thin mist could be seen clinging to the surface of the lake and diffusing the lights. Although the runway they formed was fifty yards wide and ran from one lake to the other, the overpowering hills on either side made it look inadequate for its purpose. About to make the comment, Hoppy changed his mind as Adams flashed up another message. "He says he's ready when you are, skipper."

For a moment the moonlit cradle of hills revolved more steeply beneath A-Apple as she swept westward. When she turned and levelled off again the lakes were dead ahead with the forbidding cliff of the isthmus rising into the moonlit sky. A-Apple rocked slightly and her airspeed fell as Moore lowered her wheels and flaps. As the ice-bound hills on either side began to close in like the jaws of a trap, Hopkinson could not hold back a shudder.

## 23

Feeling the cold sinking into his feet Adams stamped them up and down, packing the snow under them into a shallow plinth of ice. Far away he heard a sound like an express train as a small avalanche cascaded down a hillside. As its reverberations died away the immense silence came back. Listening to it, Adams felt it would overwhelm him if the Mosquitoes did not come soon.

He was standing thirty yards beyond the improvised runway and about the same distance from the eastern shore of the lake. Although the moonlight was bright he had to strain his eyes to see his nearest assistant. With still some mines to sow and the need to increase patrols now that the aircraft were due, Lindstrom had been able to spare him only six men to attend to the storm lanterns. Augmented by Helga, these men were spread out the entire length of the runway and with Adams needing to position himself as its far end in case an aircraft overshot, he felt as isolated and vulnerable as a fly on a white tablecloth.

The squadron's late appearance was doing nothing to improve his state of mind. Cursed with an imagination that could work miracles in such a situation, Adams' private list of disasters ranged from an emergency directive from Churchill to abort the mission to the entire squadron being caught by night fighters and annihilated.

His pessimism could not be blamed entirely on his temperament because since Helga had awoken him, Adams had been working like a galley slave of ancient Egypt. After completing the sorting out of the aircraft stores—a back-breaking job in itself—he had felt obliged to go out on the lake and help the partisans lengthen the runway. Then, acutely aware how the change in climate and altitude could affect newcomers—he had been vomiting on and off throughout the day and developed a painful throat—he had thought it prudent to check on the quarters Jensen had set aside for the squadron.

It had proved a wise decision because the tough partisans were so hardened by their privations that any hut, however damp and draughty, was warmth and shelter to them. Afraid that if the crews were so exposed some might not be able to fly, Adams had mobilized a small work force and had been kept busy until midnight stemming draughts and sharing out paraffin heaters that the Americans had thoughtfully included in the air-drop.

With no time to lose he had then rushed his small party out on the lake to mark out the runway. Here he had faced a problem, discovering that a disturbingly high number of storm lanterns had been damaged in the air-drop and could not be kept alight in the wind. Debating whether to thin out the lights the full length of the runway or pack the majority along the first hundred yards, Adams had chosen the latter alternative, arguing that once the aircraft had touched down their landing lights should be sufficient to make up for a scarcity of markers. What would happen if the wind were to swing round was something even the imaginative Adams dared not contemplate.

A gust of wind at his back, slicing through his duffel coat as if it were thin cotton, made him shiver violently. Although Adams was unaware of it, the discomfort was largely of his own making. Desperately tired and yet unable to spare the time for a meal, obsessed that the partisans should not witness his distress, he had secretly laced a cup of coffee Helga had given him with whisky.

The dose had been large and the act of a man ignorant of Arctic conditions with the alcohol opening his body's defences to the cold. Moreover, coming on top of an empty stomach, it had made him feel unreal and light-headed. As he stamped his feet again, a sudden scream of agony echoed among the hills before dying into a sob of despair. It was only an animal caught by a fox or weasel, Adams told himself, and yet found his body stiff with fear. In the bright moonlight, in the icy wind that seemed to be draining the life force from him, Adams had the sudden fantasy he had been transported to the farthermost reaches of space where the sun was only a forgotten star.

Fumbling with his gloves he managed a glance at his watch. God, they were late! He glanced up at the sky. For the last hour, moving against the ground wind, a bank of cloud to the northwest had been slowly but perceptibly nearing the full moon. With his imagination only too ready to provide a new list of calamities should the moon become obscured, Adams turned his mind back to his physical discomforts as the lesser of two evils.

The distant drone sounded for only a couple of seconds before the wind blew it away. Heart leaping in relief,

Adams listened and heard it again. About to reach down for his Aldis lamp, he remembered his orders. With the enemy aware something big was afoot, the engine might belong to a marauding night fighter.

The drone grew louder and began to fill the night sky. As one aircraft crossed the moon Adams recognized the silhouette of a Mosquito and his tight muscles slackened. Pulling off his right glove, he reached down for the Aldis, only to discover it was frozen to the ice. Panicking for a moment, he tugged hard and the lamp broke free. Above, the first aircraft was signalling as it flew down the lake. Sighting the Aldis on it, Adams began clicking the trigger.

Lights began to appear almost immediately as the partisans took their cue and ran from lantern to lantern. Through the neck of the lake navigation lights appeared as Moore prepared to make his descent. With the thunder of engines now tearing the silence to shreds, Adams' mouth was dry. Was it possible that no enemy would hear the din or see the lights? To Adams, born and bred in an over-crowded island, nothing seemed more far-fetched or unlikely.

All the lanterns now appeared to be lit. With wide gaps between the lights at Adam's end of the runway but with them more closely packed inside the neck of the lake and beyond, the effect was to make the landing strip look longer than it was. What Adams did not realize was that to crews coming in from the west the effect was the exact opposite.

Not daring to waste a second now that the runway was lit, Adams signalled Moore to land. As the squadron commander obeyed, Adams discovered to his relief that he could see A-Apple quite clearly in spite of its distance away. The moonlight was silvering its wings and its navigation lights stood out well against the sky and hills. Ideally he would have preferred Moore to have made his touchdown nearer to him so that he could judge the Mosquito's rate of descent better but he realized it was Moore's intention to touch down as near as possible to the western end of the runway so that the rest of his pilots would know the length of their safety margin.

In the event Adams' assistance proved unnecessary. With the moonlight reflecting brightly from the ice, the experienced Moore was able to dispense both with his spotlights and the advice of the flickering Aldis. Touching

170

down barely fifty yards inside the runway, he was beginning to apply his brakes before the Mosquito had entered the eastern lake. The moment she lost momentum Moore swung her round through a gap in the lanterns, ran back along the shore of the lake and disappeared into the river mouth. Satisfied the runway was clear, Adams signalled down the second Mosquito. Piloted by Harvey it made an equally sound landing, turned, and also disappeared down the neck of the lake.

Realizing his role was almost superfluous, Adams nevertheless went through the motions as one after the other of A flight came in and were guided by Moore to their dispersal points down the river. Inside the Mosquitoes relieved pilots and navigators were joking with one another as they removed their helmets and harness straps. Geared to expect all kinds of problems, some of them were already minimizing the dangers of the entire expedition.

Adams' relief was tempered by the knowledge the heavier Mitchells still had to land and their performance on ice was an unknown factor. Unable to procure special tires for them, Dunlop had come up with an ingenious compromise by dipping their tires in a powerful adhesive saturated with grit. Although the depth of this additional tread was limited by the size of the nacelles into which the wheels retracted, it was felt enough was deposited to allow at least one landing on ice. Optimists also felt the B.25's tricycle undercarriage would be of help in stabilizing her landing run.

With all these factors hypothetical, Adams' concern was compounded by the bank of cloud which was now so close to the moon its edges were turning milk-white. Signalling for haste, he guided the first Mitchell down with extra care. Its steady approach, however, told him its pilot was fully practised and although its tires shed grit that rattled against its underbelly like bullets and its weight carried it considerably further down the flarepath than the Mosquitoes, there was nothing in its landing to give Adams more than a quickened pulse.

The remaining two Mitchells landed as efficiently. By this time Adams had forgotten all about the enemy and was fully occupied in getting the remaining eight Mosquitoes down before the moonlight failed. Signalling yet again for haste, he brought five more aircraft in without trouble and was guiding down the sixth when the ice mirror suddenly glazed. Glancing up, he saw the first tendrils of cloud were creeping across the moon. Heart in his mouth, Adams was about to signal for spotlights when the moonlight returned and the Mosquito settled down safely.

The noise of the penultimate aircraft circling to land and Adams' concentration made him unaware he had company until a breathless voice made him start. "They're going to need their spotlights this time, Adams."

Turning in surprise, Adams saw Davies standing at his elbow. Although winded by the cold and his scamper down the lake, the small Air Commodore looked as if he were enjoying himself. "It's gone damn well so far, Adams. Keep it up."

As the moon suddenly slid behind the cloud and the basin of hills turned steely-grey, Adams hoped the congratulations were not premature. Visible now only by its wingtip lights, the Mosquito had completed its orbit and was starting its landing approach. It was flown by Collins and Stuart, the first of the reserve crews, and without the aid of the moonlight they could not pick out the landing strip between the rows of lanterns. As Adams tried to help, Collins switched on his spotlights. Too high as yet to illuminate the ice, they outshone the Mosquito's navigation lights and made it more difficult for Adams to monitor the aircraft's descent. Believing it was too steep, Adams gambled all and made the signal. It was a timely guess because although the Mosquito flattened out, the impact of its wheels on the ice sent it bucketing a good six feet in the air before it sank down again. Fighting to keep it from sliding sideways, Collins brought it to a halt less than a hundred feet from the two men and turned it round to join the others inside the river.

"Christ, that was close," Davies muttered. His eyes lifted to the last Mosquito that Adams was signalling down. "Who's in this one? Do you know?"

"I think it's Prentice and Lawry," Adams told him.

Davies glanced up at the hidden moon. "You should have brought the freshers down first."

Adams felt justifiable indignation. "If I had, they'd have taken longer and I might still have an entire flight up there."

Davies took a look at him and changed his tone. "Maybe you're right. Anyway, carry on."

By this time S-Sammy had completed its circuit and had its wheels and flaps down. The sweating Prentice was

172

having the same problem as Collins in identifying the height of the runway. Drawing back on his wheel he tried to pick out the ice with his spotlights. As he swept through the neck of the lake without making contact and headed on towards the eastern shore, Davies gripped Adams' arm. "He won't make it! Tell him to go round again."

Dazzled by the oncoming spotlights, Adams triggered a frantic order. Lawry, gripping the sides of his seat like a patient in a dentist's chair, also recognized the danger. "Get her up, Hugh! Get her up!"

Seeing the flarepath shrinking at terrifying speed, Prentice lost his head and pushed the wheel forward. S-Sammy thumped down, leapt forward, and thumped down again. Seeing the burning eyes of the spotlights heading straight for them, Adams gave a yell and threw himself at Davies. "Look out, sir! Get down."

Hit by Adams' body, Davies gave a grunt of shock as the Intelligence Officer fell on top of him. As the two men rolled over in the snow, the Mosquito came at them like an express train. Blinded by spotlights and buffeted by shock waves, Adams felt certain its spinning propellers would cut them to pieces. Instead its port engine swung left as Prentice, seeing the shore leaping towards him, jammed on his brakes. With a weird squeal of tires, S-Sammy went into a spectacular ground loop, recovered for a couple of seconds, then skidded equally violently in the opposite direction. Snow was hurled up in great clouds as it ploughed on towards the shore. As the half-dazed Adams climbed to his feet, there was a heavy thud, followed by a massive cracking and splintering of wood. Fumbling in his duffel coat pocket, Adams pulled out a torch and began playing it frantically around him.

Up on the shore where S-Sammy had leapt into a clump of snow-covered bushes, a huge cloud of steam was rising. Alarmed shouts could be heard down the lake as both airmen and partisans ran towards the scene of the accident. As Davies turned to follow suit, Adams grabbed his arm. Davies stared at him. "What the hell are you doing? Come on! They need help."

"Fire extinguishers!" Adams panted. "I brought two with me. They must be around here somewhere."

Davies gave a start, then joined in the search. They found the extinguishers at the foot of the shore where they had been hurled by the skidding Mosquito. Grabbing one

173

apiece, the two men threw themselves into the thick bushes. They found the Mosquito upright although its undercarriage had been shorn away and one wing and engine were almost severed. Ignoring the splintered branches that tore at them, they fought their way to the hissing engines and urgently sprayed them. Before it was certain all danger of fire was past, rescuers began arriving and pulled Prentice and Lawry from the cockpit. Although Adams was plying his extinguisher on the far side of the Mosquito, he could see one airman was already on his feet but the second was being lowered to the snow. A minute later Davies came round the aircraft to find Adams, totally exhausted by this time, supporting himself against the severed wing.

"They're both a bit shocked and Lawry got a bump on the head, but I think they'll be all right." Breathless from his own exertions, Davies had not yet noticed Adams' condition. "It could have been a damn sight worse if you hadn't brought those extinguishers with you. That was good thinking, Adams."

With the entire lake spinning round him, Adams wondered whether it was due to exhaustion or Davies' praise. Drawing closer, Davies gave a start. "You hurt yourself?"

Shaking his head, Adams pushed himself away from the wing. "No, sir. I'm all right."

As his legs buckled, Davies grabbed him and let out a yell. "Two of you—Monahan and Evans. Come over here and give Mr. Adams a hand."

## 24

Sitting on the table that had been pushed right up against the far wall, Davies, Henderson and Lindstrom appeared to be the only men in the HQ hut who had room to move and breathe freely. The rest, which included aircrew officers, ground staff NCOs and the bearded figure of Jensen, were jammed together tighter than sardines in a tin. Adams was also present, half-hidden behind the tall figure of Harvey. Because of his exertions the previous day Davies had excused him, but although crawling from his sleeping bag had felt like a resurrection, Adams had felt it his duty to attend.

Although it was 0900 hours it was still dark outside and a paraffin lamp hanging from a hook on the wall provided the only light. The shadows it cast seemed to accentuate the weariness of men who had managed only a couple of hours rest in cold and alien surroundings. Some of them, affected like Adams by the climatic change, had not slept at all and their drawn faces and pouched eyes were not missed by the observant Davies. With so many tired bodies pressed against the walls, the knife-like draughts that had chilled Adams the previous day were absent. The air stank of wet uniforms, stale sweat, cigarette smoke, and paraffin fumes.

A great believer in the upholding of morale, Davies decided an early joke would make a good preamble. "When I called you lot in here I never expected to see so many dogs' dinners at one sitting." Glancing round the assembly, he picked on the ginger-headed Young. "Take you, Teddy. You're looking worse than after our Christmas party last year. And I'd have said that was impossible."

Although unkempt, unshaven, and more tired than he could remember, the Australian did not let Davies down. "Maybe that's because I hadn't spent the night playing Scott of the Antarctic, sir."

Davies grinned his appreciation. "You know what they say, Teddy. Join the Forces and see the world."

"That must be the only flaming time they've ever told the truth, sir."

Only a few men managed a laugh. After S-Sammy's crash, they had barely got their aricraft parked in the river mouth before Davies had mobilized every man for fatigue duties. Those duties had ranged from covering the aircraft and surrounding trees with camouflage nets—no small task in itself—to dragging the wrecked S-Sammy to a less conspicuous resting place.

Davies' first hope had been that a couple of camouflage nets thrown over the wreck would suffice to hide it but on consulting Adams' partisans he had been advised this was too dangerous. With no intention that the operation should fail for lack of thoroughness, Davies had immediately announced the wreck had to be dragged across the lake into the trees. With nearly all the partisans still out sowing mines or patrolling the approaches to the lake, this had thrown the entire burden on his own men.

At first it had been thought that if enough men manhandled the Mosquito she would slide down to the ice where hopefully she would be more manageable. What no one had realized was that splintered branches from the bushes and dwarf birch had transfixed her wings and fuselage, pinning her down more securely than a butterfly to a board.

Davies had called for saws but all the partisans could provide were axes which proved clumsy tools when in the darkness men tried to sever branches beneath the Mosquito's fuselage. After an hour had passed and S-Sammy still obstinately refused to budge, Davies had suggested smashing open her fuselage to reach the branches. With S-Sammy now hated by one and all, men had swung axes on her with relish but still she remained welded to the undergrowth. With daylight only a few hours away the situation had become critical and Davies had jumped at Moore's suggestion that a second Mosquito be used as a towing vehicle. Rope now became a problem but fortunately one of the woodsmen's huts contained a full coil and this was rushed out to Davies. In the meantime Moore had started up one of the Mosquitoes and taxied her to the end of the runway. After he had swung her round, the rope had been attached to her strong points and the other end to S-Sammy's fin. As men lined themselves around S-Sammy and prepared to shove, Moore had opened both throttles.

During all this frenzied and exhausting work, Adams, on Davies' orders, had been sharing a hut with the two shaken airmen, Prentice and Lawry, and in the frosty silence the ring of metal, the thud of axes, and even the lurid curses had carried to him quite clearly. To Adams, doubtless because this time he was unoccupied, the din seemed worse than during the squadron's arrival, and when Moore had unleashed the towing Mosquito's engines, he had sat up aghast. In his fevered condition there seemed no doubt that the Germans were hearing the uproar as far away as Oslo.

The device had worked but had taken time. S-Sammy had moved a few feet towards the lake, then stuck again. Realizing a path had to be cleared for her, Davies had cursing men working in relays chopping at the tough bushes. Even when the Mosquito had slid reluctantly back on the ice, it had taken another half-hour to push and drag her beneath the trees on the southern bank and to cover her with camouflage. Nor was that the end for the partisans had then pointed out that the crushed area of bush where S-Sammy had rested might be as revealing to aerial reconnaissance as the wreck itself. As a result all the airmen had been sent back to shovel in and smooth out the snow. When Davies was satisfied at last, men had reeled off to their huts like as many zombies. After persuasion by Henderson, Davies had retired with them but only after extracting a promise from Helga that he would be awakened the moment Lindstrom returned.

The young major had entered Davies' hut at 0830 hours and after a fifteen-minute talk with him, Davies had convened the present meeting. Aching in every joint from their labours and the bitter cold, cursing men had crawled from their sleeping bags and stumbled towards the HQ hut. Inside it they had found Davies perched up on the table and looking almost jaunty. It was not entirely an act because Davies had recently received news from Lindstrom that had greatly encouraged him. On the other side of the coin, the clouds that had almost killed Prentice and Lawry had thickened throughout the night and were now down to the mountain tops. There had also been a slight fall of snow. Knowing snow storms could last for a week or longer in this part of the world Davies could not help wondering if he had brought his squadron into a death trap. His tone, however, matched his appearance.

"Sorry to have got you out again so soon, gentlemen, but while you've been sleeping we've had good news." Davies' eyes moved to Moore as he continued: "Major Lindstrom's radio operator has picked up a report that the stocks we're after moved out early this morning. If our experts are right, this means they should reach the

177

cruiser around 0700 hours the day after tomorrow. We're delighted for two reasons. One, it looks as if our journey isn't going to be in vain, and two, although we brought plenty of parachute flares with us, it suggests the cruiser intends to sail in daylight and that's going to make the job a lot easier for us."

Davies was taking in Moore's appearance as the squadron commander nodded his agreement. Although his uniform was as toil-stained as everyone else's, he was the only clean-shaven man in the hut. Making a mental note to ask how he had managed it, Davies turned to the rest of the assembly.

"This isn't the only good news. As you all know, Major Lindstrom and his men have been out all night keeping watch on the roads and passes that lead to this lake and they report no sign of the enemy. So it seems pretty certain our arrival has gone undetected." With Davies' face still chilled from exposure, his grin was somewhat lop-sided. "Which to some of you, after all the din we made last night, must seem something of a miracle."

Where fatigue allowed it, men showed relief. A firm believer in twisting the tail of fate whenever possible, Davies rounded off his sanguine preamble by commandeering the weather as an ally. "That fall of snow is a bit of luck too. It'll help to hide the mess we made last night and it'll also cover our camouflage nets."

Squashed in behind Harvey and Young, Adams heard the Yorkshireman's cynical comment. "I notice he doesn't say it might also foul up the runway."

Davies glanced at Harvey for a second but if he guessed the text of the comment he ignored it. "All right, that brings us to our duties. I'm letting you rest until noon but after that some of us will have to share sentry duties with Major Lindstrom's men. They've been working like Trojans for the last few days and as we shan't be in action for forty-eight hours I want us to share their work-load. As most of us can't ski, we shall only go to observation posts where skis aren't necessary. Naturally we'll need guides, so the idea is we go out in pairs, one Norwegian and one of us. It'll be damned cold so we'll wear all the underclothing we can and for camouflage we'll cover our uniforms with ski smocks. Naturally we'll carry Stens: in fact from now on we'll go nowhere without them because there's always the chance Jerry might stumble across us. In case that happens we must know what to do,

178

so I'm now passing you over to Major Lindstrom who'll give us the drill."

There was a hush as all eyes turned on the young major whose uniform was stained and drenched from his night in the hills. In some way the Norwegian's recently acquired stubble of beard added to his aesthetic appearance. The last few days of killing work had also taken its toll of him, his cheeks were more gaunt and his eyes deeper-set. Yet in the way a fire burns hotter as it contracts, his nervous energy reached out and dominated his audience.

"Good morning, gentlemen, and welcome to Norway. We're sorry we can't make you more comfortable but you can take my word for it that we're more than glad to have your help."

"And your whisky." The quip came from the bearded Jensen who grinned and winked at Millburn. Giving him a disapproving look, Lindstrom turned back to the silent airmen.

"I know you are all tired as we are, so I'll make this briefing as short as possible. I understand you've all been shown photographs of the area so you'll know its main strategic features. These are the two roads, the main one that runs north and south four kilometres east of the lake and the minor one that branches from it and runs west behind the hill ridge where we're camped at the moment. This secondary road crosses the river on which your aircraft are parked."

Lost in their alien environment, even the weariest of his audience were now paying attention to the young Norwegian. "In other words these two roads form a right angle south and east of us. In English terms I doubt if you could classify either of them as anything more than a country lane. They are used very little at this time of the year although they are occasionally swept of snow. Nevertheless they can carry military transports and also light armour, and if the enemy were to discover us, this is the way his mechanized forces would have to come.

"So they are the major targets for our surveillance. We can reach the north-south road by crossing or skirting the lake and then taking a pass thorough the eastern hill range. From there we can reconnoitre as far as we think necessary in either direction. As for the east-west road, we reach that by advancing upstream for three kilometres and then taking to the woods or higher ground. We must do this because otherwise the enemy might spot our footprints or ski tracks if he is carrying out a routine patrol. Civilians do not venture in these parts nowadays for fear of being taken for freedom fighters, so any tracks are an immediate giveaway. Needless to say, the routes we take to reach these roads are the same routes the enemy would use if he were to attack this camp."

A nervous cough sounded as Lindstrom continued. "Unfortunately we can't just watch the roads and leave it there. The enemy also uses ski troops and they are as independent of roads as we are. So we must also send patrols out into the hills, but as skis are essential here we shall use only our own men for this work. This might mean that later on we shall have to pair a few of you together but this is something Captain Jensen will sort out."

The grizzled Powell, one of the technical NCOs present, put up a gloved hand. "What happens if we run into any Germans, sir? Do we open fire?"

"This is a decision you would leave to the Norwegian paired with you. If you were on your own, you would use common sense. If it is obvious the enemy is only on a routine patrol, it is imperative you keep out of sight and on no account open fire. But if you are seen or it is obvious the enemy are suspicious about the lake, then you would have to open fire. In that case you would make certain no one escaped."

Towering over the assembly like a sixteenth-century buccaneer, the bearded Jensen added his own comment. "Surprise 'em and kill 'em with knives if you can. Then other patrols won't hear the gunfire." Lifting a hand he drew it across his hairy throat. "Across here, so the bastards can't yell out."

There was a dismayed murmur from the back of the hut. "Cut their throats?"

Jensen's white teeth showed in a bloodthirsty grin. "What's the matter, Englishman? Don't you like to see German blood when you kill?"

Moore was one of the airmen present who had to concede the giant's irony. In the harsh term of numbers, every flier present had probably killed a hundred more of the enemy than his Norwegian counterpart. Yet because theirs was a technical war and fought at long range only a few had seen the direct result of their actions. The ground staff, among whom Adams was a dismayed member, had in most cases never seen their enemy, much less killed any, and their concern showed on every face. Feeling Jensen's suggestion unnecessarily brutal, Davies gave him a sharp look before intervening.

"With any luck at all it won't happen, so stop worrying about it. My bet is the first Jerries to know about us will be the crew of that cruiser when we sink her. And even then they won't know where we've come from."

Following Davies' glance with a frown of his own, Lindstrom nodded. "I agree. But as we must be ready for any contingency, however remote, I want to run quickly through our battle plan if we are detected. If the enemy brings up any artillery or armour, we shall naturally first try to hold him on the main road. But if he outflanks us, and if he has ski troops with him he probably will, then we shall fall back along the secondary road. As it runs through a steep valley between two hill ranges we believe we could put up a stiff resistance there."

"If you withdrew from the main road, couldn't they continue along it and then attack across the lake?" Henderson asked.

"No, we don't think so. The snow is very deep on the far side of the hill range and we don't believe they could get armour through. And if they only used infantry, they would be too exposed on the lake."

"Then why couldn't they come over this hill and straight down into the camp? The trees would give them cover all the way."

Lindstrom explained the role of the mines. "As we haven't enough men to cover the hillside, they were our only way of sealing it off. Of course the Germans would soon rush up engineers but we feel confident they couldn't clear the mines before you had time to escape."

With Henderson showing respect for the planning that had gone into the defences, Lindstrom turned back to the assembly. "I want to make an important point here. If we are discovered, none of your squadron is to take part in the fighting." As someone gave a grunt of protest, the young major held up a hand. "No. This isn't sentiment or Norwegian hospitality. You have come here to destroy those stocks and even at the eleventh hour the radio message could be received. In which case every pilot who had got himself killed would mean one less aircraft to carry out the raid. Your job would be to stand by your aircraft until Captain Jensen or myself told you we could hold out no longer."

"What would you do then?" Millburn asked.

"We would retreat across the lake. Once on the other side we would have an excellent chance of escape."

"The lake? They'd cut you down before you were halfway across."

There was a rumbling laugh from Jensen. "You haven't seen Norwegians skate, Yank. We'd be across before you got your undercarts up."

As Millburn grinned and blew a derisory raspberry, Davies broke in impatiently. "We're getting too bogged down with speculations. If anything goes wrong we'll have to play it as it comes." He turned to Powell. "The major is keeping a twenty-four-hour radio watch, Chiefy, so we'll know the precise time the stocks arrive and go on board. This should give you reasonable time to get the kites warmed up. However, as they're going to need extra attention in these conditions, I want you and your fitters to stay down there with them and act as watchdogs during the night. Naturally this means you'll be excused the wider sentry duties. This is going to mean your using tents but with paraffin heaters you shouldn't be any worse off than the rest of us. By the way, if you get short of spares, don't forget you can cannibalize Sammy."

"We've had to do that already, sir. Flying Officer Smith's starter motor broke down coming out of Sumburgh. But we'll have the job done by this afternoon."

As always Davies found Powell's matter-of-fact manner and accent a comfort. "That's the stuff, Chiefy. Keep it up and we'll have this job wrapped up and be back home before anyone's missed us." Davies turned to Henderson, "I think the boys deserve a dram or two before they go to bed, don't you?"

The big Scot, who had worked like a labourer all night, thought Davies was having hallucinations. "At this time of the morning, sir?"

"It's hardly morning, is it?" Davies snapped. "Not seeing we've been prancing up and down Norway for the last eight hours. Where's the stuff we brought in?"

"In our hut, sir. In the chest alongside the door."

Davies turned. "Anyone volunteer to fetch a couple of bottles?"

A dozen hands shot up instantly, with Millburn's,

Young's, and Jensen's prominent among them. With a grunt Davies pushed men back and slid his feet to the floor. "All that hard work must have gone to my head. I'll go and fetch the stuff myself."

Attempting to enter the hut quietly, Davies damned the door for the prolonged squeal it made on closing. To make matters worse the gloom inside hid the low bench from him as he tip-toed towards his sleeping bag. From the clatter it made on the wooden floor Davies knew all further efforts to be considerate were futile. Nursing his shin, he swore loudly and luridly.

Two of the bedded-down men, Moore and Adams, had heard Davies the moment he had laid a hand on the door latch. Moore was by nature a light sleeper and Adams, unused to physical danger and still troubled by his sore throat, was finding sleeping difficult. He owed his presence in the hut to Davies who after the briefing had unexpectedly suggested he join the other three senior officers. The fourth member of the quartet, Henderson, was a heavier sleeper and the crash of the bench and Davies' cursing brought him upright with a start.

"What the hell's going on?"

Davies glared at him resentfully. "I've nearly broken my leg, that's what's going on. Why the hell don't they put windows in these huts?"

Henderson noticed now that the Air Commodore was wearing a ski smock. "Have you been out, sir?"

"Of course I've been out. You don't think I sleep-walk, do you? I've been down to take a look at the aircraft."

Not in the best of humours himself after his rude awakening Henderson nearly asked when he was going to settle down and let everyone get some rest. "Is everything all right?" he asked instead.

Davies scowled. "Chiefy's a bit worried about the temperature problem although it's a few degrees warmer now the clouds have come down. He asked me if he could run up an engine now and then to make sure they're O.K."

"What did you say?"

"I asked Lindstrom. He said if we must, we must, although he's obviously not keen on the idea and we mustn't do it more than necessary. One of his men has just come in with a report from Gol. Apparently Jerry is in a hell of a tizzy over our jamming job. Reserves had been told to stand by and patrols are being sent out."

Henderson showed immediate anxiety for his squadron. "Gol's less than thirty miles away, isn't it?"

"A bit more than that," Davies muttered. "Anyway, there's nothing round here to investigate, is there?"

Adams thought a word of comfort would not come amiss. "Perhaps the break in the weather is a stroke of luck after all. Otherwise they'd be sending out air patrols and the lake would never stand up to close scrutiny."

With only senior officers present, Davies could speak his fears aloud. "That's not much comfort if we can't fly ourselves, is it?" He turned to Moore who was supporting himself on his elbows. "What do you think, Ian? Could you get 'em up in this weather?"

An imaginative man who could be a pragmatist when the occasion demanded it, Moore shrugged. "All we could do is try, sir. At least some of us ought to make it."

Henderson was looking horrified. "It would be suicide. The clouds are halfway down the hillsides."

His own anxiety made Davies testy. "Don't blame me if the risks are higher than usual, Jock. Have a crack at Churchill if you feel that bad about it."

Muttering something that might have been in Gaelic, Henderson sank back and gazed at the roof where frozen moss and earth sealed the cracks. Davies moved his aggrieved face to Moore. "You're not going to like this either, Ian, but because of that leg of yours I've asked Lindstrom to excuse you all duties. I can't afford to have you crippled." As Moore opened his mouth to protest, Davies' voice rose irascibly. "Don't argue, Ian. That's an order."

When Moore sank back and no one else spoke, Davies removed his ski smock and boots and began climbing into his damp sleeping bag. "As for the rest of us here, they didn't want to use us but when I insisted they put us down for tomorrow. I suppose they think old buggers like us need a long rest after last night. You and I, Jock, go out in the morning. We're each paired with one of Jensen's men. Adams is the only lucky one."

Adams gave a start of indignation. "Why should I be left out? I'm as fit to go as anyone else."

"Who said you were left out? I said you were lucky, that's all. You're paired with the girl, Helga, in the late afternoon."

"Helga?"

"That's right. She insists on doing her share, and she chose you."

The vulnerable Adams was trying to find the fly in the ointment. "But why me?"

Davies grinned maliciously. "Maybe she fancies you. Or more likely it's because Lindstrom won't let her go far from the lake and feels you've done enough already. Anyway, you've got her. I don't know why you're complaining: she's a damned good-looking woman." To Henderson's astonishment, Davies let out a yawn. "As nobody wants us today, I'm going to get some shut-eye."

At first the Scot, whose eyes felt as if they were fighting weights to stay open, did not believe him. Then as a faint snore stole across the silent hut, he thanked God for all belated mercies and crumpled into an unconscious heap in his sleeping bag.

## 25

For the hundredth time the strap of Adams' Sten gun slipped off his shoulder. Unable to sling it over his back because of the pack he was carrying and too weary to curse, he heaved it back. He was following Helga through a wood that ran up a steep hill. Neither the man nor the girl were wearing skis. With Adams unable to ski, Helga had decided she was better able to judge what pace to keep if she went without them also. Even so, Adams, not yet recovered from his initial labours, was finding the going hard. Half a dozen yards ahead of him, Helga paused and glanced back. Seeing his distress she continued climbing for another twenty yards, then sighed and leaned her Sten gun against a tree. "I feel like a rest. Shall we have a cigarette?"

Blessing her, Adams struggled to her side. Lighting a cigarette she gazed back down the hill. "We've done well so far. We should be in sight of the road in a few minutes."

Adams, who had noticed her tact in not offering him a cigarette while he was still pumping for air, could only hope she was right. The hill they were climbing ran along the southern shore of the river. For the first mile they had taken the easy route along its level banks. Then they had climbed to the higher ground which would not only hide their footprints but would give them a bird's-eye view of the road. Although it was only mid-afternoon, a wintry mist rising from the river suggested dusk was not far away.

Ahead a hill shoulder hid the road and the steep valley through which it ran. Above, the dwarf trees climbed for another three hundred feet then disappeared into grey cloud. As his breathing steadied, Adams made his cautious suggestion. "Don't you think we've climbed high enough? If we go much further the mist might hide the road."

Agreeing with him, she gave him time to finish a cigarette before moving on. As they were now contouring the hill instead of climbing it, Adams found it easier to keep up with her. Halfway round the hill shoulder they came full into the icy wind again. Large rocks appeared among the trees and as they climbed out of a corrie a twenty-foot wall of rock blocked their way. Wasting no more than a minute surveying it, Helga handed Adams her Sten gun and began to climb. Near the top she paused on a flat rock and motioned him to follow. Adams managed the first few feet without mishap but as he reached up to hand her the Sten, his boots slipped on a patch of ice. Grabbing for a handhold to save his face from injury, he let go of the Sten which fell with a clatter into a deep cleft. Ignoring the pain from his fall, he crawled back and tried to retrieve it but discovered to his dismay it was out of his reach.

Helga, who had given a startled exclamation on seeing the gun fall, now lowered herself to his side. Finding the cleft was too narrow for even her athletic body, she tried to reach the gun's strap with the second Sten but it still remained tantalizingly out of reach. When Adams suggested he go back to find a branch she shook her head. "The others will be wondering what has happened to us. Someone will have to come and pick it up later." As she commenced climbing again, the unhappy Adams noticed she did not offer him his gun back.

They cleared the barrier of rocks without further mishap and five minutes later came in sight of the east-west lane. Covered in ice and virgin snow from the recent fall, it was flanked by another range of craggy hills that rose steeply on its far side. The frozen river passed beneath a narrow bridge and continued south through a ravine that split the range in two. Adams could see no sign of the men they had been sent to relieve but as Helga led him towards a clump of rocks, a shout echoed down. A hundred feet above them two men waved a welcome and began making their way back to camp. Helga caught Adams' arm. "We could get a gun from them."

Adams gazed up dubiously. The hillside was steep at this point and dotted with frozen rocks. "Do you think it's necessary? We're not likely to need firearms, are we?"

Eager to get back to food and warmth, the two men had already disappeared into the woods. Reluctantly Helga drew back. "They must be very tired. Very well: let them go."

To Adams' relief the rocks offered some protection from the wind. "I'm sorry about the gun. It was clumsy of me."

She responded immediately. "These things happen. You mustn't worry about it."

Wishing he could obey, Adams wriggled out of his

pack and opened a groundsheet on the snow. As she sank down on it, he offered her coffee from a thermos. "All the comforts of home," he said.

She sipped at the coffee, then looked up sharply. "You've put whisky into this, haven't you?"

"Yes," he admitted. "I thought it would help keep out the cold."

"No. It's a bad thing in this weather. And we are on duty, you know."

The dismayed Adams felt he was cutting a poor figure of a soldier. "I suppose you're right. Only I didn't put enough in to affect our judgement or anything like that."

Her eyes were crinkling at his expression and to his relief she suddenly burst out laughing. "Don't look so upset, I won't tell anyone. That is if you promise not to tell anyone I'm enjoying it."

Adams sank on the groundsheet beside her. Her face was framed in a white woolen helmet and in her ski smock she looked a picture of athletic womanhood. With the Sten gun still slung across her back, she could hardly have presented a different image to the expensively groomed, elegant, and discontented woman who was Adams' wife and yet on that windswept hill in the heart of enemy-occupied Norway Adams felt again the attraction she had for him. Always one to question his emotions, he began wondering how much a man's predilections depended on his chemistry and how much on the conditions he found himself in.

Although he busied himself pouring his own coffee, he had the feeling the extra-sensory perceptions that exist between man and woman had enabled her to read his thoughts. For his part he could feel her change of mood as she turned and gazed back in the direction of the camp. "They say there is nothing in this world that has no good in it. I suppose that even applies to war."

Unsure of her, Adams could only lift a questioning eyebrow as she turned back to him. Pausing a moment she frowned before continuing: "I think I'm trying to say that war reveals us for what we are. I know that in itself it is the supreme deceit and the supreme blasphemy, but to ordinary people it takes away every opportunity for us to deceive ourselves and to deceive others. We have to decide whether we are going to fight for the things we believe in and after that decision is made all our time is

188

taken up trying to be brave. In a strange way it is a cathartic. Do you know what I mean?"

"Yes, I think so."

"Then you must also know what it does to human relationships. Because it gives us no time for play-acting we can become the friend of a man or woman in a day or even in a minute. Have you noticed that?"

A shy man acutely conscious of the gap in years between them, it is doubtful if Adams would have made his confession in any other time or place. "I noticed it when we talked in the hut. I felt I had known you for years. All my life, in fact."

Afraid he had gone too far Adams checked himself, only to see she was smiling. "I felt the same way, Frank. That is what I wanted you to know."

Hardly knowing what he was doing, Adams removed his spectacles and began cleaning them. An act with undertones of helplessness, it brought a low laugh from the girl. "You looked so vulnerable when you first arrived. Lost and, I think, a little frightened too. But when you talked to me in that hut I realized how different you were to the others. Since then you have worked harder than anyone and all the time you have been finding more and more courage." Before the bewildered Adams knew what was happening she leaned forward and kissed his cheek. "I think you are a very special person, Frank Adams. I want you to know I like you very much."

Clearing his throat, Adams replaced his spectacles. Looking into her smiling face he had no doubts whatever—any danger or suffering was worth this moment. "I'm glad I came, Helga. I know it sounds crazy but I am."

Her hand reached out and pressed his arm. "So am I, Frank. Very glad."

Still bewildered, Adams was searching for the right words when her grip on his arm suddenly tightened. "Keep quiet! And don't move!"

Adams went rigid. "What is it?"

Her frightened eyes were staring over his shoulder. "Down on the road," she breathed. "German soldiers. Lower your head. Very slowly."

With his heart hammering painfully, Adams obeyed and then peered cautiously round the rocks. Half a dozen ski troops wearing camouflaged smocks were advancing along the road towards the bridge. With the rifles slung across their shoulders they were moving without haste and chatting to one another. Their appearance was so innocuous Adams leaned towards the girl. "Are you sure they're Germans?"

"Of course I'm sure."

"Then what should we do?"

"Nothing. We lie here and watch where they go."

Had Adams known it, the six men were part of a Bavarian Regiment stationed in Gol who had been sent out on patrol when the red alert sounded. With false alarms as much a feature of the German Army as the Allied, the men were not taking their uncomfortable duty too seriously. To the fascinated Adams, he could have been watching a squad of British soldiers as their corporal, a brawny, cherry-faced Bavarian, turned and said something that made the entire party roar with laughter. Beside him he heard Helga sigh with relief. "It's all right. It's only a routine patrol."

The road led the men round the back of the hill on which the anxious couple were hiding. When the last one had disappeared, Adams turned to Helga. "How did they get this far? I thought your brother and Jensen had sentries all along this road. And on the main road south of here."

"You're forgetting what Paul told you. If we let them know we're here, they'll comb every yard of the district. As long as they keep away from the lake, they won't be molested."

Adams realized it was the only strategy possible. "Then what do we do now? Wait until they come back?"

Before she could reply there was a sudden low rumble that echoed among the hills. Adams believed it was thunder until he heard Helga's gasp. "Your aircraft! They're warming up one of the engines."

As the rumble continued Adams remembered the permission Powell had been given the previous day. Knowing there had been problems in exchanging S-Sammy's starter motor, he guessed Powell was carrying out a test. "It's not very loud," he muttered, clutching at straws. "Perhaps the hills will screen it from them."

The words had barely left his mouth before the six Germans appeared on the road again. From six carefree young men they had suddenly turned into combat soldiers, crouched down over their skis, rifles weaving from side

190

to side. To Adams the transformation was a shock in itself and his mouth was dry as he watched them.

Motioning a second soldier to aid him, the corporal covered the entrance of the river and waved the other four men inside. Fifty yards along its banks two of them spun round and covered the trees with their rifles to allow the patrol leader to overtake them. Fascinated by this professionalism, Adams watched man after man slip behind a clump of trees and emerge without his skis. When all six men were ready, the corporal waved his arm and crouching low, the party moved down the river again. Making use of all available cover, they disappeared into the mist. As Adams' pale face turned to Helga, she jumped to her feet. "Hurry! We must get down to the road."

Before Adams could ask why, she began her frantic descent. With no other alternative open to him, Adams followed. In their haste both kept losing their foothold on the icy surface and halfway down Adams fell heavily among a cluster of sharp-edged rocks. Ignoring a sickening pain in his right leg, he hobbled after the girl and caught up with her on the road. Panting, she pointed at the bridge. "The other side. We must take cover there."

Making certain no Germans were visible down the river, she waved him across. Twenty yards down the road she scrambled over a bank of ice that the snow ploughs had left and climbed up the steep hillside beyond. Finding shelter behind some rocks she urged Adams to follow. Certain he would have a heart attack at any moment, Adams obeyed and collapsed beside her. He saw she was talking to him but with his lungs sobbing for air it was a full fifteen seconds before he could make sense of her words.

"Your leg. What have you done?"

He saw his right trouser leg was soaked in blood. "It's nothing. . . . I slipped, that's all."

She was already searching for the injury. His skin was badly lacerated and blood was welling from a two-inch gash. Fumbling inside her ski smock she pulled out an army-type bandage and bound it round the injury. "Your trousers mustn't freeze to it. Or it will tear badly when you walk."

Adams was still too exhausted from the frantic race to feel any pain. "Why have we come down here?"

Replacing his trouser leg, she drew the Sten gun strap

191

from over her head. "Those Germans will come back this way. We have to stop them."

"How can we do that?"

"We must ambush them. They'll pass no more than thirty metres from us."

Adams stiffened. "You mean kill them?"

"What else can we do? They're not likely to surrender to one man and a woman."

"But we can't shoot them, not in cold blood."

She turned to him, her voice tight with fear and impatience. "Then tell me what else we can do. Let them go and tell about our camp? Let the consignment reach Germany? Is that what you prefer?"

"Of course it isn't. But we can't shoot them down without a warning."

"Can't we? Not to save our friends from torture and death? Is our morality so precious that others should die for it?"

A pacifist by nature, Adams had come to wear uniform by asking himself that self-same question, although by accepting a non-combatant role he had often felt he had made a despicable compromise. Now life was demanding a commitment in the most brutal fashion. "All I'm suggesting is we give them a chance to surrender."

"You don't know German troops, do you?" She demanded. When Adams shook his head she searched his face for a moment, then cocked the Sten gun and laid it on the rocks before her. "They won't need to go far down the river to find traces of our camp but they will be a few minutes yet."

He discovered he was trembling so much he could barely hold the lighted cigarette she offered him. "They are such young men," he said lamely.

The smoke she exhaled was torn away in the bitter wind. "All armies are made up of young men. It does not stop them killing thousands of our people and stealing our country from us."

"I know that but aren't they just doing what they are told? These six men could be like myself and never have seen the enemy before."

For a moment anger returned to her voice. "These men you feel so sorry for are highly trained ski troops specially brought to this country to hunt down our freedom fighters. Do you know what happens to our men if they are captured? They are tortured and then they are shot. And their only crime is their determination to win their country back."

"I know the terrible things that happen," Adams muttered. "But do two wrongs make a right?"

"You keep on forgetting what is at stake here. If that consignment reaches Germany it could cost us the war."

"But couldn't the Gestapo argue the same way when they torture a man for information? That one man's agony is nothing beside the agony of thousands?"

Her blue eyes were suddenly full of dislike. "You are worse than those who fight without questioning why. You wear uniform but refuse to accept its responsibilities."

Adams felt as if a needle had jabbed into a long-festering abscess. "Do you think I don't know that? It's tortured me for years. Why do you think I volunteered to come out here?"

For the moment anger allowed her no charity. "I don't know why you came. And it seems you don't know either." As he reached out for the Sten, she snatched it away. "No. I shall do it. You shall keep your hands clean."

For the first time since he had sunk down behind the rocks, Adams realized the rumble of the distant engine had ceased. With the river entrance holding their eyes, neither spoke. When Helga finally broke the silence her tone had changed. "It was wrong of me to talk that way. We are what we are, and I was right in the things I said in the hut. If you were to kill, particularly in cold blood, it might mark you for life. Whereas these are the men who have stolen my country—I believe I can find my justification there." Before the distressed Adams could speak, she pressed his arm. "Keep still. They're coming back."

Heart hammering in his throat, Adams saw a brawny figure emerge from the dusk that was filling the river valley. Wearing skis again, he covered the road with his carbine for a moment, then waved the rest of the patrol out. Their excitement coupled with excessive caution, made it clear they had discovered the secret of the lake. As they made for the bridge, Helga settled behind the Sten and took aim.

For Adams time was standing still as one morality fought against another. It was the sight of the girl's sweating, marble-hued face that tipped the scales.

"Give me the gun," he muttered.

193

Geared to commit the act, she pushed him fiercely away. "No."

"If you don't, I'll take it away from you. And then they'll hear us."

Realizing he was right she cried something, then released her grip. Replacing the gun between the rocks Adams took aim. The men had now cleared the bridge and were almost level with them. He heard Helga's unsteady whisper. "First the corporal. He has a machine carbine."

At the last moment Adams' resolution faltered. With a cracked shout, he leapt to his feet. "Drop your guns and put up your hands! All of you!"

What followed amazed Adams by its suddenness. Like a coiled spring released by his warning, the corporal spun round and opened fire. Smacking brutally into frozen rocks, bullets whined eerily away. In a response as automatic, Adams' finger tightened on the Sten trigger and released a hose of bullets. Dropping his gun, the corporal clutched his stomach, screamed, and fell. Three other soldiers collapsed beside him. A fifth man sighted Adams and opened fire. As Adams heard the bullet smack into a rock only inches from him, his reaction was purely atavistic: to kill before he was killed. Firing again, he saw the soldier drop his rifle, spin round and fall backwards with his skis waving grotesquely in the air. As Adams paused, horrified by his handiwork, he heard Helga's warning cry. "The last man! He mustn't escape."

The sixth soldier had flung his rifle away and was skiing for his life down the lane. Forgetting his injured leg, Adams tried to run down the hillside to gain a better angle of fire. Instead he stumbled and nearly dropped the Sten. By the time he recovered the soldier had almost disappeared into the mist. Steadying himself, Adams fired a long burst and believed the man faltered. A second later, however, he drove on his skis again and vanished. Adams' shout was a mixture of panic and despair. "He's got away! Helga, he's got away!"

Although equally dismayed, Helga took command. "We must get them off the road and behind that snow bank in case any more patrols come this way. Later Jensen will send men to bury them properly."

The need to approach his handiwork seemed to Adams the final outrage. To his horror he found immense relief that all five men appeared to be dead: to have had to face their reproachful eyes would have been intolerable. Shock anaesthetized his senses until the still-warm bodies were tugged out of sight and the only remaining task was the hiding of the bloodstains. Forced until now to stay behind and help him, Helga began strapping on a pair of skis. "I must get back quickly to warn Paul. Will you be all right?"

His gloved hands filled with powdered snow, Adams was making for the centre of the road. "Yes. I know my way back."

Pushing herself away, Helga crossed the bridge. As she turned to leave the road, she glanced back. Quite motionless, with his cupped hands piled with snow, Adams was gazing down at the crimson patches at his feet as if having a vision of Purgatory. For a moment the girl hesitated. Then, with a sob of distress, she ran forward and disappeared into the dusk. Left alone Adams turned and stumbled to the roadside. With all his horror and aversion coming up at last, he vomited as if his stomach had burst.

## 26

Sitting on the bed in the HQ hut, Davies was nervously pulling on a cigarette. Three times his eyes moved to the haunted face of Adams who was slumped on a chest beside the stove. The fourth time they shifted to Helga who, seated opposite Adams, also looked pale and drawn.

Having already asked the question twice, Davies was clearly in need of a crumb or two of comfort. "You say neither of you has any idea how badly wounded that last soldier was?"

When Helga did not reply, Adams turned towards him somewhat resentfully. "We've already explained, sir. There was a heavy mist down there."

Grunting his disappointment, Davies glanced at the other two occupants, Henderson and Moore. "Lindstrom's been away a long time. What do you think's going on?"

Feeling obliged to answer, Henderson could only state the obvious. "We should know in a few minutes, sir."

Davies gave another dissatisfied grunt before the hut lapsed into silence again. In the yellow light of the paraffin lamp all three officers were showing their own brand of shock at the news Helga had brought. On Adams' return he had found the girl still closeted in the HQ hut and he had barely had time to drop his weary body alongside the stove before its occupants had bombarded him with questions. During this interrogation a partisan had hammered on the door and told Lindstrom he was wanted urgently down by the river. Telling the others to wait, the young major had run out and been absent for fifteen minutes, a time that seemed as many hours to the worried airmen.

The crunch of running footsteps on the ice outside made everyone straighten and turn. A moment later a gust of icy wind dipped the flame of the paraffin lamp and threw mis-shapen shadows on the walls. Davies' voice was hoarse as the panting Lindstrom closed the door behind him. "Well? What's happened?"

"It was Jensen. He wanted to speak to me before he drove back to the main road."

"Drove back?" Davies interrupted. "What in?"

"A German transport." Seeing Davies start, the young

196

Norwegian went on: "It appears the Germans used two transports to bring their troops into this area. Jensen was keeping a watch on them and as soon as he heard the firing he killed both drivers. He's hidden one transport north of the lake to be used later and he drove the other down the lane as far as the river to find out what had happened and to collect the remainder of the mines."

Davies had never felt so far out of his depth as at that moment. "What's he going to do with the mines?"

"As I explained yesterday, the only way the Germans can rush up troops is along the north-south road. Any armour or artillery will also have to come that way. So Jensen intends to mine the road in a cutting between two hill ranges seven kilometres south of here. It won't delay them that long but tomorrow every minute could be precious."

"But do you feel fairly confident the alarm won't be raised until tomorrow morning?" Henderson asked.

Lindstrom nodded. "Yes. It could be hours before the other German patrols return to find they have no transport, and as they will already be tired it will take them the rest of the night to get back on foot, even if Jensen's patrols don't ambush them. As for the wounded German, Jensen has already sent three men after him."

"What about radio?"

"Jensen confirms that neither truck has one. So we have no worries there."

With his beloved squadron in danger of ignominious destruction Davies was only too eager to clutch at any straw. "If your men should track down the wounded German, isn't there still a chance we might escape detection?"

"You are forgetting the Germans will send out an investigating patrol when the transports fail to return. They'll probably give them until dawn but no longer."

"Yes, but that doesn't mean they'll know about our camp here. They might just believe it has been a hit and run job. That's why I'm wondering if it's wise to mine that main road. Won't that warn them something big is afoot?"

The academic young Norwegian gave a wry smile. "You don't know our enemy here in Norway, Air Commodore. When his patrols are ambushed he always replies in great strength. This district will be combed from end to end no matter what we do, so we might as well slow him down. In any case an ambush seven kilometres away gives no indication there are aircraft hiding on this lake."

Conceding the point, Davies never thought he would find himself thanking God for the inclement weather. "At least they can't send air patrols out."

Moore spoke for the first time since Lindstrom's return. "What will you do when they break through your road block, Paul? Will you still fall back into the southern lane or will that give too much away?"

The Norwegian shrugged. "What choice do we have? The Germans are sure to send patrols down it and then it would be too late for us to establish a defence position. Fortunately, with the valley as narrow and steep as it is, we ought to be able to put up a strong resistance there. We must do so because if the Germans break through to the river they can reach your aircraft."

Henderson felt all his worst prognostications were coming true. "What are my men supposed to be doing all this time?"

"On no account to take part in any of the fighting. My radio operator on the cliff top will signal down by Aldis the moment he hears the cruiser has sailed. Your job then will be to get your aircraft away as quickly as possible."

The Scot looked both relieved and uncomfortable. "They're not going to like your men doing all the fighting for them."

If Lindstrom appreciated the sentiment behind the remark his sharp reply concealed it. "It is vitally important they obey orders and keep out of danger. Otherwise everything we are doing could be wasted."

Conscious of what a near-run thing it could be, Davies intervened. "How confident are you that the cruiser will sail tomorrow morning?"

"Like you, I can only make the assumption that because the Germans have timed the shipment to arrive in the early morning, they intend to clear the fjord in daylight. Of course if there are any delays to the train they might change their schedule but my agents along the line tell me that so far it is running on time."

Davies turned uneasily away. "Let's hope our assumption is right. Because if Jerry does get wind of us, I can't see how we can hang around here, even if your boys do their best to hold him off."

It was a remark that clearly upset the Norwegian. "You won't stay even if my men keep him out of range?"

"I didn't say that. But you can't get a squadron off the ground at a minute's notice. Not when they're bottled up in a river mouth."

"But you must give me your assurance you won't take off until you've spoken to me."

For a moment Davies misunderstood him. "You mean after your radio operator has given us the green light?"

"No. Once his signal comes you must take off straight away. I am asking that if no message comes you will not withdraw without my agreement."

Across the hut Henderson shook his head vigorously. Frowning, Davies turned back to Lindstrom. "I can't promise that, Major. Flying is our business and only we can decide when the risks are getting too heavy. What I will do, however, is warn you in good time. Can you give me a two-way radio?"

Lindstrom shook his head bitterly. "We haven't any."

Davies gave a start. "No radios?"

"No. We asked for them but we haven't been able to find the container. Jensen still has a couple of men searching for it but after that snowfall I haven't much hope."

Davies gave a whistle of dismay. "That's not going to make things any easier. All right, we'll just have to play it as it comes. I'll give you my word to stay until the situation becomes too dangerous."

Fear that at the eleventh hour his plans could come to nought brought scorn and anger from the Norwegian. "How can you assess the situation from this side of the hill? You might believe things are getting too dangerous when we are only falling back to a new defence position."

For one of Davies' temperament it could hardly have been a more unfortunate remark. "We haven't a reputation for panicking under fire, Major. We shall stay until we decide that any further delay might result in the futile loss of our aircraft. That's the most I can promise you and it ought to be enough."

As the two men's eyes clashed it seemed a first-class quarrel was imminent. The situation was saved by Helga who jumped up and said something to her brother in Norwegian. Taking a deep breath he answered her, then turned sullenly back to Davies. "I must go to Jensen now and might not see you again until tomorrow. Please

199

remind your men not to go down the river or over the hill if they hear any firing or they could kill themselves in our minefields."

As he put his hand on the door catch, Helga's anxious voice checked him. "Ta na vare da deg selv, Paul."

He nodded and managed her a smile before pulling the door open. As it slammed heavily behind him, bringing down snow from the roof outside, the four officers exchanged apprehensive glances.

Adams heard the first two explosions soon after dawn, distant sounds that reverberated flatly through the hills. His heart responded instantly, surging hot beneath his breastbone and then thumping hard. Fully dressed, he was huddled up in his sleeping bag. Although he had spent the first half of the night among the aircraft with the other three senior officers, four hours ago Davies had ordered him back to rest his injured leg.

But Adams had not slept. His leg ached intolerably and to close his eyes meant an immediate vision of the five men he had killed. More than once during those tortured hours Adams had wondered if he would ever sleep again.

The night had been one of frenzied activity for the squadron. Unable to help the partisans, Davies had decided he must do everything possible to have the aircraft ready for take-off. With Powell no longer daring to run up the engines and worried about turgid oil, ropes had been slung over the aircraft's propellers and teams of men had half-rotated the engines, reset the ropes and half-rotated them again.

Every man had taken his turn in shifts, the ground crews, the pilots and navigators, and the senior officers. The work had been tedious and brutal and no one could say how efficacious it would be, and yet because it gave men the feeling they were doing something practical and took their minds off the perils ahead, Davies had felt the idea worthwhile and it had gone on throughout the night. Although both Adams and Helga had insisted on taking part, it had soon become obvious that Adams' injured leg would not take the strain. Helga, however, had protested she was fit to continue and Davies, who was perhaps more of a psychologist than his enemies would allow, had said she could remain.

Climbing hastily from his sleeping bag, Adams had just opened the door when a third explosion came, followed by the far-off rattle of small arms fire. Although the sky was still heavily clouded, dawn was filtering through and giving shape and substance to the frozen trees. Hearing startled shouts, Adams hurried down the path and found men running out of huts and gathering around the tall figure of Harvey. They were a contingent Davies had sent to rest two hours ago. All were veterans of hazardous air battles, but they were out of their element here and many apprehensive glances were being cast at the towering hills that stood between them and the north-south road. Even the dour Harvey was frowning heavily as Adams approached.

"I suppose this means it's started?"

The news that Adams had almost wiped out a patrol of Germans had spread like wildfire through the squadron and the sudden hush that fell as men turned and waited for his reply showed the respect in which he was now held. Yet with Adams being the man he was, his only thought at that moment was that in the kingdom of the blind the one-eyed man was king. "Yes, I suppose it does. It must be coming from the road block Jensen set up."

"I wonder how long they can hold it," Harvey muttered.

The firing had started in earnest now, volley after volley reverberating through the hills. Although Adams knew the road block was seven kilometres away and that sound carried far in the icy air, the gunfire sounded disturbingly close. Millburn's curse summed up the feelings of all. "If we were allowed off the ground we could clean up the bastards in five minutes."

With every man feeling the need to discuss the situation with a partisan and yet with all the Norwegians except Helga out defending the camp, Adams suddenly remembered the wireless operator. "We could ask him what he thinks. Helga says he's Jensen's right-hand man."

The hut the operator was using was no more than thirty yards from the edge of the steep cliff. A makeshift aerial of wire stretching from the chimney to a nearby tree betrayed its purpose. Aware that apart from the Lindstroms and Jensen the radio operator was the only other partisan who knew about Skinnarland's activities, Adams had illogically expected a man of outstanding physical appearance. Instead the operator was small and

201

shaggy-haired with an unsightly cluster of warts on one side of his nose. As the contingent of airmen invaded the hut he turned enquiringly and lifted up his set of earphones.

"Can you speak English?" Harvey asked.

The man's grin showed a set of broken teeth. "I send messages to London, don't I?"

"Then what do you think is happening back there on the road? How long can your men hold out?"

"Not for long. The Jerries will get round the back of them."

"Can they hold them in the southern lane?"

The man yawned wearily. "For a time. It depends." Catching the eye of Gabby, who was the nearest to him, he pulled off his earphones and held them out. "You listen for a while, ya, while I get some sleep." Before Gabby could refuse the man curled himself up at the base of the stove and closed his eyes. Paget bent over him, then glanced up in disbelief.

"I think he's asleep already."

"It's not surprising," Harvey grunted. "Seeing the poor bastard's been on watch since Christ knows when. You can handle it, can't you?" he asked Gabby.

"Not if they send the message in Norwegian," the indignant Gabby complained.

Millburn grinned. "Didn't they teach Norwegian at that school of yours? Wake him up, you stupid bastard, as soon as you hear anything." As the men trooped out, Millburn grinned back at the scowling Gabby. "You know something, boyo? I feel safer with you in here. I've been having kittens thinking of you waving a Sten gun around."

No more enlightened than before, the airmen made their way back down the hill. As they passed the HQ hut they ran into Davies and Helga leading a party of men up from the river. Irritable from his long night, Davies gave Harvey a glare. "Where the hell have you lot been? Didn't you hear me tell you to keep away from that hilltop?"

Seeing Harvey scowl at the reprimand, Adams broke in quickly. "We've only been to see the radio operator. Gabriel's taken over the watch for a while to give him a rest."

Davies' face cleared. "Has he any news?"

"No, sir, I'm afraid not."

202

To Adams the distant gunfire seemed to be getting closer. Mixed with the rattle of small arms fire, occasional heavy thuds could be heard. The frowning Davies asked the question to no one in particular. "What are those? Mines or mortars?"

Before anyone could hazard a guess Millburn decided to try his luck. "Have you thought of sending up a couple of Mossies, sir? If they are using mortars we could knock 'em out and still have plenty of rockets left for the cruiser."

There were loud shouts of agreement from the surrounding men but Helga turned on the American angrily. "No. The Germans might not know you are here and my brother's last words were that you should stay under cover. And that is what you must do."

Davies raised a wry eyebrow at Millburn. "Does that answer your question?" When the American gave a disappointed shrug, Davies turned to Harvey. "Get your men back to the aircraft, will you? My lot are clapped out. Henderson's men can't be feeling that good either. If any messages come from Lindstrom, let me have them at once."

As Harvey led his men down the path and Davies' party dispersed, Adams drew Helga aside. At close quarters her appearance shocked him. Her cheeks were tightly drawn and there were dark bruises of exhaustion beneath her eyes. "You mustn't do any more work down there," he muttered. "It's killing work for a woman."

A series of heavy thuds followed his words and he saw her teeth bite into her lower lip. "Those are mortars. They must have come up in strength."

The unhappy Adams was aware of the paradoxical aspects of his guilt even as he spoke. "This might never have happened if I hadn't bungled up the job yesterday."

She shook her head. "No. Once shooting became necessary it was inevitable they would come. We have always known that."

"At least we'd have been sure they knew nothing about the aircraft. As it is we might be hiding here for nothing when we could be helping your brother."

Exhaustion made her angry with him. "First you feel remorse because you kill German soldiers; now you feel remorse because you did not kill more of them. War is always a muddle, don't you know that? Even a downpour of rain can change a battle. So stop torturing your-self. All my friends respect what you did. Paul more than anybody."

Praise was the last thing Adams wanted. "Respect me? For gunning five men down in cold blood?"

"Now you have forgotten how it happened. You first called on them to surrender and nearly got yourself killed because of it. But that wasn't the bravest thing you did. Do I have to remind you what it was?"

Adams felt that one day he might find comfort in her words but that day was far distant. Seeing from his expression that he regretted mentioning the incident, she turned away. "I must go and prepare the HQ hut. We shall be getting casualties in soon."

Adams, to whom the realities of war were coming too fast for assimilation, wondered why he had not thought about wounded men before. "Yes, of course. I'll come with you."

As she started along the path another heavy explosion startled a brace of ptarmigan resting on a nearby tree. Rising with startled cries they fled across the lake. Certain now the battle was coming closer, Adams limped after the girl.

## 27

With the gunfire having mysteriously ceased and the silence growing, Adams felt certain he could hear the ticking of a watch. Wondering if it was his own he glanced down and saw it was noon. He was sitting on a bench in the radio operator's hut next to Moore. Opposite him were Davies and Gabby, the latter wearing earphones. Alongside the stove the radio operator was still sprawled out fast asleep. He had been snoring loudly but a minute ago Davies had jumped up and rolled him on his side. Immediately aware how the act had betrayed his state of nerves, the Air Commodore had scowled as he took his seat again. "Why's all the shooting stopped?"

Adams had muttered he had no idea. Moore had only shaken his head. All three were showing the ravages of sleeplessness and tension. Even Moore had not managed to shave that morning and his usually immaculate uniform was filthy. Adams, not long up from the HQ hut, had thick bloodstains on his ski smock. The first of the wounded partisans had been brought in while he had been helping Helga, and with one man clutching a torn stomach and another with a deeply gashed thigh from a shell splinter, the sights had been harrowing. He had remained with Helga until she had been joined by the medical orderly Henderson had prudently brought, and then hurried up to the radio hut to bring Davies the latest news of the battle that Lindstrom had sent with the wounded.

The Germans were no longer thrusting up the main road but had followed the partisans' retreat round the back of the southern hills. During the time Jensen had been engaging them in the distant cutting, other partisans had been urgently mining the lane and setting up road blocks. This had enabled Jensen to make his present stand behind the first of these road blocks which was only two hundred metres from the main road. With the valley narrow and steep-sided, the lane was considerably easier to defend than the road but with the partisans already outnumbered and with German reinforcements undoubtedly on their way, it was clearly only a matter of time before the Norwegians were driven back to the river and the way to the aircraft was open.

Davies' problem, then, was an agonized one. He knew

that the message that could have such a far-reaching effect on the war might come at any moment. Indeed, with the stocks reaching Kranvin early that morning, on Davies' estimate it was already overdue. On the other hand, with enemy reinforcements on their way, he knew that however confident Lindstrom professed to be, every passing minute put his squadron in greater danger. With the problem compounded by the time needed to warm up the aircraft and file them out on the lake, there was little wonder Davies was hypersensitive to every change in sound of the battle. When the present silence lasted a full two minutes he let out an exclamation and jumped to his feet. "What the hell's happening out there?"

Exchanging glances, Moore and Adams followed him outside. Northwards, with the steep cliff falling almost vertically, nearly all the eastern lake was visible. The absence of friend or foe on its frozen surface confirmed that the entire German effort was concentrated behind the southern hills whose wooded slopes towered a good seven hundred feet above the hut. As Adams stared upwards he saw clouds of smoke hanging in the grey sky. With the wind still blowing from the east, the stench of cordite and high explosive reached his nostrils.

Davies was also staring up at the smoke. Looking pinched from cold and worry he was about to make a comment when there was a distant burst of Sten gun fire. As if it were a signal to recommence hostilities, the thump of mortars and the rattle of machine-gun fire reverberated again through the hills. Unaware of the irony in the relief he was showing, Davies was turning for the hut when Moore caught his arm. On the hill above branches were swaying and snow sprinkling down as someone ran through the trees. Cocking his Sten, Moore motioned the older men to take cover behind the hut but before either could move Lindstrom broke out of the trees. Bare-headed, eyes feverish, and with blood running down one cheek, he looked a desperate figure as he ran towards them. Davies' voice was brittle with alarm. "What's happened? Have they broken through?"

Fighting for breath, it was a moment before the young Norwegian could answer. "No. I've come to find out what's happening in Kranvin. Haven't you had any news yet?"

"Nothing," Davies told him. "Don't you think you should raise your men there and find out?"

206

Lindstrom pushed into the hut. Ignoring Adams who tried to examine his head wound, he stared down at the radio operator who looked as if he could sleep on until the crack of doom. "What does he think he's doing? Taking a holiday?"

Davies nodded at Gabby. "We thought we'd better take over for a while in case he fell asleep on the job."

Striding to the stove, Lindstrom prodded the man roughly with his Sten gun. "Huleste, mann. Detteer ikkestedet til a sove!"

The man opened one eye, then sat upright. "Og finn ut hua som foregar," Lindstrom shouted again.

Showing no resentment the man nodded, took the earphones from Gabby, and sat down. As Lindstrom began cranking the hand-powered transmitter, he began tapping out a message. Davies drew nearer. "What are you sending?"

Lindstrom ignored his question until the operator had finished transmitting. "I'm giving them permission to break radio silence and to tell me what is happening."

Ten long seconds passed. Then, to everyone's relief, morse could be heard in the operator's earphones. Moore shook his head at Davies' enquiring glance. "It's in Norwegian, sir."

The operator gave a terse acknowledgement as the blips ceased, then glanced up at Lindstrom. "They say the stocks went on board at dawn but the ship's still at her berth."

The young major gave a violent start. "Dawn?"

"That's what they say. As soon as there's any more activity they'll be in touch."

Trying to hide his alarm, Lindstrom turned to Davies. "That's the situation, I'm afraid."

Davies sounded hoarse. "She's still at her berth although the stocks have been aboard her for four hours? What the hell's going on? Don't your men know?"

"How can they know? They can only watch and report."

Davies resembled a small but highly wrought-up tiger as he did a round of the hut. "Christ, in that case perhaps they aren't going to sail today."

Lindstrom's protest seemed to Davies to come more from fear than conviction. "That's impossible! What would be the point of waiting?"

"You tell me." The look Davies gave Adams made the

207

Intelligence Officer wince. "How did I get into this? If they advance much further down that lane they'll be dropping shells among my aircraft. What's their full strength?"

"It's difficult to be sure but we think about sixty men. They've also got some mortars, a few self-propelled."

Davies took a grip of himself. "Can you hold them?"

"We've held them at the first road block long enough to reinforce the second and third behind us. We've also mined the lane. So there's no danger at this moment."

"But what happens when their reinforcements arrive? They'll bring armour, won't they?"

"Possibly. But we still have the bazookas and the anti-tank rifles and the lane is very narrow."

Davies was too much of an old fox not to read the weaknesses of a defence position. "I'm thinking of the extra troops they'll bring. That hill range south of the lane isn't mined and once they get round there, they can out-flank you."

"We know that. Jensen has already sent men out there. So we'll be able to check even that move for a time."

"Their reinforcements can't be far away," Davies grunted. "They might even have arrived." He put his question bluntly. "How long are you going to be able to hold out, Lindstrom? Don't give me pie in the sky: I want a realistic estimate."

Lindstrom's hesitation was brief. "With any luck, for the rest of the afternoon."

"You mean the rest of the daylight?"

"Yes. Perhaps even longer."

Davies did another turn of the hut, then faced the young major again. "You do realize I can't wait until my squadron is destroyed? But I will wait until the first shell falls on this side of the hill. The moment that happens I shall abort the operation."

Lindstrom's academic face darkened with dismay and anger. "You can't do that. Your own Prime Minister has told you the destruction of these stocks has top priority."

"I know all about the stocks, Lindstrom. But getting my squadron wiped out won't help to destroy them. We can't wait until the Germans are shooting at us, man—we need time to warm up our engines. I'll give you until the first shell lands on this hillside. Then we scramble. I've no alternative."

Frustration that he had no radio link with the squadron from the battle area made the wrought-up Norwegian shout at Davies. "You'll leave because of a single shell? One shell could mean nothing. Can't you see that?"

"Don't be stupid, man. One shell means they're within range. And that puts every aircraft at risk."

Moore's quiet voice broke into the heated argument. "Tell me about the reinforcements, Paul. Will they come up from Gol on the main road?"

He received a sullen nod. "Almost certainly."

With his own mind working on the same lines, Davies saw immediately what was behind Moore's question. "It wouldn't stop their troops, Ian."

"Perhaps not, sir, but it would slow them down and knock out their tanks. That could be critical. I know it means using up fuel and rockets but surely that's better than having to call off the operation."

Davies was never one to hesitate when the truth was apparent. "All right; get 'em moving. But not you or your two flight commanders. Send Millburn, Smith, and Machin. They're all experienced men."

Nodding at Gabby to follow him, Moore turned for the door. Lindstrom, whose startled eyes had been moving from one man to the other, stepped in front of him. "What are you doing? Not sending aircraft up?"

Moore nodded. "It's the only answer, Paul. We can knock out those mortars and stop any tanks from reaching you. It'll save you casualties and gain us time."

As he moved past the Norwegian, his shoulder was grabbed and he was swung violently round. "Have you all gone crazy?" Lindstrom shouted. "You don't start up a single engine without my permission."

Davies went pale with anger. "You're exceeding your brief, Major. I'm in charge of this squadron and my orders are that we take part in the battle. Otherwise we shall be over-run."

Lindstrom swung round on him. "What's the matter with you? Do you want the Germans to know you are here?"

Davies gave a start. "But they must know. That soldier must have got through. Otherwise why are they driving towards the river?"

"Of course they don't know," the young Norwegian shouted. "If they did, why would they bother to follow us

209

down the lane? They would be doing everything in their power to get near the lake and to drop mortar shells on it."

Davies gaped, then sank weakly down on the bench. "God Almighty, he's right. They've only to break up the ice and we're finished."

## 28

The medium tank reached the bend in the steep valley, paused like a wary animal, then came slowly forward again. As the lane opened out it lowered its stubby gun barrel and fired three shells down at its ice-packed surface. As the third resonant explosion echoed back, a fountain of smoke and mud erupted forty yards ahead.

Behind a clump of boulders up the northern hillside, the bearded Jensen slid his American-built bazooka forward and settled behind the sights. As his companion, barely more than a boy, followed his example by aiming his Sten gun at the tank, the giant pushed the gun humorously away. "It's too thick-skinned for that peashooter, lad. Keep it for the soldiers. They'll be following in a minute."

With the road mine exploded, the tank had commenced its cautious advance. On the opposite hill another anti-tank crew were lining up on it. Less patient than Jensen, they fired before it was within point-blank range and their rocket ricocheted off its heavy turret and exploded harmlessly against a wayside boulder.

The tank gunner's reactions were fast. The gun barrel swung round, steadied for a split second, then recoiled like a striking snake. The shell it spat out scored a direct hit on the partisan's hide-out and when the smoke blew away the bodies of two men could be seen lying in the snow where they had been hurled by the explosion.

Jensen was cursing fluently. "The bastard's good! Keep your head down, boy."

The tank started forward again, the grinding of its tracks a chilling sound to the thin line of partisans spread out ahead. Once again its gun barrel lowered to pump two more shells along the frozen lane. This time no explosion followed. With their limited stock of mines heavily depleted by their need to make the woods impassable, the partisans had been left with less than a dozen to sow between the main road and the river.

The tank was now a hundred yards past the bend. Bracing himself, Jensen waited until it was almost opposite him, then squeezed the trigger. His rocket struck it just below its armoured skirt, slewing it round as its starboard tracks were blown away. As it lay straddled across the lane like some mortally wounded reptile, smoke began pouring out from its air vents. Peering over the rocks

Jensen saw its hatch open and two half-stunned men crawl out. Before they could stagger to the roadside he grabbed the Sten gun from the youth and fired a long burst. Both men fell and a column of flame enveloped the tank as its lethal contents exploded. As smoke rose a hundred feet into the air Jensen winked at the pale-faced youth. "That'll give 'em something to think about, lad."

The words had barely left his mouth before a heavy explosion showered them with stones and mud. As they flattened themselves, three more explosions came in as many seconds, ringing their hide-out and sending a small avalanche of rocks and snow plunging down the hillside. More fountains of smoke opposite told that the German mortar crews were taking swift reprisals for the loss of their comrades.

The falling shells forced Lindstrom, who was sliding down the northern hill, to take cover. When the fury of the barrage lessened for a moment he began running again, taking advantage of every rock and tree. Sighting him from the hillsides beyond the road bend, enemy machine gunners opened fire. With bullets splattering at his heels, the young Norwegian dived into the hide-out and fought for breath.

Seeing the streaks of blood on his sweating face, Jensen bent over him anxiously. "You all right, lad?"

Nodding, Lindstrom allowed himself only a few seconds' rest before sitting upright. Mortar shells and small arms fire forced him to shout. "I see their reinforcements have arrived. Do you know how many tanks they have?"

"We can't be sure. But we think half a dozen."

"How many men?"

Jensen shrugged. "That's something we don't know." He nodded at the rough hillside opposite. "We think most of 'em have gone back of it to outflank us. It's looking sticky, lad."

Forced to pause again for breath, Lindstrom followed his gaze. "We can stop them, can't we?"

"Our lads will do their best but I can't stretch 'em out too far. Sooner or later the bastards will get round us and then we'll have to go—fast. You do realize it's kaput once they reach the river, don't you?"

Before Lindstrom could reply a mortar shell forced all three men to duck. The giant cursed as snow and stones showered down on them. "They've got observation posts up beyond that bend and their mortars have got us

212

bracketed. You can't move a finger without them dropping on us. Did you find out anything about the cruiser?" When Lindstrom told him the latest news, Jensen looked shocked. "At dawn? And they haven't sailed yet? What's the hold-up?"

"How do I know? It could be anything."

"Lad, this is serious. Maybe they don't intend sailing today. How did Davies take it?"

The rattle of a Sten gun almost drowned Lindstrom's resentful voice. "He says he's ordering his men out the moment the first shell falls on his side of the hill."

"You can't blame him for that. It's not going to help anybody if his aircraft are wiped out."

The young Norwegian was too worried to be generous. "He knew the risks when he took on the job. If he flies off now, he'll waste the life of every man killed here."

"Don't count your losses until your eggs break, lad. He looks a tough little bastard to me and he hasn't said he's leaving yet. I reckon he'll stay until he decides it's hopeless."

Lindstrom's voice was bitter. "That's the whole point, isn't it? What will he consider hopeless?"

Although sympathetic, the big Norwegian had his eyes fixed on the road bend where a second tank was nosing into sight. "You're going to have to be realistic, Paul. We never had many bazookas or shells and one team's already been wiped out. With tanks and mortars ahead of us and troops trying to get round our backs, I've got to watch it carefully or I'll lose every man I have."

"How long?" Lindstrom asked hoarsely.

"How can I say that, lad? But we're not going to hold out until dusk, that's for sure."

Head on arms at the edge of the table, Davies was staring blindly at the floor. Opposite him the radio operator was rhythmically chewing gum. There had been a time half an hour ago when Davies' impulse had been to tear the gum from his mouth and hurl it through the door. But now, fighting nerves and despair as he waited for the signal that never came, Davies was envying his earlier ebullition.

Hearing the crunch of footsteps outside he lifted his head and saw Adams silhouetted in the doorway. He gave a grunt. "Well! Have you got the wounded on board?"

213

Adams nodded as he limped forward. "Yes, sir. Now the bomb bays are empty we've got more room and they're all in one Mitchell as you suggested. One died in the hut from loss of blood, however. I don't think we'll be able to bury him." As Davies lowered his head again, Adams went on almost apologetically. "You do know the German reinforcements have arrived?"

Davies jerked upright. "No. Who told you?"

"A stretcher bearer. It seems they've brought tanks with them."

"Oh Christ," Davies muttered. Pushing past Adams he stood outside listening. Mixed with the crump of mortar shells there was an occasional resonant explosion. "You think those are tank guns?"

"I don't know what else they can be," Adams said.

Davies glared at the woods that soared above them. "If only we could see over that bloody hill." As he took an impulsive step forward, Adams caught his arm. "Don't forget it's mined, sir."

"So what? Lindstrom came that way, didn't he?"

Adams was beginning to wonder if exhaustion was turning the small Air Commodore light-headed. "Yes, sir, but he knows where the safety path is."

Growling his frustration, Davies turned back. "What's the situation down below?"

"I think everything's as ready as it can be. All the camouflage nets are taken down and everyone's standing by his aircraft."

Davies' groan was heartfelt. "If only we knew what to do, Frank."

With the enemy so near, it was Adams' secret belief that the squadron would be lucky to escape annihilation, much less sink the cruiser. "If the Germans have been heavily reinforced I don't see how we can expect the partisans to hold out much longer. And if there's a sudden breakthrough, will we be able to get away in time?"

Davies gave him a sharp glance. "What does that mean? You think we should start withdrawing without consulting Lindstrom?"

With Helga in mind, Adams was feeling a tug of loyalties. "I'm a bit worried about his judgement, sir. He's set his heart on destroying these stocks so much that I can't help wondering if he isn't overestimating his men's capabilities."

"I've been wondering the same thing all day," Davies muttered. Turning away he walked to the edge of the cliff. The clouds, which had been slowly lifting all day, were now level with the hilltops. "Here's another problem. If we take off now it's going to be tricky but if we leave it much longer Jerry's going to spot us from the air and then it's curtains." Davies' agony of mind was almost palpable as he took a few paces along the clifftop, then swung round. "I'm going to see Henderson. I'll send a wireless op up here to relieve you. In the meantime you know what to do if a message comes in. Use the Aldis to contact us. I've got a man standing by down there who can see you."

By the river Davies found tension as tight as a watch spring. With every preparation made for take-off but the starting up of the engines, men were standing in small groups, listening to the heavy gunfire and murmuring anxiously to one another. That aircrews should be showing the same apprehension as their ground crews might have surprised some observers but not Davies. Men used to answering aggression by aggression, their helpless role was sapping their morale. Another factor was the steep hill and winding river that hid all details of the battle from them. With imagination always painting the blackest picture, some men looked as if they expected German tanks to roll along the banks at any moment. Catching sight of Henderson talking to Moore, Davies hurried over to him.

"Is everything ready, Jock?"

The Scot swung round. "Aye, it is sir. And if you'll take my advice the sooner we're airborne the better. This place is a death trap."

Davies ignored the comment. "Send a radio operator up to the hut to relieve Adams, will you?"

Henderson stared at him. "You're surely not waiting any longer for that signal? Man, they've got tanks in that lane. If we take off now we can cover the Norwegians' retreat."

In spite of his own forebodings Davies was a man who made up his own mind. "We'll be off in good time, Jock. Send that radio operator up there, will you?"

With a glance at Moore, Henderson called Evans over and gave him his orders. As the young navigator left, Davies nodded at the small groups of murmuring men. "We'd better shake that lot up or they'll be getting morbid."

He turned to Moore. "Have you given them their order of take-off yet?"

"Yes, sir. The three Mitchells are going first. Then, apart from myself, we shall go off in the same order as we landed."

Both officers registered immediate protests. "We can't be the first to leave, Ian," Davies grunted. "It's out of the question."

"The wounded go first, that goes without saying." Henderson said. "But I'm not getting out before my men."

When handling matters of life and death within his own jurisdiction, the normally easy-going Moore could be as unyielding as steel, as many of his crews had found out. "I'm sorry but there's no other way. As Lindstrom pointed out, once Jerry finds out we're here he's going to try to break up the ice. It's guesswork how long that's going to take him but it's common sense the aircraft we send off first must be the ones that need the longest runway."

Davies, the realist, glanced at Henderson. "He's right, Jock. No question about it." As the Scot gave a growl of disapproval, Davies shrugged. "I don't like it either but you can't change the facts of life."

Realizing further argument was useless, Henderson nodded at the smoke-covered hill. "What about Lindstrom and his sister? Are they going back with us?"

"Lindstrom won't—he told me that last night. But he wants his sister to go. I've asked Adams to have a word with her."

The Scot turned towards the isthmus of ice that joined the two lakes. "If they're hoping to retreat across there, they're going to need air cover if Jerry's on their heels. Otherwise they'll be mown down before they're halfway across."

Knowing the Scot was never one to abandon his friends, Davies grinned. "You'd better make up your mind, hadn't you? A minute ago you wanted us to get the hell out of here."

He received a resentful glance. "You know what I meant sir. I want to cover their retreat. They must be in a pretty bad way by this time."

"You still haven't got it, have you, Jock? The last thing Lindstrom wants is to retreat. He intends holding on until the very last minute in case the green light comes. He's so set on it that if we took off now he'd probably go on fighting just to be bloody-minded."

216

"Once we're airborne, he'd have to quit," Henderson argued. "That's why for everyone's sake I think we should. Then they can retreat back along this river. It shouldn't be difficult to hold Jerry back long enough for them to get across and reach those two transports."

"And what if the green light comes after we've used up our rockets?" Davies demanded.

The Scot sighed. "We can't see into the future, sir. All we can do is act as we see fit."

More in sympathy with Henderson than he dared to confess, Davies became conciliatory. "Don't think I don't understand how you feel, Jock. In normal conditions I'd be ahead of you. But I happen to know more about the importance of these IMI stocks than you do, and you have to believe me it does justify our taking these risks. All the same I promise you I'll give the order to scramble the moment our aircraft are in danger. Fair enough?"

A heavy explosion made all three men turn. The barrage of mortar fire and the scream of shells that followed it made it clear the battle had reached a new height of ferocity. As apprehensive faces turned towards the three senior officers, Henderson gave a resigned sigh. "Fair enough, sir. Only I hope you can tell just when that moment is."

## 29

The silence that fell in the valley after the echoes of the last mortar shell died away made huddled partisans glance at one another apprehensively. Lying flat in a hollow, Jensen lifted his head and nudged Lindstrom. "They're getting ready to rush us, lad. Look over there."

Lindstrom's gaunt, blood-stained face lifted. Driven back beyond their second road block by relentless German pressure to within eight hundred metres of the river, the partisans were now attempting to defend a stretch of lane that had only its narrowness to commend it. Out of range of the partisans' bazookas, five tanks were drawing up nose to tail. The hoarseness of Jensen's voice betrayed the strain he had been under since the battle started. "They'll come at us under a mortar barrage. Any minute now. Lad, I think this is it. I want you to go back to Davies and tell him to start his aircraft up. And then take Helga across the lake. We'll join you as soon as we can."

As Jensen expected, the young major's response was fierce. "No! We've still got some bazooka shells left. And then we can fall back on the bridge. I'll go and tell Larson to blow it up."

Jensen caught his arm. "Lad, the river's frozen. They can drive straight across it."

"All right, then we'll retreat beyond it. They still don't know about Davies. We'll act as bait and lead them away."

The giant's voice was almost gentle as he shook his head. "You know we can't do that, Paul. Someone's sure to take a look down there and then Davies wouldn't stand a chance. We have to fall back down the river and try to hold 'em while the aircraft get away. But it'll be a close thing, so go now and tell Davies to get moving. In the meantime I'll call my lads back from across the road."

As he reached for a Very pistol, Lindstrom snatched it away. "No. That message could still come. At any moment. I'll tell you when to retreat. That's an order."

For a moment it seemed the giant Norwegian would take the pistol from him. Then, as he stared into the young man's tortured face, he sighed and dropped back. "Very well, lad. We'll wait a bit longer and see what happens. But I hope you realize that if those tanks break through they'll cut off our lads on the other side of the valley."

The nerve centre of the German thrust that was causing such concern to airmen and partisans alike was a cluster of rocks high up on the southern hillside. Three men occupied it, a colonel, a major, and a corporal radio operator. The colonel was Helmut Walcheim, a forty-three-year-old infantry officer who had served for two years on the Russian front. The frostbite scar that ran down from his chin to his lower neck was a legacy of that ordeal. Sent up with the reinforcements to take charge of the operation, he had brought with him six medium tanks and nearly seventy more men. The young major beside him was the officer he had superseded. Both men were showing intense curiosity at the fierce resistance they were encountering. Although Norwegian partisans had been a thorn in German flesh for the last two years, their methods of resistance to date had been the standard guerrilla tactic of surprise and withdrawal. To encounter a group as large as this and one prepared to stand and defend its position was a new experience for both German officers. Searching for a reason, Walcheim had been examining the hill range that ran between lane and lake for the last couple of minutes. Lowering his binoculars, he turned to the younger officer. "What have they got here that is so important? We've no reports of anything unusual in this area, have we?"

"No, sir. The entire area is a wilderness."

Walcheim's tone was dry. "A wilderness they have sown with mines and given many lives to protect. It is an odd wilderness, Klein." Scanning the hill again, Walcheim came to a decision. "I am going to fire a few shells up there. At the worst they might explode a few mines."

The young major looked puzzled as he took the microphone from the radio operator. "Just into the woods, sir?"

"No. Into that fold of hills beyond. I think it is beyond the range of the mortars so tell the tank crews to fire a couple of salvoes."

In the lane below the remaining tanks were in position to attack. Behind each one a small party of infantrymen was assembled. Further back still were half a dozen heavy mortars mounted on the back of transports. Although geared to launch the attack that everyone hoped would finally break the partisans' resistance, the Germans' mood was grim rather than enthusiastic. Having already tasted the Norwegians' fighting qualities all of them knew that a direct advance down the narrow lane was going to be costly. As a consequence Walcheim's order, delaying as it would the ordeal for a few more minutes, was welcomed by the tank crews although gibes that only an infantry officer would give such a damn-fool order passed between the men as they raised their 37mm guns to the towering hillside.

Watching through his binoculars, Walcheim gave Klein the order to fire the first salvo. As the resonant explosions echoed back, he saw five shell bursts register on the second sweep of hills. Nodding at Klein again, he waited. This time he saw only four explosions and turned to the young major. "Did all of them fire that second round?"

Klein addressed the microphone, then glanced back. "Yes, sir. They say so. Do you want another salvo?"

Grinning wryly, Walcheim sank back. "No. It was just a shot in the dark. Tell the mortar crews to be ready. I want all the cover we can get when the tanks go in."

As Klein gave the order, the mortar crews below could be seen crouched over their guns, shells in hand. Receiving Walcheim's nod, the young major was about to give the order that would start the attack when a distant rumble sounded from behind the hill. Walcheim caught his arm. "Wait a moment!"

As they listened, a second rumble augmented the first. "What is it?" Klein whispered. "Thunder?"

Below puzzled soldiers could be seen gazing at one another. As Walcheim looked up at the hill he gave a sudden cry of understanding. "Aircraft, Klein! It's aircraft engines!"

Klein looked at him as if his mind had gone. "Aircraft? How can aircraft operate here?"

Walcheim, who had not served in Russia for nothing, ignored him and snatched away the microphone. "Attention, all tank crews! This is urgent! Go back to the main road and try to reach the lake. Report to me what you see there. I repeat, this is urgent!"

There was immediate confusion below as tanks began slewing round and men and transports fought to get out of their way. The rearmost tank was the first to break free and snow spewed out from its tracks as it drove at speed along the lane. The thunder was now reverberating loudly among the hills as yet more engines started up. Klein's eyes were large with bewilderment as Walcheim gave a laugh and slapped his thigh. "Now it becomes a race, Klein. If we lose it they will destroy us. But if we win it, we have them trapped."

220

## 30

The Germans were not the only ones to hear the aircraft engines. Lindstrom gave a violent start, then leapt to his feet. "You hear that? Damn them! Damn them!"

Cursing, Jensen dragged him back. "What's the matter with you? Do you want to be killed?"

The young Norwegian was trembling with despair. "What are they doing? We could have given them another thirty minutes. Perhaps even more." Turning, he tried again to climb out of the hollow. "I must stop them."

Jensen dragged him back and held him with sheer strength. "Try to understand, lad. It's over. And it's for the best. With those tanks moving off I can get my boys back across the valley." Still holding the struggling Lindstrom he turned to the youth beside him. "Get back to the camp and tell his sister to cross the river. And tell the Englishmen to hurry. The Jerries are going to smash the ice."

Nodding, the youth jumped out of the hollow and with his body bent double dashed for the wood. Watching until he was safely away, Jensen turned back with a somewhat shamefaced grin to Lindstrom. "You going to be a good boy if I let you go?" As the distraught young major threw off his hand, his tone changed, "It's over, Paul. You've got to understand that."

Breathing heavily, Lindstrom appeared stunned by disappointment but as Jensen picked up the Very pistol and raised it, he gave a shout and threw himself forward. "No! Not yet!"

The giant's massive strength held him back and a second later a red flare soared into the grey sky. With a cry of despair, Lindstrom turned and smashed his clenched fist down on a rock. As he dropped to his knees, the wincing Jensen saw his palm had split and blood was staining the snow. "You've done your best, lad. We've all done our best. So stop punishing yourself."

The look he received made the giant wince again. "You! Of all people! The one man I thought I could trust!"

Jensen's voice was as gentle as a father comforting a child as he bent over him. "We couldn't let our men die for nothing, could we, lad? Go back and take care of Helga. We'll look after things here until Davies gets away and then we'll join you across the lake."

It seemed for a moment as if Lindstrom had not heard him. Then, with an exclamation, he jumped up and ran from the hollow. As a machine gun began chattering Jensen's face tightened but although Lindstrom made no attempt to evade the fire he reached the trees safely. Free now to show his grief, the giant Norwegian turned heavily and began making his preparations to retreat to the river.

The HQ hut stank of sweat, blood and antiseptics. With all the wounded and dead evacuated and the rest of the casualties detained down on the river, it was empty but for Adams and Helga. The girl's face was hard with determination. "It's no use. Please stop arguing with me. I'm not leaving my friends. Neither would you."

With no idea how much time he had left but aware it might be counted in minutes, Adams had a feeling of panic. "But it's what your brother wants. It's the last thing he told Davies."

"Of course he did. It's what any man would say. But how will I feel when I am safe in England? Have you thought of that?"

"But he'll be recalled by the Americans if the stocks escape. And what can you do here now the Germans suspect you?"

Even as he argued Adams knew there was no relationship between logic and loyalty. As if she could read his thoughts, her expression changed. "I can cook for them and tend to their wounds, Frank. But most of all I can let them know that in this treacherous world there are some who care and some who are faithful. Is that such a small thing?"

Adams cleared his throat. "I never said it was a small thing. But you have to see it from their point of view. They'll be worrying night and day in case you are captured. Is it fair to burden them like that?"

She turned sharply and went to the door. Her anorak and slacks were heavily daubed with blood from the wounded men she had attended. "How does one ever know what is right and what is wrong? One can only do what one's heart feels. Please go, Frank."

Adams tried to play for time. "At least come down to the river with me. The least you can do for Paul is cross the lake and wait for him there."

She glanced up in the direction of the radio hut. "No.

Arne will stay on watch until Paul gives him permission to leave. I'm not leaving him alone. In any case Paul is certain to come back this way."

To Adams' shame, throughout the entire conversation he had been listening to the sounds of battle and wondering how much longer Davies would wait. At present there was a lull in the firing and wondering what it portended he followed the girl outside. As they listened they heard a sudden fusillade of gunfire. "Tank guns, I think," Adams muttered at the girl's enquiring glance.

A few seconds later they heard the burst of the shells. Although the explosions were hidden, Adams counted five. A second fusillade followed a moment later. This time Adams distinctly heard the scream of a shell and glancing upwards saw a flash and column of smoke on the lakeside crest of the hill. Helga turned to him sharply. "What are they firing at up there?"

Before Adams could reply an urgent whistle began shrilling down on the river. Knowing what it meant, Adams turned pale. Helga said something in Norwegian, then turned away. "So it is over. All that work and suffering and loss—all for nothing."

Adams winced. "Don't blame us, Helga. Davies has already waited longer than he should. He can't stay until the squadron's wiped out on a point of defiance. Wars aren't won that way."

She stood motionless for a moment, then turned back to him. "I'm not blaming anyone, Frank. You are quite right. And this war must be won. Now more than ever."

Below there was a cough, then a rising roar as the first engine fired. The dam of Adams' restraint burst at last. "You said you couldn't leave your friends. Yet that's what you're asking me to do. Come with us, Helga. For all our sakes."

Her hand was lifting to his arm when there was the slither of footsteps behind them. A couple of seconds later Evans, looking overjoyed, burst out of the trees. As he ran towards them Adams closed his eyes.

"Did you hear that whistle, sir? It means we're getting out."

All Adams could do was nod. Helga drew the excited navigator's attention with a smile. "Mr. Adams is coming now. Please go down and tell them."

Giving Adams a puzzled glance, Evans ran on down

223

the path. Removing his glasses, Adams began cleaning them. It was an act that seemed to bring the girl to a decision. Touching his arm, she made him turn and face her.

"There is something I want you to do for me, Frank. After the war you must come back to this country. I want to prove to you how beautiful it is." When Adams did not speak, she braced herself. "I also want you to meet my husband. The three of us will have a marvellous party. Did you know the Norwegians are very good at parties?"

Adams was standing very still. "Your husband?"

"Yes, Rolf. He escaped from Norway soon after the Germans invaded and since then he has been serving in the British Navy. There hasn't been much time to talk about ourselves, has there? But you will like my husband and he will like you. Will you come back?"

Adams stirred. "Yes. Yes, I'd like to." Straightening, he replaced his glasses. "But if you came over to England you could see him when he is on leave. Isn't that a good reason for coming with us?"

In spite of herself, her voice faltered. "It is so like you to think of that. But no, I must stay here with my friends. Rolf will understand."

Below a second engine burst into life. As Adams' stricken face gazed at her she gave a sob of distress and threw her arms around him. "Don't look so sad, Frank. I can't bear it."

Before he could speak she pushed him down the path. "Go now, please. Go home to England and try to forget what has happened here."

He stumbled a few paces forward, then turned. His last memory was of her standing in the hut doorway smiling at him. Her voice carried to him clearly over the noise of the engines. "At least we tried, didn't we, Frank? We tried as hard as anyone could have tried."

The hundred things Adams wanted to say choked him. He did not look back again.

## 31

Down on the river the activity was intense. With the impression, rightly or wrongly, that the bursting shell above meant enemy troops would flood down the banks at any moment, men were working in a frenzy to get the aircraft out of the death trap that the river entrance had become. As the heavy-duty accumulators strove to fire the turgid engines, Chiefy Powell could be seen skating about the ice like a middle-aged circus performer as sweating mechanic after mechanic sought his advice.

One by one the half-frozen engines burst into life. To everyone's relief, and no doubt because they were air-cooled, the Mitchells' were the first to fire and the B.25 carrying the wounded men was manoeuvred round to clear the entrance. Just as she was about to taxi out on the lake, Moore was obliged to halt her as stretcher bearers arrived with two more casualties. As they were hastily loaded aboard, the startled airmen learned that German tanks had driven eastwards, almost certainly in an attempt to break up the ice.

The news was a supreme test for the discipline and morale that were the hallmarks of the unit. Aware that if haste turned into panic all would be lost, officers and men alike took a fresh grip on themselves. If this was to be their last battle, the squadron would not lose it as a disorganized rabble. In many ways the next half-hour was one of 633 Squadron's finest victories because it was a victory against itself.

On Adams' arrival he had been immediately whisked into the second of the B.25s. To their mutual disgust Davies and Henderson had been bundled in with him. In charge now that flight operations were under way, Moore was determined to get all three Mitchells airborne as quickly as possible. Once inside the aircraft Davies had commandeered the co-pilot and navigator's seats and installed Adams in the empty bombardier's position in the nose. When the pilot had expressed discontent, Davies had snapped that if and when navigation was called for, the crew would be reinstated. At the moment, along with a number of ground staff NCOs, they were seated in high dudgeon beyond the bulkhead. Other mechanics were lying uncomfortably in the empty bomb bay.

With orders to operate independently, the first B.25

wasted no time once she reached the western end of the runway. Engines bellowing, she began picking up speed. In spite of the calls being made on them, Moore and his two flight commanders ran out on to the lake to watch. With all three B.25s packed to capacity, her performance was the yardstick on which the other two Mitchells' chances could be assessed.

Anxious eyes followed her as she thundered down the runway, throwing back a cloud of snow. When she was less than four hundred yards from the eastern shore and her wheels were still glued to the ice men believed she was overloaded, dug their nails into their palms, and looked away. But the Mitchell's screaming engines clawed her up at the last moment and she banked unsteadily away from the hills. With her pilot under orders to head immediately for the U.K. the B.25 climbed and disappeared westwards, using cloud cover for protection.

The Mitchell's struggle to become airborne was not a welcome sight for Davies and company, who were next to go. For Adams in the very nose of the aircraft it was a terrifying experience as rutted ice flashed past and her engines screamed their protest. Thudding down on her wheels as if they would never break free, the B.25 finally skimmed less than a dozen feet over the spot where Prentice had crashed. Remembering the hill range ahead, Adams felt certain he was only seconds from an exploding fireball and oblivion.

Yet Adams was soon to realize how lucky he had been. As Davies ordered the Mitchell pilot, a freckle-faced Canadian, to go into orbit just below the cloud ceiling to keep watch on the situation below, a sudden fountain of snow rose five hundred yards from the eastern shore of the lake. Knowing what it meant, Davies' mouth turned dry with fear as he ordered the pilot to turn back. "Find those tanks! The boys must knock 'em out before they get within range of the lake."

Sweeping back and crossing the eastern hills, the B.25 entered the wide valley that contained the main north-south road. Staring down Davies could see the tiny shapes of half a dozen transports but no armoured vehicles. He glanced at the pilot. "We haven't flown over 'em, have we?"

The Canadian shook his head. "I don't think so, sir."

Behind Davies, Henderson was looking equally con-

226

cerned. "Can't you see anything, Frank? You've got the best view of anybody."

Henderson's earphones responded somewhat shakily: Adams had not yet recovered from the take-off. "No, I can't see any sign of them. Could that explosion have been mortar fire?"

Davies frowned down at the ribbon of road. "What—from those transports? They must be three miles from the lake. That's well out of mortar range, isn't it?"

Adams tried to focus on the misty panorama of snow and rock-strewn hillsides that was flashing beneath him. "I don't see what else it can be, sir. It looks as if the tanks must have gone back into the lane."

On Davies' orders the B.25 turned southward. Dense clouds of smoke told that the partisans were still resisting although by this time they had been driven back to the river. As the Mitchell banked over the steep valley four grey shapes could be seen heading down it at speed towards the fighting. Davies could not decide whether he was relieved or not. "Then that must have been a mortar shell. But why have the tanks left the lake?"

"They probably couldn't get over the hills," Henderson said. "The snow looks pretty deep on its eastern slopes."

The Scot's guess was correct. In sending his armour to attack the lake Walcheim had proved himself no tank commander by over-estimating the vehicles' ability to operate in snow. The prevailing winds had built up deep corniches on the eastern hillside and when the tanks had left the main road they had found no track firm enough to take their weight. When one tank had sunk too deeply in a snowdrift to be dragged out, their commander had asked Walcheim's permission to withdraw.

Knowing from the sounds reaching him of the frantic efforts the squadron was making to escape, Walcheim had taken personal charge of the mortars and rushed them up to the lake. Bolted as they were to the transports the heavier ones had proved useless but the light mortars could be manhandled and Walcheim had ordered their crews forward. The explosion Davies had witnessed had been a crew's first attempt to establish their range. Seeing the shell fall well short, NCOs were spurring their crews forward again.

During this time, while armourers had been ripping out the safety pins of bombs and rockets, mechanics had

227

been working frantically on the remaining engines and most of the aircraft were now lined up on the western perimeter of the lake. Two engines, however, had failed to start, the port engine of Machin and the starboard engine of Collins. Collins and his navigator had accepted the situation with resignation but when Machin was told no more time could be spent on him he had begged permission to try out the Mosquito's legendary one-engine take-off capability. As flight commander, Harvey had told him not to be a bloody fool and had sent him and his navigator packing to the third Mitchell already out on the lake. The Yorkshireman had wanted to stay to the last with Moore but the young squadron commander had ordered him out on the lake with the others and the scowling Harvey had been forced to obey. Keeping A-Apple's engines running, Moore had then given the long-awaited signal to the ground crews. As they ran out with relief towards the waiting B.25, Hoppy had tossed a couple of hand grenades into the two crippled Mosquitoes. As the two aircraft exploded the Cockney caught sight of the first of the partisans as they retreated down the river.

Although Moore had initially decided to send all three B.25s off first, he had then realized that should any of the Mosquitoes' engines stall he would need his fitters and the third Mitchell was under orders to wait until A Flight was airborne. Then Davies' radio message about the first mortar shell had been received and forced Moore to revert to his original timetable. It proved a wise decision because the Mitchell had barely cleared the ice before a second shell exploded, this time less than a hundred yards from the lake. With range-finders marking the burst and other mortar crews running into more advanced positions, the battle of the lake had reached a crucial point. Had Walcheim not made his original tactical blunder of sending up tanks instead of mortars, there is no doubt the squadron would have been trapped and destroyed. As it was the issue could not have been more finely balanced.

With neither bombs nor rockets on his B.25 Davies could do nothing to attack the four tanks and ordered his pilot back to the lake. As he orbited just below the hilltops he could follow every movement in the deadly game being enacted below. Inside the river mouth the fires from the blazing Mosquitoes were staining the ice crimson. Beyond the isthmus the remaining thirteen Mosquitoes were jostling one another in readiness for take-off. The last Mitchell, carrying its shaken mechanics back to the U.K., had already vanished into the clouds. As a third mortar shell dropped on the very shore of the lake, Davies' voice was sharp on the R/T. "Get them moving, Moore! They'll be dropping shells on the ice at any moment."

With Moore insisting the Mosquitoes retain their landing order, Harvey was the first pilot to follow the B.25. With snow pluming from its racing propellers, his Mosquito had a meteor-like appearance as it skimmed down the runway. Needing a shorter run than the Mitchells, it was airborne a good six hundred yards from the shore and Davies was about to make a reassuring comment when he heard a horrified exclamation from Adams. Glancing down again, he saw ice and snow rearing up from the very fringe of the lake. Little damage could be seen at first but as the airmen stared down, a second shell fell in almost the same place. This time a deep crack appeared, followed by black water that began swilling over the ice around it. Davies was close to hysteria as he yelled his warning to Moore at the far end of the lake. "They've got the range, Moore! It's breaking! For Christ's sake get your boys away!" Then remembering who he was, Davies became a good field commander again. "Tell every man to hunt for those mortars the moment he's airborne."

The experienced Harvey needed no such order. His Mosquito was already skimming over the southern hills like a wolf casting for scent. Catching sight of one of the forward gun crews crouched in a hollow he swung round on a wingtip and opened fire with both cannon and Brownings. Two men tried to escape but were cut down before they had run ten yards. The third man died over his gun. Levelling off only a few feet above the snow, Harvey raged off in search of other mortars.

They proved difficult to find. The hillsides were vast and the outcrops of black rock acted both as camouflage and cover. Nevertheless Harvey's attack afforded a respite while other mortars were rushed forward and in the lull another Mosquito cleared the ice and immediately joined in the hunt.

With every second precious two more Mosquitoes in echelon were already moving at speed along the runway. As their tails lifted a fountain of snow and ice rose a full hundred yards from the shore as a newly positioned mortar began firing. As long cracks radiated out, Adams heard Moore's voice on the R/T and marvelled at its calmness. "How bad is it, sir? We can't tell from this end."

Itching to help his men, Henderson broke in before Davies could answer. "Keep them going, Ian. You've lost about a hundred and fifty yards of runway so far."

As both Davies and Henderson fell quiet, Adams heard Moore giving his crews instructions. With an icy death threatening all of them, the Mosquitoes were swinging into line as if on an exercise. Until that moment Adams felt he had never understood the meaning of discipline.

The two Mosquitoes cleared the runway safely and immediately fanned away in search of mortar crews. Two more were already racing through the isthmus, two more were taxi-ing forward. In spite of himself, the imaginative Adams was fascinated by the deadly game. Every additional Mosquito that escaped added its threat to the gun crews and tilted the scales in the squadron's favour. Until a new crew crept forward, dropped a shell deeper into the lake, and tilted the scales violently back again.

One such mortar crew, led by a tough and determined NCO, had driven well ahead of its colleagues and found protection from the marauding Mosquitoes by two huge rocks. As the fourth brace of Mosquitoes roared overhead, the crew fired their first shell. Lobbing high into the air, it fell about four hundred yards into the lake. Although the explosion was to the left of the runway, it brought a horrified and unprintable comment from Henderson. A second shell broke a huge ice flow from the runway.

With nothing to lose now Moore sent the last of his Mosquitoes off almost in one another's slipstream. Shells were falling in greater numbers as more and more mortar crews came within range. To Adams it seemed half of the eastern lake was now awash with black water, bobbing ice, and widening cracks. With the southern boundary also beginning to break up, the runway looked like an ice flow itself.

As if tied together by string the four Mosquitoes came skimming through the isthmus. As the distance between their leader and the black water shortened, Adams barely dared to look. The end of the runway could not have been fifty yards from the Mosquito when, like a skier leaping upwards, it broke free and began to climb away. As the second and third aircraft followed, the onlookers above began to breathe again. The fourth Mosquito, however, still had her wheels on the ice. Perhaps the cause was an engine giving insufficient power, perhaps a propeller had slipped back in pitch. Whatever the reason, the gap between aircraft and broken ice was shrinking at terrifying speed. The hoarse shout over the intercom could have come from either Henderson or Davies. "Get her up, lad! Ger her up!"

There was a last flash of ice ahead of the Mosquito and then time and space ran out for the crew of V-Victor. As the desperate pilot heaved back on his wheel, the Mosquito lifted like a drowning man making a last effort to save himself, then its undercarriage dropped into a deep fissure. Instantly it somersaulted and exploded. When the high column of spray and water subsided only eddying black water marked the grave of Spencer and Cross. The exclamation that broke from Davies sounded suspiciously like a sob but neither Henderson nor Adams were in any state to notice it. Recovering, the small Air Commodore addressed the R/T. "What are you waiting for, Ian? Get moving, for God's sake."

With the last of his men gone, Moore was already moving along the runway. Through the isthmus ahead shells could now be seen falling indiscriminately, some dropping short into the water, others adding to the disintegration of the icefield. With the smoke from the crashed V-Victor a reminder of the peril ahead, Hopkinson was sitting pale and rigid in his seat. Yet the Cockney was still able to pass a quip as Moore thumbed the throttles forward. "They'll never get me doing winter sports after this, skipper."

Moore's eyes crinkled in appreciation. "Make that two of us, Hoppy."

Adams felt his eyes sting at the men's banter. Below A-Apple was now streaming out smoke and snow as Moore gave her engines full power. With water and broken ice spreading back towards the centre of the lake the effect was to make the Mosquito appear to be doing twice her rated speed as she ate up the remaining runway. Davies, who a moment ago had been urging Moore on, now went silent as if fearing his voice might make the fractional difference between life and death.

The broken ice was less than a hundred yards ahead of A-Apple when Moore eased back on the wheel. When the aircraft's wheels thumped down again, someone let out a thick curse. Holding the Mosquito down to the very edge of the broken ice, Moore tried again. For a moment she faltered and Adams distinctly saw a flash of spray from her spinning wheels. Then she recovered, her engines screaming with the effort. But although her wheels escaped the black water she remained only a couple of feet above it and no one knew whether she could not lift or whether Moore was deliberately holding her down to build up speed. Then her nose began to rise and everyone breathed again.

Yet the ordeal for crew and onlookers alike was not yet over. As Moore neared the shore a shell dropped and exploded on an ice flow only a few yards from his starboard wing. As the Mosquito rocked violently it seemed her opposite wingtip must strike the water. When she recovered and cleared the eastern shore Davies' croak suggested he had escaped a heart attack by the same narrow margin. Henderson muttered something in Gaelic but the sweating Adams found his mouth too dry for comment.

Shouts and cheers filled the radio channel as men witnessed the escape of their popular leader. Adams barely recognized the authoritative voice that silenced them. "Valkyrie leader to squadron. Cut your cackle: you've a job to do. Forget the mortars: they can't harm anyone now. Red Section: take the lane behind the southern hills. Green Section: we're giving cover in the river area. Watch out for collisions where the lane and river intersect. That's all. Go."

It was an order that brought immense satisfaction to the wrought-up crews and to no one more than Young as he led his Mosquitoes towards the bitter fighting at the river bridge. Through the dense smoke, long flashes could be seen from the four tanks that were now firmly established on either bank of the river. Their fire was directed at the rearguard of the partisans who, led by Jensen, were fighting desperately to hold the position while the squadron escaped and their comrades crossed the lake. But with shells exploding among the trees and hurling steel and wood splinters among them, the partisans were being driven back by sheer fire power.

Young knew nothing about the details of the fighting but the fire from the tanks told its own story. As tank commanders read the threat and hastily swung their turrets round, the six Mosquitoes curved like a piece of string and came diving back. Picking his own target, each pilot released a rocket and opened fire with his cannon. When the thunder of the last aircraft was reverberating away in the hills, two tanks were burning fiercely and two were lying askew with their turrets destroyed.

The task for Harvey's Green Section was more difficult. With no armour down the reaches of the river and with German ski troops wearing camouflage smocks like their Norwegian counterparts, it was difficult to identify friend from foe. Realizing the airmen's predicament and that the aircraft were capable of holding the enemy infantrymen back, Jensen ordered his men to break off the action and run for the lake. With the German soldiers not daring to follow them down the river banks, it was soon possible for the Mosquito pilots to locate the limit of their advance and to open fire. With plenty of cover from the flanking trees, the enemy casualties were not heavy but the object of the squadron's intervention, to give the partisans time to reach the lake, was entirely successful.

Still orbiting in the B.25, Davies and his officers were able to see the pitifully thin vanguard of Norwegians crossing the isthmus. Pressed against the perspex bomb hatch Adams was searching for a glimpse of Helga but the Mitchell's speed and distance away made the task impossible. As Young's Mosquitoes swept back over the southern hills, he heard Davies talking to Henderson. "I wonder if that radio operator has left the hut yet, Jock?"

It was a comment that made Adams realize the small Air Commodore was still hoping for a miracle. On his orders the Mitchell swept low over the cliff but it proved impossible to tell if anyone remained in the cabin. As the B.25 circled the eastern lake again, another party of Norwegians could be seen crossing the isthmus. With many of them supporting wounded comrades they were clearly the rearguard. As the Mitchell swept towards them a bearded figure waved a Sten gun in appreciation before disappearing into the trees.

Following Moore's instructions, Young's Red Section was now giving the squadron fighter cover. Harvey's section was still busy holding back German infantrymen. Filtering through the trees, some had managed to reach the lake and were courageously trying to chase the Norwegians across it. Although they scattered and ran as three Mosquitoes strafed them, it was obvious they would be across the lake in strength once the aircraft withdrew.

Their persistence posed a new problem for Moore. With the clouds now perceptibly lifting as the short afternoon drew to its close, it was certain German fighters would be racing towards the lake. Yet with so many wounded men to carry to their transports, the partisans needed all the time they could get. Aware what his request meant in terms of finality, Moore lifted his face mask. "Valkyrie Leader to Linchpin. Have I your permission to bomb the ice?"

It was a question that jolted Davies both by its obviousness and its implications. With the number of rockets and bombs that would be needed to make an effective barrier, there would be no point in attacking the cruiser later even if the all clear were to come. For a moment Davies felt aggrieved that such a crucial decision should fall on to his shoulders and not the broader ones of Staines back in England. Telling Moore to wait, he ordered his Mitchell pilot to make one last run over the radio hut. This time Germany infantrymen could be seen swarming up the hillside that led to the cliff top. Deciding that no man, however dedicated, would wait and throw his life away for what now seemed a hopeless cause, the heavy-hearted Davies gave his answer. "Permission granted, Valkyrie Leader. Only hurry it up or we could be in trouble."

Neither Moore nor his men needed the advice. A-Apple was in a dive almost before Davies had finished speaking and two heavy rockets went streaking down towards the isthmus. Harvey came next, aiming his rockets at the place where Moore's had struck. Seeing huge chunks of ice hurled upwards, Adams was about to make a comment when a faint, flickering light caught his eye. Turning his head he saw the light was coming from the top of the cliff. As he read the message his heart began hammering and he gave a shout of disbelief. "Sir! It's Lindstrom! He says it's Valkyrie."

With the Aldis hidden by the pilot alongside him, Davies clearly believed Adams was having visions. "What did you say?"

By this time Adams had remembered Helga's last words. "Lindstrom must have retreated over the hill and taken the radio operator's place. Can't you understand, sir? He's telling us Valkyrie is on."

Shouts could now be heard over the air as other men noticed the Aldis but none of them matched Davies' yell which nearly blew the valves of his radio. "Moore, do you hear that? It's Valkyrie!" Almost betraying to the enemy the object of the mission in his excitement, Davies swung round on Henderson. "It's on, Jock! The operation's on!"

234

It was a moment when all Henderson's Highland phlegm rose magnificently to the surface. "Aye, I heard Adams, sir. We're in luck, aren't we?"

Davies blinked. Then, as two Mosquitoes went diving past, he remembered his earlier orders and grabbed his face mask. "This is Linchpin to all crews. Forget the ice and keep your rockets. I repeat—keep your rockets!"

Moore, who had turned towards the cliff the moment the Aldis was seen, heard the order but his eyes were held by a dozen infantrymen who had burst out from the trees. As they appeared, the frail but defiant figure of Lindstrom stepped out from the side of the hut and began firing at them. Urging A-Apple on, Moore banked steeply and opened fire. Two men fell, the rest ran back for cover. As Moore went into a climbing turn he heard Davies' sharp, high-pitched voice. "Valkyrie leader, get your boys together! We haven't a minute to waste."

Seeing Moore ignore the order and swing round on a wingtip, Adams wanted to cheer. Yet although A-Apple went raging down with all guns firing and Harvey and his flight in line astern came swinging in after her, it was clear the young Norwegian was doomed. Trapped on the cliff top by his dedication he was showing his defiance by refusing to take cover or be captured. As he advanced towards the trees firing his Sten gun, a bullet struck him and he fell to his knees. Even then his defiance did not end. As Mosquito after Mosquito plunged down to protect him, he lifted an arm and waved it southwards. Only then did he fall forward and lie motionless.

It was a final act that said everything. Although frowning at the flagrant disobedience of his orders, Davies was looking as moved as anyone. As Moore was heard ordering his pilots to formate behind him, Davies glanced at Henderson. "I want to see this to the end, Jock. What about you?"

The grim-faced Scot stirred. "Aye, sir. We must. Get Moore on the blower before he leaves us behind."

Forward in the bombardier's hatch Adams was discovering, if he had not known it before, why he was not the stuff military leaders are made of. With the Mosquitoes withdrawing from their protective role, fifty or more German soldiers were already in hot pursuit across the lake. To Adams, feverish with concern for Helga and for men who had become his friends, it was a betrayal and his head sank in despair against the icy perspex window.

235

## 32

The scene of the final battle might have been set by the old Norsk gods themselves. With darkness little more than forty minutes away, the blanket of cloud that stretched from horizon to horizon had turned black and forbidding. Yet the setting sun had broken through a gap in the mountains and was staining the fjords and snow the colour of blood. Out in the northern fjord, with its bow wave making a huge arrowhead, the cruiser resembled an impregnable castle around which the crimson waters divided. Even the Wagnerian music was there: the scream of airfoils and the thunder of engines as the god Odin watched his warriors prepare to do battle.

Knowing that all fighter bases for two hundred miles would have been warned of the Mosquitoes' presence, Moore had ordered strict radio silence before making for the fjord. He had also flown perilously low. With the lake and fjord far apart, the chances were fair the enemy would not put two and two together. At the same time Moore was disappointed by the weather conditions. With all his crews bad weather specialists, he had hoped the clouds would stay on the mountain tops for the rest of the day. Now that they had lifted a critical thousand feet more it seemed certain the tough German fighter pilots would be carrying out an intensive search for the enemy who had risen so daringly from their midst.

As the tight phalanx of Mosquitoes with the single Mitchell tucked away in its midst swept towards the fjord, Moore saw with relief his hope was realized and the cruiser had not yet received a protective umbrella of fighters. Had he known it, the reason was less poor guesswork from the fighter controllers than the common problem raised by tight security. With the Germans having to keep secret the true nature of the cruiser's cargo, controllers who would normally have made intelligent guesses about the Mosquitoes' objective were having to seek advice from superiors who were as ignorant of the facts as themselves.

At the same time there was not a man in the squadron who was not aware of the fine limits of survival. German defence systems were always efficient and the cruiser would already be in touch with controllers who in turn would be vectoring fighters towards the fjord. If the ship was not sunk within the next few minutes the Mosquitoes would be trapped at zero height among the mountain tops. To make matters worse the ceiling of cloud meant fighters could mass undetected and so become an even greater threat.

Despite the need for haste, however, the complex network of crimson fjords and mountain ranges forced Moore to orbit the terrain once before deciding how to launch his attack. The northern tributary from Kranvin ran into the Hardanger fjord at a point where the main fjord turned ninety degrees south-east. At present, three miles or so from the mouth of the tributary, the cruiser was protected on both sides by steep mountains but once she entered the main fjord her flanks would be exposed until she was past the bend when the mountains of the Hardanger would close round her again. These were less steep and wider apart than those of the tributary but it would still take great skill to attack the cruiser's flanks. Moreover it was along this stretch of water that the banks began to shelve and made a beaching possible.

Ideally, then, the ship should be attacked when crossing the wide bend in the main fjord. Unimpeded by mountains, aircraft could strike at her from all sides and in doing so thin out her flak defences. But she would be minutes before she reached the bend and with hungry fighters racing in, minutes were more precious than jewels. Moore made his decision. "Valkyrie Leader to squadron. Red Section—give cover! Green Section—follow me and watch those mountains!"

On the cruiser below the frantic hoot of sirens had sent helmeted men racing to battle stations. Gun turrets were swivelling round and a couple of pom-poms had already opened fire. As Green Section swept towards the fjord an ominous screen of bursting shells began to open up before it.

Witnessing his first air strike, Adams was marvelling at the calmness of it all as he heard Moore ordering a line-astern attack. Falling back and swinging into their new formation with all the skill and discipline for which their unit was famous, the six pilots dived over the mountains and bending like a drawn bow came sweeping back at the cruiser from the stern. The fascinated Adams at least knew the theory. Attack from either the bows or stern to avoid as much flak as possible and try to knock out the gunners with rockets or cannon fire. Then, when the defences are weakened, come in for the kill from the beam—if you can. What even Adams' vivid imagination had never succeeded in capturing was the overwhelming brutality of such battles. Like all large naval units, cruisers carried massive fire power and the barrage they could put up against aircraft was terrifying.

Moore was the first to attack, coming in at a slight angle in a twenty-degree dive. Taking the rear starboard gunners as his target, he first released a rocket and then, as the cruiser leapt up towards him, opened fire with his cannon. As the Mosquito shuddered under their recoil, Moore had a blurred glimpse of a twin LMG that seemed to be hurling tracer straight at his windshield. In the three or four seconds that it took him to traverse the length of the ship, his mind recorded sights like a hypersensitive film: the heavy winch and derrick his rocket had hurled away . . . tracer zipping past his cupola like blue electric sparks . . . a rating on a lower deck being thrown like a carcass of meat against the ship rail. Then A-Apple was past but the LMG gunners in the bows now had an unrestricted view of her. Feeling hammer blows on the armoured shield behind him, Moore dropped down until his slipstream was ruffling the black water and weaved out of range. Only then was he able to glance at Hoppy and he saw the Cockney was unhurt. Noticing his concern, Hoppy gave vent to the resentment of all Mosquito navigators. "When the hell are we getting armoured seats, skipper?" When Moore shook his head ruefully, the Cockney glanced back and gave a whistle of dismay. "You sure she's only a cruiser? She looks as big as a battleship to me."

One by one the crews of Green Section followed into the hell of bursting shells and trident thrusts of tracer. Harvey's rocket struck a davit and a lifeboat swung crazily down to dangle by its bows. Matthews' cannon fire smashed into the wrap-around armour of a pom-pom and killed two gunners. Paget's rocket hit a capstan on the stern and hurled murderous chunks of metal in all directions but as he swept on he ran into the combined fire of a pom-pom and two LMGs mounted at the base of the cruiser's front funnel. Fragments of wood and metal flew from the Mosquito and a long tongue of flame leapt out from its starboard engine. Skimming over the black water like a fiery meteor it suddenly broke up and plunged down like a stone. The two chess players, Paget and Smith, had become pawns themselves in a bigger and deadlier game. The horrified Adams heard a voice call out "Oh, my God" and took a few seconds to realize it was his own.

Full of fight and with guns to spare, the cruiser was giving her attention to the aircraft circling above as well as those attacking her. With the fading light adding to the effect, the multi-coloured shells she hurled up looked like bubbles rising from soda water. As her heavy guns bore for a moment on the Mitchell, Adams heard for the first time in his life the heavy cough of flak. Cringing as red-hot steel sheared past, he marvelled at the courage of men who could face such terror every day of their lives.

Orbiting just beneath the black ceiling of cloud, Young's section were like gladiators witnessing the carnage in the arena before their turn came to fight. Below, the cruiser's captain had ordered full speed ahead. Fully briefed against all contingencies, he knew about the stretch of shelving shoreline just inside the Hardanger fjord and was determined to get nearer to it in case fighters did not arrive in time.

The emergence of the cruiser into the wider water of the main fjord came as West, Harvey's last pilot, came climbing out of the flak with his tail unit a mass of scars and his navigator mortally wounded. Moore raised his face mask. "Valkyrie Leader to Red Section. Beam attack. In you go!"

As Young's men came peeling down, Green Section took their place to give them cover and allow its own crews to lick their wounds. Over the R/T Harvey could be heard asking the condition of West's navigator. West's reply made Adams wince. "He's in a hell of a mess, skipper. He's lost an arm."

"Can you get a tourniquet on?"

West sounded close to tears. "I don't see how, skipper. He hasn't any shoulder left either."

"Then all you can do is give him a shot of morphia. Can you get back home?"

"Not without a navigator, skipper."

Harvey's sigh said it all. "All right, lad. Stay out of range until we've finished the job."

The sun was now a red ball between the western mountains and its rays were tinting the smoke that rose from the fjord. Here and there the effects were beautiful, a column of pink that swirled gracefully upwards or a mauve cloud that floated away in the dusk. For a moment the gunfire from the cruiser had lessened as its crew prepared for the next attack. In the dusk fires could be seen burning on both her fore and aft decks with shadowy figures fighting to control them. To the imaginative Adams, Odin had set the scene to perfection and was now ready for his awe-inspiring maidens to scream down and select the dead for Valhalla. Not for the first time Adams wondered whose inspiration had provided the code-name.

With Young's Mosquitoes in position, they commenced their attack, one unit coming in on the cruiser's port beam and the other on her starboard. As rows of coloured shells spewed out from the ship, reflections could be seen in the black water. Both Young and Millburn released two rockets apiece. One rocket blew a great hole in the gun deck, another two struck the armoured hull of the cruiser and exploded. Although there were jubilant shouts over the R/T, they died as the cruiser sailed on without displaying serious damage.

Orbiting above Davies was growing concerned at the resistance the ship was showing. At the most generous estimate German fighters could not be more than five minutes away. About to interfere, Davies was relieved of the need as he heard Moore's sharp order. "Nos. 11 and 12. Get your sights down. We need rockets around her waterline."

With the blizzard of fire being hurled at them, crews were having the utmost difficulty in keeping their aircraft steady enough to take aim. Ellis was about to launch his two rockets when a 37mm shell scored a direct hit on his port engine, smashing its complicated system of pipes and valves into a fused mass of metal. Somehow he managed to avoid collision with the cruiser but as his crippled Mosquito reeled across the fjord its wing tanks exploded and it fell in a sea of flames on the opposite bank. Larkin, who had seen his rockets fly high and explode on the superstructure, gritted his teeth and closed right in firing both cannon. The daring and ferocity of the attack caught one gun crew by surprise and men were slaughtered and hurled in all directions. Pressing home his attack until the last second, Larkin had a piece of aerial dangling from his tail-wheel fairing as he leap-frogged the ship.

Van Breedenkamp, the young South African, had more luck. Striking the ship's stern, one of his rockets must have damaged her engines because her speed was noticeably reduced as his shell-torn Mosquito weaved away. Yet with

240

precious minutes ticking past, Moore knew that the cruiser was winning the battle. Banking steeply over the mountains, he addressed Harvey's men. "Valkyrie Leader to Green Section. Stand by. I'm trying something different." He glanced at his tense navigator. "Tail fuse both bombs, Hoppy."

The experienced Cockney did not need to ask his intention. Skip bombing had been regular squadron practice until the advent of rockets and still had its uses when ships had armour as thick as this cruiser's. As A-Apple's bomb doors opened, Hoppy fused both bombs and watched Moore closely.

Keeping in the heavy shadow of the mountain, A-Apple began her attack. As she dived over the thick woods that lined the main fjord and lowered her belly to within a few feet of the water, the cruiser opened fire with all its starboard guns. With the multi-coloured shells reflected in the mirrorlike surface, it seemed she had suddenly doubled her fire power and even the battle-hardened Hopkinson flinched at the sight.

As the vectors shortened the cruiser turned from a ship into a towering castle of steel whose fires seemed only to proclaim her invincibility. As A-Apple shuddered from a shell that took a six-inch strip from her port wing, Hoppy saw Moore jerk his head and he pressed the bomb release. With the Mosquito only a few feet above the surface, the bombs had no chance to find their natural trajectory. Instead they struck the water horizontally and like flat stones went bounding towards the cruiser. One of them, fitted with a clip-on tail fin, lost the unit after its second bounce and the bomb toppled over and sank like a stone. The second, fitted with a modified fin, went bounding on towards its target.

With the flak blinding them, neither Moore nor Hopkinson had time to follow its progress. Intent now on survival, Moore banked steeply away to avoid the blast. As he weaved eastward a huge flash lit up the dusk and the Mosquito reared alarmingly. A yell came from Hoppy. "We got her, skipper! Right amidships."

All gunfire from the cruiser momentarily ceased. Above, breathless onlookers saw flames leaping out of a huge hole in her side. What they could not know was that the bomb had struck on an upward trajectory and so the hull below the waterline was not critically damaged although tons of water were pouring in. The discovery brought fresh heart to the cruiser's captain. A tough product of the old German Navy, he knew time was on his side and his voice over the damaged tannoy revived his half-stunned gun crews. "Fighters are nearly here. And if necessary we can beach her in a few more minutes. So hold on, lads. Hold on!"

Matthews was the next in line. In an attempt to harass the gunners and draw away some of their fire, Moore led the rest of Green Section in a nose to stern attack. He knew that one or more of his aircraft might fly into the blast of Matthews' bombs but by this time he felt any risk was called for. As the multi-coloured flak began reaching out for Matthews' frail aircraft, Adams heard Henderson's frustrated voice. "Why the hell didn't we bring some stores ourselves instead of sitting up here like a bloody wallflower at a party." The fact Davies did not take the comment as a criticism against himself told Adams much about the Air Commodore's own state of mind.

Although Matthews pressed home his attack in his usual reckless way, it proved a failure. A bullet or shell cut the electrical lead that ran to one of his release hooks. Consequently only one bomb fell and it missed the cruiser's stern by a good twenty feet. Frustrated, Matthews flew deeped into the blizzard of fire, grabbed the bomb button from Allison, and tried to release the faulty bomb himself. His emergence unscathed from the dense flak suggested his confidence in his immortality might have some foundations after all.

To Adams the ship had now turned into an invulnerable monster prepared to accept all night the fiery spears being hurled at her and he felt little hope as Monahan and Ellis began their attack. By this time the cruiser had reached the shadow of the Hardanger mountains and the effect was dramatic with her fires glowing redly and staining the swirling water around her. With their upper-wing surfaces painted white, the Mosquitoes looked like moths flitting to their doom as the rest of the flight went in to harass the gunners.

A few seconds later all the guns opened fire again, turning the fjord into a giant kaleidoscope of colour and movement. To the hypnotized Adams, still up in the crimson sunlight, the sight was both beautiful and evil, a sorcerer's *son et lumière*. To Monahan and Ellis, the reflections in the black water made it difficult for them to judge their height in multi-coloured shells seemed to be flying both above and below them. Seeing the sweating Monahan nod his head, Ellis pressed the bomb release and felt the Mosquito leap upwards as the bombs fell. His task completed, Monahan tried to find escape from the blizzard of shells that howled around him.

From above, the path of the bombs could be followed by their white splashes. One was ahead of the other and as it passed beneath the ship's bows Davies gave a groan of disappointment. The second one went plunging through the crimson arrowhead that surrounded the cruiser and disappeared. For endless seconds, while the frail moth that was Monahan's Mosquito weaved away to escape the vengeful flak, nothing happened and Davies' nails dug deeply into his palms. Then there was a brilliant red flash. As a huge column of smoke and water reared upwards from the cruiser, Davies let out a cry of triumph.

It was a cry that changed immediately to disappointment when he saw the battered ship was still making way, although another fierce fire was burning amidships. Realizing that by this time her momentum alone would carry her to the shelving beach, Moore decided he must order a mass onslaught by all the Mosquitoes that had rockets left. Because of the narrow confines of the fjord it would mean the chances of collisions were high but the battle had reached a stage when all risks had to be discounted. He was about to give the order when a shuddering red flash lit up the shadowy fjord. It was followed by another a couple of seconds later. A yell made Moore's earphones rattle. "She's going. She's going at last."

Davies was right. Monahan's bomb had blown away a main bulkhead of the cruiser's magazine, allowing a raging furnace to pour in among the packed shells. As the breathless crews stared down, another flash seemed to run the full length of the ship. It coalesced into an enormous ball of fire and debris that rose at terrifying speed towards the orbiting Mosquitoes. Realizing their danger, pilots banked sharply away, only to feel their aircraft rear violently as the massive blast reached them.

As the water cascaded back and the smoke veered away, the transfixed Adams saw the cruiser's back had been broken. The stern was a glowing hulk of metal with detonation after detonation tearing it apart. The bows were some two hundred yards away and slowly rearing on end as hundreds of tons of water poured through ruptured bulkheads.

The end came quickly for the stern as a final explosion tore it open. Great clouds of steam rose and merged with oily smoke as the huge segments disappeared, leaving hundreds of small fires burning behind them. The bows took half a minute longer, sliding in backwards as the water flooded in. Catching sight of tiny black figures leaping into the crimson fjord, Adams realized to his astonishment that some men had survived the titanic explosion. But the sight he knew he would never forget came from the very prow of the sinking hulk. Unhurt by some quirk of blast, still defiant by some miracle of the human spirit, an LMG crew were still firing at the orbiting Mosquitoes.

Not a single cry of triumph was heard as the bows slid from sight and water doused at last the defiant tracer. It was the battleshocked crews' way of paying their respect to a valiant enemy. Adams found he was beyond emotion. His only thought was that if there was a Valhalla, the gods would surely be playing host to both friend and foe tonight.

Davies was the first to recover. Calling his congratulations to Moore he was just turning to Henderson when a distant shout on the R/T made him stiffen. "Look out, skipper. Bandits. Look. . . ."

As the warning ended in a cry of pain, all crews glanced anxiously at the cloud above. Just below its base a thin tongue of flame could be seen. It lengthened rapidly as it slithered earthwards. Watching the drama in which they had played so important a part, Monahan and Ellis had forgotten the maxim that in the air a man must never relax.

With the Mosquitoes caught in the last rays of the sunset, they were a perfect target for the Focke Wulfs who came plunging down like gannets. Having been switched hither and thither by the controllers in their efforts to find the mysterious squadron and now, having found it, discovering they were too late, the German pilots were determined to exact some revenge for their humiliation. For the Mosquito crews, reacting from days of strain, it was a moment of extreme danger which Moore was quick to recognize. As the fighters came raging in and his aircraft milled about in confusion, his calm but forceful voice restored order and discipline. Forming a defensive

244

circle that momentarily held the Focke Wulfs at bay, the Mosquitoes and the lone Mitchell fought their way up to the clouds and disappeared.

As the grey mist closed around the B25, bringing its own sense of security, Adams felt he had been at war for a thousand years. Behind him, excited beyond measure at the success of the mission, Davies was recovering fast. "We've done it, Jock! We've dropped the IMI consignment right to the bottom of the fjord. The P.M. and the C.-in-C. will dance a jig when they get the news."

Henderson sounded as drained as Adams felt. "Yes, sir, I suppose they will. But it's been very costly, hasn't it?"

Davies was grinning like a jubilant elf. "I wonder if Moore's sent the code word back yet? Staines'll bite off the end of his cigar when he hears it." When the big Scot only shook his head, Davies became impatient. "Cheer up, Jock, for Christ's sake. Anyone would think the thing had gone sour. Instead we've pulled it off and we're going home."

With his leaden eyes closed, Adams caught only two words—"going home." Alongside Davies the Canadian pilot made a request for his navigator. The small Air Commodore hesitated, then nodded. "All right. We don't want to get lost at this stage in the game, Adams, come out of there! We're swopping places with the crew."

There was no reply from up front. Frowning, Davies tried again, "Adams? What's the matter with you?"

When there was still no reply, Davies gave Henderson a look of concern and lowered himself into the crawlway. Seeing Adams huddled up with his face mask askew and his head resting on a metal moulding, Davies frowned anxiously and pushed forward to investigate. Bending over the motionless Intelligence Officer he gave a grunt of disbelief. Haunted by bitter memories, shocked by the loss of young friends, and facing hundreds of miles of dangerous skies before the long ordeal was over, Adams had found solace at last. He was fast asleep.

# JOIN THE 633 SQUADRON

The original 633 SQUADRON, written a number of years ago, has become a classic of air literature, translated into many languages. The British author, Frederick E. Smith, had not planned any further books until he was deluged with reader inquiries from all over the world asking for more information about the members of this Yorkshire-based Special Service Unit. He finally was persuaded to continue the series of books about this legendary Mosquire Squadron of the RAF. The results are rousing, action-filled stories which are now being published in the United States for the first time.

## 633 SQUADRON

(now available)
The mission was called Vesuvius, and the invasion of Europe depended on it. The squadron's target was a Norwegian fiord where Germans were developing something so secret that even the RAF crews were told nothing about it. But everyone knew this was a dangerous, almost suicidal, mission. Caught between the attacking German aircraft and the grim mountain walls, the 633 Squadron plunged into the howling valley of death.

## 633 SQUADRON: OPERATION RHINE MAIDEN

(available April 1st)
Under the young, brilliant, new Commander Ian Moore, the squadron flew a mission to thwart the new German anti-aircraft rocket which posed the

most deadly threat to Allied invasion plans. The squadron had to come in on a daylight bombing run to wipe out the rocket factory and strike an underground target buried deep in a Bavarian valley.

# 633 SQUADRON: OPERATION CRUCIBLE

(available May 1st)
Autumn 1943. To restore world confidence in the RAF, which had been blamed by a British correspondent for heavy U.S. losses over Europe, the RAF and the 8th Air Force top brass chose the 633 Squadron to perform their most hazardous mission yet—giving ground support to American troops going in on a daring Dieppe-style landing against totally unforseen odds.

# 633 SQUADRON: OPERATION VALKYRIE

(available June 1st)
February 1944. The squadron was called on to destroy a large consignment of heavy water being smuggled out of Norway to Germany. To succeed in this mission seemed impossible until Intelligence Officer Frank Adams came up with a bizarre scheme—the only hitch was that it would put the entire squadron in great peril.


*633 SQUADRON books are published by Bantam, to be available wherever paperbacks are sold.*

# BANTAM WAR BOOKS

These action-packed books recount the most important events of World War II. They take you into battle and present portraits of brave men and true stories of gallantry in action. All books have special maps, diagrams, and illustrations.

| | | | |
|---|---|---|---|
| ☐ | 12657 | **AS EAGLES SCREAMED** Burgett | $2.25 |
| ☐ | 12658 | **THE BIG SHOW** Clostermann | $2.25 |
| ☐ | 13014 | **BRAZEN CHARIOTS** Crisp | $2.25 |
| ☐ | 12666 | **THE COASTWATCHERS** Feldt | $2.25 |
| ☐ | *12664 | **COCKLESHELL HEROES** Lucas-Phillips | $2.25 |
| ☐ | 12141 | **COMPANY COMMANDER** MacDonald | $1.95 |
| ☐ | 12578 | **THE DIVINE WIND** Pineau & Inoguchi | $2.25 |
| ☐ | *12669 | **ENEMY COAST AHEAD** Gibson | $2.25 |
| ☐ | *12667 | **ESCORT COMMANDER** Robertson | $2.25 |
| ☐ | *11709 | **THE FIRST AND THE LAST** Galland | $1.95 |
| ☐ | *11642 | **FLY FOR YOUR LIFE** Forrester | $1.95 |
| ☐ | 12665 | **HELMET FOR MY PILLOW** Leckie | $2.25 |
| ☐ | 12663 | **HORRIDO!** Toliver & Constable | $2.25 |
| ☐ | 12670 | **THE HUNDRED DAYS OF LT. MACHORTON** Machorton | $2.25 |
| ☐ | *12668 | **I FLEW FOR THE FÜHRER** Knoke | $2.25 |
| ☐ | 12290 | **IRON COFFINS** Werner | $2.25 |
| ☐ | 12671 | **QUEEN OF THE FLAT-TOPS** Johnston | $2.25 |
| ☐ | *11822 | **REACH FOR THE SKY** Brickhill | $1.95 |
| ☐ | 12662 | **THE ROAD PAST MANDALAY** Masters | $2.25 |
| ☐ | 12523 | **SAMURAI** Sakai with Caidin & Saito | $2.25 |
| ☐ | 12659 | **U-BOAT KILLER** Macintyre | $2.25 |
| ☐ | 12660 | **V-2** Dornberger | $2.25 |
| ☐ | *12661 | **THE WHITE RABBIT** Marshall | $2.25 |
| ☐ | *12150 | **WE DIE ALONE** Howarth | $1.95 |

**\*Cannot be sold to Canadian Residents.**

**Buy them at your local bookstore or use this handy coupon:**

---

Bantam Books, Inc., Dept. WW2, 414 East Golf Road, Des Plaines, Ill. 60016

Please send me the books I have checked above. I am enclosing $_____ (please add 75¢ to cover postage and handling). Send check or money order —no cash or C.O.D.'s please.

Mr/Mrs/Miss _____

Address _____

City _____ State/Zip _____

WW2—5/79

Please allow four weeks for delivery. This offer expires 11/79.